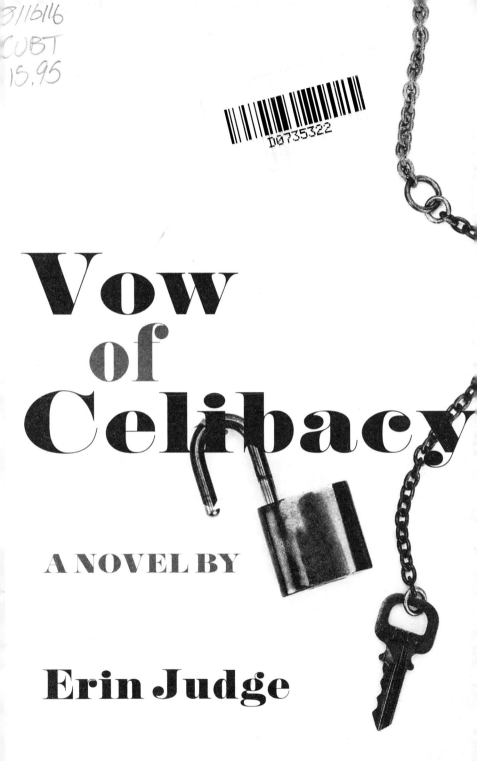

Vow of Celibacy

A NOVEL BY

Erin Judge

A GENUINE RARE BIRD BOOK

Los Angeles, Calif.

Vow
of
Celibacy

A NOVEL BY

Erin Judge

THIS IS A GENUINE RARE BIRD BOOK

A Rare Bird Book | Rare Bird Books
453 South Spring Street, Suite 302
Los Angeles, CA 90013
rarebirdbooks.com

FIRST TRADE PAPERBACK ORIGINAL EDITION

Printed in the United States

Set in Minion

10 9 8 7 6 5 4 3 2 1

Publisher's Cataloging-in-Publication data

Names: Judge, Erin, author.
Title: Vow of celibacy : a novel | by Erin Judge.
Description: First Trade Paperback Original Edition | A Rare Bird Book | Los Angeles,
CA; New York, NY: Rare Bird Books, 2016.
Identifiers: ISBN 9781942600725
Subjects: LCSH Bisexual women—Fiction. | Sex—Fiction. | Dating (Social customs)—
Fiction. | Fashion—Fiction. | Models (Persons)—Fiction. | Friendship—Fiction. | Body
image in women—Fiction. | Humorous stories. | BISAC FICTION / Contemporary
Women.
Classification: LCC PS3610.U52 V69 2016| DDC 813.6—dc23

For my smart, beautiful Mom

Vow of Celibacy

I, Natalie, hereby swear to abstain from
sex of any kind until I finally figure out
what the hell my problem is.

Signed: *Natalie, Nov 3*

Witnessed: **Anastaze, Nov 3**

Wazzoo

ANASTAZE CALLED ME AT 6:57 a.m. this morning. I left my ringer on for this very reason.

Anastaze (pronounced "anna-STAYS") is an adorable hipster with a personal style so perfectly calibrated that even her mild bow-leggedness comes across as a deliberate element of her self-presentation. She's also a professional web designer, a widely read anonymous blogger, a music geek, a UK citizen, a genius, and my best friend. And a virgin.

So when she called me at 6:57 a.m. today, my mind went straight to one thing. I answered the phone with confidence.

"Is this the news I've been waiting for?"

Anastaze just sobbed back. I sat bolt upright.

"Staze? What happened? Where are you?" I demanded.

"Sorry, Nat. I'm alright, I'm safe," she said, sniffling. "I'm being a baby."

"Oh kiddo, you're not a baby. Do you want me to come over?"

She let out a shaky sigh. "Can you meet me at the New Town Diner? Very soon?"

I glanced at my alarm clock. I had a meeting at a nearby mall at nine-fifteen, but I figured I could stop by to see her and still make it. I had no other option. Anastaze never does this.

"I'll be there in half an hour," I said. "Order me a coffee, OK?"

I found Anastaze at New Town fiddling with a menu, her puffy eyes magnified by her black-framed glasses. She saw me, and the corners of her mouth began to twitch. I kneeled on the blue vinyl bench beside her and wrapped my arms around her slight frame. She heaved two quick, hot sobs into my shoulder, then pulled back and rubbed her brown eyes. I switched around to face her without a word and started plotting the merciless evisceration of whoever did this to her.

"This is ridiculous," she said at last. "I'm ridiculous." She dropped her face straight down onto the table and did not pick it back up.

"Whatever it is, you can tell me."

"It's incredibly naff, Natalie."

"Staze. Just spit it out."

She lifted her head and pushed her wavy brown bob back behind her ears. "Last night, I went to a reading by Sam Elliot Jacobs," she began. I nodded. Sam Elliot Jacobs is, of course, that iconic and depressing writer who allegedly defines something or possibly everything about his/our generation. In addition to his two short story collections and single massive inscrutable novel, he also edits a literary magazine with a cover so minimalist it's literally blank. A different color of blank each month. I tease Anastaze that her sacred collection of these publications looks a lot like my sacred collection of paint chips. She is absolutely what the kids would call a Sam Elliot Jacobs superfan.

"How was it? Did you talk to him?"

"No. I just went and listened. I love his voice, it's mellifluously hot." This is how she turns a phrase, *mellifluously hot*. "But then came the question and answer portion, and someone—"

She fell silent and looked away as the waitress dropped off two coffees without a word. I threw her a grateful smile and returned my attention to Staze's tale of bookstore woe.

"She's gone. Continue. Somebody asked a question?"

"A woman asked if he was seeing anybody, which is a bit of a joke because he's chronically single. We all laughed, and Sam laughed too, but then, out of nowhere, he introduced his fiancée." *Oh shit*, I thought. I knew she'd had an epic crush on this guy for years, but suddenly I wondered if a part of her had been— "And I've been saving myself for him!"

"Oh shit!" I blurted. "Seriously?"

"Yes! No. I don't know," she said, shaking her head. "I suppose I imagined we were soul mates, Natalie, and now he's got some fiancée. And it gets worse."

"There's more?"

She took a deep breath and sipped her black coffee. I poured a bunch of cream in mine and glanced at my watch. It was already after eight, and I was worried about my meeting and my growling stomach.

"After that, someone else asked who his favorite new writers might be. I was already trying to sneak away by then, so I was behind a bookshelf when I heard him say it." She shot me a hard look.

I gasped. "He said you, didn't he?"

She paused, and her head fell to the side with exasperation. "He said, 'I find the weblog Broken Hope Chest very intriguing, and I would love to meet the writer behind it, *whoever she or he might be.*'"

My jaw dropped. Months ago, rumors swirled around the Internet that Anastaze, who writes anonymously but from a decidedly female perspective, was actually a dude. Essentially, a bunch of writers decided that Broken Hope Chest, my shy and brilliant friend's beautiful body of work, was so astute and incisive that its creator must actually have a Y chromosome. Comments sections and message boards erupted with pure speculation. Anastaze spent weeks ranting to me about trolls and flame wars and other medieval-sounding insanity. She agonized over outing herself, but she truly believed she would not be able to write Broken Hope Chest anymore if her real identity came to light. I'm the only person in the world who knows that Anastaze writes this famous thing (aside from my now-former therapist Jeanette, because I had to tell somebody, and poor Jeanette doesn't know the difference between an email and a tweet, so it's probably fine).

After a couple of weeks, the shitstorm died down, as all Internet-related shitstorms quickly do. But the fact that Staze's favorite-ever writer—a man whom she fantasizes is her soul mate—would still publicly entertain the sexist controversy over her work's provenance made his tremendous compliment so much more bitter than sweet.

"Staze, that is awful. It's not stupid at all."

She looked at me with her pink-and-brown eyes. "I feel like such a coward, Nat." I shook my head and thought, *No, you're not a coward. You're brave enough to make art for art's sake.* She misinterpreted. "You think I should just reveal myself."

"I used to," I explained. "I used to think you should tell the world right away, yesterday if possible. But now I believe you need to wait until you're absolutely certain the time is right."

"But what if something happens to me? What if I get hit by a bus?"

"Staze, if you get hit by a bus, I will throw the biggest press conference in the history of online literature, and all the hip kids will flock to your grave like you were Jim Morrison or something."

She half-smiled. "You think they'd let me in at Montparnasse? For *le weblog*?"

"Maybe not. But I'm fairly certain we could get you into the Cambridge Cemetery."

"With Henry James?" she asked earnestly.

"With all those crazy Jameses." I love that the idea of sharing an eternal resting place with a stodgy novelist and his neurotic family actually restores Staze's pluck. I looked at my watch again. "Staze, I have to run. I'll call you this afternoon, OK?"

She waved me out the door. "Go. I'll get the coffee. Thank you. I love you. I still feel like an idiot. Have a nice day." As I headed toward the door, Staze leapt up, jumped in front of me, and gave me a squeeze. Then she bounded back over to the blue booth and resumed fiddling with her menu.

She's the cutest little genius you ever did see.

I hopped into my green ten-year-old Camry (passed down from my father) and raced to my meeting at the Shops at West Newton. Working in fashion production is occasionally quite glamorous, but I also spend a lot of time in malls. At a red light, I discovered a plastic container of raw almonds in my center console, and a wave of relief flooded over me. My now-former shrink Jeanette believes that skipping meals is particularly harmful to my recovery.

I've come a long way with my eating issues thanks to Jeanette. She's a diet addiction recovery specialist, according to her business card. I found her a few years ago after I fainted at the fabric store while attempting the infamous lemon-honey-cayenne cleanse. Instead of counseling me to lose weight, she has helped me become more comfortable with food and my natural size. I'm not all the way there. But I do have half a pan of brownies in my fridge that I haven't demolished, and all the clothes in my closet fit me right now. No more aspirational skinny jeans from middle school that I expect my adult body to shove back into someday. And while I know I don't eat perfectly, I also know that nobody does. Diet ideations are few and far between these days. I'm coming gradually to accept, and even enjoy, the way I look: I am rounded, plump, big-boned, ample. I am large, I contain multitudes. White lines of thin skin cut trails along my hips, thighs, and arms, all the places I expanded too fast. My small breasts are suspended over a high, narrow waist that melts into my wide hips, which jut out in most directions. (Had I been born in a different century, I would've saved a bundle on bustles.) My silhouette tapers again at the lower half of my strong, thick thighs. My skin is pale, marked with a few freckles and a scar I got from climbing over a broken television. I have red hair and blue eyes and I look kind of like Botticelli's Venus whenever I find myself standing naked on a giant scallop shell.

I'm not entirely healed or balanced or sane, but I did quit therapy a couple of weeks ago. Well, technically I'm doing what Jeanette suggested: taking a three-month therapy vacation.

The fact is, I know exactly what I need to deal with next, but I can't bring myself to get into it with her. Jeanette is *lesbian*. Not *a* lesbian, but *lesbian*, from an era and a terminology that far predates my own. I imagine she referred to her first girlfriend as her "lover" and read Adrienne Rich in a consciousness-raising group and worked at a women's book/textile/organic food co-op. Forgive me, *o feminism*, for my generational prejudice, but I do not feel comfortable dishing about my salacious sex life with Jeanette. She just feels so straight to me. For someone so lesbian.

For one thing, I do not want to tell her about my recent vow of celibacy. Vows of celibacy used to be a clever little ruse of mine: I would announce to everyone within earshot that I was swearing off sex in order to goad potential partners who seemed to enjoy a challenge into my bed. I must actually mean it this time, though, because there's nobody around to call my bluff.

I decided to take a genuine break from it all a few weeks ago when I found myself neck-deep in the wreckage of Hurricane Alex, the super hilarious term I coined for my most recent interpersonal disaster. Even though we were spending almost every night together, I still found myself showing up dateless to important events. After the whole thing blew up so spectacularly, I finally decided it might be a good idea to take a step back and contemplate my past. I've never had a problem getting physical with captivating people. I always figure out a way to seduce any intriguing individual I set my sights on: musicians, professors, doctors, and more, all reduced to puddles of surrender at the touch of my hands and my lips. I get what I claim to want from all of them, sometimes for months and even years.

But Anastaze believes that what I seek sexually is an echo of a previous experience, a yearning that might seem old and irrelevant but apparently gapes wide and unfulfilled in the corners of my mind and my heart. The truth is, I'm often a mystery to myself, and I can't look around at the disaster radius of Hurricane Alex and pretend it's all new stuff. Some of it is really old, and it's followed me around for half a lifetime.

And so, I wrote out a vow of celibacy, which Anastaze witnessed, and I promised to confront my whole story and figure out why the intense sexual connections I spend my life chasing always seem to leave me emotionally high and dry. It's time for me to face the whole truth about all of it, which means going back. Way back, in fact. All the way to ninth grade.

§

THE CHALKBOARDS AT MY high school were green instead of black and very rarely used. Most of the teachers relied on overhead projectors, with their tarnished metal parts sheathed in industrial hues of nubby plastic casing and their searing bulbs and their whirring fans. Ms. Stewart, freshman English, abused the ugly contraption almost daily. Between that and her bland fashion sense, I naturally sought out other beautiful things around me to absorb my gaze.

Fortunately, there was Tyler, the bassist. His hair was an impossibly dark, almost-purple auburn, and his thick black eyelashes circled his clear green eyes as if for emphasis. He would glide into class in his flat-soled skateboarding shoes and oversized T-shirt with a thin cord of leather around his neck, drop his books on the desk in front of mine (thank you, alphabet), and, as he removed his outer layer, usually a thrift-store flannel or army surplus jacket, he would look at me and nod and sometimes even speak.

"Natalie. It's Boobs Day," he said one spring morning near the end of the year.

I raised an eyebrow. "Excuse me?"

"We watch the old *Romeo and Juliet* movie, and at some point Ms. Stewart stands in front of the TV so we don't see Juliet's boobs."

"Doesn't that make it Not Boobs Day?" I replied. "And how do you know about this?"

"Fisher told me. He has English first," he explained. "Maybe Stewart will get distracted and forget. So it's at least Potential Boobs Day."

I shook my head. "No way, dude. Look at her dress. She must've worn that just to mess with Boobs Day." Indeed, Ms. Stewart's awful frock du jour featured actual bell sleeves. We cracked up.

"Ladies and gentlemen!" Ms. Stewart said, pushing the television cart to the front of the classroom. "Bring down the volume!"

"First she's going to make it Not Boobs Day, then she's off to the Renaissance Fair," he whispered, and I laughed even harder. "Oh, Fair Lady Stewart! Why must thou ruin yon Boobs Day?"

"Looks like she's having some trouble with ye olde laserdisc player," I whispered, still giggling. "Maybe she'll accidentally start it right at the boobs part."

Tyler grinned and looked at me sideways. "Why are *you* so interested in looking at some chick's tits anyway?"

"Tyler!" Ms. Stewart barked. "Tyler, why is it that I see the back of your head so frequently?"

"Sorry, miss. I had to ask Natalie a question about *Romeo and Juliet*," he said, and I kicked his chair.

The truth was that I had no idea why I was so interested in looking at Olivia Hussey's tits, but boy was I interested! At fourteen, my sexual feelings for other girls formed a tidal wave of envy, desire, shame, and thrill that rose up as suddenly as it died down again, leaving only confusion and fear in its wake. Hormones are a bitch. And that's probably the real lesson teens need to learn from *Romeo and Juliet*, though most of us absorbed very little from the film that day. While Mercutio performed his manic rant and Tybalt bit the dust, I mostly just stared at Tyler. I stared at Tyler staring at Heather Boyle, who sat beside him. Sometimes I would find myself staring at her, too.

Heather Boyle was beautiful and popular and still mostly sexless. She wrote her class notes in big loopy print with stylized lowercase a's that looked like typeface instead of just an o with a stick on it like the rest of us. In addition to being effortlessly pretty, Heather was a bright student and a gifted athlete who chose volleyball over cheerleading when a conflict arose, which was pretty cool. Still, perhaps because she didn't need moves to get attention, she seemed uninterested in high school flirtation and unaware that any of it was going on around her. As the minutes crept by and I gazed at the back of Tyler's freckled neck, I followed the path of his eyes to Heather's tanned knees and downy thighs and wondered if she'd ever been kissed. I never had.

Fortunately for me, this was about to change. Some girls never manage to extricate their own sexuality from the desire to be desired that is cultivated in us from a very young age. But if you're a lucky girl, like I was, then your sex drive kicks in early, and you do what you do because it feels good, not to prove anything or to please anyone else.

And in a way, it all began that day, after Ms. Stewart made sure to block our view of the sex but not the murder or the suicide, and after the bell rang. That's when Tyler called to me. "Hey, Natalie."

I spun, already armed with my backpack and halfway to geometry. "Yeah? What's up?"

"You were right," he said. "Not Boobs Day."

I shook my head wistfully. "Alas. Not Boobs Day."

"Are you going to the Wazzoo Festival on Saturday?"

"Yep," I replied, trying to hide my excitement. "Got my ticket."

"Cool. See you there."

Tyler breezed past me and exited the classroom. And, although I already knew the answer, I wanted to hear her say it.

"Hey Heather, are you going to Wazzoo on Saturday?"

"Wazzoo? What's Wazzoo?"

I smiled. "Nothing. Never mind."

Wazzoo Unlimited was (and perhaps still is) a line of skateboarding and surf gear out of Australia, and, for a time that happened to coincide with my teen years, they sponsored an annual touring music festival. Every spring, the tour would come through the mid-sized metropolis near the sprawling suburb where I lived. I went three times, in ninth and tenth grades and then again senior year. That last one was something of a goof. It's incredible how short the turnaround time is on ironic nostalgia when you're a teenager.

Wazzoo my freshman year featured two of my favorite bands, Pull and the Jennifer Eights, plus a few solo artists like Jack Cazenove, long before he was famous. I went with some girls who I've since lost touch with. We arrived early in the afternoon, and my companions headed straight for the field in front of the main stage to stake out a good spot. Being a bigger music geek, I wandered around the periphery toward the side stage, which would feature local musicians for a while and then give way to national up-and-comers. The paths between the stages teemed with vendor tents, and as I strolled through, I began to understand why my parents were so reluctant to let me attend an outdoor summer concert sponsored by Australian extreme sports apparel. Nobody was selling anything wholesome or educational on those merch tables, though I was certainly learning a lot. The air was filled with what I now know to be an amalgam of marijuana, clove cigarettes, and patchouli. At the time I could identify zero of those odors.

I knew that my ignorance regarding many of the items for sale must not be indicated to anyone. I tried to eavesdrop and analyze context clues as I nonchalantly fingered the blown-glass wizard figurines.

"…because my old piece has a broken slider, so I just need to replace it…"

"…designed so the carb is covered by your middle finger instead of your thumb…"

"…need a new one-hitter. My parents nabbed my old one…"

I knew that voice. I looked up.

"Tyler?" I asked, poking my head out from behind the black light posters.

He stared at me, brow furrowed. I started to panic.

"Uh, we have English class? And—"

"Dude, Natalie, I know who you are!" He laughed a dry laugh and gave me a hug. He held me there, arms wrapped around my waist, chin tucked behind my shoulder. No pats. "It's awesome to see you. You should come over and meet my friends. Well, like, they're my brother's friends, but they're awesome."

He grabbed my hand and started leading me out of the merch tent. My stomach climbed up into my throat and then bungee jumped back into my lower abdominal cavity.

"But what about your…one-hitter?" I attempted.

"Oh, right." He marched back over to the dreadlocked woman with the metal cash box, who herself seemed unfazed by his rude departure in the middle of a transaction. She opened a small tin filled with what appeared to be fake cigarettes, and Tyler selected one. He slid the item behind his ear, stood stock still for a few seconds, then pulled out his wallet with a flourish, as if paying for his purchase were some kind of brilliant idea.

That's when it finally occurred to me that he might be chemically altered in some way.

Looking back on it, he was obviously stoned, but I had no notion of the telltale signs at the time. It's a bit jarring to remember my own state of ignorance, or innocence, with respect to narcotic highs and lows and just about everything else around me that day.

Tyler grabbed me by the hand again and led me over to his group. They were all juniors with cars. "Everybody, this is Natalie. She's cool as shit," Tyler announced. He dropped my hand and walked over to the person I assumed based on looks and familiarity to be his brother. Juniors usually ignored me, along with sophomores and seniors, but these kids smiled and waved and greeted me warmly. The peace and love attitude cultivated by board short marketing must have infused their souls with goodwill. I smiled, too.

"Hey," I said, stretching out the word in order to sound as chill as possible. Tyler took a set of keys from his brother and pulled me away again. "Bye!" I said, perhaps too cheerfully, to my cool new junior friends with cars.

"Natalie, Natalie, Natalie," Tyler said. "I'm really glad you're here."

He led me directly to the gate where a burly guy with sideburns stamped our hands for reentry. I didn't ask where we were going. What I really wanted to know was *why*. As we strode through the parking lot, Tyler seemed a bit more clear-headed than he had a few minutes before. He looked at me and smiled. "We've never really gotten a chance to talk to each other, you know? Except in English."

"You're not going to *drive* somewhere, are you?" I asked, instantly mortified for sounding like such a narc.

"Nah," he replied. He stopped next to a blue Honda Odyssey minivan, shoved the key in the lock, and slid open the rear passenger door. "I just thought we'd hang out here for a while. There's Gatorade and snacks and stuff."

We climbed inside. Tyler reached for the cooler, handed me a bottle of water, and parked himself on the bench seat beside me.

We sat there.

We sipped water.

We sat there.

And we sat there.

The temperature in the car was comfortable, but I felt like I might suffocate from the awkwardness.

I looked over at Tyler's profile as he stared straight ahead, and I was gripped by a boldness that is now so familiar to me but at the time I had no idea I possessed. I reached up and touched him. His neck muscles contracted as I pulled his new one-hitter out from behind his ear, grazing his earlobe with my fingertips.

"How does this thing work?" I asked. "I'm a dork, I know."

He laughed too hard. "You've never used one of these before?"

"I've never smoked pot before."

"Seriously?"

"I mean, I want to," I told him. "But I don't, like, have a cool older brother to show me the ropes."

"Well, the idea with this thing is…"

After that, conversation came easy. We talked about drugs and parents and siblings. We talked about music and school and friends and his band. We talked for two solid hours. When the opening notes of Pull's latest album streamed in through the minivan window, I put up my hand to silence him and groaned.

"Ugh! I can't believe we're missing this!"

"Do you want to head back?" he asked, placing his hand on the minivan door. And I did, but not nearly as much as I wanted to hold on to what was happening right then. Tyler and I had our own lives at school, and none of the same friends, and one measly class together for the few short weeks of the semester that remained. If this whole experience was going to make us weird around each other forever, like I knew that it would, then the least we could do was try to make it count.

I didn't answer him. Instead, I reached for his earring, and he turned his head and swallowed. I thumbed the silver ball floating on his lobe and fingered around the steel post in back. I committed to every brazen impulse. I leaned over and gently blew around the edges of his ear. I placed my right hand on his left leg. He was trembling.

He turned his head toward me, his gaze vacillating between my nose and my mouth. His green eyes looked kind of puffy and sleepy, suspended in pinkness, encircled by those long black lashes that were practically hitting my face. I felt my lips curl into a faint smile, and I kissed him.

He didn't kiss back. His mouth was moist and motionless, and when I opened my eyes, it was obvious he had never even closed his. My face flushed crimson and my racing brain berated me for making the worst possible call and misinterpreting all his clear signs of lack of interest and purely platonic friendship.

Then, with a sharp exhale, he pushed me down across the bench seat.

We made out and made out and made out. He felt around on top of my shirt and I didn't stop him, so he reached beneath it and touched my bare stomach. I felt more than just the taste and thrill of another person; I was getting volumes of fresh information about myself, too. Everything was new, but the rhythms seemed familiar and comfortable. I rocked and grinded and heard myself make faint little sounds. Other than school, I'd never been a natural at anything: not sports or music or social politics. But I knew I was made for this.

Tyler seemed comfortable too, but I was sure he had tons of practice, until he tried to flip me on top of him and accidentally threw me off the seat.

"Whoa!" I cried, catching myself on the driver's side headrest.

"Oh shit! Sorry. I was—shit!" He was wide-eyed and unduly concerned. I laughed.

"It's OK, I'm fine," I assured him. He slid onto his back and I propped myself up on my side next to him.

"I've never done this horizontally before," he confessed. I stroked his face with my fingertip.

"Well, you're doing just fine," I replied, surprised to hear myself come out with something so coy. How I had so much game by that age is still a mystery to me. Some of it must be biological. The rest is probably attributable to cable television. I climbed on top of him. "Is this where you wanted me?" I whispered, and we pressed our mouths and clothed bodies together again.

After a few more minutes of undulating, I was hit by a wave of adolescent self-consciousness. I realized that I was *bigger* than Tyler. I became aware of his boney hips beneath me, much narrower than my own, and I felt my thick thighs pressing against his spindly legs through his giant skater jeans. *I must have twenty pounds on this kid,* I thought, and before I knew it I had dismounted and assumed a kneeling position on the van floor.

"What's wrong?" he asked. He searched my face. Determined not to reveal my hand, I gave a wry smile and placed my hand at the top of his thigh. He grabbed the back of my head and pulled my face toward his mouth.

I unzipped his jeans and slid my hand past the elastic waistband of his boxers. I moved my fingers toward the knob of flesh that had been alternately bruising my hip and electrifying my pubic bone as we straddled each other moments before. I grazed the head with my fingertips, and Tyler's breath quivered. It was the softest skin I had ever felt in my life.

Our kissing tapered off after that, and we both started to get a little shy. I reached for another bottle of water while he fixed up his clothes. "So," I said. "Ready to head back?" He nodded. We tumbled out of the minivan, vibrating with excitement. The Jennifer Eights had just started their set, and I pulled Tyler along, pleading with him to hurry. As we jogged back to the venue, he let out a low chuckle.

"What?" I asked, grinning.

"I guess you're not a lesbian then."

"I guess not."

"Don't get offended," he said. "It's just, I'd been wondering."

I'd been wondering, too. Now I had solid confirmation that both my mind and my body were definitely into boys, which was a tremendous relief. Still, I started to get the feeling that my interest in this boy in particular would ultimately turn out to be a burden. One day I was a nerdy freshman waiting impatiently for her first kiss, and the next thing I knew I'd racked up a whole litany of sexual experiences in the course of a single afternoon. And with my crush, no less. My bass-playing, honors-English-taking, way-cooler-than-me crush.

This was definitely going to end badly.

Tyler and I parted ways as soon as we got back through the gates. His high had evaporated, and inside the walled city of the giant venue, we were definitely no longer the only two people on Earth. "I better go find my brother," he said.

"Yeah. OK. Uh. Bye," I said, not knowing if I should tell him to call me or ask to come with him or what other follow-up phrases to offer.

"Later on," he said. And he turned and walked away.

I found my friends at their spot in front of the main stage. I'd half expected them to be worried about me, but it turns out that while I was experimenting with sexuality, they were experimenting with a flask of peach schnapps. They leaned against me, languidly drunk and smelling like sickly-sweet candy. They told me what a fun time I'd missed and wondered where I'd been.

"Oh, the side stage," I lied. "I was up really close so I decided to stay there the whole time."

Somehow I knew that what had just happened with Tyler needed to be a secret, and not for the sake of *my* reputation. At school, I was a nice girl, a smart girl, maybe even a funny girl, but I was not a hot girl. My body buzzed with desire and the anticipation of more, but the cold stadium lights bore out the reality of the tan girls in bikini tops that I would never be.

I turned my attention to the Jennifer Eights and fixated on the bassist. I watched as she rocked her hips against her instrument, emanating talent and confidence and sex in the tiny black baby T that revealed her perfect stomach. Suddenly I felt like I'd been kicked in the solar plexus.

$\mathscr{S}$

I PULLED INTO THE mall parking lot a half an hour after leaving Anastaze at the New Town. Bloomingdale's recently hired us to produce an in-store fashion show for a new designer collection. After spending the morning talking production details with the store manager, I headed to the food court to interview models. One of the quirks of my job is how often the food court doubles as my office, where chicken patties marinated in pickle juice sublimate in the deep fryer and meld with the odors of the artificial buttery baked goods and sugary burgers. It's quite the olfactory experience.

I work for a small fashion production company. I started out as an intern, juggling my duties with a barista job to pay the bills. It went on like that for a few years before the company started generating enough business to hire me on as a third full-time employee. And back before my intern years, it was just Melanie and Stephanie, working out of Steph's basement.

These days, M&S Fashion Productions operates out of a warehouse space in Somerville. We share the floor with a printer and a chocolatier and a few visual artists. It smells like cocoa and gesso and burning hair, which is way better than fake-baking pretzels and spilled grape soda. It's a fun space, but I spend very little time there. I'm out in the field more than Melanie or Steph, who are both moms these days and happy to man the website and deal with intake and billing. I work out of my car, rely heavily on my coffee-stained laptop and aging Android, and hold many meetings in the food court, close enough to get a whiff of the ubiquitous samples of crispy orange chicken.

I'm usually pretty on top of things at my job, but I found myself bizarrely unprepared for the interviews I conducted today.

I sat alone at a big table near the Panda Express, reloading Staze's blog on my laptop and contemplating the last few French fries in the bag. As I sat there, I noticed a woman looking at me, trying to make that uncertain blind-date eye contact. I looked back at her, wondering if she sat behind me in Econ in college or something, but her face didn't ring any bells. I just knew that I was waiting to interview a model named Gwendolyn, not some regular lady who probably eats French fries. Finally the woman walked right up to me.

"Hi, can I help you?" I said, looking up from Staze's unchanged website.

"I'm sorry," she said hesitantly. "Are you Natalie?"

"Yes," I replied slowly.

"Oh, hello!" She smiled. "I'm Gwendolyn Santos."

I stared at her for an uncomfortable number of seconds before I finally realized that Gwendolyn must be a plus-size model and the new line at Bloomingdale's must be a plus-size line.

Actually, my post-interview perusal of the documentation revealed that the new Bloomingdale's collection is not a new acquisition for the store but an extension of an established high-end brand. Stephanie had booked all the models for me to interview, and I hadn't read the specs for the event very carefully.

"So, Gwendolyn," I began, pulling myself together. "How long have you been modeling?"

"Over a decade," she replied. "Before I moved here, I worked in New York with the Forbes-Banks Agency. Mostly print. But I've got plenty of runway experience, including several Full Figured Fashion Week events." She handed me her résumé.

"Wow," I said. Her runway castings read like the itinerary for a dream trip around the world, and her print gigs included every major fashion house that's ever even attempted plus clothing. I looked up at her. While she was clearly beautiful, she also just looked like a regular person. Modeling is a very physically demanding job, and I was sure she was uniquely qualified. But I was used to the models I work with looking pretty damn different from all the other people sitting around at the food court.

I must've paused for quite a while, because she felt compelled to continue the conversation. "Do you come from a modeling background yourself?"

"Me? No. No, of course not," I replied, flummoxed. I've never even considered modeling, what with my size, which I suddenly realized was pretty much the exact same size as her size. "I'm more of a production person," I covered. "I'm interested in the light design, the choreography, those elements. Thank you, though, that's a very flattering question."

"I just assumed. You've got the cheekbones. That's ninety percent of it." She flashed a gorgeous smile.

"Well, Gwendolyn, you're way overqualified for this event, and we're lucky to have you." I filled her in on the pay rates and call times, and I told her I'd email her a contract before the end of the day.

Now I had only to contend with Staze. She still hadn't posted anything since the bookstore incident. I loved her dearly, but sometimes I didn't know how to help her. We were so different, but somehow she always managed to give me great comfort and advice. I was heading over to her place that night to throw away sharp objects and confiscate her shoelaces. Actually, I would be making dinner. I could at least try to get her to eat something. And I could listen.

§

I SERIOUSLY CONTEMPLATED SKIPPING school that Monday after the Wazzoo festival, faking some kind of concert hot dog–induced illness. I was definitely plenty nauseated. I'd had one of the best afternoons of my life with the person I was about to see, and I had no idea whether we would even acknowledge it.

When third period rolled around, I gathered all the nonchalance I could muster and strode into my English classroom. Tyler showed up a minute later, walked past my desk, threw his books down, and took off his jacket without looking at me. I watched him in my peripheral vision as I pretended to copy down the homework. The bell rang.

Then, Tyler turned around, and, without a smile, he winked at me. I blinked my eyes slowly back at him, woozy with his energy. His nostrils flared, and he looked away. After class, he dropped a piece of paper with his phone number onto my desk.

Thus began our summer of sexploration in bedrooms and basements, dodging parents and siblings, scrambling for clothes as cars pulled into the driveway, bonking heads, learning where not to put our teeth. Maybe teenagers fumbling all over each other is not our favorite thing to think about as a society, but plenty of us did it. I personally believe I'm much better off for that experience. Still, I'm sure as a parent I'd feel at least a little bit obligated to do or say something, and my own mother did try, in her mortifying way.

"Are you going steady with that boy?" she asked, not understanding anything about anything.

"No, Mom, we are not 'going steady.' He's my friend."

"Is he your *boy*-friend?"

"He's just my friend. He's, uh, teaching me how to play the bass. Bye!"

My mom, a third grade teacher, had summers off, too, so tyler and I spent most of our time over at his place, where his brother was the only other person around to avoid. As an only child, I could never quite understand the complex combination of friend, rival, relation, and acquaintance that comprises a sibling. Tyler and Jason were less than two years apart, and even though they never looked directly at one another, they seemed to notice everything about each other. Jason, for example, noticed us sneaking apprehensively past his bedroom, and he relished the easy ribbing he could dish out just by acknowledging my presence.

"Why, hello there, Natalie," Jason said as we passed behind him one weekday. He never looked away from his computer screen.

"Oh, hey, Jason!" I blurted as Tyler yanked me away and Jason smirked, motionless except for his fingers.

Tyler pulled me toward the basement stairs. We bounded down and flopped onto the hideous couch with the eighties cruise ship upholstery. I spent hours on that couch. On the afternoon in question, we started out doing what we did for a relatively healthy percentage of our time together. We talked.

"What's up with Jason?" I asked, worried by his mischievous tone. "Is he going to tell your parents or something?"

Tyler balked. "Is he going to *tell*? No. No way. Besides, we're not even doing anything."

"I guess, but I really don't want to have a conversation about what we're not doing with your parents."

"Relax," Tyler said, dropping his shopping bag. "Jason won't say anything. He's got secrets of his own." I didn't ask for details, but based on Jason's laser-like focus on Halo and lack of female companionship, I assumed Tyler meant drugs.

I picked up the bag containing Tyler's most recent discount CD store purchases and pulled out a box from the copy shop. "What's in here?"

"Those are the flyers for Morbidica's next show," he explained, "Morbidica" being the unfortunate name he and his friends gave to their very first band. He opened the box and handed me one.

I lit up. "Elmwood? You're playing at the Elmwood? Oh my God!" It really was thrilling. The Elmwood Lounge hosted every decent mid-sized indie band that came to town, and I actually owned a fake ID declaring me to be eighteen whole years of age for the express purpose of getting into that place.

Tyler beamed. "It's an early slot, but it's still pretty cool." I realize now that the Elmwood would book local high school bands at odd hours just to take a cover charge off their friends and family and kick them all out after forty-five minutes. That's not necessarily a bad thing, but the bands didn't audition for the honor. They pretty much just had to sign up.

"I will totally be there!" I exclaimed, and Tyler's face fell minutely but perceptibly.

"Uh, yeah. Yeah, absolutely," he said absently, fiddling with his new CDs. I sat there confused until he eventually looked up at me and lunged, tackling me onto the couch. And I'm certain I squealed with girlish delight.

I showed up at the Elmwood for Tyler's show all by myself. Tyler traveled with his bandmates, and I was hoping to tag along with them after the show, so I didn't want an entourage of my own to negotiate. After milling around the periphery of the Elmwood for a few minutes, I finally noticed a familiar face.

"Why, hello there, Natalie," Jason said. He leaned against the wall next to me.

"Oh, hey!" I replied, grateful for his companionship. I'd noticed a few guys from school near the stage, but nobody I would approach. Half of Morbidica attended our cross-town rival high school, so I wasn't too surprised to see a whole coven of girls in black lipstick that I didn't recognize. "Are any of your friends here?" I asked Jason, remembering his band of merry travelers from Wazzoo.

"No. I'm meeting them after this over at Insomnia." Insomnia was a coffee shop down the street from the Elmwood. They sold T-shirts that said *I Drink My Coffee Black Because Black Is How I Feel on the Inside* and served tremendous milkshakes made with four shots of espresso plus some tarry grounds thrown in for extra jitters. "What about you?" he asked. Just then, the room went dark.

On stage, the lead guitarist started a simple, catchy riff. The lights came up on him and the drummer, and the singer stepped out from the back. Despite the name, Morbidica had more pop undertones than crunchy metal sounds, and their first song bounced along joyfully. But through the first verse, something was missing: the bass.

Along came the chorus, and Tyler burst out of the wings, laying down a serious funk groove as he half-danced his way onto the stage. I squealed and clapped before I could catch myself. Fortunately, everyone else in the room was just as delighted by him as I was. Even the bartenders and bouncers, who clearly loathed these kiddie events, all stopped and smiled and applauded for Tyler.

The fact is, the band teemed with talent, and Tyler stood out as the most gifted among them. In addition to playing some solid original songs at the Elmwood that day, Morbidica also covered the Red Hot Chili Peppers. Tyler didn't simply nail Flea's bass part, he actually managed to make it his own. He was the real musician of the bunch, and he still is. He plays bass and drums with a couple of bands down in Austin, which I learned one day when a google search auto-completed his name. After I entered the first eleven characters.

When the set was over, the guys rushed around unplugging and coiling and breaking down so another high school band could take the stage. Jason and I lingered against the wall.

"I gotta admit, the kid's good," Jason remarked with a conciliatory smile.

"He really is," I swooned, drunk on a cocktail of awe, desire, and pride. I noticed Tyler crouched over by the monitor. "I'm going to congratulate him."

I walked over just as the gaggle of girls in plaid skirts and fishnets converged at the base of the stage too. Tyler noticed them first. "Hey. I'll be done in, like, seven minutes," he told them. He still didn't see me, so I kind of raised my hand and waved from the other side of the speaker.

"Hey, I just wanted to say nice job!" I half-shouted. Tyler saw me and jumped.

"Yeah, you guys were great," added a girl from hell's Catholic school.

"Um, thanks. Thanks," Tyler said, glancing between us.

One of the girls looked at me skeptically. She turned to Tyler. "Aren't you going to introduce your friend?"

"Oh, sorry," he said, wiping his hands on his jeans and standing up. "Gretchen, this is my friend Natalie. Natalie, this is Gretchen. My girlfriend."

I believe I actually left my body then, just for a split second. I heard a loud ringing in my ears as I came back, and I locked my knees to keep from crumbling all the way down to the floor. I turned to face Gretchen, examining the purple streaks in her hair and her size-zero corset top. "Hi," I managed, as she looked me up and down. "I know him from English," I attempted, trying to explain to both of us what the hell I was even doing there.

"That's cool," she said, throwing her friends a smirk.

I vaguely recognized the sound of my name being called from far away. I thought it might be God or Jesus or a long-lost relative urging me to just go ahead and die of shame.

"Natalie! Hey, Natalie!" I whipped around. Jason. "Are you coming? To Insomnia?"

"Oh. I...I have to go with Jason," I mumbled to Tyler and the girls. I felt like I might throw up, but instead I looked at Gretchen and said, "Nice to meet you."

I hurried out of the club in the wake of Jason's long, purposeful strides. Outside, he lit a cigarette and offered me one. I just stood there. He put the pack away and leaned up against the brick wall, taking long drags.

"He's a little asshole," he said eventually, to nobody in particular.

"No, he's not. We're not—we were never—" I stammered.

"He is. I *told* him. Forget that kid. Let's just go." He pushed off and strode across the street. I wasn't fully conscious of how nice Jason was being to me that night. All I could muster was a dazed, compliant sort of gratitude. I trotted behind him like a melancholic puppy.

We walked into Insomnia and sat down with a group of rising seniors. For once, I was too out of it to care if I seemed cool enough to be hanging out with them. A guy in a cape invited me to play chess—"Fancy a game of chess?"—and I accepted because it gave me an excuse to sit still and be quiet. As I pretended to contemplate my next move, I chastised myself for being so blindsided. What I'd said to Jason was true. Tyler was never my boyfriend. I was never his anything. Whether or not I wanted to be was moot from the very inception of whatever it was we were doing. I knew where I stood all along. So what gave me the right to feel so hurt?

"It's not so wretched," my opponent said.

"Huh?"

"You said 'wretched,' but you actually have a lot of good options. You could move your rook here, or..."

I nodded and tuned him out. I hadn't said "wretched" but "Gretchen," just once, under my breath. Gretchen. He had never mentioned her. Were they having sex? Technically, Tyler and I were not, technically, having sex. Technically, I was still a virgin. And technical virginity means a very great deal to otherwise-sexually active fifteen-year-old girls. But I wanted to know about her. I wanted to know if he was more intimate with her body than he was with mine.

After I lost a few games of chess, Jason offered to drive me home. I directed him to my house, and as he pulled up to the driveway, I made a feeble attempt to thank him.

"I guess I won't be seeing much of you anymore…" I trailed off, gulping down tears that I knew would come hard and staccato and snotty and rough.

"I wouldn't be so sure of that," he said with a sympathetic smile. I took that to mean he was rooting for me with Tyler. I had no such optimism.

"Yeah, well, thank you, Jason. Thank you for everything." And with that, I climbed out of his aging red Honda and slammed the door. I walked inside, exchanged a few brief pleasantries with my parents, trudged up to my bedroom, and fell apart.

§

On the topic of falling apart, I arrived at Anastaze's apartment off Harvard Street in Allston around six, lugging the makings of dinner and a bottle of wine. I let myself in and found her splayed out on the couch, surrounded by Sam Elliot Jacobs books and many copies of his magazine. Mournful French lyrics poured from the iPod dock. I dropped my bags and shook my head.

"Seriously?" I asked, gesturing around at her little scene.

"Listen to this, Nat. 'Autumn upbraided him for his misspent summer with its effortless transition from novice green to vibrant red.'"

"That sounds like something you'd write."

"I know!" she cried, burying her face in a pillow. I gave her a moment to sulk while I chopped onions and opened wine.

"Staze," I said, handing her a glass, "Maybe the whole 'she or he' thing shouldn't break your heart so much as make you realize that you don't actually love this person. You don't even *know* him."

"Not personally," she conceded. "But I know his voice, and I love it. I believe he sees the world the same way I do."

"Isn't a person's ideas about men and women and what they're capable of a big part of *her or his* world view?" I argued.

"He probably didn't mean it," she minimized. "He enjoys courting controversy. He's pugnacious."

"'Pugnacious.' Does that mean cute? I forget."

"No," she explained. "'Pugnacious' means eager to fight."

"Oh. I get confused because pugs are so adorable."

"Think of a pugilist, like a prize fighter," she suggested. "'Pugilist' is etymologically related to 'pugnacious.'"

"Oh, of course, I'll just think of a pugilist," I quipped.

"That sort of thing doesn't help you?" she asked sincerely.

"Um. No." We're pretty different, Staze and me.

We returned to the topic of her ill-fated crush for the better part of an hour. I asked leading questions and hugged her while she cried and even persuaded her to eat a little plate of pasta.

"Thank you for taking all my codswallop seriously, Natalie," she said, pouring herself the last few drops of wine.

"It's not hard to take you seriously, Staze, until you say something like 'codswallop,'" I teased, and she finally cracked a smile. "I'm happy to be here for you, especially after all the hours I spent prattling on about Alex."

"But that was an actual relationship," she said.

"Depends on who you ask."

"How's the vow of celibacy going?"

"So far, so good," I replied. "I'm trying to reflect on my past."

"Your past is fascinating," Staze replied. "Maybe you're the one who should write a book, Nat."

"Nah," I said with a smile. "Anything I write would wind up with a pink high heel on the cover. I refuse to be dismissed and mocked by high-minded writers like yourself."

"Oy, I've read my share of chick lit," she protested.

"You think Jane Austen is chick lit," I shot back.

"And you think *Bridget Jones's Diary* is serious literature!"

"It is!" I insisted. "Just like *West Side Story* is serious theater!"

Staze stood up, walked over to her bookcase, and started tossing novels at me. "What about *Blindness*?"

"Sounds depressing," I said, examining the back flap.

"Please, Natalie," she begged. "Why don't you read something contemporary and challenging?"

"Staze, I already slog through seven hundred pages of *Vogue* every month," I argued. "That's more than enough abstract imagery for me." At that, Staze pretended to faint dead away, and I lost myself in peels of laughter. Stunning pratfalls are just one of Staze's many hidden talents. When I finally recovered, she climbed back onto the couch next to me and reached for her beverage.

"I feel so lonely, Natalie. Like nobody knows me."

"I know you, Anastaze."

"Of course you do," she said. "But I want something different. A boyfriend. Maybe a family."

Staze doesn't talk to her parents. That's a whole huge can of worms when it comes to her anonymity as well.

"Well, I'm in your life, and I'm not going anywhere," I offered. "But of course you want a boyfriend. I get that. It's a different thing."

"I have all these readers who quote-unquote '*love*' me," she said, gesturing redundant air quotes.

"You mean like you '*love*' Sam Elliot Jacobs?"

She paused. "Touché."

"Staze, you have fans because you're talented. But of course nobody can love the real you if you don't share yourself with them," I pop-psychologized. "I think all this Sam Elliot Jacobs stuff isn't about being in love with him so much as wanting the public writer's life that he has."

"So, what is that, projecting? Am I projecting, Natalie?" she asked, a bit annoyed.

"Well, do you really want to design websites and corporate logos for the rest of your life?"

"Please, Nat. Not now. I can't think about any more today," she said.

I hesitated, but I didn't want to let the moment pass. "I believe that if you decided to reveal yourself, or even if you just responded to that agent who wants you to publish under your pseudonym, you'd find yourself opening up to more people in your personal life, too."

"Well," she sniffed. "Thank you for employing your vatic powers on my behalf."

"'Vatic?'"

"'Vatic.' Oracular. Prophetic. It's from the Latin for 'seer.'"

Of course it is.

§

IN THE DAYS FOLLOWING my surprise introduction to Gretchen, I spent a lot of time sulking in my room. When I wasn't sulking in my room, I would creep down to the kitchen and avail myself of whatever sat in the refrigerator: cold spaghetti, leftover chicken, that nasty low-fat coffee chip marshmallow swirl ice cream my mother bought by the gallon. After my third day in a row of cleaning out everything prepared and edible, said diet-conscious mother delivered a stern lecture.

"Natalie, you already need to lose some weight. This is not helpful," she said, shaking an empty lo mein container in my face. "Have you been exercising at all this whole summer?"

My pattern with food was utterly banal. When I ate, I felt soothed and spacey. When I stopped eating, I squirmed in my own skin, hating my body and my stupid illogical broken heart. Mom scolded me and I agreed with her, just as Tyler and the whole wide world agreed with her, that I didn't look right, that something was wrong with me, that my appearance was shameful. I fed myself to offer some peace, then I loathed myself for accepting the comfort and failing to beat back my growing body, then ate some more to assuage the loathing, rinse, repeat. I spent late nights researching diets on the Internet, choosing the most extreme ones and failing at them by mid-morning. I wanted a different body yesterday. I wanted to wake up as Gretchen six months ago.

My pants started to get tighter. Prior to that, the thrills of my salacious summer had taken inches off my waistline, although I had barely noticed. Now, with flesh spilling out of my jeans, I actually had concrete evidence that I was gross. I bought some ugly oversized T-shirts from a discount store and sat around in my new unflattering wardrobe, dreading the first day of school.

I wear horizontal stripes on the outside because fat is how I feel on the inside.

Then one day, about a week before sophomore year, the phone rang. It was Tyler.

"Hey, what's up?" he asked casually.

"Hi," I replied, trying to sound as affectless as possible. "I haven't heard from you in a while."

"Yeah, we just got back from Glacier today." *Glacier.* I completely forgot that his family had been planning a two-week camping trip. They were scheduled to leave a few days after the Elmwood show. "So, you want to come over?"

"Um." I glanced up at the mirror in my bedroom. My eyes were pink and swollen, my face was puffy, my skin was ghostly pale. "How about the day after tomorrow?"

"Wednesday?" he asked. "Sure. Come by around noon, cool?"

I spent the next thirty-six hours jogging, laying out in the yard, and forcing down gallon after gallon of water. I had no idea what Tyler expected from seeing me again, but I didn't want to appear as devastated as I was either way. I tried to convince myself that he probably just wanted me to swear an oath never to tell anyone about his ill-advised hook-ups with nerdy chubby unpopular

Natalie from English class. But I couldn't fight my inklings of hope. I longed to kiss him and kiss him and never ever stop.

On Wednesday I put on makeup: concealer under my eyes, eyeliner, mascara, lipstick. Then I decided I looked like a desperate poseur and washed it all off, leaving only a stubborn residue of black goo around my eyes. I pulled on my loosest jeans and an innocuous black T-shirt, brushed my teeth for the fiftieth time, and walked over to his house.

Tyler answered the door without a shirt on, looking for all the world like he'd just returned from Sun Tan Push-Up Camp. "Natalie," he said, hugging me close.

I followed him down to the finished basement and sat hesitantly on the couch. Tyler started fiddling with the CD player, searching for some particular track. "So what's up with you?" he asked.

"Um. Nothing." I didn't say another word. I picked at a loose thread on the cushion next to me, waiting for the other shoe to drop.

"Camping was pretty fun. We saw a grizzly," he said. I didn't respond. "Why are you being weird?"

"I'm not being weird," I replied. "I just—"

"Dude, are you wearing *makeup*?" he asked, and he leaned in to study my face. He smiled slyly and the next thing I knew he was on top of me with his lips on my lips and his hips on my hips.

Wait, some part of me said. *Stop. What is this? What does that mean?* But those questions quickly fell away as I tumbled out of my head and into my body.

When I think about the war I waged against my poor young self during those weeks I didn't hear from him, I can't remember a single moment when I didn't want to rip off my own skin. I felt trapped, imprisoned by the flesh around me. But the moment Tyler kissed me, I experienced a surge of pleasure implicitly tied to inhabiting my own body. I surrendered to that glittery rush of excitement and passion, just like I had in the minivan months before. I felt more than just wanted. I felt alive. I felt *good*.

So, in other words, sexual activity granted me a reprieve from my otherwise-constant body hatred.

Well. That's something.

Tyler and I kissed and groped and grinded until we heard the basement door open and slam. We bolted up and flew apart as footsteps crashed down the stairs and Jason appeared before us, a blur coming into focus from the bottom up. Jason did a double take when he saw me. Then he glared straight at Tyler.

"Come on, man! What the fuck?"

"What?" Tyler responded, taken aback.

"What is she doing here?" Jason demanded, pointing at me but staring down his brother. Tyler just stood there, shirtless and ambushed.

"Look, mind your own business, Jason," Tyler asserted, his tone turning defensive. "Why do you get to have an opinion all of a sudden?"

Jason paused, fuming. Finally, he exhaled. "You shouldn't treat her that way," he said, his lips curled in anger. Then he turned to me. "You shouldn't let him." He shook his head and disappeared back up the stairs.

Tyler and I looked at each other, stunned. Slowly, a gooey sludge began to envelope me. The blob of shame, formed at the Elmwood and fed by my bingeing and now Jason's disgust, had finally grown large enough to swallow me whole. I stood up. "I'll go," I said, tears welling up in my eyes. I hurried up the stairs and out the door and all the way home, where I promptly collapsed into hysterics in the first-floor bathroom.

It never occurred to me back then that Jason might have been defending me, that two sexy brothers had just quarreled over my honor. I just felt exposed, like somebody had finally seen me for what I was, and it turned out I was a pathetic slut with no self-respect. I couldn't see the situation any other way at the time, not even after I answered the phone the next day and heard a familiar voice on the line.

"Tyler?" I said, hoping.

"It's Jason," came the reply. "I'm heading downtown tonight. My friend's getting a tattoo. Do you want to come?"

And so I went, and I bore witness to the birth of Jason's friend Zephyr's Celtic armband, and afterward I sat around with his posse drinking coffee and wondering what, exactly, I was doing there.

And again the next night, I found myself in the company of a big group of rising seniors, buzzing on late-night caffeine, talking about music, playing board games and card games. I started to wonder if this was a permanent state of affairs, and, if so, if I needed to buy some new clothes. I'd been rotating my limited black T-shirt collection all week.

A few days later, school started, and I found myself seated directly behind Tyler in sophomore honors English. (Fuck you, alphabet.) After twenty minutes of ignoring each other, he turned to me with a flat expression on his face and asked, "Are you dating my brother?"

"We're just hanging out," I replied, and after class I immediately switched my schedule around so that I wouldn't have to see him anymore. I had to feign a sincere interest in Textiles and Design in order to convince the guidance counselor to agree to the shift.

It turned out to be the best thing that ever happened to me.

Fabric and My Life

THE RECHARCHE SHOW AT Bloomingdale's came uncomfortably close to full-on disaster. For one thing, we wound up with more than 250 RSVPs for a department store event in the middle of a weekday. It turns out plus-size women get pretty excited about the idea of being taken seriously by hot designers. Usually we plan for half the RSVPs to show up, plus about thirty more to account for walk-ups and interested shoppers. We've never planned for more than one hundred attendees before, so we had to scale up to a larger seating area, more staff, and more models, since part of the model's job is to walk around and greet customers after the show. With only a week to go before the event, I had to redo everything: the catering, the equipment rental order, the lighting design, the music, even the runway looks and model castings. Although it wasn't an ideal situation, it also was not the kind of thing I would normally have any trouble handling. I might sometimes fail to prepare for informal mall interviews, but the shows are the big deal part of the job. I *never* fuck this stuff up.

But I guess I've been way too distracted by all the sex I'm not having lately, because I stood there that afternoon in Bloomingdale's with my clipboard and my walkie-talkie and twelve looks and eleven models.

I counted and recounted the names on the list over and over again. Nine-ten-eleven. Nine-ten-eleven. I somehow doubled-up a model assignment when I transferred the casting list over to the master, so it was a stupid transcription error. Unfortunately, I discovered my mistake less than an hour before the event. I have a Rolodex packed with extremely professional and reliable standard models to call in case of emergency, but plus models are a different story. I stared at the orphaned outfit in the program, a gorgeous floor-length chocolate brown strapless dress with pale blue detailing. I grimaced at the thought of omitting it.

I spotted Gwendolyn in the makeup chair and made a beeline for her.

"Hey, Gwendolyn! You look great! Listen, can I have a word with you for a moment?" I blurted as buckets of adrenaline comingled with the caffeine already coursing through my blood.

"Hi, Natalie. What's up?" She talked like a ventriloquist, barely moving her mouth as Jeff (the very best makeup artist in New England) expertly highlighted her stunning cheekbones. I threw Jeff an embarrassed look.

"I was just wondering… I just need to know if…" I took a deep breath. This was no time to be timid. "I'm short one model. Do you know of any plus models that live nearby?"

"Oh, that sucks!" she declared as sympathetically as she could without moving her face. "Did somebody get sick?"

"No," I replied. "It's an error. On my part."

"Oh," Gwendolyn said, with a touch of trepidation.

"It's awful, I know. This never happens," I said.

"It's true," Jeff vouched. "Natalie's the best. I've never seen a problem at any of her events. Smile please, Gwendolyn."

"Thank you, Jeff," I said, grateful for his reassurance.

"Well, everybody makes mistakes," Gwendolyn said through her glowing grin. "I'm trying to think if I know anybody this far west. The only people I can think of are probably at their day jobs."

"Yeah," I replied, dejected. "I'll have to drop a look. It's a shame, because I made this." I held up the program so Gwendolyn could see it in the mirror.

"Done!" Jeff announced, and Gwendolyn spun around and grabbed the paper from my hand.

"Shit," she said, studying the full-color brochure promoting all twelve outfits as well as the accessories I coordinated with each of them. She looked at me. "I can go twice if you want."

Relief washed over me. "Could you? I would be so grateful. It's look number eight. I'll get you a dressing assistant, and I will absolutely make sure you are compensated additionally for—"

"Hang on," Gwendolyn interrupted. "Do you have a strapless bra?"

"What? No, not on me, but I'm sure we can find you one down in lingerie."

"No, I've got one," she said, reaching for her bag. She rifled around for a moment and proudly produced the undergarment. "Perfect! I'll wear number eight, and *you* can wear the number twelve outfit in your regular bra. Don't you think?" She turned to Jeff, handing him the program. He paused, considering her suggestion, and then looked at me and nodded.

"Wait, *me*?"

"What were you planning to wear out there?" Gwendolyn asked.

"Um, *this*," I said, gesturing at my jeans and button-down shirt.

"Natalie. A real outfit will be much better," she said, plucking look number twelve off a rack and thrusting it into my arms.

"Hang on. That can't happen," I protested. "I have to emcee from the sound booth."

"So emcee the whole thing, then walk out yourself at the end," Gwendolyn said breezily, as though strutting down a runway in front of a couple hundred people was no big deal. "Besides, that number twelve is a bit conservative for me. Eight will let me show some skin." She winked at Jeff. "It's win, win, win!"

"Oh yeah? Who gets the third win?" I asked, still sure as hell I wouldn't be walking down that runway.

"That would be me," declared Jeff. He grabbed me by my shoulders and pushed me down into the makeup chair. "I've been dying to do this for years," he said, rubbing my face with a wet wipe while grabbing fistfuls of compacts from the red metal toolboxes he repurposed for his trade.

"But there are a million things to do! I can't just be sitting here," I said, raising my voice.

"Stop! Don't move your face!" Jeff admonished.

"See? Sitting still is *work*," said Gwendolyn, slipping into her strapless bra a few feet away, her back to Jeff and me. "Welcome to my world."

And as I sat, I racked my brain for anything I absolutely had to do in the next forty minutes. I usually run around, triple-checking all the elements that the consummate professionals I hire have already taken care of. But really, people just need to know where to find me if they have questions, and Jeff was making me a lot harder to miss. After just a few minutes in his capable hands, I already looked amazing. Randy, the adorable geek who helps me out with sound and lighting, wandered over to us.

"Hey, Natalie. Whoa." He startled at the sight of me with a face full of cosmetics. "You look really good."

"Thanks, Randy," I replied. *What a sweet kid.* "How can I help you?"

"Uh, twenty-minute warning," he said. "Do you need anything from me?"

"Just please go tell the models where I am if they need me. And Claudia." Claudia is the events manager of Bloomingdale's. She usually spends preshow overseeing the setup out front and encouraging shoppers to come gawk at the spectacle.

"Roger," Randy said with a nod. "And you just need one wireless mike, as usual?"

"Yup," I answered.

"What's the range on that mike?" Gwendolyn interjected. She was hovering nearby so she'd be on hand to start bullying me anytime I threatened to back out.

"Pretty good. I'd say eighty feet," Randy replied. "Seventy-five for sure."

"Perfect." Gwendolyn looked at me in the mirror. "You can stand out in front and announce the whole show."

"Oh, I'm sorry," I said. "I thought I was in charge here."

"You were, until you proved to be a very poor judge of your own best assets," she said with a wink. The woman loves to wink.

After a few minutes with Jennifer, the hair stylist, and a full-on assault on my décolletage by Gwendolyn, involving padded cups, an ACE bandage, and yards of athletic tape, I noticed Claudia pacing around the dressing area.

"Claudia!" I called, waving.

She cocked her head and paused. "Oh! Natalie!" she said, finally recognizing me. "You look so special!"

"Thank you," I replied.

"So. Looks like we're ready to go," she said. "It's quite a turnout."

I gathered the models together for a last-minute review. "Please line up in order, and remember to mingle and meet-and-greet after the show is over. Try to memorize as much as you can about your outfit from the program: price, size range, who did the shoes and accessories, all that good stuff. OK?"

The models voiced their agreement. I'd never worked with any of these women before, but they seemed to be paying particularly close attention. It occurred to me that my striking appearance might have something to do with it. As they lined up, I took one final glance in the mirror. My hair was piled high with loosely pinned curls. I had dramatic black eyeliner with pale lips, like a plus-size Pia Zadora. I wore a gold scoop-neck top with a structured waist-length jacket, tapered cigarette pants, gold bangle bracelets, and purple-strapped heels. I looked stunning.

Stepping out of the dressing room, I learned that "quite a turnout" was quite an understatement. All the chairs were full, and women stood crowded along the sides of the audience and crammed between the makeup counters beyond that. I couldn't even see where the crowd ended. Perhaps this would've prompted some performance anxiety, but I was too busy worrying about whether the sight lines and sound would be good enough for the guests at the back. And forget about the catering. There was no hope of everyone getting a canapé.

My intro music swelled, and, instead of setting up backstage with my notes and my wireless microphone, I walked out into the lights and onto the wing next to the runway. It dawned on me that I should probably introduce myself, since everybody could see me.

"Hello," I said, my voice shaking. I took a breath. "My name is Natalie, and I, along with M&S Fashion Productions and Bloomingdale's, would like to welcome you to the debut of Recharche's new Recharche Woman line of apparel." Applause. I had made it through the improv portion of the afternoon. I smiled and relaxed.

As I read introductions off my index cards, I noticed how the models bounded down the runway gleefully, flirting and swinging their hips. Standard models are as disciplined as infantry. Their steps explode with rigid confidence while their faces remain expressionless. It seemed like these plus models had been trained in a completely different skill set. They were engaged, friendly, interacting with the crowd. And the audience seemed more entertained than usual, like they were watching a concert instead of a lecture.

"Next, our penultimate model," I said. I love to say "penultimate" because it makes me think of Staze. "Elizabeth is wearing the cocktail-length A-line Jewel dress in black. Her shoes are Valencia, and her bracelet, earrings, and necklace are by Samantha G."

"And finally," I declared, dropping my arms a bit to show my clothes, "I am wearing the Recharche Woman Scoop top in gold, with the Moto jacket and the Luxe pant." I noticed all the eyes turning to me, and suddenly I was ice cold. "Shoes by Tidal Wave, bracelets by Samantha G," I blurted. I pivoted about fifteen degrees on my heels, the epitome of discomfort. I didn't so much as look at the runway.

"Now, let's have a round of applause for all of our models and for the Recharche Woman collection at Bloomingdale's!" I declared at last, and I watched as the carousel of beautiful models marched out before me for the finale. As Gwendolyn passed, she caught my eye. "*WALK!*" she mouthed sternly, and so, after Elizabeth emerged in her Jewel dress, I begrudgingly picked up the rear, strutting as best I could, pivoting the way I'd seen my models do a million times. I felt my face start to burn as I stomped hard and too quickly back up the runway and, finally, offstage.

Afterward, at the meet-and-greet, I talked to dozens of smiling customers. Usually the audience fails to associate me with the disembodied voice they hear announcing the show, so nobody asks me anything or seems quite sure why I know so much about the clothes. This time, everybody had a million questions just for me, and it was fun being able to talk about the outfits I'd put together and make a few specific recommendations.

By the time we finished mingling and striking the production area, it was almost four o'clock. I headed back to the dressing area to change my clothes. I crouched at the mirror, poised to wipe off my makeup, when Gwendolyn stopped me.

"No way. You're not getting off that easy," she announced, grabbing the towelette right out of my hand. "We're going out."

"You know what? I am not going to fight you on that one," I answered, sitting down. "But I am definitely going to change my shoes."

"Great show, Natalie. You did very well out there," she said.

"Please. I'm no model. But, we made lemonade, right?" I replied.

"Seriously, you did *very well*," she emphasized, but she could tell I was in no mood to hear her praise. She lowered her voice. "On an unrelated note, Jeff is straight, right?"

"Oh yeah. Completely. Those tool boxes: so ironic," I explained with a smile.

"That's what I figured. I just didn't know if they were seriously ironic or fabulously ironic, you know?"

"I do know. The best is how many people stop him and ask if they can borrow a hammer or an Allen wrench," I said, lacing up my pink and black sneakers. "He just hands them some mascara and insists it should do the trick."

"That's too funny," Gwendolyn said. She paused. "I think I'll ask him out."

"Oh," I replied. "I don't know, Gwendolyn."

"Does he have a girlfriend?"

"No, but he dates mostly models. Standard models, I mean," I said, catching myself. "And you know how that can be."

"Tell me about it. I used to be one," she replied.

"Oh. Uh," I stuttered, unsure of what I was trying to say in the first place. "Well, invite him out with us. We'll get a couple of drinks in him and you can read his vibe at the end of the night."

"No," she said, turning to look for Jeff. "I think I'll ask him out right now. I'm not really an end-of-the-night kind of girl."

I watched her walk right up to him. Where do I get off thinking I'm so bold?

§

THE FIRST TIME JASON tried to kiss me, I bloodied his nose. I didn't cold deck him or anything. It was an accident. That must have been almost halfway through sophomore year. Was there somebody else before that? Elvis maybe? The timeline gets a little confusing. I do remember a few things from tenth grade, though, very distinctly.

Textiles and Design met from 10:00 a.m. until 12:30 p.m. every day of the week. The program held on long after most other vocational tracks at my public high school got cut. TexD, as we affectionately called it, successfully morphed from a job training program into an art and fashion school application portfolio incubator.

I'd spent my academic career up to that point hovering around the middle of the top track, keeping up with my accelerated classes and toeing the honor student line. One summer, I'd dusted off my grandmother's old sewing machine and constructed a few no-frills purses from scraps of worn-out clothes I didn't want to part with. Other than that, I hadn't so much as sewed on a missing button before I walked into the TexD studio that fall.

I started the year rocking my new ugly T-shirt collection. My hair hung shapelessly past my shoulders, and I wore the same black Chuck Taylor All-Stars every day. Meanwhile, TexD teemed with teen fashion plates, in their stylish glasses and their angular haircuts and their fierce shoes. My first day was the second week of class, so everybody was already immersed in their own work by the time I arrived. I observed the steady rhythm of activity for a moment, then made my way to the instructor.

TexD was taught by a woman named Melissa Castignaglisi or Calcaglioni or something impossible like that. We all called her Miss C, which was very close to her first name. She wore her fire-engine red hair in a short pixie cut and rotated through an impressive collection of eyewear frames from a line she designed herself. Although she was pushing sixty, her hip style and boundless energy made her seem younger than most of her colleagues.

I approached and handed her my transfer form, still debating whether devoting myself to a craft for almost thirteen hours a week was a reasonable price to pay for avoiding a boy. She looked at me and smiled.

"Natalie. Welcome, Natalie. I'm Miss C." She perused the form. "You are but a sophomore? You're our only one." With that, she headed toward the front of the studio and motioned for me to follow. A small boom box sat pumping out Bob Marley, and she turned the volume down all the way. "Excuse me, TexD?" she said, and the sounds of chatter and scissors and sewing machine pedals all ceased. "This is Natalie. She'll be joining us for the year." I felt overwhelmed by this public introduction, and just as I started to turn red—

"Hi! I'm Minh!" piped up the Asian girl in the front, smiling. Her hair was parted on the side and pulled into two sharp ponytails. She wore an orange jumper dress and floral dark blue tights. I noticed a pile of rings and bracelets sitting in a basket at her workstation.

"I'm Brooke," volunteered a brunette with sleepy eyes and a slow smile. All the kids introduced themselves. Seven girls and four guys. I would be the twelfth student. I noticed a few workspaces remained open.

Miss C set me up at a station along the wall opposite the windows and handed me a stapled packet. "You can fill out all this paperwork tonight and bring it in tomorrow. Don't worry about being behind. There's plenty of time, and most of what we do in here will be driven by your own projects anyway. Last week we made pillows, and I'd really like you to do that just to get a feel for the machine." She gestured at the clunky black Singer clamped to the end of my table, then hustled over to the supply wall and loaded me up with swatches and stuffing. I had my foot on the pedal ten minutes after I walked in the door.

Later that night, I signed the equipment waiver and initialed all the safety information in the TexD intro packet. The last page was a questionnaire filled with intense and provocative questions designed to turn a feckless teenager into a purposeful artist. The final question asked what we wanted to focus on as a general project for the year, and I thought long and hard on that one. I pictured the TexD juniors and seniors in their hip clothes, all unique and self-expressed. I'd tried shopping at the thrift stores and sifting through the mall, but I could never find clothes I liked that fit my stubbornly pear-shaped frame. With determined inspiration, I wrote down the words, "I want to make a whole new wardrobe. For myself."

I continued to spend weekend evenings and occasional weeknights hanging out at Insomnia with Jason and his friends. A group of us would commandeer a particular corner of the joint, annexing surrounding couches and two-top tables as our contingent grew. Jason usually gave me a ride, but sometimes other people were kind enough to chauffeur me around. My memory of that group is a hazy amalgam of trench coats, cigarette breaks, long hugs, and deep conversation. They loved to talk philosophy and religion, muddled through Kant and Kierkegaard in their spare time, blew off the banalities of school in the pursuit of purer truths.

They also really liked to get high.

If pot is the gateway drug, then not enough is said about the throngs of people who spend their lives loitering at the gate. They seem to have no intention of passing through to anything else, but they sure do love marijuana. It's possible that some of them were self-medicating, but I happen to know plenty of people who have healthy and fruitful relationships with pot. As for the white girls with dreads lost in the clouds, perhaps we're not all meant to be seriously productive members of society. Perhaps some of us are filling a niche by procuring tiny nose rings and bongo drums and spending our twenties working as migrant laborers. All I know for sure is that Jason's friends were very kind, and nobody ever crashed a car or got in a fight, which is more than I can say for the very first keg party I ever attended.

I would occasionally step out into the alley and take a hit or two off the joint, but pot made me hyper and giggly, in contrast to the mellow contemplation it seemed to evoke in everyone else. I'd tried smoking two or three times during my Summer of Tyler, and that was fun, but we were usually too preoccupied with our music talk and making out to bother doing drugs. I was a total pot novice compared to the seasoned professionals in the Insomnia crew, and I hated doing anything that might call attention to the fact that I was younger than the rest of them.

Still, I enjoyed slipping out back with Elvis, who had graduated from our high school the year before and matriculated at the local city university. A couple of the Insomniacs (as I secretly called them) attended the same college as commuters, and they aspired to scrape together enough money to get an apartment together in the spring. I liked to watch Elvis work his vices. He would dip his one-hitter into his pouch of marijuana, occasionally sneaking a stealth hit of the good stuff in between drags of his hand-rolled cigarettes. The dude was pretty tall and rather imposing in his all-black attire, leather duster, dark goatee, and steel-toed boots.

"Excuse us, all," he would announce to the rest of the crew with a polite nod. We'd walk out the back door and lean against the wall opposite the dumpsters. He'd pull out his sundry stashes and sources of fire from his plethora of pockets. "Anything for the lady?" he'd ask, and I would decline. He nonetheless offered every single time.

"It is so cold out here," I remarked one November night, shivering. Elvis, ever the gentleman, took off his enormous duster and placed it over my shoulders. It weighed about three thousand pounds.

"That's OK," I said, peeling it off and returning it to him. He put it back on, then placed his hands in his pockets and wrapped his arms around me like giant leather wings. I felt electrically warmed, cocooned up next to his body. When I noticed his heart pounding, I thought, *What the heck.* I looked up at his face, stood on my tiptoes, reached my arms around his neck, and pulled his mouth toward mine. He kissed me back slowly. His hands emerged from his pockets, and, with his coat still enveloping me, he placed them on my waist. Everything felt frozen, enchanted, ethereal. Fucking *romantic* is what it was. I opened my eyes for a split second and saw the sincere tenderness on his face, then closed them again and lost myself in our gentle embrace.

After that, we started ducking out back for longer and longer stretches of time. Sometimes Elvis would drive me home and we'd park down the street and make out for an hour or so. It never went beyond that, not even mild groping. I thought about it, but somehow the lengthy kisses felt complete, like they were all we were ever meant to share.

By mid-December, our prolonged absences from the coffee shop started to baffle everyone, as snow and ice covered the already slick back alley. We slipped and slid over to the far wall, then propped ourselves against the freezing brick and wrapped ourselves up in each other. One day, a good six weeks into this kissing routine, a girl named Liesel came out and caught us in the act.

"Oh. Hey there, guys," Liesel sputtered. We released each other. As I stepped back, I slipped on the ice and landed hard on my left hip. Elvis scrambled to help me up, but I caught the look Liesel shot him as he did.

Naturally, I took her judgment to mean that I was a shameful choice of girl, slatternly and plump and otherwise devoid of positive qualities. So when Elvis drove me home that night and pulled right up to my house, averting his eyes and bidding me goodnight, I believed it was because he never actually liked me, and our discovery by one of his comrades meant that our ridiculous antics must come to an end.

I realize now that he was probably thinking that he, a nineteen-year-old adult man, should not get involved with a fifteen-year-old high school sophomore. He probably decided that the right thing to do was to back off before things went any further. But to me, at the time, Elvis felt like my peer. And to me, at the time, I chalked his sudden distance up to my ultimate undesirability. Sure, I could conjure an odd sort of trickery when I had a guy alone. I could fool him, distract him from my unattractiveness with my willingness, my chutzpah. But in the cold light of another's gaze, all the fun had to stop. I just wasn't cute enough.

After the New Year, I stopped frequenting Insomnia and started hanging out instead with the TexD kids or, alternately, all alone with my grandmother's sewing machine. My father helped me construct a Styrofoam and duct tape mold of my torso and another of my lower body. I sewed a couple of simple pencil skirts first, and then, even though dresses are easier, I skipped right over to shirts. I ruined five yards of plaid fabric before I started making real progress on that first fitted button-down with cuffed short sleeves.

One evening, I walked home after flinging swatches around with the TexD kids in the studio for a couple of hours. My mother told me a boy named Jason had called for me. I reached for the phone and froze. I had never actually *called* Jason before. What if Tyler answered? I'd seen Tyler in the hallways a few times, always managing to avoid eye contact. Jason and his senior friends occupied another part of the campus, though I'd sometimes bump into them when I made my way to and from TexD in the vocational tech building. I decided the safe thing to do was to avoid using the phone. I pleaded with my mother to drive me to Insomnia, and she relented. ("But none of those *obscenely* huge milkshakes, Natalie. Do you understand me?") I found Jason and the crew in our usual spot.

"Hey, I heard you called," I said, plopping down on the cushion next to him.

"Hadn't seen you in a while," he replied, barely raising his eyes. "Just making sure you're doing OK."

"Yeah, I'm good," I said, pulling off my jacket. "Do you like my shirt? I *made* it!"

He glanced at me. "Impressive," he remarked, and then he returned to his book. I grabbed the novel I had to read for class and smoldered with regret that I'd made the trek all the way downtown. I could've been back home churning out more one-of-a-kind Natalie couture. I decided to lift my spirits by flagrantly defying my mother, so I stepped over to the counter and ordered a mint chocolate espresso shake. I stood at the pick-up window waiting for my order, and suddenly Jason was right behind me.

"I'm taking off. Can I drive you someplace?" he asked. He seemed anxious to leave.

"I just got here," I replied. "I'm waiting for my thing."

"Just get it to go!" He must've heard how clipped he sounded, because he softened his tone. "Come on, I want you to hear this song."

I grabbed my coffee shake and a straw and followed Jason out the door. I wondered if he was going to tell me to stop hanging around, that my make-out sessions with Elvis meant I was no longer welcome in the caffeinated high-energy metaphysics club. The coolest—and most surprising—part was that I really didn't care that much. I started spending time with the Insomniacs because of a strange twist of fate, and I found myself much more drawn to my new artsy design crew. They smiled a lot, wore brighter colors, and listened to far more enjoyable music.

This became all too clear as I sat there in Jason's parked car inhaling second-hand smoke and trying to grok his noise rock. Jason's musical taste veered away from the pop melodies his brother preferred and toward the weird and buzzy and absurd. The unlistenable. I sat there trying so hard to understand what the fuck could possibly be entertaining about the cacophony spilling out of the car speakers that I didn't notice Jason's face in the immediate vicinity of mine.

And that's when I spun around and head-butted him right in the nose.

"Ow! Fuck!" he blurted, whacking the steering wheel with the palm of his hand.

"Oh shit! Jason! I am so sorry," I said, yanking some napkins out of my bag. I passed him a stack, then leaned over the parking break and gently blotted his face. He looked at me, his eyes watering from the impact.

"Oh no," he said softly. "Your shirt."

There wasn't too much blood overall, but I looked down and saw that, indeed, a little had gotten on my sleeve and the corner of my collar. "Oh dude, please. Don't worry about that."

"But you made it yourself," he said, sniffing. I was touched and pretty damn surprised by his concern for my lovingly handcrafted apparel. And, come to think of it, what *had* his nose been doing millimeters away from my face?

He seemed almost done bleeding, so I leaned over and put my tongue in his mouth. He kissed me back, but it didn't feel particularly sexy. It didn't really feel like anything.

I stopped kissing him, threw open the car door, and bounded into the house with a coy little wave. Then I stood by the door and listened. Jason didn't start up the car and drive away for what seemed like a long time.

I went upstairs to the bathroom and carefully unbuttoned my shirt. As I immersed it in a sink full of freezing water and started to scrub out the blood, the reality of my data set started to soak in as well. Three boys, all independently—more or less—seeing me this way. I caught a glimpse of myself in the mirror, standing there in my baggie jeans and pink bra, and asked out loud to my own reflection:

"Am I *hot*?"

$$\mathcal{S}$$

AFTER RELATING MY HUMILIATING tale of Bloomingdale'sian woe to Anastaze this evening at my place, I asked her what was up in her own life.

"Oh. Nothing. Not much," came her shifty reply. This is why we've never played poker. Taking her money would be way too easy.

"What are you not telling me?" I demanded, and she grinned and blushed at the same time.

"I guess I sort of met a guy," she admitted, raising her eyes to meet mine. I grinned right back.

"Well hot damn!" I actually slapped the end table. "Tell me everything."

"Well. We've had coffee a couple of times. I like him. He is very nice and gregarious and all that."

"Yeah? That sounds great, Staze! Where did you meet him?"

"And we have a lot in common," she continued, buzzing past my question. "He's a reader, an avid reader. He's conversant in a variety of topics I find engaging, and—"

"Fantastic," I interrupted. "*Where did you meet him?*"

"Oh. Well. I don't know if I want to tell you that," she replied, enunciating a little too deliberately.

"Look, Staze, I'm not trying to meddle in your business. I'm just curious! Did you meet him online?"

"Yes. In a way," she hedged. I started to feel like a police interrogator.

"Anastaze. Are you going to tell me where you met him or not?" She looked at me sheepishly. "If you say no right now, I'll drop it."

I watched as her tan corduroy–clad knee bounced and her fingers poked out of her blue and white argyle sleeves to drum the table. She was an absolute tangle of tics.

Finally, I broke the silence. "Dude. How bad can it be?"

"We met at a get-together for this online group we both belong to," she managed. "It's for people who share a common interest." She sounded like she'd been reviewing her testimony with her attorney for hours.

"OK, that's nice," I patronized. "And what exactly is said common interest?"

"Well, Natalie, it's this weblog," she said, tossing back a healthy glug of wine.

"OK, and which blog would that b—oh no. Oh no! Staze, what are you telling me? Do you mean to tell me that—"

She buried her head in her hands and shook it wildly. "No! Don't say it. Don't say it, Nat!"

"You mean to tell me that you met a guy *at your own fan club meeting*?" And with that, she threw her tiny body off my reupholstered red velvet armchair and onto my purple shag rug.

"Wow. Fucking…wow," I said, slowly absorbing the information.

"Stop. Please," she begged, her face still buried in the floor.

"Staze. What were you thinking?"

She sat bolt upright. "I was *thinking* I wanted to meet a man who was *interested* in me, and I *reasoned* that this was a surefire way to meet a man who is interested *in me*!"

She looked back at me. I could see that she had thought this through, that she had been as logical as possible in constructing her personal action plan here.

I lost my shit. I cracked up beyond control, and we laughed so hard wine came out of our eyeballs. She hurled a few throw pillows at me. She's a literal one for sure.

Once we calmed down, I tried to be optimistic. "So, what's his name? Where does he live?"

"His name is Howard, and he lives in Somerville. He's an adjunct professor. At Harvard."

"Howard from Harvard," I said. "Does he know your dad?"

"Probably not," she replied. "Howard is at the Divinity School. He lectures on the Torah and the Talmud."

"Deep stuff, huh?"

"No, not really. They're survey courses. He doesn't get too deep into rabbinical questions. It's not yeshiva."

"So it's Jewish thought for the goyim?" I asked.

"*Everything at Charvard iys for theh goyim*," Staze replied in a perfect Eastern European accent. "I don't know," she continued, back to her normal English boarding school manner of speech. "I'm a bit worried that he might be too religious for me, but judging his adequacy as a partner hardly seems fair, considering I'm concealing my identity from him entirely."

"Meaning you didn't tell him that you are his favorite blogger, and what else?"

"We are on a strictly first-name basis at present," she replied.

"Yeah," I said with a nod. Staze's life in her father's long shadow has never been easy, not for a single moment. "I don't think you can rule him out based on the religious stuff. Isn't there a wide range of opinions out there about what Judaism means?"

"Obviously, Nat," she replied. "Some think Judaism is itself the question of what Judaism means."

"Deep," I said.

"Circular," she countered, shaking her head and losing herself in boozy contemplation.

"Staze, is Sam Elliot Jacobs Jewish?"

She sighed. "Of course he is."

"And what does it mean to him?"

"Well, it suffices to say that he and I are pretty much on the same page," she replied, sitting up. She grabbed the green Zin bottle and took a swig directly from its mouth.

"I realize I'm going to have to figure out everything that happened with Ben," I told her.

"Ugh, *Ben*," she growled. "He was such an abominable dickhead to you, Nat. A truly puerile cad." She handed me the wine. I gulped and passed it back.

"I don't know, Staze. He was…" I paused. "Torn." It's strange now to think that when Staze and I were getting to know each other, Ben was usually there too.

"Perhaps revisiting that phase of your life will bring to light some important truths," she suggested.

"I guess. We'll see. I've been thinking about all the hooking up I did before him, back in high school," I revealed.

"What have you learned?"

"Some stuff about my feelings toward my body, which probably made standing on the runway at Bloomingdale's even more surreal than it otherwise would have been," I admitted.

"What do you mean standing on the runway?" she asked.

"Oh, did I not mention that part? I wound up wearing one of the outfits in the fashion show. It was a plus-size event thing," I said, with a wave of my hand. "It was nothing."

Anastaze's face lit up. "No! No, you did not *mention that part*! You modeled? Natalie, you *modeled*?"

"I sure did," I admitted. "Is that the craziest thing you've ever heard?"

"Oh, that is perfect!" She actually clapped her hands with glee, like somebody had just given her a pony for Christmas. *Here it comes*, I thought.

"So it's, what, comical? Absurd? The living end?"

"No, silly, it's *perfect*," she insisted. "Will you do it again? I would love to come see you model!" She was beaming.

"Hang on, Staze. You're pleased about this?" I asked, perplexed.

"Natalie, I'm so proud of you!"

"Proud?" I scoffed. "Honestly? Being a fashion show producer is brainless enough. I thought modeling would prompt you to friend-dump me for sure."

"Item one: I will never friend-dump you. Item two: you are so beautiful and outgoing! I love the idea of you taking the spotlight for once!"

"Says the famous anonymous blogger," I chided.

"Come on, Natalie. Let me be happy for you."

"The thing is, Staze, it's not a thing to be happy about. I screwed up logistics and my penance was having to parade around in front of people who kept looking me up and down." I felt the muscles seize up in my abdomen all over again just thinking about it.

"I'll bet you were magnificent," she gushed.

"Right, so anyway, body image, sex life, blah blah blah," I said. "I'm still digging deep into my various exploits. At least Ben always made me feel smart. He used to call me his 'thinking-man's shiksa.'"

"That's a terrible word," Staze spat. She's particularly defensive of me when it comes to Ben. "It means filth. Abomination. Don't ever call yourself that."

"I think it's lost those connotations, Staze. Like on *Seinfeld*."

"Still," she protested, shaking her head. "That word is not a joke to me." I figured this might have something to do with one of the many family traumas she endured in Europe. I met Staze moments after she first arrived in the US, when we were housed in the same freshman dorm.

But before I head off to college, I guess I should probably finish high school.

§

I KEPT MAKING OUT with Jason for far longer than I should have. I never felt a thing for him, not one iota of attraction or revulsion or anything: just white noise buzzing inside my head. But Jason seemed to think we shared a connection, so I tried my best to figure out what we might have in common. We barely talked. I would ask him questions, and he'd deflect them: "Why does *that* matter?"

Ironically, when I wasn't making out with him, all I could think about was sex. Of course, my only physical experience of lust at the time had been with Tyler, who I still saw in the halls almost every day. He had apparently moved on from Gretchen and was now joined at the hip with one of the naughty pep squad members who smoked cigarettes and wore black nail polish. Every sighting of the two of them together made me want to choke myself with his wallet chain.

By April, I had finished my entire TexD wardrobe: six shirts, two skirts, two pairs of pants, and three dresses. My fashionista friends, all relieved by their acceptances to RISD and FIT, took me gallivanting all around town to celebrate. We shopped for basics and accessories to round out my wardrobe and then sat around refreshingly well-lit diners looking impossibly hip. Well, they all certainly did. I was their chubbier, younger, less hip attaché. People probably assumed I was their intern.

One Friday, my TexD friends helped talk my way into the eighteen-plus gay dance night downtown. Minh and Brooke distracted the straight male bouncers while David M. and David G. flirted us past the door guys, saving us the cover charge and scoring alcohol bracelets for themselves.

Inside, the atmosphere was pretty disappointing. The music sucked: undanceable gothy crap that wasn't even beat-matched dripped morbidly out of the speakers. Both Davids disappeared into dark corners while Xavier, Minh, Brooke, and I lingered by the bar, sipping our sodas and feeling letdown. After about an hour, Brooke started waving her car keys.

"Anybody want to go to my place? We can watch HBO or something," she suggested, and, just as we all admitted we were ready to give up, the second DJ of the night started his shift. He must've suffered through the previous guy's set too, because he immediately bombarded us with hits: Erasure, Madonna, New Order. The entire club spilled out onto the floor. My friends and I bounced around gleefully. David M. even managed to stop flirting with strangers long enough to come dance with us for a few songs.

In the middle of "Blue Monday," I felt somebody brush against me from behind. I assumed it was David G. finally finding his way back to us, but when I turned around I instead found an adorable girl with cropped brown hair looking at me with giant brown eyes. I know now that the proper term for her would be "baby dyke," but at the time I had no such vocabulary.

I turned around to face her and danced, flattered by the attention. When she put her hand behind my hip and pulled herself closer, I wasn't quite sure how to handle it. I contemplated explaining that I was straight, but instead I just kept moving my body side to side, closer and closer to her. And then came that feeling, that all-the-way-into-my-body feeling, that precious dissolution of anxiety and neurosis that I hadn't experienced since my last kiss with Tyler. Before I could even form the word "LESBIAN" in my mind, I grabbed her by the waist and kissed her to a haunting chorus of *ahhs*.

We made out hard in the surging crowd, our hands grasping at each other's bodies and shoulders, our backs arched, pressing our torsos together. I couldn't think about what it meant. I just absorbed the sensory input: the flashing lights behind my closed eyes, the pounding beat, the driving cadence of the melody, and the glorious sensations of her slender arms and delicate mouth. I know it's a cliché but girls are *soft*. They're also supple and smooth, and they smell really fucking good.

The song ended, and we broke apart. I thought we might talk over the bar, but instead she disappeared into the crowd with a shy smile.

A couple of hours later, I got to be the center of attention for the entire car ride home.

"Can we talk about Miss Natalie here? And her exploits?" David M. demanded as we all shoved our way into Brooke's mother's minivan.

"Oh my God, yes!" Minh chirped. "Do you know that girl or what?"

"No, not at all," I replied, still kind of dazed. "I don't even know her name." Everybody squealed.

"So she came up to you and just started kissing you, out of the blue?" David M. asked.

"Actually, I kissed her," I said with a silly grin.

"Hot. That is completely hot," he opined.

"Natalie, have you been holding out on us?" asked Xavier. "Have you been a lesbian this whole time?"

"Wait a minute," Brooke interjected. "Natalie, don't you have a boyfriend? Who's that guy with the red Honda?"

"There's a boy. Sort of," I replied.

"Do you like boys?" asked David G.

"Oh, I like boys. Not really that one, though," I admitted. Suddenly there were no limits on my candor, not with myself or anybody else. We pulled up to a red light. Everybody turned to face me, and I basked in their curiosity.

"So, does that make you a *bi*, Natalie? A *bisexual*?" David M. asked. And with that, the light turned green in front of the car and inside my head. There it was. That was it. I didn't have to wonder anymore.

"Yeah. Yeah," I said, a bit dreamily. "I'm a bisexual. That's what I am." We paused, soaking it in.

"I love it," David M. declared, and we giggled and gossiped our way back to the suburbs.

I climbed into bed as soon as I got home, but I must've stared at the ceiling until 4:00 a.m., my body buzzing with the frightening thrill of girl-kissing comingled with the sense of relief that my new label brought me. The questions wouldn't stop coming: Will it always be easier just to pass for straight? Will I tell my parents? Will people think I'm a lesbian in denial, or just a great big slut? *Am* I just a great big slut?

I quickly settled into a very comfortable place with my sexual orientation, or lack thereof. And I would never call myself—or anybody else—a slut. Honestly, it's the "great big" part that more reliably makes me cringe.

$$\mathcal{S}$$

I ACTUALLY MADE IT over to our Somerville offices this morning. The nondescript industrial building off Webster Street is one of the few places in all of Eastern Massachusetts with a free parking lot. I pulled up in my Toyota after grabbing coffee and a pastry from one of my favorite cafés in nearby Union Square and climbed up the metal staircase to the back entrance. The freezing-cold railing shocked my hand, waking me up a bit. In just a few weeks, this entrance will become a perpetual tiered skating rink, and I'll have to enter by the front door or risk breaking my neck.

The back door is my preference, though, because I get to walk past the chocolatier. I make it a point to amble slowly and wear loud shoes in a shameless attempt to be noticed by the guys who work there. Today was no exception.

"Natalie, come here!" a voice called as I sauntered by. I looked over with feigned surprise and saw Sean, the co-owner.

"Hey, Sean," I said as I headed into their suite. The space is wide open and undivided, and it contains several cauldron-like apparatuses bubbling with chocolate, a few industrial ovens, and lots of other stainless-steel equipment I can't identify. And it smells like heaven.

"I need your help," Sean said, furrowing his brow. "I'm worried about this batch of chocolate cranberry cookies. I think they may have been poisoned."

"Oh my word!" I gasped, playing the straight man.

"There's only one solution. You and I should both eat one. In the interest of public safety," he suggested sternly.

"It's our moral obligation," I said with a nod. He motioned for me to follow him, and I marched solemnly behind the counter and around to the cooling racks by the cracked window. The late-autumn air rushed in and collided with the dry heat from the ovens. Sean slid a tray off the top and offered it to me. Every cookie was flawless, a perfect specimen, almost identical in size and shape and teeming with chocolate and nuts and fruit. I chose one, broke it in half, and inhaled as fragrant steam poured from the thick center. Sean grabbed a cookie and chomped into it, chewing quickly, with an expression of concentration on his face. I slowly took a bite.

"Definitely not poison," I declared.

"What? Oh, yeah." Sean snickered, remembering our little game. "Do you think it's too much cranberry?"

"No," I opined. "It's really balanced." He nodded, scrutinizing his half-eaten cookie it in the sunlight. Between the apron, the Red Sox cap, and the grizzly beard, he could've been the centerfold in *Edible Somerville*. I chuckled at the thought.

"What?" he asked, self-conscious at my giggling.

"Nothing," I said, smiling. "I have to head to the office." As I walked away from the delicious smells, I called back, "Thanks for the cookie!"

"What? Oh. No problem, Natalie," Sean hollered, distracted by his baked-good perfectionism.

I polished off my perfect cookie just as I stepped through the blue M&S door. Stephanie threw me a thumbs-up as she hurried somebody off the phone.

"Yes. See you then. Bye. Natalie, you rock star!" she gushed without missing a beat. "Claudia from Bloomingdale's could not stop raving about the Recharche show."

"There's Miss Natalie," Melanie said, emerging from the kitchenette. "Very nicely done."

I smiled and shrugged. Normally, I enjoy such praise, but in this case I had actually fucked up royally, and the only reason the show came together was because of Gwendolyn's quick thinking.

"Claudia's already sending us more business," reported Stephanie. "Two other shows at her store, plus referrals for events at Nordstrom's and Saks."

"I guess I better get cracking then," I said, throwing my bag down on my desk.

"I can handle the downtown shows," Melanie volunteered.

"Oh, Natalie," Stephanie said, handing me a yellow sticky note. "A woman called for you. She wants to talk about a 3-F thing. She says she got your number from a Gwendolyn Santos?"

"Yeah, that would be the Gwendolyn you're cutting a time-and-a-half check for. She's a plus model. A *fantastic* plus model." 3-F is short for Full Figured Fashion Week. One of the many perks of my arrangement with Melanie and Stephanie is the geographic boundary on event referrals. I'm permitted to take freelance design work anywhere, but I must refer all New England event production and fashion show gigs to M&S. However, if I get the chance to produce a show anywhere else—including New York City—then it's all mine.

I sat down and dialed. A woman answered immediately. "This is Lily."

"Oh, hello! My name is Natalie, and I received a message about an event for Full Figured Fashion Week?"

"Natalie. Natalie," the woman said, shuffling some papers. "Ah. Natalie. Referred by Gwendolyn. Well, it's an afternoon runway show. Small label, brand new. It's their first Full Figured Fashion Week."

"OK, and what's the budget?" I asked, clicking my pen.

"I'm sorry, why would you need that information?" she replied.

"Well, if I'm going to produce an event, I need to know what I'm working with." I paused for a moment. More silence. I continued.

"You can get back to me if the designer isn't prepared to answer that question yet."

"Hang on," Lily replied. "I'm sorry, *I'm* running the event. I called to hire you as a model."

"*What*?" I blurted, stunned.

"I should have been more clear," she continued. "Gwendolyn mentioned that you worked as a producer, but she said you were also breaking into plus modeling. This gig is not very highly paid, but it would look great on a new résumé."

My mouth went dry. I almost turned her down right then, but I decided that might not reflect well on my new friend and savior Gwendolyn, so I stalled.

"You know, Lily, I'm going to have to give you a call back later. Would that be OK?"

"Well. Fine. But please get back to me as soon as you can," she said. "In the meantime, I'll email you the specs."

I recited my email address and hung up. Then I dialed Gwendolyn.

"Hello?" Her voice sounded groggy and dry.

"Did you tell a woman named Lily to call me about a gig?" I demanded.

"Natalie?" she said. "What time is it?"

"It's time for you to explain why you told this woman that I was a *model*!" I could feel Stephanie trying to eavesdrop behind me.

"Calm down. It's an easy gig," she mumbled, and I finally realized I had woken her. I looked at the clock: 8:45 a.m.

I took a deep breath. "I'm sorry I called so early. I just have no idea why you mentioned me at all."

"She's on a shoestring budget," Gwendolyn replied. "She asked if I knew any plus models without a ton of experience who might be cheaper to hire, and you were the first person who came to mind."

"Well I certainly don't have a ton of experience, considering I have *zero* experience," I declared.

"What about the Bloomingdale's show?" Stephanie chimed in. I whirled around, but she didn't look up from her paperwork. "Claudia mentioned that you modeled. She said you did great."

"This is not happening," I announced.

"OK, Natalie, I'm awake now," said Gwendolyn. "Listen, I planned to call you before you heard from Lily, but she's apparently so type A that she couldn't wait twenty-four hours. This is just a suggestion. If you don't want to do it, you definitely don't have to. But I think you'd have fun. I'll help you with the process if you're interested."

"I really don't know what to say," I replied.

"Just say yes and stop freaking out about it," Gwendolyn advised.

"Do it!" Stephanie chirped. "Don't be so uptight, Nat."

Uptight. That's a thing I never want to be.

"All right, fine," I relented.

"Woo hoo!" cheered Stephanie.

"Great. And try not to sound too excited," Gwendolyn teased. "It's walking down a runway, not getting all your teeth pulled."

"But I need a bunch of stuff now, right?" I asked, opening up my email. "Lily says I need a shoe bag, and she wants my measurements and headshots. Headshots?"

"Natalie, you of all people know the drill here," Gwendolyn replied. "A shoe bag is no big deal. And you can come over to my place some time this week to do measurements and head shots. And drink martinis."

"OK, I'm beginning to see the bright side," I joked.

"Good!" Gwendolyn said. "I'll ask Jeff if he can do your makeup for the photos. Hey, Jeff?"

He was right there next to her. Jeff who dates models. Standard models.

Perhaps Gwendolyn can be my new guru.

First Time for Everything

O N MY FIRST FULL day as a newly-minted teen bisexual, I woke up with a sense of resolve. I met up with Jason and told him I kissed somebody else. We never officially broke up, but we were never officially a couple in the first place anyway, so that seemed fine. He stopped calling me, and I never showed up at Insomnia again. I spent the summer at my new haunts, mostly twenty-four-hour diners and bookstore cafés.

When junior year rolled around, I started hanging around the kids from my academic classes again, and I volunteered to make costumes for the drama department. I strutted around campus in my handmade clothes, and soon half the girls in school were commissioning custom garments from me. It was a fun little business, and it helped cover the cost of my addictions: expensive fabric and concert tickets.

I passed the second half of high school kissing people at parties and not going on any official dates. I missed both proms and both homecoming dances. Maybe I was disappointed on some level, but it all seemed so irrelevant to my life. I wasn't the girl you took to the prom, I was the girl you dared to make out with your girlfriend at the *Godspell* cast party. And that suited me just fine.

I finally spoke to Tyler again at the Wazzoo Festival that I quasi-ironically attended toward the end of senior year.

I remember the group I went with: some drama club members and a handful of friends from my AP classes. The theater kids and I had spent half our lives at shows, but a couple of the sheltered honors kids had never even been to a concert, so I dragged them along for the experience. As soon as we arrived, we lit up a bowl and got the nerds super high. One poor girl became convinced she was dying and begged us to call her mother. Fortunately, we were able to calm her down with the help of some overpriced French fries.

Around dusk, I got kind of melancholy and wandered off alone. I remember thinking that I probably wouldn't stay in touch with any of those people. I missed the Insomnia kids and my TexD friends from tenth grade. I moped around the venue, listening to the late-afternoon guitar music and wondering if I would once again find people I could connect with at college.

I strolled into the vendor tents with the wizard figurines, only this time I could identify all the head shop gear for sale. As I wove through the stalls, I noticed a group of fellow seniors standing by the venue's back wall. Graduation was only two weeks away, so we had definitely entered the clique truce honeymoon period that magically happens at the end of high school. I recognized a cheerleader and a couple of lacrosse guys chatting it up with some hard-core stoners. I couldn't decide what was more bizarre: the tableau of them all standing together, or the fact that they saw me and motioned for me to join them.

"Hey, Natalie, right?" asked Andre, one of the captains of the lacrosse team, as I approached with my hands stuffed into my homemade pockets. "What's up, Natalie?"

"Hey, Andre. I'm good. What's up with you guys?" My standard-issue greeting was met with smiles and nods and not a lot of words. That's the problem with senior truce: just because we're all suddenly friends doesn't mean we can all suddenly relate. Fortunately, I had an ice-breaker. I reached into my messenger bag and produced my tiny pipe, which I'd packed earlier. "Does anybody want a hit of this?"

As the gang passed around my drugs, the cheerleader attempted to chat me up. "Natalie, is this your first Wazzoo?"

"My third, actually."

"Wow, that's a lot! Is this like a lesbian thing?" she asked, glancing around. I scanned her for cruelty, but she seemed sincere.

"Um, no, I don't think it is. I just really like music," I said.

"That's cool, Natalie," said Andre in a whisper, holding in his hit. He blew it out. "All of us, we've never been before. But we heard, you know, it's a fun place to hang out, smoke some weed." He flashed a killer smile. You don't get to be cocaptain of the lacrosse team at a suburban high school unless you're oozing charisma, as Andre always did.

"Who are you here with, Natalie?" asked the cheerleader as she passed me the pipe. Popular people say your name a lot.

"Some drama club kids," I replied.

"We're here, the group of us, from, you know, the team, and you know, some other friends." Andre clung half-heartedly to his ability to make sense as the weed snaked around his brain. "We came, all of us, with a friend who, you know, has been to the show before."

"Speak of the devil," the cheerleader said, looking over my shoulder. I heard a familiar voice approaching from behind.

"OK, I got sodas and some fries. I figured we could share."

I didn't have to turn around to know who it was. He walked right up next to me and started passing around the food. I watched as he handed Andre a greasy white container, grabbed a couple of fries between his fingertips, and shoved them in his mouth.

"What's up, Tyler?" I said softly. He looked over at me. "Fancy meeting you here."

"Natalie brought us some fun," said the cheerleader, swiping the pipe out of my limp hand and handing it to Tyler. He accepted, his glassy green eyes still fixed on my face.

"She did, didn't she?" he said. Tyler hit the pipe and passed it to the lacrosse player next to him without taking his eyes off me. The bowl was promptly cashed, but Tyler's new friends repacked it with their own stuff, lost in their hazy world. We stared at each other like they weren't there.

"What are you doing here, Natalie?" His question was warm and quiet.

"Oh, you know. Wazzoo," I replied, looking down. I felt nauseated and thrilled, shy and sheepish, but eventually I managed to meet his gaze.

"You look amazing," he said, and I liquefied. High school kids do not say that kind of thing to one another, not in some public context. Maybe that's what prom is for, to hear and say that kind of thing, but I missed all that, and I missed Tyler achingly, even though I saw him every single fucking day for three fucking years.

"I miss you, Tyler," I whispered, and I saw him buckle inside like I had a moment before. He grabbed my hand.

"We'll be back," he told the others as he yanked me away from the circle. We trudged past the vendor tents and rounded a corner, where he promptly threw me up against a cement wall and kissed me hard. I kissed back, pulling his shoulders as he pressed his whole body into mine. We were still close in height. He was maybe an inch taller than he'd been, and deliciously familiar.

"Natalie," he whispered as I bit his earlobe. We matched each other movement for movement, rhythm for rhythm, push for pull, and before long it overwhelmed me. I felt out of air, sick to my stomach, with a sudden ache behind my left eyeball. I pulled my face away from his.

"Tyler, I have to go find my friends," I said, sliding his hands off my waist and slipping out from his grasp.

"Natalie," he said again, shaking his head.

"Call me. Tonight," I instructed, and I turned and walked, trembling, into the crowd.

Eventually, I found my gang of nerds and actors. "Natalie, where have you been? You missed so much fun!" This from the girl who, hours earlier, pleaded with us to take her to the hospital for acute cannabis poisoning. I tried to enjoy the company and the last three bands for the rest of the evening, but my mind was elsewhere. After the festivities wrapped up, I drove my friends home and hurried back to my empty house.

My parents were out of town that weekend, which would be a fun detail if the circumstances for their absence hadn't been so awful. Mom and Dad actually spent a large chunk of my last year at home away from our house. Dad's father was dying of cancer, and mom's brother had gotten himself into a huge legal mess by embezzling from his company to buy cocaine. My parents ferried themselves back and forth between Grandpa's house and Uncle Greg's drug rehab facility most weekends during the whole ordeal. At first I enjoyed the peace of independence, but mostly I felt antsy and depressed. I puttered around the empty house, ordering take-out with the twenty-dollar bill my father would leave for me. Sometimes I took my mom's car to a party or a show, but mostly I watched movies and made clothes and wished for a best friend.

The phone rang a little after midnight. I'd been carrying the portable unit around with me, my thumb on the "talk" button.

"Hello?"

"Natalie?" His voice was quiet and unsteady.

"Yeah, it's me."

"I'm not sure why I'm calling. Maybe you told me to?" Tyler said in a whisper.

"Can you get out?" I asked. "My parents are gone for the weekend."

"Um, yeah," he replied. "Yeah. I'll be right over."

"Park down the street," I instructed. "And don't ring the bell, just knock on the door when you get here." Even though my family barely knew our neighbors, I wanted to keep a low profile.

We hung up. I'd already showered and put on clean clothes and changed the sheets on my bed. I ran upstairs, changed my clothes again, and worried at my hair for what must've been about thirty seconds but felt like two hours. The minutes crawled by. I distracted myself by trying to guess how much alcohol we could plunder from each bottle of liquor without my parents noticing. Finally, I heard thumps on the door, and I hurried over and yanked it open. I will never forget how Tyler looked in that doorway: his brow furrowed, his face pale, his skin shining with a thin layer of sweat. He still wore a single cord of leather around his neck.

Tyler stepped through my front door. I invited him into the living room, and we sat down on the couch.

"Do you have any weed?" he asked, his leg bouncing frantically.

"Sorry, no. Your new best friends from the lacrosse team finished mine," I teased. He didn't pick up on my playfulness.

"Oh, I'm sorry. Sorry about that," he stuttered.

"Do you want something to drink?" I offered. "My parents have everything, gin, vodka, Kahlúa, whatever." I stood up and moved toward the liquor cabinet, but he grabbed my arm and yanked me down on top of him. He kissed me, but something about it felt off. His touch seemed limp and watery, like he was eight thousand miles away. I pulled my face away from his and looked into his eyes. He didn't look nervous; he looked downright scared. I stroked his cheek tenderly and climbed off him. "Follow me," I said, and I led him to the kitchen.

I put the kettle on to boil and retrieved two oversized *Friends* mugs from the cabinet. "Do you want to be Monica or Chandler?" I asked, and he let out a loud laugh.

"Can I be Joey?"

"No, Joey shattered all over the floor the first day we got him," I said. "I keep loose buttons in Phoebe. Don't even ask about the other two." I watched as Tyler studied the cups, turning them slowly on the countertop, bending over to examine them at eye-level.

I retrieved the honey and two bags of ginger tea from the cabinet, then popped into the dining room to grab my father's bourbon.

"What are you making?" Tyler asked.

"Toddies," I said. "My mom's been giving me these since I was in kindergarten." I portioned out a tea bag, a generous squeeze of honey and another of fresh lemon, and a shot of bourbon into each of our mugs. I poured in hot water and stirred until the honey dissolved. I removed the tea bags—they're hardly the point anyway—and handed Tyler a cup.

"I wanted Monica," he said, and I obliged. He followed me back out to the living room and sat down on the couch, and I threw a fleece blanket over his shoulders.

"Oh. Thanks," he said. "That feels nice."

"You seemed upset," I said, curling up next to him. "You can relax." He put his arm around me, and I placed my hand on his knee. We sat there in silence, sipping our respective drinks. After a little while, I tried moving my hand up the inside of his leg, but he stiffened.

"Natalie, I need to tell you something," he blurted, banging Monica down on the coffee table. I turned to face him. "It's about today, about this afternoon."

"What, Tyler," I demanded, expecting to hear that he had a girlfriend, that he was sorry for kissing me, that he had made a mistake. "What is it?"

"I, uh," he stammered, grabbing his hair with his hands. "Natalie…"

"Spit it out, dude."

"Uh," he sniffed, rubbing is whole arm across his face. "Me and those kids? Andre and them? We took some acid. LSD."

"OK, and?"

"And I am *freaking out*," he said, tears welling up in his eyes. "It's mostly over now, but this has been the worst shit ever."

"Oh, Tyler." I wrapped my arms around him. I held him there on my couch, his whole body heaving, until his breathing became steady again. When he raised his head, his face was covered in snot and tears and sweat and exhaustion.

"Can I spend the night?" he asked, sounding like a little boy. "I don't want to sleep alone."

"Of course."

I led him upstairs, and we talked softly in my bed for hours. I held him while he tried to calm himself and make sense of his day. He explained that he didn't have visual hallucinations so much as the sense that he was not inside himself, that he had completely lost any connection to his own identity. I stroked his head and tried to imagine what that must've been like.

"And you don't know those people very well, right?" I asked, referring to Andre and the gang.

"Barely at all," Tyler replied, gazing at my ceiling. "That's why I was so fixated on you at the show. It felt like you were the only person alive who still knew who I was."

"You seemed completely fine. I had no idea."

"I was just coming up," he explained. "It got a lot worse after you left."

"Fuck, Tyler," I said. "I wish I'd stayed with you."

"Nah, that would've been terrible, too," he said, shaking his head. "But thank you, thanks for saying so. And thank you…" He looked over at me and held my chin in his hand. And then, at last, he kissed me, and it felt real. I let out a laugh, even as our lips pressed together.

"What?" he asked.

"You're back," I whispered, and he smiled and kissed my forehead.

"Natalie," he said, gazing into my eyes.

"Yes?" I answered, ready to say yes and yes and yes again.

"I *really* need to sleep," he confessed. "I still feel fucking…not good."

"Oh," I replied.

"Is that OK?"

"Of course," I said, stroking his face. "I understand."

He rolled over and pulled my arm around him. Come to think of it, that was probably my very first experience with spooning. So at least we were breaking some new ground that night.

Tyler fell asleep almost instantly. He must've been so exhausted. Personally, I had a bit of a harder time dozing off, what with my screaming case of blue balls. I tried to get comfortable, but my arm kept falling asleep. Eventually, I rolled away from him and nodded off.

The sun was up when I started to stir. I felt too comfortable, like I had suspiciously much room to move around. I opened my eyes. Tyler was gone. Just then, I heard the front door slam. My bedroom window faced the street, so I looked outside. Despite all my fears and insecurities, I remember being absolutely certain that he wasn't going to leave. I watched him from the second floor as he walked to his car and opened the passenger door. He rifled around in his front seat for a minute and emerged with a cigarette dangling from his mouth. He stuffed some indecipherable items in his pockets and headed back toward my house.

I stood in my bathroom with the door open while I waited for him to finish smoking. I had slept in my perfect outfit, and we had both seen better days. I washed my face and was brushing my teeth when he bounded back up the stairs.

"You're awake," he said. "Move over."

I made room at the sink as he produced a toothbrush from his back pocket.

I spat out my foamy mouthful and laughed. "I see you came prepared."

"I'm in a band!" he argued. "I sleep places."

"I'm sure you do," I said, raising my eyebrows. He laughed and shook his head. I probably should've felt hungry or tired or in need of caffeine, but I just felt living, charged. I watched him in the mirror as he finished brushing, and we made our way back to my bed.

"I feel one million times better," he said.

"Good, I'm glad."

"When are your parents coming home?" he asked.

"Not for a while," I told him. "They'll call before they leave."

"So we have some time then," he said, already unbuttoning my shirt.

We'd been getting hot and heavy for a few minutes when he stopped and emptied his pockets on my nightstand: cigarettes, an unmarked CD, and a three-pack of condoms.

"Is that OK?" he asked.

"I'm not sure."

"That's totally fine," he said. "We don't have to."

"Oh, the condoms are definitely OK," I replied. "I'm just skeptical about your choice of music."

He grinned at my joke and popped open my blue boom box. "How do I put it on random?"

"Push the play button twice, I think."

He fiddled with the buttons and adjusted the volume. To my surprise, the opening strains of "Dreams" poured out of the speakers.

"Dude, is this *Fleetwood Mac*?"

"You know it."

We kissed for a little while longer before I pushed him back. "I cannot believe you're playing *Rumours* right now."

"Do you hate it?" he asked.

"No, I like it just fine," I said. "It's just surprising."

"I've been listening to it a lot lately," he explained. "For some reason it's always reminded me of you." I felt tears well up in my eyes, so I shut them tight and pulled him close.

Tyler and I spent pretty much the whole day in my bed. The actual sex we had remains vague and impressionistic in my memory. I tend to recall sex as glimpses and sensations, momentary snapshots, sometimes even colors. I only retain the hard clinical details of very bad sex, and I've had mercifully little of that in my life. What I know for sure is that my first time with Tyler still ranks among the best sexual experiences of my life. The part where he put on a condom and entered me felt both momentous and incidental, like an extremely big deal and an insignificant combination of parts and motions all at the same time. One second I was a virgin, and then Tyler pulled out his finger and stuck in his cock and something about me fundamentally changed? It seemed surreal at the time, and it doesn't feel any less so looking back. What's clear to me is that my true transformation took place in that minivan my freshman year, when my clit first swelled and my cheeks first flushed and I first soaked through my underwear.

Maybe most people have amazing first times. Maybe the idea that it's usually fumbling and premature ejaculation in the back seat of a car is a myth, a holdover from a bygone era before *Our Bodies, Ourselves* and HBO liberated us all from such sorry deflowerings.

But no matter what you read or see ahead of time, you can only really learn it with your own body. Good sex the very first time can happen if you manage to transform into a sexual being well before that first time comes around, and if you have sex with a person who brings that creature out in you. On some level, though, it was luck. I was lucky. I can't really tell how it was for Tyler. It's hard to remember anything but his timing, his tenderness, his rhythms, the way his body made mine feel. I don't know. He is a musician. Maybe he dances that beautifully with everybody.

My parents called around four to say they were headed home, which gave us a few hours to order a pizza and bask in the afterglow.

"What was up with you and Jason?" Tyler finally asked me as we helped ourselves to second slices.

"I don't know. We didn't really click," I explained. "Did you guys ever talk about it?"

"No. We have definitely never mentioned you," he said.

"We just kissed. It never quite worked out. It wasn't like…" I trailed off.

"Yeah." Tyler put his slice down. "Natalie, I should probably tell you something."

"You have a girlfriend," I ventured, half-joking.

Tyler paused. "OK, I should probably tell you two things."

I rolled my eyes. "What's her name?" I asked. "No, don't tell me. I actually don't care."

"You seriously didn't know that I have a girlfriend?" Tyler asked skeptically.

"Dude, I try not to keep close tabs on you anymore," I answered. "What's the other thing?"

"I'm leaving the day after graduation," he said, averting his eyes. "We're going on tour."

"For how long?"

"Until the end of August. And then I start conservatory," he explained.

I had no idea how I was supposed to respond to any of this. I noticed a familiar throbbing behind my left eye, which I chalked up to caffeine withdrawal. Wordlessly, I walked into the kitchen area and put on a pot of coffee. Tyler just watched.

"That's cool about the tour," I said finally. "And conservatory. Wow."

"Where are you headed and when?" Tyler asked, grabbing a third slice.

"Stephen Easton College. It's in New York, the Hudson Valley. I leave sometime in August," I replied.

"That sounds cool," Tyler said. I stared at the coffee maker. As soon as a little black liquid had gurgled into the pot, I grabbed the handle and poured it into my cup. Scalding droplets flew, and a few sizzled on my skin. I didn't care.

Coffee and pizza in the late afternoon. It's always been one of my favorite things: that hazy post-coital time when you're loose and exhausted and starving and buzzed. I miss that so much right now.

As difficult as it was to hear all the things he'd just told me, my heart was still hovering far above its normal position. As long as Tyler remained in my house, sharing food and conversation, I didn't have to think about him, didn't have to obsess about him, didn't have to wonder when and if I would see him again.

He left about an hour later. We made out a bit before he took off, and I started to long for him the moment he shut my front door.

§

My evening playing dress-up with Jeff and Gwendolyn proved to be exactly the kind of fun lift I've been desperately needing lately.

The dead snowless gray of early Boston winter has really started to bum me out, and contemplating the physical high points of my sexual history is beginning to wear on my abstinence resolve.

Gwendolyn lives in a converted second-floor dentist's office in the South End of Boston, just off I-93. It's a grid of industrial spaces recently converted into lofts, wine stores, and places to buy your purse dog a sweater. Her apartment has everything I pictured: exposed brick walls, dangling pipes, and a ledge with high stools that divides her tiny kitchen from her living room and which she uses pretty much exclusively as a bar.

I rolled up just as the sun was setting way too fucking early in the afternoon. Jeff buzzed me in, and I heard the unmistakable sound of a cocktail shaker as I climbed the painted cement stairs and banged on the metal door. It swung open, and there stood Gwendolyn in a floor-length green satin dress with spaghetti straps, three-inch pumps (pretty striking on a 5'10" woman), and a tiny glittering tiara.

"Look, Jeff! It's our mutual friend Natalie!" she announced. Then she stepped back and welcomed me in with a wordless sweep of her arm.

"Hey, Natalie," said Jeff, glancing up in my direction as he distributed the contents of the shaker into three martini glasses.

"I hope two of those are for me," I said, slumping onto a stool. "I've had a hellish day."

"No complaining until after your first drink," Gwendolyn insisted. She plunked an olive-laden toothpick in a glass and handed it to me.

I took a sip. Delicious, clean gin. I gave it a lazy stir and slipped an olive off the stick with my teeth. It oozed with buttery umami. "Yum!"

"Gorgonzola," Gwendolyn informed me. "I stuffed them myself."

"I'm feeling a bit underdressed," I said, noticing Jeff's burgundy blazer and purple bow-tie over his T-shirt and jeans.

"We always dress for cocktail hour in this house," said Gwendolyn. "And we didn't want you to feel out of place. Because we are about to doll you *up*, my friend."

"I'm all yours. Do what you will. I hereby relinquish control to the experts," I conceded.

"Good!" Gwendolyn pushed my beverage toward me with a wink. "Drink up. That's what we're looking for in these headshots: woozy and willing."

"I know that's what I'm looking for," I replied, raising my glass to my lips.

Gwendolyn winked and disappeared into her closet to pull some clothes for me while Jeff grabbed fistfuls of tubes and brushes out of his toolboxes. I wandered around admiring the woven wall hangings and framed photographs of gorgeous women giggling in front of the Eiffel Tower. A couple of *Playboy* bookends held up some books I recognized from Jeanette's collection: *Appetites* by Caroline Knapp, that Marya Hornbacher memoir, a few Buddhist-leaning volumes on radical acceptance. I scanned the shelves for images of Gwendolyn during her standard model days, but those didn't appear to have made the highlight reel.

Jeff perched me up on a stool in the living area and had started shellacking my face when the door buzzer rang. In breezed Kylie and Jo, two impossibly tall friends of Gwendolyn's from various arenas of the biz. Kylie carried a sizable camera bag, and they both lugged hard plastic cases of lights.

After Jeff perfected my makeup, Gwendolyn brought me into her bedroom to try on some outfits. We were all a good martini and a half into the evening at that point. She plugged in her oversized curling iron and started chucking tops onto her duvet for me to review.

"Do you want to pick out your own clothes, Madam Stylist?" she asked from inside her walk-in closet.

"Oh no," I replied. "I shouldn't be involved. I'd drive myself nuts. I'm sure you'll pick something great."

"Well, I've got plenty of options," she replied.

"Your friends seem so fun," I said. "Have you known them long?"

"I have. Jo's a model, obviously, and Kylie is a former model turned photographer, and much happier with her life now," Gwendolyn explained.

"You were all models?"

"Yep. Paris, Milan, the whole nine yards," she answered. "You know, the food in Italy is so incredible, some of it even tastes good coming back up."

"Gross!" I blurted.

"Sorry. Dark humor got me through."

"So when were you all working together?" I asked, wondering about the timeline and all the changes they'd clearly been through.

"It must've been eight or nine years ago now." She paused. "Another one of our friends, she died, and obviously it really affected all of us."

"Oh no," I said. "I'm so sorry."

"Thank you," she replied. "Sarah did too much coke, and her heart was fucked up anyway from puking all the time, so, there you go."

"Jesus."

"Yeah, and we all kind of went through a 'there but for the grace of God' thing after that." She sat down on her bed and rubbed her eyes. "I was supposed to fly back to New York, but instead I went to my *abuela*'s house in Puerto Rico and just let her feed me for a month."

"Wow," I said, not sure what else I could offer.

Gwendolyn shook her head and stared off into space. "She was so happy. I have this vivid memory of eating serving after serving of *tembleque* while she stared at me and cried."

"That's quite an image," I said. "This little old lady watching a size zero girl eat."

Gwendolyn shrugged. "Well she wasn't *that* old. She got married at seventeen, so she must've been, what, like fifty-nine maybe?"

"Ha! That's so young!"

"Yeah, she would make me a huge pork-filled breakfast every day, then rush off to the law firm," Gwendolyn mused. "Anyway, after that I figured I would never model again. But then my body settled into this, and I had a whole second career."

A burst of laughter poured in from the next room. "I definitely admire the vibe you've got going on here, with your crew," I told her. "It's so glamorous and chic."

"Nah, it's just goofy stuff," she said. "I guess I still think of the standard runway life as 'glamour,' with all its sharp corners and opulence. In reality it was a bunch of miserable bullshit."

"Well, this must be the upside of glamour then," I said, feeling bad for inadvertently bringing up a tough subject. I tried to redirect the conversation. "How are things going with Jeff?"

"A whole lot of fun," she said with a grin, picking up a button-down top. "Really, really good times. Here, throw this thing on and I'll do your hair."

"Aye aye, Captain," I replied. I sucked down the last drops of my second martini—Jeff insisted I drink from a straw after dedicating minutes to my lip line—and buttoned up Gwendolyn's black French-cuffed top in front of her vanity. I sat down at her white dressing table while she tested the curling iron's temperature.

"So what about you?" Gwendolyn asked, as she transformed my frizzy mess of winter hat hair into a graceful cascade of spirals. "Any special guys in your life? Or ladies?"

I raised my eyebrows. "Jeff told you, huh?"

"It's a fun fact," she said.

"Well, right now, I'm trying to avoid getting involved with humans of any gender," I explained.

"Tough breakup?" she asked. I hesitated, and she backtracked. "Obviously we don't have to talk about this if you don't feel like it."

"No, it's cool," I said. "Something ended. Badly. I've never really had a breakup, though. Not officially."

"Really? You seem like you've been through the ringer of relationships and heartbreak your fair share of times."

"Well. Heartbreak, sure," I explained slowly. "I guess I'm not the relationship type."

Gwendolyn nodded. She picked at a few strands of hair and stood back. "Take a look," she said. I turned to face the mirror.

I don't really have the words for how beautiful I looked.

"Holy shit," I said, turning my head from side to side. "You're a miracle-worker."

Gwendolyn winked. "It's all about having the right tools and knowing how to use them. And Kylie's a total pro. These photos are going to blow your mind."

We headed back to the living room, and Kylie and Jeff spent the next hour swirling around me while Jo and Gwendolyn joked and opined and shook up more cocktails. Kylie took at least two hundred shots from every angle and with a million different lighting combinations.

"How much do I owe you for this?" I asked toward the end of the session.

"I usually charge three hundred," said Kylie as she scrolled through images on her camera. "So how about...ninety-percent off?"

"Thirty bucks? No, Kylie. I can't," I protested.

"Sure you can," interrupted Gwendolyn. "I roped you into this gig, so how about you just rely on the kindness of my friends here, OK?"

"At least let me pay for dinner," I argued. "Order sushi, anything you want. It's on me."

"I already ordered Thai," said Gwendolyn. "And dinner is on M&S. I *accidentally* got a time-and-a-half check for that Bloomingdale's job."

"Because you volunteered to go twice and bail me out!" I insisted.

"*Mira*, Natalie, you bailed *yourself* out," she said with a wave of her hand. "And I wound up in a hot dress with a cute boy." She stole a kiss from Jeff. "Win, win, win."

We concluded the evening with pad thai and curried vegetables and brown rice and a walking lesson. I noticed Jo didn't touch any carbs. Gwendolyn, on the other hand, managed to take second helpings of everything.

"I have to maintain my womanish figure," she quipped, her mouth full of rice noodles.

I laughed and followed her lead.

§

THE SUMMER BEFORE COLLEGE crept by at a snail's pace. I didn't work enough, didn't see my friends enough, and more or less pined for Tyler as the clock counted down the hours until I left home forever. I checked his band's website every day, hoping for updates that never came frequently enough in the era of dial-up. With high school over, I didn't even have access to the normal market for personalized garments from the girls in my classes. Out of sight, out of mind, I assumed.

So I was quite surprised when, one afternoon in late July, I got a phone call with an order.

"Hello, may I please speak to Natalie?" asked the voice on the line.

"Yup, this is Natalie," I replied, taking a big swig of my vanilla latte.

"Hi," came the warm reply. "This is Heather, Heather Boyle. I don't know if you remember me." Like I could forget Heather, Heather Boyle, the self-same Heather Boyle who I spent half my total time in ninth grade English watching Tyler ogle and the other half ogling myself. "We had a class together freshman yea—"

"Of course," I blurted, interrupting. "Of course I remember you, sure."

"Oh, great!" she said. "Well, the reason I'm calling is because, you know, Natalie, I really love the clothes you make."

"Really?" I asked, confused. My styles always tended toward the funky end of the spectrum, so it was odd to hear praise from a girl who still donned mostly Keds and khakis.

"Oh yes!" she chirped. "In fact I was wondering, if you have the time, if you could maybe make me something?"

"I would be happy to," I answered, looking around for a pen and paper. "What kind of a thing did you have in mind?"

"I guess I'm not quite sure," she replied.

"I could do, like, a custom shirt? A dress? A skirt?"

"Natalie, I'll level with you," she said. "I'm headed to Washington in the fall, Washington State, and I'm worried that my clothes aren't really…interesting enough. You know, for that world."

"Well, I'm a big believer that people should just wear what they like," I replied. "But, if you want me to make you something, I bet I could do a dress that would be to your taste and also a little on the edgy side."

"That sounds wonderful," Heather gushed. Every word out of her mouth was coated in sugar and honey. "Would you be able to come to my house? Maybe this Tuesday?"

Fast forward to Tuesday: I pulled up to the Boyle estate in my mother's Acura. Their house was easily twice as big as ours, situated on a corner lot complete with a pool and a hot tub in the extra-large backyard. And behind that sat one of our town's toniest golf courses; everybody who lived in the Boyles' development automatically retained membership at the attached country club. I started contemplating the ethics of jacking up my price twenty percent.

I rang the bell and soon Heather's long figure appeared behind the glass and opened the door. In my memory, she's wearing tennis whites. I can't imagine she actually was, but for some reason, when I recall that afternoon, I see a white polo shirt, a white pleated skirt, and pristine white sneakers contrasted against the impossibly even tan of her skin.

"Natalie! Welcome!" Her voice bubbled over with sweetness. She fiddled with the doorknob.

"Hey, Heather," I said, juggling my coffee mug, keys, purse, and giant bag of fitting supplies.

"Here, let me help you," she offered, plucking the bag off my arm. "Hi!" she said again, and she reached around with her free arm to give me a half-hug.

Did she really smell like baby powder, or is that just another invention of my memory?

"Thank you so much for doing this!" she exclaimed as we stood in her entryway.

"No problem. Thanks for thinking of me."

"Let's go up to my room," she said, and she bounded up the staircase. I walked behind her, taking it all in. The foyer opened on both stories, and the whole front of the house was bathed in light by a series of picture windows that faced the back and the golf course. From the stairs, I could see five or six girls in bikinis giggling around the pool, taking turns practicing somersaults into the water.

"My sister and her friends," Heather explained from the top landing. "Sorry, they're loud and annoying. They won't bother us, though."

"Oh, it's fine, whatever," I said absently. "It's not like a fitting requires too much concentration."

I followed Heather past the banister and down a hallway with doors on either side, then through an open space with a big-screen television, a bar, and some beanbag chairs. "That's the game room. Nobody ever uses it," she explained, which seemed incredible to me. Personal space was definitely not hard to come by at chez Boyle.

"And this is my room," Heather announced, opening the door to what can only be described as a one-bedroom apartment. She had an anteroom with a giant window seat, a tremendous main room filled with gorgeous brushed metal furniture, and a bathroom with a separate Jacuzzi bathtub. I started to wonder exactly how many water jets these people were paying to operate on a daily basis.

"Damn," I declared, shaking my head. "Wow."

"Thanks!" she said. "It's actually the master suite. My mom agreed to give it to me if I made the cheerleading team, but she forgot to stipulate that I actually had to *join* the squad." She flashed a gum commercial smile. "Sometimes having lawyers for parents can have its advantages."

"I bet she wishes she'd been more careful with the original contract," I said, still in awe.

"She learned her lesson. My sister probably won't be getting away with anything like this."

"So," I said. "Should we get started?"

"Oh! Sure!" Heather replied, her voice shimmering with enthusiasm. She handed me the fabric bag. "Just throw stuff on the bed, that's fine. Natalie, you like music, right?"

"Yep," I said absently, pulling out my swatches and pattern book. I'd spent a few minutes the night before marking styles I thought might work well for Heather, although obviously she could wear anything. I stood there absorbed in my set-up until I noticed what was playing. "Is this Portishead?" I asked.

"It is!" Heather replied. "My half-brother got me into them. He goes to college in New York City."

"Nice," I said, nodding my head. "See, you don't need my clothes to be hip."

"Trust me, I need all the help I can get," she said, and she flopped dramatically onto the bed in front of me. "This CD is probably the coolest thing I own."

"Well, don't worry," I said, sitting down next to her with the pattern book. "I'll make you something that'll have those Pacific Northwest hippies thinking you were born with a hacky sack between your feet."

"Natalie, you're so funny," she said, flashing another glittering smile. Her knee would not stop bopping up and down. *What a metabolism*, I thought.

"So, this one is just your basic halter dress," I explained, flipping open to my first Post-it bookmark. I reached for some swatches. "It's kind of a preppy style, but we could do it in an interesting plaid, or maybe a wide stripe."

Heather leaned over my shoulder, pressing her mostly-bare thigh against the puffy pocket of my olive cargo pants. "This one looks really fun!" she exclaimed as she reached across me to grab a piece of cloth, rubbing her entire upper body against my lap in the process. *Straight girls are so oblivious*, I thought.

"Uh, yeah!" I said, turning pages furiously. "We could also do a shirt dress, or this other one with the cap sleeves…"

"No, I like the first one. That's the one I want," she said, absently smoothing the fabric swatch she had chosen across her leg. "What next? Do I need to get measured?" she asked, eyes locked on her orange-and-red-paisley knee.

"OK, yeah, if you're sure." Most of my customers hemmed and hawed over the few choices that had to be made for at least an hour, so Heather's quickness caught me off guard. I spun to dig for my measuring tape in the bag behind me. *She's so decisive,* I thought.

By the time I turned back around, Heather was standing directly in front of me in her underwear. Which was not white. Not at all. Pink bra. Purple panties. Purple panties with a pink ribbon.

I looked straight at her and then immediately averted my eyes. *Shit. Come on, Natalie, be professional*, I thought. I fixed my gaze on her nonsexual belly button and wrapped the tape measure around her waist.

Purple panties. Pink bra.

Now, I was in no way a thirteen-year-old boy. I didn't gawk at Farrah Fawcett posters or Christie Brinkley calendars or whatever masturbatory swimsuit-issue fantasies straight adolescent males get off on. I'd seen most of the girls I made clothes for with their shirts off, and it was never a sexual thing. But this…was different.

I remember learning about Titian's *Venus of Urbino*. A woman lying in a bed making eye contact with the viewer, staring back at you, *that* means sex; if she's looking away, the beauty of her form is the only point. I didn't—and I still don't—ever objectify any of the women I had to see half-naked in the course of doing my job.

But there Heather stood, centimeters from my knees, arms by her side, staring right at me. Wanting me to look. Daring me.

The backs of my fingertips brushed her navel. She sucked in her breath.

"Oh, sorry, are my hands cold?" I offered, and my voice cracked. Maybe I was more of a thirteen-year-old boy than I thought.

"No." Heather replied firmly. "No, it just feels…" She trailed off, and she fixated on my face, slightly below my eyes, for a fleeting moment.

The next thing I knew, the top scorer on my high school's volleyball team had me pinned down on her bed with her tongue halfway down my throat.

"Whoa," I blurted, pushing her off me.

"Sorry! I'm sorry!" she exclaimed. She bolted away and crouched at the corner of her bed, covering her mouth with both her hands.

"No, don't apologize," I said as reassuringly as I could, still totally stunned.

"I thought," she attempted, shaking her head rapidly. "I'm sorry, I thought..."

"Heather, it's OK. It's OK," I repeated. At this point we were talking over each other. "You just startled me, that's all, it's fine!"

She shuddered. I felt awful for reacting so forcefully, but I had not seen her coming at all. Upon reflection, however, I started to understand the real circumstances that brought me to the Boyle house that afternoon. I'm not the only queer kid who came out in high school to wind up with a story like this one. We sat there on the bed for a few minutes as I contemplated my role in the unfolding situation. Finally, she started to talk.

"Natalie, are you a lesbian?" Heather asked. She looked at me with the full-contrast intensity of her blue eyes and dark brows.

"No," I told her. "I'm bi."

"You're sure? Like, you definitely like boys?"

"Yes," I said with a nod. "I definitely like boys."

Heather looked away and hugged her knees to her chest. She stared at her pristine ivory duvet cover. I sat across from her, waiting to hear whatever she had to say.

"So how do you know you like girls?" she asked, wriggling her painted toes.

"I guess I just do," I replied. "I have for a while."

"When did you know?"

Oh, around age fourteen, when I spent hours upon hours staring at your legs, I thought, but that didn't seem like the right answer to give. "Just after sophomore year, I guess? That's when I first kissed a girl."

"Yeah, I heard that you did that," she said. "Not specifically, just that you kissed girls. In general."

"Yeah, it gets around."

"But you're sure that you like boys too?" she asked, puzzled. "Like, you don't think that you're in some kind of transition?"

It's not an unreasonable question, given the way most people perceive straightness and gayness and the many false binaries of life. It's definitely one of the more common inquiries I've heard in my umpteen years playing host for the popular pastime I call "Ask a Bisexual."

"I like boys and I like girls," I explained. "In my limited experience, my body seems to respond to both, so that's the information I have to go on."

Heather nodded, her brow still furrowed with an alarming intensity. She looked away and contemplated her comforter and her ruby toenails for what seemed like a long time.

"I don't think I like boys," she eventually managed, softly but resolutely.

"That's totally OK," I said, placing my hand on her knee. Just then, another thing hit me, and I pulled back. "Wait a minute. What about Jorge?"

Jorge was the goalie of our high school lacrosse team, and a cocaptain with Andre, but a much more straitlaced and upstanding scholar-athlete type. I thought of him as very serious and very religious. I also knew that he and Heather had been going together for years. They were voted "cutest couple" in our yearbook something like three times, and they'd won the dreaded "most likely to get married" distinction in our senior superlatives.

I imagine that kind of pressure would prompt any reasonable girl to dyke out, if only in defiance of such ridiculous expectations.

Heather shrugged. "He's nice. I don't know. Usually it seems like we're more friends than anything else."

"Don't you guys, like, hook up with each other?"

Her face was blank. "He's saving himself for marriage," she said.

"OK," I replied. That didn't surprise me. "But what about—"

"Nothing below the waist," she interrupted. "Ever."

"Oh."

"Yeah," she said, and at last she cracked a half-smile. "And I don't even like the kissing stuff when we do it."

"So, I mean, I'll ask you the same question you asked me. Are you a lesbian?"

We sat there in silence. My idea of her as another late-blooming straight girl started to fall away. I noticed her double-pierced ears for the first time, and the downy fuzz she left undepilated above her top lip.

"I don't know what I am. Maybe I'm asexual. That's a thing, right?" She slumped back and banged her head against the wall a couple of times.

I inched closer to her and swept her hair behind her ear. "I doubt you're asexual," I said in a low voice. I leaned in and slowly kissed her neck. Goosebumps erupted on her shoulder. I put my hand back on her knee and kissed her neck a few more times. She turned her head and placed her mouth on mine.

Kissing drunk girls at parties or dykey girls at dance clubs was fun and exciting and mildly exhibitionist. Kissing vulnerable, confused, mid-coming-out Heather was an entirely different animal: intense, quiet, private. I had never been alone with a girl like that before. I knew I was supposed to take the lead, but I hesitated. I didn't want to push her too far or move things too fast for her comfort. Besides, I barely knew what I was doing myself. *A little kissing, that's all,* I thought. *A little kissing should be just fine.*

Heather, type A as ever, was apparently underwhelmed by my lightweight beginner's agenda. After a few minutes of soft-core making out, her aggressiveness returned. Before I knew it, she was on top of me, only this time it didn't occur to me to push her away.

When she pulled my shirt off, I didn't object. When she relieved me of my bra, I just went with it, the heat of her body and breath and energy carrying me along for whatever ride she wanted to take me on. I reached around and unhooked her hot pink clasp, slid off her bra, and tossed in onto the floor.

That state of things—us rolling around kissing with no shirts on—lasted an eternity. Like most late-adolescent sexual encounters, it felt simultaneously so naughty and so silly, and the longer it went on the more self-conscious I became. At the beginning I managed to focus on the sensations, but after a few minutes I found myself opening my eyes more often, for longer stretches of time, and I started to notice the stark differences between Heather's tan muscles and my pale flab. I became concerned that she might try to take off my pants, and not for prudish reasons. I've always hated my hips and thighs the most, and the idea of Heather Boyle seeing them filled me with middle school gym locker room dread.

And so, when Heather, ever the go-getter, eventually did reach for the drawstring on my cargo pants, I grabbed her hand and interlaced our fingers instead.

"What?" she asked.

"Nothing," I said with a wry smile. "I thought this might be a good time to, you know, check in."

She laughed, shaking her head. "You really are so funny."

"So, is the jury done deliberating?"

"About what?" she asked.

"Do you like girls?"

"I don't know. I like *you*, Natalie. I think you're funny, like I said," she volunteered.

"But what about, you know, what we're doing here," I prodded. "Let's call it 'recent events'?"

"Um. Fun? I think it's fun?" she answered, the light bouncing off her skin. She seemed pretty relaxed, especially given the miserable identity crisis she'd been having just minutes before.

I pushed her hand above her head, flipping her onto her back and rolling over onto my side. "I wonder how much fun," I said, narrowing my eyes, and with that I slid my right hand down her stomach and past the purple elastic waistband of her underwear. I remember being terrified but, as always, propelled by my desire to dance with the limits, to push things as far as they could possibly go. Her stomach heaved and trembled as I moved my hand over her pubic hair. "Is this OK?" I whispered, and she inhaled deeply and nodded yes. My hand hovered just above the part of her I was so scared to touch. She nodded again. I slipped my middle finger just barely into the groove. She was so wet, impossibly wet. The smell of her filled my nostrils. "Woah," I gasped.

"What?" she said, slightly more alarmed than amused.

"Nothing. Just..."

"Just what?" she demanded.

"Just, this," and I moved my hand around, spreading her wetness around so that she could feel it too.

"OH MY GOD!" she shouted, and once again she had skittered away from me and across the bed before I even knew what was happening. She leapt off the other side of the mattress and froze there, half-turned away from me, still wearing her purple panties, with an expression of pure horror on her face.

"Heather, what is the matter?"

She looked down at her lap. "Oh God, is it my period?" she asked, dropping into a whisper for the p-word. And with that, she took two giant gazelle leaps into the bathroom and slammed the door.

Poor Heather. If you ask me, the fact that a high school graduate—the salutatorian!—could be so utterly clueless about the workings of her own anatomy is a sad testament to the failure of our public education system.

The moment clearly ruined, I found my shirt and threw it on, not bothering with the bra. I knocked on the bathroom door. "Heather?" I said, to no reply. "It's OK, it's a thing that happens. I mean like it's supposed to, it's a thing that's supposed to happen." I heard the shower turn on, which I took as my invitation to disappear.

I gathered my belongings and raced down the stairs, exiting the Boyle mansion in a cloud of awkwardness. I knew Heather was embarrassed, and probably would be in an entirely new way once she did a little independent research. But I was also starting to realize that the way I related to sex was not the way everybody related to it. Up until that point, I had been operating under the assumption that what was blossoming in me, the comfort and the enthusiasm, was normal. I thought that any non-hyper-religious red-blooded American would probably approach sex the same way I did. Instead, I was finding out that my largely uncomplicated sexuality was itself a kind of complication. Most people didn't, and don't, and wouldn't, and won't, feel the same easy-breezy fun-times kind of way about that stuff, and all too often my comfort breeds discomfort, even suspicion, in others. I certainly find this to be true now. And even though Heather had initiated almost everything, even though she had carefully engineered our entire encounter in her bedroom, I still left feeling like I was the sex freak.

I tried phoning Heather a couple of times, but she never returned my calls. In what remained of July, I sewed together a red, orange, and pink paisley halter dress based on a single waist measurement and a few educated guesses, and I left it in the Boyle family's mailbox with a note wishing Heather the best of luck up in Walla Walla.

And I returned to my pre-matriculation routine of reloading Morbidica's website a few hundred thousand times a day.

$\mathcal{S}$

ANASTAZE MAY HAVE ACTUALLY gone off the deep end this time. She is currently dating an entirely different unsuspecting member of her own fan club, bringing her grand total now to *three*. It's not that she didn't like the other two; they just started to get too close to her and, rather than risk exposure, she simply dumped them instead.

"Why are you doing this to yourself?" I demanded over breakfast at the diner.

"I haven't the slightest idea, Nat," she said, looking exhausted and wan. She had circles under her eyes darker than any I'd seen since she procrastinated on her senior project and stayed awake writing about Virginia Woolf for two straight weeks.

"You haven't been sleeping," I declared accusingly. "Staze, this is getting serious."

"I know," she said. "But it's as if I'm not even the one driving. Some external force picks me up and drags me to these fan gatherings and out with these men. The only time I feel like myself is when I'm writing."

And her blog really is enjoying an artistic renaissance right now. Every day brings another breathtaking entry, and her narrative snippets have given way to other forms: lyric poetry, character sketches, a simultaneous broadening and deepening of her work. It's heartbreaking to see how low she's been laid by all of this, and it's a bit chilling how fruitful her suffering seems to be for her art.

"What's the new guy's name?" I asked.

"Don't bother learning it," she replied. "At this rate, he'll be gone in a week."

"Careful, you're starting to sound like me," I joked. "Or the old me, I guess."

"Indeed, enough about my bizarre turn," she said with a wave of her hand. "What's going on with you?"

"I still haven't slept with anybody," I declared, and Staze gave me a round of applause. "Thank you, thank you. I'm learning some stuff, I guess, but I don't really know if I'm getting anywhere."

"Just keep it up," she said. "You'll get somewhere."

"The power of perseverance?"

"It's certainly worked for me. I've maintained the same writing project for over a decade, and now I have tens of thousands of readers every day," she said.

"And where has it gotten you?" I asked.

"What the hell is that supposed to mean?" she snapped.

"You brought it up, dude," I said, and she looked down at her untouched scrambled eggs and dry white toast. Again, I'll never understand people who lose their appetites in a crisis. The tiniest disruption to my own life and I become a food vacuum, roving from fridge to cupboard, mouth agape.

We sat there in silence for a little while, me gulping coffee while she pushed yellow curds around with her fork. "Staze," I said gently, placing my hand on her wrist. "You have to eat something." She nodded and took a reluctant bite of her toast. Wincing, she swallowed hard and looked up at me with her wide brown eyes, and I gave her a standing ovation.

Do the Right Thing

MY PARENTS DROPPED ME off in the Hudson Valley right after Labor Day, and by the time the leaves turned red and yellow, I had finally found a very best friend. Anastaze, savvy from her pre-college years in boarding school, initiated me to the rites of quasi-independent dorm living. We stuffed the industrial laundry machines with both of our loads, strung Christmas lights to offset the soul-sucking fluorescents in our rooms, and stockpiled pilfered hand fruit and plastic bowls from the dining halls. We took long walks to nearby waterfalls and into town to visit the chintzy antique stores and buy mediocre coffee from the unassuming local bookstore. And we talked.

We talked about religion and philosophy and sex. We talked about my reserved father and overbearing calorie-counting mother; we talked about Anastaze's artistic English mother and stoic scholarly father. She told me about things I'd never seen, like the Eiffel Tower and Prague and the Dalmatian coast ("blue water, pink pebbles, and hot Croatian soccer players"). I filled her in on the quirks of three-way kissing ("tricky, but somehow easier when drunk").

By the end of first semester, Anastaze had developed a hopeless crush on her Russian literature professor. She enrolled in *LIT 222: Pushkin, Tolstoy, and Dostoyevsky* thinking it would be a cake walk, since she'd written her high school International Baccalaureate Extended Essay (which is a thing, apparently) on *Crime and Punishment.* Professor Liam Donaldson, however, gave her a compelling reason to continue her studies in the field.

"He's incredibly learned, Natalie, a proper intellectual, and so engaged in the material," she gushed to me by the side of a tiny stream near campus. "And he has kind eyes. And his beard is just so..."

"*Gray*?" I interjected, taking a swig. "Anastaze, he's like my parents' age."

"He's forty-five!" she shouted. "He's *only* forty-five!"

"Saying 'only' doesn't make forty-five sound any younger," I insisted. "I'm telling you right now, your first kiss cannot be with a beard like that."

She groaned, flopping onto her back in the grass. "But boys our age are so *dull*, Natalie."

"Man, are you spoiled," I replied. "If you think these smart hippie college guys are boring, you've definitely never been to a high school pep rally."

"Pep rally?" she asked, furrowing her brow. "What is a pep rally?"

And so began the odd-couple friendship we still enjoy to this day.

In addition to the excitement of finding Anastaze, college provided a number of other social benefits. Easton parties featured excellent music, stimulating conversation, and a very sex-positive vibe. I hooked up with a handful of people during those first months of freshman year. I remember some more clearly than others.

Julian could've been Tyler's long-lost cousin, only with longer hair and a much higher tolerance for THC. He lived in my hall, and his room was decorated with a single Arabian-patterned tapestry and a plastic-framed poster of Jimmy Cliff. We started hanging out once he arrived on campus, after orientation, when I was drawn into his room by Toots and the Maytals. And I suppose he's the first person I ever actually had casual sex with. We hung out and groped each other and talked about music, but his penchant for cannabis quickly became intolerably boring. I think the main thing I got out of Julian was those initial experiences with a supervision-free environment, the liberty to have sex in the afternoon or at night or in the morning, whenever we felt like it. It was a privilege of adulthood I found intoxicating; it made me voracious and curious and outwardly focused. Unfortunately, Julian just wanted to crawl inside his bong and never come out. We started to drift apart around early October and stopped hanging out after Columbus Day.

Esther's father spent years abroad as a Christian missionary; her mother was his Korean bride. Esther had one of those SoCal childhoods that involves mostly church retreats and Bible camp and a surprising dearth of beach culture and surfing. Still, her huge public high school exposed her to tremendous possibility, and she came out as a lesbian at fifteen. Fortunately, following the initial freak-out, her parents wound up being pretty chill about it. She was a sophomore at Easton when we met, and the social chair of the campus chapter of Amnesty International. She helped organize big parties where everybody sent postcards petitioning for the freedom of a prisoner of conscience. We only spent one night together. Esther was cute but also kind of twitchy and hyper, and we never made much of an effort to see each other after that one slightly intoxicated encounter.

Luke was a very good-looking varsity baseball player: strong jaw, brown eyes. We had halfway-decent sex one night after my first and only Jennings Hall (aka "the jock dorm") party. He avoided eye contact with me in the cafeteria the next day. I got the message and duly reciprocated.

And that was pretty much it for my entire first semester. I thought for sure that I would rack up a freshman fifteen casual sex partners, but the two one-night stands I managed taught me that those aren't really my thing. If you really share a connection with somebody, why not keep doing it? And if you don't, then what's the point of doing it in the first place?

Anastaze and I both decided to take a short Christmas break that year and return to campus for the January session. So few freshmen opted in for Jan-mester that we got our entire dorm floor to ourselves. We enrolled in a class together, a survey of iconic American film from 1960 to 1990. I figured a syllabus that included Spike Lee might help Anastaze improve her knowledge of popular culture, which was woefully lacking. The class met for five hours a day, four days a week, for four weeks. The instructor was a post-bac rellow—our college's equivalent of a super-senior, usually somebody trying to pad his or her CV before applying to PhD programs—named Ben McNally. Associate Lecturer Benjamin McNally. I began the Jan-mester knowing nothing about diegesis or "the gaze" or the matrilineal nature of Judaism. I had a working vocabulary in all three by Groundhog Day.

The first day of class, Anastaze and I trudged through the snow to partake in a particularly jarring 9:00 a.m. mandatory viewing of *Psycho*. Everyone in the room knew exactly what was coming the minute Janet Leigh stepped into the shower. Everyone except poor Anastaze.

"How the hell did you know to expect *that*?" she asked during our lunch break. "I thought you'd never seen the film before."

"Staze, there's a reason the class is called 'iconic,'" I said. "That scene is super famous. It gets referenced all the time."

"Brutal," she said, pushing aside her untouched bowl of soup. I had to sit in the bathroom and chat with her every time she showered for the whole rest of the term.

After a quick in-class essay on Hitchcock's use of light in the parlor scene, we were already on to *Dr. Strangelove.*

"Now *this*," declared Ben, our post-bac lecturer, "is one of my favorites." And it really is a great film. It's dark, and it makes you feel a little crazy to watch, but if you're willing to go with Kubrick on it, it's actually quite funny. *Gentlemen, there's no fighting in here! This is the war room!* I cackled out loud at that one, breaking the silence in the lecture hall as my fellow students struggled to stay awake for a black-and-white movie first thing in the morning. Thirty heads whipped around to look at me, including Ben's. His eyes met mine, and he smiled.

Ben immediately returned his attention to the movie, but my eyes lingered on him. He kept his chestnut brown hair long, and on days when he didn't tie it up, his curls fell around his face past his angular jaw. I noticed how deliberately he dressed his tall, thin frame to differentiate himself as a teacher: a button-down shirt, corduroy pants, even a blazer with actual elbow patches.

Staze loved *Dr. Strangelove* too. She particularly enjoyed the idea that the Russians would build a Doomsday Machine as a deterrent and then neglect to mention it to anybody. "Frighteningly plausible," she sniffed. After class, we hung around to chat with Ben about Kubrick.

"Wait a minute, you've never seen *A Clockwork Orange*?" Ben practically hollered at Staze.

"She's never seen anything. She went to school *abroad*," I teased her. "In *Eng-lund*."

"I'm pretty sure they have *A Clockwork Orange* in England," Ben replied, having a point.

"I attended an experimental boarding school *abroad*," Staze explained, elbowing me in the ribs. "And I was raised *abroad* with artist parents and no television. Although it's true that I've never seen the film version of *A Clockwork Orange*, I did try to muddle through the book when I was about eleven."

"When you were *eleven*?" Ben blurted, shaking his head. "That's insane. But you really have to see the movie. Do you guys want to come over to my place and watch it tonight? I'm in the Head of Hall apartment in Shropner, and it's deadsville over there." Shropner was a small, relatively remote dorm with mostly freshmen in residence, so I imagined Ben really was all by himself.

I looked at Staze, and she seemed up for it. "Sure. We don't have any plans."

"Awesome. I'll have some food and wine and stuff," said Ben. "Say seven?"

"That sounds great," said Staze. "Really, I'm eager for all the education I can get. Natalie's giving me a crash course in pop music," she explained.

"Yeah? Like what?" he asked me.

"Everything. There are big holes in her Michael Jackson knowledge, so we covered his early stuff yesterday. Jackson 5 through *Off the Wall*. Just the hits. I'm going to make her watch *Thriller* this afternoon."

"Right on," said Ben in his Bay Area cadence.

"What's *Thriller*?" Staze asked. "Is it anything like *Psycho*?"

Ben and I looked at each other. "Not really?" he offered.

"All right, we should grab lunch. We'll see you tonight," I said to him. As we walked away, I realized that I was trying to show off my musical knowledge to him, hoping he'd be impressed. "So,

Thriller is an album and also a song, but most importantly it's a thirteen-minute music video..."

$\mathcal{S}$

FULL FIGURED FASHION WEEK is days away, and I'm starting to lose sleep over it. I can't believe how nervous I am. I talked to my mother on the phone this morning, which did little to assuage my anxiety.

"Natalie, sorry to call you at work, but I need to know, are you available to drive down next weekend, because we've got a few things going on, and you still need to clear some of the crap out of your old room, because we're getting ready to finally renovate and—"

My mother is incapable of ending a sentence on the telephone. The only way to converse with her is to cultivate a willingness to interrupt.

"Sorry, Mom," I interjected, hurrying out to the bare warehouse hallway in front of the M&S office. "But I have to go to New York next weekend. It's a work thing."

"Well, that sounds exciting, Natalie, so what exactly will you be doing there in New York, you know I haven't been there in, what is it now, five or six years at least and—"

"It's a fashion show, Mom. I'm working on a fashion show." I could hear my voice echoing through the corridor. I hoped nobody else could.

"That's great, because, you know, I often think Boston is kind of a bizarre choice for you, given your industry, and I know you've produced things in New York before, and maybe this will lead to other opportunities to produce in New York, and maybe even relocate there, which we would love, since you'd be so much closer and —"

"Actually, Mom, I'm not producing," I explained. I have no idea why I didn't just let her believe whatever she wanted to believe and wrap it the hell up.

"Oh Natalie, please tell me you're not assistant producing, because you're beyond that level now, and you've been working at this job for many years and—"

"I'm in the show, Mom," I blurted, already furious with myself for the decision I was in the process of making. "I'm modeling in the show. I'm working as a model."

Silence.

Un-fucking-precedented telephonic silence. From *my mother*.

I tried to explain. "It's no big deal, just a one-time thing. I did an event for a plus line at a department store around here, and, long story short, I wound up walking down the runway. And a model saw me there and recommended me for this gig in New York, so I figured, why not? You only live once, right?" I struggled to tag on a lighthearted laugh.

After a long pause, Mom sniffed. Then, she sighed.

"Oh, Natalie." She sighed again.

"What?" I demanded. "What, Mom? Tell me what the problem is." I started to pace around the hall.

"It's just…" Sigh number three. "Natalie, you're a beautiful girl, a beautiful woman, you know that, and it just seems a shame that instead of finally getting in shape, you've just *resigned* yourself to being *obese*, which is very unhealthy, not just physically but psychologically and—"

"Mom!" I barked. "I just told you I've been hired as a model. How are you twisting this into a bad thing?"

"A *plus-size* model, Natalie, you said a *plus-size* model, and, I mean, come on, honey, doesn't that bother you? Doesn't it make you feel sad or disappointed or, I don't know, *embarrassed*, maybe, or—"

"No, Mom, it doesn't. I am plus-size. So no, it does not make me feel embarrassed to be modeling plus-size clothing. Not at all."

"You know, Natalie, I do my best to be accepting, I really do, I try very hard, and I always ask you if you're dating any interesting young men *or* young women, and I think I deserve some credit for that, but calling yourself plus-size, that's something I have a hard time just flat-out accepting and—"

"Listen, Mom," I snapped. "If me getting a side job as a professional model somehow makes you ashamed of me and my appearance, then let's just not talk about it."

"Oh Natalie, I am not ashamed of you, honey," Mom said, her voice getting quieter. "I'm just concerned about you, sweetheart, because I love you, and I would never be ashamed of you, not at all, and in fact your father and I are proud of you, but I worry about you, because for one thing, *are* you dating any interesting young men or young women, Natalie, because you haven't mentioned anyone to us and—"

"I've just been really busy lately," I deflected. She was poking around dangerously close to a nerve. "Anyway, *changing the subject*, I'm planning to come down for Thanksgiving in a few weeks. What do you need me to deal with besides the stuff in my room?"

"Well, I suppose I should tell you now that the day before Thanksgiving I'm going to be having a little surgery, nothing to worry about, just a little procedure and—"

"Is it a mole? Did you have a biopsy?" Ever since Mom's father died of metastatic melanoma two years ago, the specter of skin cancer has been a frightening concern for both of us.

"No, Natalie, it's nothing like that, honey, it's actually, well, as you know your father and I are planning a cruise this summer for our thirty-fifth, and I've decided to treat myself to a little lipo, just a bit under the arms and—"

"You're getting *liposuction*?" I spat. "You have got to be fucking kidding me."

"Natalie, watch it with the f-bombs, all right? I am your mother, and I know we talk like friends, but I don't like that kind of casual swearing, and you know that, and I sent you to college, so at the very least you should be able to express yourself without—"

"Fine, Mom. I'll express myself. I'll even drop some of that expensive book learning on you, ready? Liposuction is one of the most dangerous surgeries you can get. Any sane person would conduct a basic *cost-benefit analysis* and decide against it."

"Listen, honey, I hear that you're concerned, but I have this fabulous doctor, and he and his staff have assured me and reassured me that—"

"Who's your doctor?" I demanded, yanking out a pen and paper. "Give me the name so I can do my own research."

"Well his name, his name, honey, is Dr. Shelley, and—"

"Ha. You're sure it's not Dr. Frankenstein?" I quipped. "Sorry, just a little literary joke from all that college you paid for."

"I attended a free seminar called 'Achieving Summer Arms' at Dr. Shelley's clinic and—"

"Whoa, whoa, wait a second. Is this Dr. Shelley as in Dr. Mortimer Shelley? The guy with the billboards?" Back home, the downtown area is peppered with ads for this guy, right next to the highways piping people in an out from the suburbs.

"Why yes, *Natalie*, as a matter of fact, he is," Mom replied, and I could tell she was starting to lose her temper. "He has an extremely large practice due to the quality of his work!"

"Or his long-term financing," I muttered.

"Enough, young lady!" she barked. "I have determined that this is the best option for me, and I do not need your editorial comments at this point, not at all, because I've made my decision and I remain firm in that choice, which is mine to make and—"

"All right, Mom, all right," I replied, already exhausted. Talking on the phone with my mother must be equivalent to ninety minutes of cardio. "Just email me the details, please, and I'll stick around that weekend and help Dad, or whatever."

When we finally hung up, I found myself all the way at the other side of the building, near the metal back stairs. I threw open the fire door and plunged into the icy morning air. I took a few deep breaths and watched the puffs of vapor emerge from my lips. The shock of the cold was bracing and I felt instantly better, until I realized that the door had latched behind me and I was outside in the cold without my coat or my keys.

"Fuck!" I yelled, pounding my fists against the door. "Hey! Can somebody let me in? Fuck!"

My teeth began to chatter, and I was just about to give up and attempt the frozen staircase when the door opened, just a crack.

"What is it, little girl? Are you selling something?" asked a man's voice, pitched to sound like a *Monty Python* version of an old woman. "Because we don't want any!"

"Sean?" I asked. He pushed the door open, and I slipped inside.

"Oh, Natalie, it's you!" he teased. "I assumed you were still busy yelling at your mother."

"Shit," I said. "You heard that?"

"Bits and pieces," he replied. "You want some hot chocolate?"

"Um, sure," I said. "I'll take a taste. But I'm not a huge hot chocolate fan."

"Yes, because you've never had *my* hot chocolate," he bragged. "Follow me into my lair." His retro New Balance sneakers squeaked against the buffed hall floors.

"I swear I don't normally yell at my mother, " I explained as we stepped into the chocolate suite. "It's just...she's...she's being..."

Sean grabbed a tiny paper cup. "I heard something about plastic surgery?" He sucked his teeth.

"Yeah," I said, as I watched him pull off a metal lid and ladle out some syrupy liquid. His concoction smelled like so much more than chocolate. The air filled with the aromas of mocha and pepper and cinnamon. "Yeah, I guess it scares me. And it bums me the fuck out."

"I don't blame you," he said, handing me the cup. "Kinda sucks when the person you're supposed to look like doesn't like the way she looks."

"Exactly!" I blurted, a little too loud. "Thank you!" I raised the chocolate to my lips.

"Careful!" he cried, and I pulled the cup away from my mouth. "Sorry, but it's basically hotter than molten lava."

"Ah," I said, blowing on my chocolate. "Good to know." A kitchen timer started beeping in the background, and Sean sprinted away without a word. "I'll leave it on my desk for a few minutes before I drink it!" I shouted.

"OK, cool!" Sean called back.

"I will! Literally!" I replied.

"What?" he asked.

"Nevermind! Thank you!

I strolled back to my office and forgot all about the hot chocolate. By the time I noticed the white cup sitting next to my coffee mug, the whole serving had turned solid. I guess I missed my window.

Ten hours later, it was squarely the middle of the night, and sleep was not happening, so I stared up at my white ceiling fan and thought about Ben.

§

THE NIGHT BEN INVITED us over to watch *A Clockwork Orange* turned out to be the coldest of the year. Staze and I bundled up as much as two uninitiated college freshmen possibly could for the ten minute walk to Shropner. Frankly, a four-hundred-dollar shopping spree at a high-end outfitter probably couldn't have prepared us for the weather that night. The sun set almost three hours before we headed out into the freezing cold wind. It must've been zero degrees with a wind chill of twenty below. By the time we arrived, all of our extremities and exposed skin ached and tingled; we could barely breath. I remember whimpering with pain as I stood there waiting for Staze to swipe us through the door with her card key. The lock sprung open and we tumbled in, shoving the heavy door closed behind us and crying out in agony.

Head of Hall apartments in Easton dorms sit at ground level, presumably so the residence "mothers" could monitor students' comings and goings back in the day. Ben opened the door to his place and chuckled at us. Over his shoulder, I could see deep mahogany wood tones, a red oriental carpet, and an actual roaring fire. He was holding an oversized wine glass, about a fifth of the way full.

"A little balmy out there?" he asked with a grin.

Staze exhaled with a gravelly groan. "Ugh! It's horrifying!" I stood there shivering, too frozen to respond.

"Here, just throw your coats and shoes in the hall and come on in. I've got a fire going," Ben invited. We ripped off our icy gloves and hats, struggling to untie our boots with our raw fingers, and stumbled into the apartment. I threw myself down in front of the fireplace, offering my wind-bitten cheeks and hands up to the flickering flames. After a couple of minutes, my teeth finally stopped chattering, and I looked around.

"This place is amazing," I said, noticing the woodwork on the wainscoting and mantle. The courtyard-facing wall even had a couple of stained glass windows.

"Yeah, it's pretty nice," Ben replied, turning side to side with his arms outstretched. "All this and more can be yours someday, if you're too scared to leave college after four years!"

"Really, Ben, why did you decide to do post-bac?" Staze asked.

"Oh I'm serious," he said. "I had no idea what to do after Easton, so I just kind of lingered in denial until second semester of senior year, at which point I freaked out and broke down crying in Professor Case's office."

"You're kidding," I blurted with a gasp.

"Nope, no, unfortunately I am still completely not kidding," he said, disappearing behind the countertop that separated the living area from the tiny kitchenette. "Shiraz?"

"Oh, yes, please!" said Staze.

"Uh, sure," I consented, throwing Staze a puzzled look. "What's Shiraz?"

"Red wine. This one's South African. It's great," Ben answered, emerging with two more goldfish-bowl-sized wine glasses and a bottle. "Anyway, Case suggested I apply for post-bac, mostly because I was a film studies major and enrollment in the department's courses was growing faster than the faculty. He thought I could ease the teaching burden while I figured out what the fuck to do with my life. Which brings us to now."

"And so what are you going to do after this year?" asked Staze.

"Jeez, Anastaze, what are you, his mom?" I scolded.

"Thank you, Natalie," said Ben, pouring a tiny splash of wine into a glass from high up so that it sloshed up the other side like in an advertisement. "You get the first taste."

"Cheers," I said, grabbing the glass. I gulped down the mouthful. Staze and Ben stared at me.

"Well?" Ben asked. "How is it?"

"Um. Good?" I said.

Staze giggled. "Natalie, do you know how to taste wine?" she asked.

"I know that I just tasted some wine," I replied. They stared some more. "What?"

"All right, Natalie. When you open a bottle of wine, you never know for sure whether it's going to be good or if it has turned bad," Ben explained, pouring small tastes into the other glasses for Staze and himself. "So the first thing you need to do is smell it." Staze swirled her wine under her nose and closed her eyes. Ben stuck the entirety of his ample schnoz deep into the bulbous glass. I cracked up.

"What? What's funny, Natalie?" Staze asked, blushing.

"I guess I'm finally getting that liberal arts education, huh?" I remarked. "How do you guys know so much about wine?"

Ben looked at Staze. "From growing up, I guess. My mom has a big thing for Côtes du Rhône."

"My father loves Côtes du Rhône too," Staze agreed. "Also Montepulciano."

"My father thinks Pert Plus is the greatest invention in world history," I added, still laughing. That got Ben going.

"What? What is a Perth Plus?" asked Staze, catapulting me into hysterics.

"Perth Plus?" managed Ben. I was laughing so hard I couldn't speak. "Perth Plus is an Australian ice wine," he deadpanned, sending me over the edge. He cracked up too, and I laughed until my sides ached.

Once we finally calmed down enough to explain to Anastaze the wonders of two-in-one shampoo plus conditioner, Ben and Staze continued their crash course in oenology. I actually learned a lot, particularly vocabulary: "bouquet," "vintage," "legs," "finish." The evening's lesson probably saved me from some serious embarrassment down the road, when my lack of wine manners could've made me feel ignorant and exposed in a much less playful context.

Then, Ben uttered five words that I will never forget, for they indelibly altered the course of my life:

"*I'll go get the Brie.*"

Once upon a time, you couldn't simply roll into any big box grocery store and pick up a tray of sashimi and a tub of artichoke pesto. When I entered college, I had never eaten eggplant pizza or bitten into a sweet date, let alone one that was stuffed with goat cheese and wrapped in bacon. Nowadays you can get a caprese sandwich with a side of mesclun greens—complete with arugula and radicchio—at your local TGI Chainfood's, but back when I started school, the ubiquity of such simple gourmet pleasures was yet to arrive on our national landscape. Before Whole Foods and the Food Network turned being a foodie into an accessible pastime for millions of suburbanites, I got my first taste of that world while hanging out with Ben and Anastaze.

"Staze! What's Brie?" I whispered as Ben vanished into the back corner of the kitchenette.

"Oh God, Natalie, it's cheese! It's French cheese. Lord."

"Have some mercy, dude!" I retorted, showing her my palms. "I didn't react like that when you said you'd never heard of Snoop Dogg."

"Shut up!" she snapped back. She looked in Ben's direction, straining to see if he heard me.

"Anastaze," I said, dropping my voice even quieter. "Do you like him?"

"What? No! Be quiet, Natalie!" she scolded, waving her hand to silence me.

Ben returned holding a wooden cutting board covered in delicacies: Brie, apricot preserves (to pair with the Brie, obviously—obvious to anyone but eighteen-year-old Natalie, of course), Kalamata olive tapenade, herbed goat cheese, and a box of almonds covered in chocolate and sea salt. He put down the board and whipped an extra-long baguette out from behind his back.

"Did you carry that bread in your waistband?" I asked, squinting at him.

"You bet I did!" he responded.

"Classy," I chided.

"Hey, I'm all class, baby," he fired back with a smile that reminded me of the look he shot me when I laughed at *Dr. Strangelove* earlier that day. He gave us a quick rundown of the contents of the cutting board, and we tucked into the delightful spread. Suddenly, the room lit up with a flash, followed closely by an echoing boom.

Staze jumped. "What was that?"

"Lightning? With snow? Is that even allowed?" I asked, rushing over to the window.

Ben joined me. "Yup. Storm's a-brewin'," he remarked, looking around.

"I think storm's a-happenin'," I replied. The wind whipped through the courtyard, and it looked like we were trapped inside a particularly tumultuous snow globe.

"Yup," Ben agreed. "Storm's a-here."

"I am not looking forward to heading back out into that," I said.

Ben turned his attention to his laptop. "Wow. That's unheard of."

"What?" I asked, still gazing out at the swirling snow.

"They just canceled classes for tomorrow," Ben replied.

"But they haven't canceled classes in eleven years!" said Anastaze, who read every word of every campus guide and admissions brochure before matriculating, turning herself into a treasure trove of Easton trivia in the process. "True," said Ben. "But Jan-mester is only three years old, so this was probably bound to happen." He closed his laptop and turned to face us. "So, would anyone care for some Kubrick?"

"How about we drink every time we see a phallic object?" I suggested.

"Um, no, we'd all get shitfaced," Ben fired back. "Now shut up and enjoy the comic violence."

"Aye, Professor," I said with a salute.

"Hey, that's Associate Lecturer McNally to you." Ben shoved me playfully with his shoulder. I got goose bumps. *Shit*, I thought. *I really hope Staze doesn't like him.*

We watched *A Clockwork Orange,* slightly drunk and giddy with that childlike school's-canceled glee. I saw the movie a couple of times in high school, but it took on a unique significance in my life after that night in Shropner. I can't think about it without remembering Ben's wicked smirk or the many times he elbowed me and said, "This is the best part." (It was no fewer than five.) Come to think of it, I haven't seen *Clockwork* in years. I wonder if it still feels as loaded now as it did back then. Perhaps I'll glue my eyes open and force myself to watch it again sometime.

That night in Shropner, as we experienced the droogs, and as my head grew lighter and dizzier with wine, I found Ben's hand creeping toward the small of my back, his index finger coming to rest somewhat oddly in the belt loop of my pants.

When the movie was over, I turned to him. "Even fucking weirder than I remembered. Where's your bathroom?"

"Through the bedroom on the right," he said, gesturing with his head. When I tried to get up, he yanked me back down by my belt loop.

"Ha! Me first!" he cried, levering himself up off the couch and making a beeline for the bathroom.

"Hey!" I shouted in protest. Then I lowered my voice. "Anastaze," I said, my face flushed with booze and attraction. "You have to tell me *right now* if you like him."

"Please. Of course not," she whispered with a furrowed brow.

"Then why didn't you want him to hear me teasing you about Snoop Dogg?" I asked, trying to smoke her potential secret crush out of its hole. I had already promised myself that I would never compete with Anastaze for a guy.

"Natalie, I was a bit shy because he's my teacher! He's *our* professor, remember?"

"Associate Lecturer," I corrected, suddenly skeptical of what I'd perceived as Ben's obvious moves.

"Do not develop a thing for him, Nat," she admonished. "I've seen that film before, many times. When I attended school *abroad.*"

"But that was high school," I argued. "This is college. Plus, you're in love with your Russian lit prof even though he's a million years old."

"I admire Professor Donaldson from afar," she clarified. "I do not sit on his couch watching movies and inching ever closer to him."

"Staze, he's just a fifth year student," I whispered, trying to convince myself as much as her. "There's nothing inappropriate about it. He's only twenty-three."

Staze paused. "I suppose that's true. Still…" She trailed off as Ben returned to the room.

"Oh, is it my turn now?" I said with a sarcastic smirk. "Be my guest," he replied with a valiant bow.

"My, what a gracious host," I teased, disappearing into the bathroom.

When I emerged, I heard Staze demurring on something. I hoped it wasn't the offer of more wine. "Oh, no, we couldn't. Thank you, but no."

"What's up?" I asked, drying my wet hands on my pants. (What is it about the Y chromosome that renders hand towels anathema?)

"I'm trying to convince Anastaze that you guys should stay here tonight," Ben informed me, and the goose bumps returned to my neck.

"Well, it is mighty shitty out there," I said, looking out the window. The wind howled between the buildings, whipping snow everywhere.

"But it must have warmed up some if it's snowing like that," Staze remarked, eliciting puzzled stares from Ben and me. "I know a bit about weather."

"You're the expert," Ben said. He shrugged. "Personally, you couldn't pay me to go out there tonight. Your call, ladies."

Staze and I looked at each other. I tried to bury my desperate pleading somewhere behind an expression of fated resignation. Staze relented. "All right, we'll stay," she said.

"Thank you so much, Ben. It'd be hell trying to get back across campus." I looked at my watch. It was only one-thirty. "Does anybody want to watch another movie?" I suggested.

"I'm kind of an early riser," Ben said. "Left over from my rowing days."

"Did you row crew for Easton?" Staze asked.

"All four years," he replied, opening up a closet and pulling out some blankets. "It kind of sucks, because I still have my NCAA eligibility, but Easton doesn't want me to row this year. Post-bac rules."

"Really?" asked Staze.

"Yeah, they try to keep us separate from the students, you know, since they're paying us to teach," he said. I stared at the courtyard while Anastaze attempted to drill holes into my skull with her laser-like stare. Ben yanked the cushions off the couch and pulled out the bed. He set us up with sheets, blankets, and pillows, and he fetched us two glasses of water. "Do you guys need anything else?"

"Nope. This is perfect," I said, attempting a flirtatious smile. "Thanks for taking care of us."

"No prob," he said. "Sleep well." And with that, he retired to his bedroom and closed the door.

Despite my body image issues and Staze's modesty, we stripped down to our base layer tops and took off our jeans. It turns out that even just one semester at a hippie school like Easton with its four annual naked parties can have a pretty stunning effect on one's attitudes toward one's own body. We climbed into the couch bed, whispering and giggling for a few minutes before Staze drifted off mid-sentence, an adorable habit of hers that persists to this day.

I, on the other hand, was wired for sound. My whole body buzzed with an electrifying full-tilt attraction more intense than I'd felt in a while. I'd expected to find this all around me at college, but the very first person to push those buttons for me was, unfortunately, my professor, or at least my post-baccalaureate associate lecturer. But he was basically a peer, I reassured myself. I stared at the ceiling, wide awake, rationalizing and fretting and twitching with desire. *I just want some good sex,* I told myself. *What's the big deal if he's sort of my teacher?*

I remember saying that to myself: *I just want some good sex.* But when I think about it now, the sex I'd had with Julian felt pretty good for what it was. He turned me on; he got me off. No real complaints, except that he didn't quite hold my interest beyond that. I was eighteen years old. Had I already sublimated my desire for genuine connection into a specious quest for "good sex"?

That's what I do now, obviously. I obsess about my "sex life," but I could be having sex any night of the week if that was all I wanted. Good sex to me means sex with somebody who really intrigues me. I've known for years that I'm not particularly interested in random romps with just anybody. But I label it all "good sex:" the intellectual satisfaction, the mental attraction, the fucking *feelings.* I'm comfortable wanting sex. I know I'm good at it. I know I'm fun. I don't think sex is too much to ask.

After convincing myself that all I wanted from Ben was physical pleasure, I decided to throw caution to the wind. I waited until Staze had been asleep for a while, then I slid off the pull-out bed. I headed for the bathroom, which was, of course, through Ben's room. Slowly, I opened the door and crept in. Ben was still and silent. I walked into the bathroom. He had left a nightlight on, and I wondered if he did so for our benefit or because he always did. I stood there in the dim light of the tiny bulb and looked at myself in the mirror. I had on black panties, no bra, and a well-worn pale pink V-neck T-shirt, which fell to just below my belly button. My hourglass shape bulged out at the tops of my thighs, just above where the sink cut off my reflection. But I remember thinking that I looked sort of sexy.

I threw some warm water on my face, drying off with the bottom of my shirt, then swung open the bathroom door and stepped out. I looked at Ben again and saw him blink in the snow-brightened room. I lingered silently next to his bed for what seemed like an eternity, watching him watch the ceiling. Finally, when neither of us had spoken or moved for a good two or three minutes, I turned back toward the living room.

Ben grabbed my hand and pulled me down into the bed. He flipped me under him and moved into a push-up position, hovering above me. "We can't tell anyone, Natalie," he whispered. I nodded, and he softly touched his lips to my neck. A faint whimper escaped from my mouth. "Shh," he said, flashing a more intimate version of his sly smile. His eyes scanned my face.

"I'll be quiet," I uttered, barely audibly.

"At least try," he said wickedly, brushing the back of his hand against my thigh. I bit my lip. "That's hot," he whispered.

"I know," I mouthed, wrapping my arms around his neck and pulling his lips to mine.

Today when I think of a twenty-three-year-old American male, I picture a gangly, overgrown child. But when I was eighteen, Ben seemed like a fully fledged grown-up, like a real adult. He took charge, moving and manipulating my body, flipping me over, pulling my legs around his waist. He kept condoms in a little drawstring pouch that hung from his headboard, as opposed to mood-murderingly buried in some remote sock drawer halfway across the room like the other guys I'd slept with at college. And he talked to me, which was a first. It wasn't quite dirty talk; it was more of an intimate play-by-play, telling me what he was going to do to me, telling me what he wanted, telling me how hot I was.

I loved it.

By the time I tore myself out of bed with him, the clock read 4:22. I remember watching a couple of minutes tick past, knowing I should wake up next to Anastaze. I wanted Ben to see that I knew how to be cool about the whole situation. I stood up and gave him a last kiss on the lips.

"Natalie. Thank you. I enjoyed that very much," he said. It seemed like an odd and somewhat formal thing to say, but he was already half asleep.

"It was my pleasure," I replied coyly.

Anastaze didn't even stir when I crawled in next to her. We both woke up the next morning around seven-thirty when the sun rounded the building across the yard and bombarded us full-blast through the undressed stained glass windows.

"Let's just go," I said to her as we got dressed. "He's probably still asleep."

"You think?" she asked, puzzled. "Seven in the morning is rather late for a crew captain."

I gave her a pointed look. "Well, he had a long night," I whispered.

"Not really, though, I mean, I think we all went to bed before two, and…." A light bulb went off. "Oh my God. Oh my God, Nat!"

I put my finger over my mouth to silence her. "I'll tell you, I will," I whispered. "Let's just get going."

"Wow," she said, shaking her head. She pulled on her sweater. "You are quite a goal-oriented person, aren't you?"

I grinned. "Right now, my goal is breakfast," I said, opening Ben's apartment door as quietly as possible. "Dibs on the waffle iron." We geared up in the Shropner foyer and trudged back to the dining hall nearest our dorm, and I swore Staze to secrecy before telling her absolutely everything.

§

STAZE TEXTED ME WHILE I was waiting for my pizza last night and asked if she could drop by. I know she can tell I'm having a hard time too, but for now our focus continues to be on her problems, and rightfully so. Talk about a fucking roller coaster. One minute she's over the moon about her burgeoning relationship or her new heights of literary creativity, and the next she's pulling out her eyelashes. Literally. It's that bad. I told her to come on over and bring beer. She arrived just as the delivery guy left.

"So at least tell me his name, if it's bothering you this much," I said as we shared my couch with the flat white pizza box.

"Jeremiah," she told me. "He's a writer, the same guy from a couple of weeks ago. We've been seeing one another steadily."

"And you're still on a first-name basis?" I asked, taking a sip of my IPA.

"He knows my surname, and he didn't ask any further questions," she said with a shrug. "Maybe he'll google me and find out about my father, but so far it hasn't come up at all."

"And? What do you guys talk about?"

"Mostly we discuss Broken Hope Chest, since it's been such a frenzy of activity lately," she said, shaking her head.

"Staze, do you find yourself blogging with a mind to what you'll talk about with Jeremiah the next time you see him?"

"Of course I do, Natalie," she confessed. "It's crazy, I know. It's completely bizarre. But then, inspiration is inspiration, I suppose..." She trailed off.

"So what else do you talk about?"

"Other than that, we haven't been doing very much talking," she said, averting her eyes.

"But you haven't slept with him," I verified.

"No." She cracked open one of the Belgian wheat beers she likes. "Almost. But no."

"Wow," I said. "This is no joke, is it?"

"I feel like the most duplicitous person in the world," she said morosely.

"Now, I think I know the answer to the following question, but can you please tell me in your own words why you can't just reveal to this one very special person the truth about who you are?"

"Jeremiah is the organizer of the fan group, Natalie," she explained.

"Oh, Anastaze," I sighed.

"Yes. And also, Broken Hope Chest is written by an anonymous thirty-one-year-old virgin. As in someone who's never had sex before," she continued.

"And you told him that you weren't a virgin?"

"Well, when you're thirty-one, most people assume you're not. And I haven't exactly clarified my situation." She traced the stitching on my couch cushion with her finger.

"But why can't you also be a virgin, independently of your mutual favorite anonymous blogger?" I asked.

"It just seems like too much in common, too much overlap," she explained. "I guess I don't want him to piece it together."

"Well then maybe you should just *tell him yourself*, Anastaze," I urged.

She paused for a long time, still following the lines of the pillow. Finally, she looked up at me. "I know I have to tell him, Natalie. But when I do that, I also have to tell everyone. I'm terrified."

"Staze, here's the thing," I said, grabbing her hand. "I don't believe in God or fate or messages from the universe or anything like that. But I do think that we create crises for ourselves when what we really need to do is change."

"Yes, of course, I get it, Nat," she said, waving her hand dismissively.

"No, I'm serious," I continued. "You know what my main regret is about Ben? It's how long I allowed myself to suffer. And you were telling me all the while that I should get out, and I just didn't listen."

"But Natalie," she argued. "That's just where you were at the time. Your heart was not going to allow you to extricate yourself from that situation until you were utterly worn out." She looked at me again. "And I had to accept that, even though it hurt me to see you in pain."

"I still don't know what I learned from Ben, exactly," I told her. "Probably most of what I retained is not entirely positive. And yes, it's probably time, or past time, for me to figure it out. But, Staze, I don't think this is about Jeremiah, or about sex, or about any of that stuff. I think this is really about your work."

She picked at a slice of pizza and paused. "The plot thickens," she said at last. She reached into her messenger bag and pulled out a folded tabloid-size newspaper with a series of blocky headlines. The thickest, blackest letters on top read *Manhattan Review of Books*.

"What is this?" I asked, grabbing at it. "And who does the graphic design?"

"Don't get me started," she snarled. "It's intentional. The font is evocative of the golden age of newsletter-based pseudo-intellectualism. That thing is like the coelacanth: it's a living fucking fossil."

"Whoa," I said. "What'd it ever do to you?"

She yanked the bottom half down for me to see and pointed to a small blue headline. *Gender and Anonymity: Sam Elliot Jacobs on Internet Literary Communities.*

"Shut. The fuck. Up," I whispered, flipping furiously to the contents page.

"I hate him," she spat. "I hate his posing, hackneyed, misogynist guts."

"Well, that's a reversal," I said. I threw open the article and started to skim it. "So does he flat-out say you're a dude, or what?"

"Basically, yeah!" She leapt up and started to pace furiously and gesticulate even more so. "And he has the audacity to quote V. S. Mishra. V. S. Mishra! Of course he writes beautifully, but I happen to know firsthand, *firsthand*, that he is *dreadful* in person, as I've been forced to dine with him on several occasions, and—"

"Staze, hang on," I interrupted. "All I'm reading in here is this guy singing your praises."

"Well, at the beginning, he mostly explains what a weblog is to the borderline Luddite geriatric readership," she ranted. "Read the end."

I flipped to the final few paragraphs and read them carefully. When I was done, I put the paper down and picked up my beer.

"Anastaze," I began. "How long have you loved this Jacobs guy?"

"I don't know, perhaps ten years? But I don't love him anymore. Absolutely not. Let's be crystal fucking clear about that."

"And before this, did you ever see him as a misogynist?"

"Maybe. A little," she attempted. "No. Not at all, honestly."

"And do you mention his work in your blog?" I asked. She gave me a look. "I mean, I read the thing, but I probably wouldn't pick up any references."

"Occasional allusions may appear now and again, yes," she admitted.

"Staze. He's goading you," I said with a smile. "It's so obvious. He adores your work, and he wants the literary world to take it seriously. And I think he wants to meet you."

"What, then, Natalie? Are you implying this is some kind of a trap?" She took the paper and waved it in my face.

"I would bet that he believes that you're a woman, but he knows you well enough from your writing to assume that you would not be able to stand it if he stated publicly that you might be a guy."

"What?" she asked, dropping back down onto my couch and grabbing her forehead.

"He's a fan of yours, Anastaze," I continued. "And he is using his position to create a context for you to come out and take your rightful place in this mad world of brainy writers. That much is clear to me. *Crystal fucking clear.*"

Staze sat silently for a long time. She picked up the paper and read the last few paragraphs again. Finally, she finished her beer, opened another one, and plunked her head down on my shoulder.

"When I was in school, the *Manhattan Review* published a four-part series on my parents' tumultuous relationship, penned by my mother. Lots of betrayal. Plenty of sexual detail. I was barely sixteen."

"Gross, dude," I blurted. In my defense, that was an attempt at empathy. I tried to envision a scenario in which anybody would give a shit about the nitty-gritty details of my parents' marriage, but it's nearly impossible to imagine what half of Staze's experiences as a kid must've been like.

"I just don't want to answer any questions about my family," she said, tears filling up her eyes. "I'm so afraid that's all anyone's going to care about."

"First of all, that's just gossipy bullshit. It might get some play initially, but it will not be what ultimately matters to people," I assured her, wrapping my arms around her slight figure. "Second of all, if you want, I'll be your publicist. You can direct any and all inquiries to me, media or otherwise."

Staze let out a big sigh and wiped her tears. Then, she reached for her iPhone. "December the first, then?" she said resolutely. "I appear to be wide open that day."

"Uhhh," I said, stunned, scrambling for my Blackberry. "That's, like, three weeks away."

"Indeed," she said. "Are you in?"

"Completely," I told her.

And so, this weekend I take the train to New York to work as a model, then I head to my parents' house to play dutiful post-lipo holiday nurse, and after that I return to Cambridge just in time for my stint as Anastaze's public relations director.

In the meantime, though, I'm still moonlighting as my own shitty, hapless, sleep-deprived sex therapist.

Three of Us

BEN, STAZE, AND I became an inseparable trio for the rest of the Jan-mester. Ben had a car, and he drove us all around the area in search of new culinary experiences for them to expose me to. We ate sushi in Rhinebeck and dim sum in Poughkeepsie. We made pesto with an actual mortar and pestle in the Shropner apartment kitchenette, and we drank bottle after bottle of very average red wine. After a long dinner and sometimes a movie, Ben would either drive us back to our dorm across campus, or we would walk, always heading out reasonably early out of respect for Ben's holdover crew team sleep schedule.

And every single night, regardless of whether we had already spent the entire evening together or not, I would walk, alone and freezing, all the way back to Ben's apartment. In the morning, Ben would wake me before seven, say his ritual thanks, and send me on my way. I would trudge back to my dorm, climb into my own bed for another hour and a half or so, and then rush off to film class to stare at the teacher I was screwing. By the time our three-day weekends rolled around, I was so wiped out I'd sleep until noon, missing most of the scant and precious winter daylight.

Staze, for her part, didn't pass too much judgment, at least not initially. For the first couple of weeks, she even conceded that Ben was pretty attractive. And she always relished hearing any details I was willing to share.

"Wait a minute, Natalie. He *pulls* your *hair*?" she asked, incredulous, as we wiled away a weekend afternoon in my dorm room.

"Yeah, he does," I replied. "It's like something out of a movie."

"I'm afraid I've never seen that kind of movie," she quipped.

"I mean, where does a guy like Ben pick up moves like that?" I wondered. "Maybe he had an affair with an older woman."

"Don't you know anything about his past?" Staze asked. "Do you discuss relationships?"

"We barely talk at all when we're alone," I explained. "You've been present for every real conversation I've ever had with him."

"That seems odd."

"Not really," I said. "I just show up at his place late at night, and then we do it." And that pretty much summed it up.

The following Thursday, as the three of us wandered around a depressingly-lit grocery store in the early evening darkness, a smile broke out across Ben's face.

"Hey Staze," he said. "Let's make Shabbas dinner tomorrow."

"Oh, I don't really observe..." Staze said slowly with some shyness.

"Come on, it'll be fun," he urged. "I bet you know how to make challah."

"Of course I know how to make challah," she said. "But I don't know, Ben, it seems like an awful lot of—"

"There's this little Russian store near here," he interrupted. "They'll have everything we need."

"I think it sounds fun," I piped up.

"Totally," said Ben. "Anastaze. Think about it. Are we really going to take Natalie all the way to Poughkeepsie for Chinese dumplings and never even feed her kreplach?"

Anastaze rolled her eyes. "Fine," she relented. "But this doesn't mean I'm going to shul with you."

"I don't go to shul unless my mom's in town," he replied.

"Guys?" I said, preparing to ask the obvious question.

"Synagogue," they said in unison.

"'Shul' means synagogue," Ben explained, jangling his keys. "More or less."

When we arrived at the Russian market, Anastaze took charge, yanking unintelligible can after inscrutable package off the shelves and tossing them into Ben's basket with a flourish. She marched over to the deli counter and had a whole foreign language exchange with the butcher, followed by what seemed like a pretty heated discussion with the middle-aged woman at the register. All Ben and I could do was tag along behind her with our mouths hanging open, struggling to keep up.

"Is everything…OK?" I asked Anastaze as we loaded packages into the car. "With that lady?"

"Oh, yes," Staze assured me. "We were just discussing the best route back to Easton from here."

"In *Yiddish*?" Ben asked, incredulous.

"Mostly, yeah," Staze replied. "A little Russian. The deli guy spoke to me in Yiddish."

"Holy shit," he muttered, shaking his head in amazement. "Do you speak anything else? Hebrew?"

"French," Staze answered as we piled into the car. "I learned just enough Hebrew to get me through my Torah portion."

"Dude. I had no idea," I said to her, still stunned.

"Eh," she shrugged. "It's one of the benefits of a peripatetic childhood. And believe me, such benefits are few and far between."

Ben and I fired questions at Anastaze all the way home, and, being Staze, she gave a lot of vague and curt answers. She's always been a private person; I think it's how she manages to cultivate an individual identity. When your parents are as famous as hers, deflecting the probing questions of even those closest to you just kind of comes with the territory.

Ben dropped us off back at our dorm that evening, and we made plans to spend Friday together. "We'll need to start preparing the brisket on the early side, perhaps around nine or ten in the morning," said Staze. "And the challah will be best if we get it going right around that time as well."

"That sounds perfect. We'll make a day of it," Ben said to us through his car window. "I'll supply the Manischewitz."

"*Blech!*" said Staze with a smile. "All right then, see you tomorrow."

As usual, I crept away from my room late that night, walked half a mile, and swiped myself into Ben's building. He opened the door to his apartment and slid his hands around my waist.

"Natalie," he said in my ear, a half-whisper. He always said my name like it was a simple declarative sentence, a new word or concept he'd just acquired, one that he liked the sound of in his own voice. "Natalie. Natalie."

I'm not entirely sure why I remember that one Thursday so clearly. We'd spent at least a dozen nights together by then. I'd become familiar with his patterns, his moves. Maybe it was the music.

I slipped off my snowy boots and strolled into Ben's bedroom while he paused in the kitchen to fetch us a couple of giant tumblers of water. (The ancient, overactive heating systems at Easton always rendered the residence halls uncomfortably warm and dry in winter.) While I waited, I poked around the music files on his laptop.

"See anything good?" he asked, shutting his bedroom door behind him.

"Uh, yeah, sure," I replied. "Lots of stuff." I double-clicked on the Cowboy Junkies' version of *Sweet Jane*, and the ethereal opening tones rang through his speakers.

"Oh, this is a great one," Ben said to me. "Do you dance?"

"Uh, sure," I replied a little shyly. "Sure, I mean, I go out dancing from time to time."

I expected him to get up and spin me around the room a few times. Instead, he scooted back and propped himself up against the headboard. "Will you dance for me?"

I balked. "No! What? No!"

Then he looked through my eyes, past my underdeveloped teenaged frontal lobe and directly into my squishy, horny lizard brain. "Natalie. Dance for me."

What else could I do? I slipped off my scarf and started to sway. I felt hot all over, like a full-body blush, and I felt Ben's eyes fixed on me, but I couldn't bring myself to look back at him.

Now, I've been hauling around a double-digit sized ass since before I turned twelve, but I'll say one thing on behalf of this bod: it moves pretty well to the music. I closed my eyes and rotated in a gentle circle, throwing in a couple of slow-motion body rolls. I tossed my head back and threw my arms in the air. By the time the bridge came along, I even dared to glance at my audience. Ben just sat there, transfixed, and I could no longer suppress a smile. I looked firmly into his eyes, climbed onto the bed and crawled toward him, slowly, in tune with the rhythm. He didn't move. I straddled his lap and pressed my forehead against his, but I kept my hands away. We stayed there for a moment, blinking at each other, too close up to see much, savoring the pause before the flood.

"Thank you," I uttered at last, "for this special lesson on the male gaze."

"Ha," he said, placing his hands on the tops of my thighs. "Experiential learning."

"Come to think of it, being with you reminds me of the movies a lot," I mused, stroking his hair.

"I'll admit, I strive for a certain cinematic aesthetic in my world," he told me. "What's like the movies right now?"

"Well, the music is diegetic," I continued, "because we're the characters, and we can both hear it."

"Indeed," he said. "And your little narration is expository."

"Well, it's intended for the audience joining us right now, *in medias res.*"

"OK, sure, if that's what you're into," Ben teased.

"You know what this scene really needs," I prompted, "…is a montage."

"A montage," Ben said, almost at the same time, and we collapsed into each other.

An hour later, sweaty and spent, I stood up to drink some water. Ben looked at me with a contemplative, almost puzzled expression.

"Natalie. You're smart," he said. He cocked his chin. "Very smart."

"Thank you, I think," I said, chugging from my plastic tumbler. "Are you just now figuring that out?"

"No," he replied. "Not exactly."

I flopped back down and propped myself up on my left arm. "Because you look like Data from *Star Trek: The Next Generation* trying to comprehend human emotion."

"Hm. I am trying to figure you out, I guess," he said. He yawned and flopped onto his back. "There's a lot there."

"Again, thank you, I think," I replied, falling onto the left side pillow, and we both drifted off right away.

Ben shook me awake around seven in the morning. I opened my eyes, flinching as he threw back the curtains.

"Oh, I thought..." I said, groggy from my full week of late nights and class days. "You know, the whole Sabbath thing..."

"Yup," Ben said. "I'll see you guys back here in a couple of hours."

I took that to mean I wasn't welcome to hang around and drink coffee until Staze showed up. He had to recognize what a totally absurd charade it was, but I guessed it was important to him to at least try to maintain appearances. He was, after all, my teacher, and Anastaze's. He was the one taking a risk, and I knew that and did my best to respect it. I rolled out of bed that Friday and bundled up without complaint.

I stuck a note on my door telling Staze to head over without me, then proceeded to sleep past noon. When I finally made it over to Shropner, the brisket was already in a slow oven and Staze was punching down the challah dough.

"Natalie's here!" Ben cried as he opened the door. "That means I get to put the klezmer music back on!"

"Ugh, fine," Staze relented. "But only one or two songs, or I'll come after you with this paring knife."

"Wow," I said. "I don't need any cultural experiences that involve such a high level of trauma for you, Staze."

"Funny you should mention trauma," Staze said. "Ben and I were just discussing my adolescence."

"Ha," I said, with a nod to Staze's dark sense of humor. "Fun times."

"You're probably sorry you asked, aren't you, Ben?" Staze hollered over to him.

"Actually, it's pretty fascinating stuff," he said as some up-tempo woodwind jams filled the apartment. "Sounds like it probably sucked for you, but still."

"Well, thank you for your empathy, I suppose," Staze quipped as she puttered around the kitchen.

"Can I do anything to help?" I offered.

"No, it's not a lot of work," she explained. "It just all has to be done in a particular order. Ben, how long until we light the candles?"

He looked at his watch. "About three and a half hours," he said. "Hey Natalie, how about you help me drink this?" He pulled out a clear liquor bottle with a white label containing a purplish, nearly wine-colored liquid. Staze immediately started snickering.

I might've been a clueless neophyte to most of Judaica, but even then I recognized Manischewitz as something of a joke. Still, I played along, mostly for their amusement, and partly to gauge how naïve they really believed me to be.

"Man-issue-its," I said slowly, playing phonics with the bottle. "Well, I better taste it like you guys taught me." I unscrewed the cap and poured a tiny amount into one of Ben's giant red wine glasses. I gave it a good swirl and stuck my nose in as far as it would go. "Well, the legs are a bit weak, but it's got an interesting bouquet," I commented, putting on my best concentration face. "Maybe it just needs to open up a bit." I swirled it around some more and took a tiny sip. "Wow," I said, feigning a startle. "That might just be the most delicious wine I've ever tasted."

Ben grinned wide and looked over at Staze. I expected her to be laughing hysterically, but instead she just stared at me, dumbfounded. "Natalie, you cannot be serious," she said with undue gravity. "Please tell me you're joking."

"Staze, this stuff is incredible," I said, taking another sip. "It's so…complex. I love the earthy aroma, the bold finish."

Ben turned back to face me. "You're kidding." I looked up at him innocently. "She's kidding. Natalie. Come on. You're kidding, right?"

Finally, I broke. "Yes, of course I'm kidding! It's awful! It tastes like grape juice left out on the radiator."

"Oh, thank God," sighed Staze.

"Jesus, Anastaze," I chided. "What do you take me for?"

"That is not the sort of thing to have your fun about, Natalie, not with me," she explained, her face powdered with flour. "I cannot be best friends with a person who sincerely enjoys Manischewitz."

"Heaven forbid," I teased, flicking her with a dish towel.

And so we switched from Manischewitz to Cabernet and from the klezmer classics of Leo Fuld to French hip hop. We joked around, talked, and watched Staze cook. She even let us help braid the challah. I still have some photos from that day in a shoebox labeled *COLLEGE*. They look simultaneously eons old and as though they were taken just yesterday.

The sun started to dip out of the sky way too early in the day, of course. "My mom said to light the candles at 4:27," Ben reported.

"Is she very observant?" I asked.

"Yeah, you could say that," Ben replied. "She's a rabbi."

"Oh. Wow," I said. Staze instructed me to move a few dishes onto the table while Ben set up two tall candles in holders.

"Staze, get over here and bless these things," he said. "It's 4:25 right now."

"Hang on, just one more second," she bellowed, her head halfway inside the oven. "I need to pull out the challah."

"Why don't you do the blessing?" I asked Ben.

"Nah, that's women's work," he said with a smile.

"Give it a rest, Ben," Staze commanded. "Don't indoctrinate her inaccurately."

"You'd be a lot more convincing as a defender of feminism if you weren't covered in flour and wearing an apron," I teased her.

But Staze was all business. "All right, it's *berakhah* time."

Ben grinned. "Stop! Berakhah time!" he said, and I giggled. Anastaze looked puzzled. "It's a song reference," he explained. "Sorry, we're very serious." I noticed the yarmulke on his head for the first time. He must've gotten it out when he fetched the candles.

Anastaze lit the two tapering candles and waved her hands over them. "*Barukh attah, Adonai Eloheinu, melekh ha-olam...*"

When she finished, Ben said, "Amein," and I followed suit. Then he turned to Staze. "Shabbat shalom," he said with a nod.

"Shabbat shalom," she replied. "And thank you for convincing me to do this. I forgot how much I enjoyed Friday cooking. I've never done it all by myself before."

"Really?" I asked, taking my seat. "Because this looks absolutely amazing." Staze really did go all out. In addition to challah and brisket, she made noodle kugel, beets, and big bowl of braised greens with garlic. Ben contributed a heaping pile of potato latkes with applesauce.

"They're generally more of a Hanukkah food, but we wanted to cut across all the holidays and give you a real taste," he explained.

"You just wanted to make latkes," Staze teased as we ripped apart the bread.

Ben shrugged. "It's the only Jewish thing I know how to make!"

"So where does matzo come in?" I asked, prompting Ben and Staze to deliver the Cliff's Notes version of Jewish history, faith, and culture. Passover, seders, Elijah, the lamp oil, Sephardim versus Ashkenazim, on and on. Ben eventually got to talking about his bar mitzvah.

"I gave this really overwrought speech about ridding the world of all nuclear weapons," he said with a chuckle. "I guess it was pretty typical."

"What about you, Staze?" I asked.

"Well, my bat mitzvah was pretty fucking awful, actually," she said, putting her fork down. "Once the rabbi realized there would be a couple of press photographers there, he refused to let my mother anywhere near the bimah."

"What? Why?" Ben balked.

"Because she was a convert," Staze explained. "He didn't want some Protestant-looking English lady standing up there being Anglo-Saxon and raising eyebrows. Of course, her conspicuous absence prompted more supercilious questions than it prevented."

"Yikes," said Ben.

"Ben, did your father convert?" I asked.

"Actually, no," he explained. "My parents weren't married for very long. After they split up, Mom did some soul-searching and decided to go to yeshiva."

"And where's your father?" Staze said.

"No idea," Ben said. "He drinks. Like, professionally, pretty much. I haven't seen or heard from him in years."

"I have a naïve question," I began.

"No need to qualify, Natalie," Ben teased. "All your questions are naïve."

"Thanks, Professor," I quipped back. "You're really helping me to cultivate a lifelong love of learning here."

"Sorry, sorry," he replied. "Please. Ask away."

"Can a person be half-Jewish?" I asked.

"What do you mean, Nat?" Staze replied.

"Well, each of you has one parent who wasn't raised Jewish," I clarified. "Does that matter in some way?"

Ben and Staze looked at each other for a few seconds. Finally Ben spoke. "This is actually a somewhat controversial issue you've touched upon, Natalie."

"Yeah?" I said. "I'm sorry. We don't have to talk about it."

"No, no," Ben assured me. "Questions are always good."

"Technically," Staze explained. "Judaism is matrilineal. To the Jewish people, you are automatically a Jew if your mother is a Jew."

"So that's why it doesn't really matter that Ben's dad wasn't," I said.

"Right," said Ben. "And that's probably also why Staze's family dealt with some degree of…" he hesitated momentarily, searching for the appropriate phrasing. "Antipathy?"

"'Bullshit,' I believe, is the word you're looking for," she suggested.

"All right," Ben grinned. "We'll call it bullshit, then."

"It's just so dreadfully antiquated, don't you agree?" Staze asked Ben. "The idea that one should marry within one's own tribe…it seems artificially constricted at best."

"Well, you and I have very different experiences with that question, I guess," Ben hedged.

"What do you mean?" Staze asked.

"I mean that you had a Jewish father who married a hot blonde, and I had a Jewish single mother who never married again, despite her dedication to her community," Ben said. I just sat there, stunned to be privy to this type of discussion. I went to college just after the nineties-era reign of extreme political correctness, and that lingering mindset dictated that nobody was really allowed to contribute to or even listen in on the internal debates of other cultures.

"You have no idea what my mother went through," Staze snapped. "She loved my father when he was nobody. She even converted to his faith, forsaking her own family's wishes. In the end, she wound up humiliated and alone."

"Anastaze, don't get me wrong. What happened to your mother was terrible," Ben continued. "I'm more concerned with the question of Jewish men and our tendency to date and marry non-Jews."

"But like, what about the randomness of who you happen to fall in love with?" I asked. "Isn't it kind of an open question? Isn't it outside of our control?"

"Nah, that's just in the movies," Ben declared. "In real life, you can't fall in love with somebody unless you allow yourself to."

"So are you saying you would never date a gentile?" Staze asked.

"Not seriously, no," he replied, at which point Staze shot me a look so conspicuous that I had no choice but to distract Ben with a joke.

"What about if you were just kidding?" I said. "Like, 'I'm dating you! Wait, no I'm not! *Psych!*'"

Ben laughed. "'Look at us, we're dating! Oh wait, it's Opposite Day!'"

I giggled. "Opposite Day. That's old school."

Staze just sat there, perplexed and horrified. "Ben, how can you say that you wouldn't date a person who wasn't your own kind? That smacks of racism, *supremacy* even, and—"

"Look, I'm not saying that Jews are better than anybody else, and I'm not saying that no Jew should ever marry somebody outside the faith," he explained. "And I'm *definitely* not saying that converts or their kids deserve to be treated like shit, because that's wrong. Very wrong." Staze softened. Ben continued: "I'm just saying that I am uncomfortable with how often Jewish men just plain categorically reject Jewish women."

"But like, is it your job to fix that, though?" I asked him.

Ben sighed. "It's my job to not be part of the problem, I guess," he said.

"Right," I continued. "But your *main* job is to rid the world of all nuclear weapons."

"Yes, let's not lose sight of that," Ben said with a slight grin.

"You guys, let's make a pact," I suggested. "Let's all promise never to make, own, or even attempt to get our hands on a nuclear weapon. Ever."

Ben looked at me with a phony furrow of his brow. "But what about if the shit is really going down? Like in some kind of post-apocalyptic *Mad Max* scenario?"

"Not even then," I said, trying to remain as grave as possible. "We all have to do our part for nonproliferation."

"And be part of the solution," Ben added, picking up his wine.

"I suppose I can get onboard with that one," Staze relented, finally relaxing into a smile. She raised her glass. "To the Shropner Accords," she declared. We all clinked glasses over the center of the table.

"That toast is totally binding, you guys," I said, still dead serious. "If either of you acquires an A-bomb someday, I will be really ticked off."

"Irked," said Staze.

"Peeved," I said.

"POed," said Ben, and we all broke out laughing, busting through any remaining tension.

"So, tell us, Natalie," Ben said to me as he opened up another bottle of wine and poured a healthy portion into my glass. "What do you make of all this?"

I could feel Staze's eyes on me. I stared at the burgundy liquid swirling in my glass. "I mean, I think it's amazing," I finally said. "You start with all this centuries-old tradition, and then it takes on even more gravity and significance in the last century." I hesitated, but I pressed myself to ask the question that was weighing on my mind. "Did either of you have family in the Holocaust?"

"My mother's mother is a survivor," Ben said. "Her parents and siblings all died."

"My father and his parents fled Poland when he was four years old," said Staze. "By the end of the war, everyone they knew before was dead."

I nodded and sat there quietly for a few moments. "I guess the strangest thing for me is that I don't have anything like what you have. It's not that you're Jewish and I'm something else comparable. It's like, you're Jewish and I'm nothing."

"Isn't your family Christian?" Ben asked.

"We celebrate Christmas," I explained. "But we never went to church. My mother's parents are vaguely Presbyterian, and my dad's an engineer like his dad. Neither of them ever had any interest in religion."

"So you're secular," Staze said. "Most Jews are secular. You're still an American. That's your culture."

"I'm sure to you I have a very obvious culture," I said to her. "But it's hard for me to see what that might be. I grew up in the suburbs. Our culture is cable television and shopping malls."

"So you feel like you lack something," Ben suggested.

"It's not an absence so much as an overarching lameness," I explained. "It's all so very bland, so very *Good Morning America*."

"So the suburbs didn't really agree with you," Staze suggested.

I shrugged. "Some people like it. They go to church, they eat dinner with their families, they feel safe. I always preferred hanging out with my friends in the city, going to all-night diners and gay dance clubs."

"That sounds like a rich cultural tapestry to me," Staze said, sipping her wine. "I spent all my time locked away at boarding school, or else gallivanting around the world with a motley crew of middle-aged intellectuals. I never really got a chance to enjoy any city with my peers."

"I just studied all the time," said Ben. "My mom was pretty strict. She expected a lot."

"What about once you got here?" I asked.

Ben gazed at the candles, which were burned down to almost nothing. "College is—was—really fun. I guess that's why I can't leave," he added with more than a hint of self-deprecation.

"Speaking of leaving," I said, noticing Staze nodding off into her half-eaten latkes. "It's getting late. We should get out of your hair. Right, Anastaze?"

Staze startled. "What? Oh, I'm sorry. Yes, we should leave. Thank you for hosting us, Ben."

Ben stood up and gave Staze a big hug. "Thank *you* for making us this wonderful meal," he said to her. "You are incredible." Staze just smiled and slipped out into the hall to start lacing up her boots.

"Thanks again," I said, wrapping my arms around him.

"I'll see you later, I hope," he whispered into my neck.

I pulled away. "I'll see you sometime," I said, and I left to go bundle up in the hall.

Staze showered me with pity and frothed up a great deal of righteous indignation on my behalf as we made our way back to our dorm. I couldn't help but side with Ben.

"But we're not dating," I insisted. "Neither of us has ever indicated a desire to be dating. We're just friends who have sex."

"Oh, come now, Natalie," Staze pried. "You cannot expect me to believe that you don't love him."

"I *don't* love him," I insisted. "I mean, as a friend, sure, but…"

"You spend all your time with him, and you're sleeping together," she argued. "If that isn't a relationship, then I don't know what to call it."

"It's friendship, and it's sex," I said. "Everything doesn't have to fall into some nominal category, Anastaze." It sounded fairly convincing, even to me.

In truth, however, I felt perplexed and confounded to my core, and I ultimately passed that night in my very own bed. The long day of food and wine had rendered me groggy and bloated, and Staze's well-intentioned cross-examination made me feel even worse.

But really, there was something else. I didn't feel rejected or betrayed so much as guilty—personally responsible—for what was going down between Ben and me. Just like with Jason and Elvis and even Tyler, I blamed myself for being…a temptress? An all-too-willing object of forbidden desire? My ambivalence about people wanting me always stemmed from my own empathy with how bad I was for them, how toxic I could be for their self-perceptions or reputations. My sense of myself as a poisoned apple had already grown substantial roots. Anything anybody risked in order to sleep with me seemed like it must be at least partially my responsibility, my fault. And now, Ben's desire for me felt like an affront to his family, his people—a bad deed, something profoundly insensitive I was doing to them, even perpetrating against them.

So, as that Friday clicked over into Saturday, I privileged Ben's stated beliefs over my own stirrings of emotional connection or what might be construed as romantic love. I lay there awake, alone in my freshman double, feeling the weight of what I demographically symbolized as well as the much more familiar weight of my bulging thighs and hips. I couldn't sleep, but I didn't go back to Shropner.

And although I didn't know it at the time, that was the last time I would manage to refuse an invitation from Ben ever again.

§

I'M IN NEW YORK at the Water Street Hotel, sharing a suite with three models. Three *other* models. The show is tomorrow afternoon. We had a brief meeting with Lily, who hired me, after we arrived today, and there's a fitting in four hours. We're supposed to be resting, but I'm way too worked up for that. The first and only time I ever modeled, I didn't have a whole lot of lead time to think about how many people were going to be sitting out there gawking at me. I know this is a plus event, but I'm still convinced that my stomach flab and upper-arm cellulite will compel the designers, stylists, and audience to all simultaneously vomit into their high-end purses.

I've found myself pulling up Jeanette's number on my phone on more than one occasion. I come very close to pressing the green button, then inhale sharply and hit the red one instead. I know she'd want me to call her, given how much anxiety I'm experiencing, and how much this event activates all of the most challenging issues from my past. And now I'm dealing with my mom and her surgery too. Still, I am not ready to call. A big part of me wants to see this through, to handle this on my own.

Well, not entirely on my own. Gwendolyn sat next to me on our train from Boston, driving the conversation with quips and gossip and a few casual pointers. She could clearly tell how freaked out I was.

"Natalie. Calm it down," she said to me somewhere outside of New Haven. "It's other people's jobs to make sure you look good at this thing. All you have to do is walk."

"But I thought you said that it's much more than just walking, that it's hard work!" I argued.

"Well, you also have to sit still," she said.

"I can barely sit still now, and nobody's gluing shit to my eyelashes," I pointed out.

Gwendolyn reached for her purse. "You want a Xanax?"

"Huh? Oh. No thanks," I replied. "I've never taken it before, and the last thing I need is another variable to worry about."

"Once you've taken a Xanax, it becomes impossible to worry about having taken a Xanax," she explained. "At least until the next day."

"Still, no, thanks," I said. "I have a weird thing about work drugs."

"Yeah?" she asked. "Tell me more."

"Well, interning at fashion houses, I saw a whole lot of people taking antidepressants because their jobs made them miserable, or taking uppers to work all night, or taking their friends' or even their kids' Adderall or Ritalin when they needed to focus," I explained. "It just seems like you shouldn't need drugs just to do your job."

"That's very wise," Gwendolyn complimented. "I only take the Xanax when I fly, mostly because my doctor told me I could enroll in a six-week aversion therapy course or I could just take a pill whenever I get on a plane."

"Maybe I could just take a pill whenever I model, meaning just this one single fucking time."

"Babe, if you don't like it, you really don't ever have to do it again," Gwendolyn assured me. "I happen to think it's a great fit for you, and a way to get a cushier job in the industry than the one you've got."

"I like my job," I replied. "It's busy, but it's definitely a level of stress I can handle. Plus they pay me well."

"But did you honestly get into fashion to do production?" she prodded. "It seems like you do a lot more event-coordination-type stuff than styling."

"It ebbs and flows," I explained. "But I do enjoy my work, at least comparatively. When I got out of college, I moved to New York and started working in some mid-sized houses, but I burned out pretty quickly."

"What did you want to do?" she asked.

"Design," I explained. "I've wanted to design clothes ever since I was in high school. But it was super competitive, and I was largely self-taught. All the other kids in New York had graduated from fashion school, and there I was straight out of some hippie-dippie liberal arts college in the Hudson Valley."

"Huh," Gwendolyn said. She scrutinized my face. "I never would've pegged you as a designer."

"Well, neither did anybody doing entry-level hiring in New York," I said. "I bounced around at low-paying internships for a few years, but then it just got too expensive and crazy to live there. And there was other stuff, too…" I trailed off.

Gwendolyn took the domed top off her thermos and poured some coffee into it. "What other stuff?" she asked.

I looked around the train car. It was almost full, but most people seemed absorbed in cell phone conversations or by their traveling companions. I sighed. "I kept sleeping with the wrong people," I admitted. "One very wrong person in particular."

"Ah," Gwendolyn said with a nod. "New York will do that to the best of us."

"Yeah," I agreed. "And there was more. I guess I can talk to you about this, because you've been on both sides."

"Both sides of what?" she asked.

"Gwendolyn, I have never been thin," I told her. "I've tried. I've dieted, and I was probably as thin as my body can get without drastic measures when I was in college," I began.

"Go on," she prompted.

I took a deep breath. "Back in New York, no matter who I was or what I did, it seemed like the big problem was always my body. I know I was more qualified for some of those jobs than the people who got them, but they were all extremely thin. And they got hired over me."

"Of course. I'm sure that was a factor," Gwendolyn agreed. "Most people in fashion are totally psychotic about body size. It boggles the mind."

"And with the guy, the very wrong person I kept sleeping with," I continued. "I knew that the only reason he didn't want to be with me was because I wasn't thin."

Gwendolyn looked at me skeptically. "That was the *only* reason?"

"It was the only reason I could control," I explained.

"But Natalie, you just told me that you can't control it," she argued. "Not without, what were your words? 'Drastic measures?'"

"All the time I spent talking to him, laughing with him, comforting him," I said. "It ultimately proved to be exactly as fruitful as the thousands of hours I put in running around Manhattan doing bullshit errands for entry-level designers, which is to say not at all. It's obvious my time would've been better spent starving myself."

"Starving yourself isn't something you do, it's something you *don't* do," Gwendolyn clarified. "Takes no time at all, and leaves you to go crazy at your leisure."

"I'm sorry, I don't mean to be so glib about it," I said.

"Oh come on, I'm thick-skinned, as you can see," she quipped. "And I can also tell you every single advantage of being extremely thin, and there are *many*. It's nothing compared to the cost, though."

I paused for a long time, my head swimming with regrets about my time in the City and everything that went down between Ben and me. "You know, I've been doing a lot of thinking lately about that guy, the one in New York," I told her. "And my job with M&S is great, so I don't feel too bitter about not getting some precarious position at a fashion house. But that guy…"

"You honestly think he would've loved you if you'd been thin," she prompted.

I nodded. "I know he would've."

Gwendolyn poured herself some more coffee. "Well, I'm not going to say you're definitely wrong. But let me ask you this: did he approve of, like, your music collection?"

I had to think about that one. "Some of it, sure," I said. Then a memory flooded back. "Actually, there was this one time when he deleted a whole bunch of music off my computer without asking me. It was just silly stuff I liked in high school, Green Day and No Doubt, and I still had all the CDs. But he just dumped it all off my laptop when I wasn't looking."

"Not cool enough for him?" she asked.

"I guess not," I replied.

"Natalie, I know that guy," Gwendolyn said to me.

"You know Ben?" I asked, confused.

"His type, I mean," she clarified.

"Oh, right," I replied. "I'm a little slow on the uptake right now. Bundle of nerves and all."

"Right," she said. "So, this guy, he had very particular taste, right?"

"Uh, yeah, I guess," I replied. "He tended to either love or hate any given movie, that's for sure."

"Were movies his thing?" she asked.

I nodded. "Film studies major. Film studies professor, these days."

"Wow," she said, raising one eyebrow. "Yikes."

"What?" I asked.

"I dated a guy for a while with a meticulously curated life, back when I was a standard model. Nothing I did or enjoyed was ever OK with him. Man, he was *brutal*. He ridiculed me. He belittled any opinion I had that was different from his," Gwendolyn said, gazing past me out the train window. "And God forbid I should open my mouth in front of his friends."

"Yuck," I replied.

"Yeah, it sucked," she continued. "But I stayed with him for years, because he had me fooled, too. He had his well-appointed world, and I guess I thought it was cool, or *authentic*, ironically."

"Well, Ben's not some suave international bachelor," I argued. "He's just some nerdy kid from San Francisco working as an adjunct professor."

"It's possible he grew up," she said. "Some people figure out who they are a little later. I know I'm a completely different person than I was ten years ago."

"The thing is, I don't know if I am," I confessed. "My life is different. I have a real job now, and I bought an apartment. But other than that, it's as if I'm still that same chubby high school freshman pining after the kid who sat in front of her in English class."

"Natalie, Natalie, Natalie." Gwendolyn patted my leg a few times. "This fashion show sounds like just what you need right now."

My stomach contracted at the very mention of my impending runway doom. "Why did you have to bring that up?"

"You mean that distant, far-off event that we're traveling to New York City for right now?" she teased.

"Yes, that one. Let's not discuss it. I feel ill," I said, putting my head between my knees.

Gwendolyn clasped her hands. "Ha! Perfect!" She rubbed her hand over my back to comfort me. "I'm telling you, this is going to be so good for you. Better than skydiving!"

"Can't we just go skydiving instead?" I pleaded.

"Too cliché," she joked. "Strutting down a runway in front of an audience sounds like exactly what the doctor ordered for your condition."

I thought about Anastaze and her blog and my mom and her surgery. "You know, I really don't want to be stuck forever."

"Then you won't be," Gwendolyn said with a wink. "That's how it works."

And now she's sound asleep in a comfy hotel bed, and I'm half freaking out about the show and half contemplating what was really going on inside my head for all the years I stayed so hopelessly hung up on Ben.

§

BEN CALLED ME ON the phone for the first time ever that Saturday after I failed to show up in his apartment the night before. He would always dial Anastaze's extension when he wanted to get in touch with us and make plans. I figured it was all part of his cover, the additional layer of discretion that our situation required. But then there he was, boldly phoning me with six whole full days of Jan-mester to go.

"Natalie. It's me," he said in a low voice when I picked up the phone. "It's Ben."

"Hello there, Ben," I sang, trying to sound friendly and upbeat. "What's the haps over in Shropner?"

"I missed you last night," he replied, still in his low tones. "I waited for you until late."

I started to wonder if this was going to devolve into short-distance phone sex, which seemed far too silly even for us. I hurried across the room and shut my door. "Well, after our conversation, it just didn't seem appropriate to—"

"Can you come over tonight?" he interrupted. "I have a thing with some friends down in Poughkeepsie, but I'll be home around eleven."

"I'm supposed to make dinner with some sophomores on the third floor," I hedged. "Then we're going to play charades, so it'll probably be a really late night…"

"So come over after," he pleaded. "Natalie. I'd love to see you."

And I relented. After that, we fell back into our former pattern, every night for the rest of the month. Staze wrote her final paper for film class on Sydney Poitier's rebuttal to his father in *Guess Who's Coming to Dinner*, which she rationalized as an important issue for herself and her own family but I recognized as an impassioned defense of me. She was probably right to be concerned. I was up against his professional responsibilities, his mother, and four thousand years of religious tradition. And Staze could plainly see that I'd fallen for him. I had no power at all.

I worried a lot about how things would change once Shropner filled up with students again. Ben was assigned two large Intro Film classes to TA during the spring semester, along with the small seminar he would teach all by himself. He had a busy schedule complete with hundreds of new students ahead of him, plus it would be a lot harder for me to slip undetected into a dorm that was fully populated with underclassmen. I told myself that our affair would surely fizzle by February, a notion I used to justify losing myself utterly in Ben's bed for the final few nights of January.

The day before the other students were scheduled to return, Staze and I went over to Shropner for an end-of-Jan-mester celebratory dinner. Despite all the subtexts and open secrets, the three of us still managed to have a genuinely good time hanging out as friends. I don't remember too many details about that evening, but I know that the three of us called it a night a little on the early side. It probably goes without saying at this point that I trudged home with Staze and then subsequently returned to Shropner. When I completed my round trip, I noticed a little hatchback parked out front loaded up with luggage and a few chairs. I hesitated before swiping myself into the building.

I found Ben standing there in the dorm entryway, talking and laughing with three girls, one of whom I recognized from my art history class. He noticed me and shot me the iciest, most stern look I'd ever seen cross his face. I wanted to turn and run back out the door, but I knew that only would have made the situation worse.

"Natalie!" said Lucy, the chick from *ARTHIST 103: The Impressionists.*

"Oh hey, hi Lucy," I stammered. I made eye contact with Ben, attempting to communicate my panicked inability to come up with a single viable excuse for my presence.

"Hey look, guys, it's my friend Natalie, from my film class," said Ben. "What's up, Natalie?" he asked, leaving me standing there holding the fucking bag. I could've throttled him.

Instead, miraculously, some suave, breezy voice rose up from deep within me, and I smiled. "Oh. Well. I was just heading back to the Res Quad from my car, and I thought I'd drop by and ask if I could borrow your copy of *A Clockwork Orange.*"

Ben relaxed and nodded, and I knew I'd just passed a critical test, a pop quiz that neither teacher nor student knew was coming. "Sure thing. I'll go get it," he said. "And then I'll help these guys unload their car."

Ben disappeared into his apartment while I made idle chitchat with my classmates. He returned with the movie and handed it to me. I could feel an index card slipped underneath it. I thanked him and headed outside.

Once I was a few feet away, I read the note: "Meet me between Shropner and Billings in ten minutes." Billings, the campus facilities management building, was a big concrete bunker that sputtered and hummed loudly from its strange nest in a recessed pit behind Shropner. Just behind Billings was the faculty garage, which was next to the arboretum; beyond the Latin-labeled flora sat the exiled freshman parking lot. Of course, I didn't have a car that year, but I took the gamble that Lucy would never follow up and catch me in my lie. I wandered aimlessly through the trees outside Ben's dorm for a while, then hiked partway down the steep hill toward Billings. I stood there shivering, a little freaked out by my near-total isolation. Finally, a curly-mopped silhouette appeared and approached me.

"Hey, the coast is clear. Come with me. Hurry," he commanded, and I scurried behind his long strides back around to Shropner's front door. He swiped the card key and gave a look around before waving me in. I bolted for his open apartment door and slid inside, out of sight.

"Quick thinking back there. Well-played," he complimented as I started to take off my coat. "Hang on. I want to show you something."

Ben grabbed my gloved hand and led me through the living room all the way to the back of the kitchenette. He opened the door to the long closet across from the refrigerator and proceeded to step inside.

"Come on," he said, yanking me through the door. I crouched and climbed in behind him, dodging brooms and dustpans. He banged hard on the far surface and suddenly another door sprang open and crunched against a pile of snow. I ducked under the low jamb and stepped through.

There we stood, in the dimly-lit freezing cold, surrounded by dumpsters. I realized we were in the back alley behind Shropner. *You have got to be fucking kidding me*, I thought. Ben just looked at me with raised eyebrows, his mouth emanating puffs of humid condensation.

"What's this?" I asked, as if I hadn't already figured it out.

"It's a way out," he explained. "Since some students are already back, you'll have to leave through here." I just stared at him. "What?" he asked.

"Ben," I said. "It's dark. And steep. And how do I even get back up to the path from here?"

"I'll give you my flashlight. You can figure it out," he assured me. "Besides, it'll probably be light when you leave in the morning." I could tell he was choosing his words carefully. Heaven forbid he commit to a scenario in which I would use that door to enter or leave on a regular basis, or even at any point in the future. Me exiting through the back of the kitchen pantry was simply the plan for the next morning.

I rubbed my gloved hands together and shivered. "Listen, Ben," I began.

"Natalie." He wrapped his arms around me and whispered into my neck. "I'm glad you're here." He slid his hands up through the back flaps of my coat and inside my shirt. He caressed my bare skin and pressed his mouth against mine. Our kiss warmed me, made me feel hot. I opened my eyes and noticed the sultry vapor pouring out of his throat and nostrils. I pulled my body away, then wordlessly led him back in through the clutter of mops toward his bedroom.

Admittedly, we're talking week four of the seven-fucking-year Ben saga, and already our young heroine has lost every shred of her precious dignity. But, in my defense, the sex…

Let's take that night, with the pantry and the dumpsters, just for example. I closed Ben's bedroom door behind us and we started kissing, standing in the dim lamp light a few feet away from his bed. He ran his fingers up the back of my neck and through my hair, then abruptly pulled my shirt up over my head. He reached around and undid my bra with his left hand and slipped it off my shoulders, all in one seamless motion. We stood there kissing for another moment, and then he spun me around and pressed his body against my bare back. He kissed me between my shoulders and brushed his lips against my neck.

"Natalie."

He maneuvered us both another quarter turn so that we were facing the full-length mirror on the back of his bedroom door. I looked at us, at my topless body in the warm light, at his nose stroking the left side of my neck. He took off his glasses and placed them on the dresser, and his chestnut curls fell over his dark brown eyes.

"Natalie," he said, making eye contact with my reflection. "I want you to watch yourself."

Ever obedient, I watched as he circled my nipple with his fingertips and kissed my neck and squeezed my breast and bit my earlobes. I watched as he ran his right hand all the way up my thigh along the outside of my pants over and over again, then unbuttoned my fly and plunged his hand into my jeans, stroking me through the thin strip of cotton that covered my flesh. And I watched as his fingers found their way inside that layer as well, as his eyes grew heavy and his mouth grew slack and his nostrils flared. The reflection of his eyes again met mine, and he smiled, pressing his lips to my ear and filling it with the brave and filthy words that described what he wanted to do to my body. I could hardly breathe.

Forgive me, but I agreed to climb through a maze of dumpsters in the snow in exchange for a thrill that intense. I'd probably do it again.

§

AND SPEAKING OF INTENSE thrills…

I, of course, slept fitfully the night before the fashion show, despite the eight hundred–count hotel bedding. Our hair and makeup call wasn't until two in the afternoon, so I spent the whole morning trembling in bed. Gwendolyn tried to get me to eat an actual meal, but a few bites of scrambled egg were all I could manage. That, plus what must've amounted to several generous pots of coffee.

"Natalie, how about maybe you take it easy on the caffeine," Gwendolyn suggested. "Aren't you worked up enough already?"

"I think I need the bathroom again," I said, clutching my gut. The harsh black coffee combined with my catwalk fright were wreaking havoc on my usually iron-clad stomach. I shut the door behind me and shouted through it. "Gwendolyn, I don't think I'll be able to do the show in this condition."

"Nonsense," she replied. "You'll calm down in the makeup chair. Trust me. Besides, if digestive distress prevented anyone from walking down a runway, the entire fashion industry would've crumbled long ago."

"True," I agreed, climbing into the shower. I turned it on, shut my eyes and stood under the hot stream. I have a transcendent recurring dream that I can breathe underwater. Exposing my face to falling water is the closest I can get to that ecstasy in real life. I stand under a pounding shower, inhale through my nose, and feel the magic. I know it's the ecological equivalent of driving a team of Hummers to Argentina or whatever, but it comforts me in my worst moments. Gwendolyn practically had to rip me out "Come on, Natalie!" she shouted. "The cab is waiting!"

I took a few final deep breaths, and I swear I was reaching for the faucet when she threw open the door and turned the knob all the way to cold.

"Gwendolyn!" I shrieked.

"We're leaving right now," she demanded. "Jesus, there's enough steam in here to power a small engine."

I grabbed a towel and stepped out. "I thought I could maybe open my pores wide enough to kill me."

"You wish," she retorted. "Leaving. Right now."

"All right." I threw on my most flesh-concealing underwear and sturdiest bra and topped that with a boring grey jersey dress and some lame black boots. Then I twisted my soggy red locks into a moist bun. I figured if I was going to wind up exposed as a huge fraud and a bitter disappointment anyway, why not dress the part?

I grabbed my coat and my shoe bag off the back of the door as Gwendolyn dragged me out of the room. We hurried down the stairs, and she shoved me into the last remaining cab next to Deena, one of the New York–based models. Deena, dressed in a sharply tailored black shirt and tight black pants with lots of ornamental zippers and pockets, took a long look up and down at me, followed by another. At last she returned to her compact. As the taxi pulled away, she spoke, never lifting her eyes from her gloss application. "Gwendolyn, why did you let this poor girl wear a dress that pulls up over her head?"

"Oh, fuck me," blurted Gwendolyn. "Natalie? Don't you know that rule already?"

"I guess I never thought about it," I replied, shivering, too cold to feel embarrassed. "But it's probably because I'm supposed to get my hair done in these clothes, right?"

"It's standard operating procedure, but it often proves pointless," Deena explained. "We show up in our button-downs and zippered dresses only to wind up crushing our up-dos with some narrow-necked top moments before trotting out on the runway."

"Isn't that the worst?" chuckled Gwendolyn.

"So this really is your first gig?" Deena asked me, snapping her mirror shut and pressing her lips together.

"I produce shows up in Boston. That's my main job," I told her. "But this is my first time working as a model, professionally. I'm amazed at how many details you guys just take care of. I've never put 'wear a button-down' on one of my spec sheets, but now that I think about it, the models always do."

"The designer put a real emphasis on RPMs for this one, wouldn't you say so, Gwendolyn?" Deena said with a smirk and an arched eyebrow.

Gwendolyn paused to think. "Wow, you're right!" she agreed. "How about that?"

"RPMs?" I asked.

"Real Plus Models," Gwendolyn replied. "A lot of quote-unquote 'plus' models, especially for print but also sometimes runway, wear a size eight."

"I've seen six," Deena reported.

"So we have a little acronym for ourselves, those of us who actually wear a size fourteen," Gwendolyn explained.

"Size eighteen, thank you very much," declared Deena with a slow, sly smile. I looked over at her, admiring her fitted clothes and erect posture. Her bright blue eyes hid behind her short hair, which was dyed jet black, a stark contrast to her pale skin. Her waist was quite narrow, though I noticed how much longer her thighs were than mine. Her knees hit the back of the driver's seat. She was statuesque, graceful, magnificent.

Gwendolyn grinned. "Now I'm downright excited to be representing…what's this label we're working for called again?"

"Phoebe Hipp," said Deena.

"Phoebe Hipp. Is she the designer?" I asked.

"I suppose that's possible, but Phoebe and Hipp are also two famous Amazons," Deena said. "So it would be quite a coincidence." Gwendolyn cackled, and even I managed a few ha-ha's, though they quickly turned to dry heaves.

Deena noticed my distress. "Natalie, relax," she soothed. "Gwendolyn and I know what we're doing. We'll look after you." I couldn't tell if she was flirting or just being kind, mostly because I was rendered temporarily incapable of eye contact. The taxi lurched and swerved through Manhattan, as taxis do, while I tried desperately to hold on to my scrambled eggs.

We arrived at a warehouse complex on the far west side and piled out of the cab. Having been to NYC's Fall and Spring Fashion Weeks in the past, I can say that I was relieved to find that this event was a notably scaled-down version. We were a healthy distance from Bryant Park. Furthermore, the venue and time slot Phoebe Hipp occupied reflected the fact that the brand was small and new, and I for one was happy about the distinctly modest profile. We walked into the building and followed some handwritten signs to the makeshift-but-ample backstage area. The models—the *other* models—had already arrived.

The next forty-five minutes collapsed into a frenzy of hair, makeup, chatter, and wardrobe. Tiny, angular Lily rushed around in a black turtleneck, black slacks, and a black headset, carrying a brown clipboard, spazzing and twitching and barking commands and contradicting herself. Watching her, I realized how great I am at my job, and, oddly, the more amped up she got about producing, the more I calmed down about modeling.

Occasionally, I would catch a glimpse of a serious-looking woman with cropped blonde hair wearing a tailored white pantsuit. She appeared to be about five-foot-four in her three-inch heels. Even with models towering over her, something about her ensemble and her carriage made her seem quite tall. She looked spectacular.

I realized that, aside from Lily (who was more C-3PO than human), I was the scrawniest woman in the room.

"Ten minutes!" shouted the sound guy, prompting Lily to lose her mind.

"TEN MINUTES! TEN MINUTES EVERYONE," she screamed, her eyes bugging out of her head. "LINE UP!"

"Excuse me," I volunteered. "But I'm not dressed yet."

"Oh! Oh my God!" sputtered Lily. "You most certainly are NOT." She grabbed me by the arm and dragged me over to the wardrobe area. "Where's Nancy? Where the fuck is Nancy?"

"Calm down, Lily. I could get Natalie's clothes on and off five times in ten minutes," said Deena. "If she'd let me."

"Stop it!" Gwendolyn chided. She whacked Deena on the behind. "I told you to behave yourself."

Just then, the woman in the white suit emerged from behind a partition. "What's the problem, Lily," she half-asked, half-declared, calm as she could be.

"Nancy! This model isn't dressed yet and we're at..." She checked the stopwatch hanging around her neck. "...NINE minutes now. Nine minutes!"

Nancy took it in, unfazed. She stepped back and looked me up and down over and over. She took her time, studying me intently, and finally spoke: "What's your name, hon?"

"Natalie. I'm Natalie," I said.

"Natalie's the black cocktail-length, Nancy," barked Lily, flipping through the pages on her clipboard. "On the rack right behind you." She grabbed the dress she'd assigned to me at the run-through and held it up for her boss.

Nancy ignored her. "I'm Nancy Shafer. I own Phoebe Hipp," she said as she spun my body with a firm tug on my shoulders. "Thank you for doing this. Natalie, what's your cup size?"

"Small C, large B?" I replied.

She turned me back around, still evaluating my figure. "Can I put you in a halter?"

"A halter?" The plain black dress felt safe and inconspicuous, which was exactly how I wanted to feel on that runway. "Really? Because I don't know, with my arms…"

"Oh, I love that! A halter would be perfect for you, Natalie," interrupted Gwendolyn, butting in on behalf of whatever I might be afraid of, as usual. She wore a floor-length, pink evening gown with a broad decorative waistline and wide shoulder straps. She, like every other woman in the room, looked utterly captivating.

Nancy glided over to a clothing rack and returned with a vibrant blue halter dress with a silver metallic skirt sparingly augmented with asymmetrical embellishments: blue and green rhinestones and white lines in the pattern of delicate feathers.

"Oh, wow," I said, in spite of myself.

"Thank you, Natalie. It's one of my favorite pieces," said Nancy, showing no change in emotion. "Take off your dress please, hon. And your bra. This one has support built in." She unzipped the dress and slipped it over my head just as I finished yanking off my dreadful gray dress and neutral bra. "Can we get some hair over here please?"

A stylist came and stood on a step stool in front of me. He started picking and spraying and tamping down individual hairs while Nancy tugged at my outfit.

"THREE MINUTES!" cried Lily On the Verge of a Nervous Breakdown.

"Don't stroke out, Lily," muttered Nancy, still focused on my look. She stepped back and evaluated her work. Apparently satisfied, she gave a subtle nod and looked me in the eyes. "Shoes."

"I have a shoe bag!" I attempted. "I have neutral and black and—"

"What size, Natalie?" she interrupted.

"Nine!" I blurted, and she zipped open a plastic wardrobe to reveal a whole secret stash of heels. She put her hands on some silver pumps and plopped them down in front of me.

"They're eight and a half," she declared. "Put them on please."

Obediently, I shoved my feet into the half-size too small shoes. They weren't the most comfortable I'd ever worn, but I could handle them for a short while. "Yeah, I can do these," I said with a slight smile.

"PLACES!" cried Lily.

The next twenty minutes were a complete blur. I think I went fourth or fifth, but I don't remember for sure. Once I figured out it wasn't my job to think, everything became a lot easier. I watched how Gwendolyn and Deena both steeled themselves and posed before stepping through to the break in the curtain, and I did my best to emulate them when my turn came around.

At the end, Nancy walked down the runway and the rest of us followed in a V-formation behind her. I brought up the rear on the right side. Nancy bowed several times for her applause, then turned to face the back. That was my cue to pivot and exit through the curtain.

And then it was over.

The decibel level backstage skyrocketed as we squealed and chattered and giggled away our nervous energy. The whole thing had gone off without a hitch. Lily practically collapsed on a folding chair.

"Can I have everyone's attention please," Nancy stated, with her characteristic lack of interrogative upspeak. "On behalf of myself and the rest of us at Phoebe Hipp, I want to thank you. Our budget was pretty low for this event, and I was concerned about the caliber of model we would be able to get. I so appreciate the models who agreed to work today at a reduced rate. As for those of you who walked runway for the first time this afternoon, as far as I'm concerned, you are all consummate professionals." Gwendolyn, standing beside me, reached up my back and gave my hair a tug. I was embarrassed that I hadn't realized there were other brand-new models in the group. "Now, we need to clear this space immediately, so please help yourselves to the clothes you're wearing and meet me in thirty minutes at the hotel bar. Drinks and food are on Phoebe Hipp. Thank you again, everyone." Nancy started clapping, and we all joined in, cheering and whistling for her, for one another, and for ourselves.

At the bar, I grabbed a glass from the tray of martinis Gwendolyn had procured, forgetting that I'd barely eaten a thing all day. After a few sips, I started to get pretty fuzzy, plus I was already abuzz with a well-earned performance high. I really did do a hell of a job. I was a huge drama queen all morning, but when it really mattered, I proved capable, flexible, resilient. Nancy and Gwendolyn projecting such confidence on me helped a lot, but mostly I just had to get out of my own way and treat the modeling like what it was: *work.*

After getting surprisingly drunk off half a martini, I put away a couple of meatball sliders and baby spinach quiches and started to feel normal again. I struck up a conversation with a blonde model named Summer, a student at Columbia.

"I love the dress you're wearing," she said, complimenting my halter. "I wish I'd gotten to model something I could've worn to the bar."

"But I loved that floor-length piece you had on, with all the buttons," I gushed in between bites and sips.

"This line is amazing. I wish she had more casual stuff, though," Summer said.

"Coming next fall," declared a voice from behind our table. I spun around and saw Nancy, carrying a fresh glass of champagne. "May I join you," she stated, taking a seat.

"Of course," I said with my mouth full. "Please."

"Sorry to eavesdrop," Nancy began. "A casual line is in the works. For now, we're still gowns and dresses. I started Phoebe Hipp because a friend couldn't find anything to wear to her high school reunion. We shopped everywhere, and she spent half the day crying and the other half laughing at her hideous options. I couldn't believe the lack of youthful or even classic styles in plus-size formal wear."

"Oh, it's awful," Summer said. "I have a friend back home who wears a size twenty, and the best thing she could find to wear to prom was a floor-length plain black dress with a black jacket."

"Exactly," Nancy agreed. "Larger women get stuck with formless, top-heavy, sequined old lady outfits, or headed out to senior prom dressed like a concert fucking cellist."

"Ha!" I honked, still pretty buzzed. "Yeah, it totally sucks," I agreed, this time in my indoor voice.

"And I'm not a designer," Nancy continued, sipping her champagne. "I started out in finance. I worked as a stylist for a little while, but I see myself primarily as a businessperson."

"Did you go to business school?" asked Summer. "I'm considering it."

Nancy nodded. "Harvard MBA, class of ninety-seven."

"Hey, I live in Cambridge," I piped up. "Wait, hang on. How old are you? I mean, if you don't mind saying. To us."

"Why do you ask that Natalie?" Nancy said with a smirk.

"Well, I guess I thought you were, like, my age. I'm thirty-one, but I graduated from high school after you finished grad school, which is kind of surprising," I sputtered.

"Oh honey, I went *back* to business school," Nancy said. "I didn't go to HBS until I'd already spent years on Wall Street. Then I returned to finance for a couple of years, then threw it all out and had a whole career as a window dresser. I'm forty-seven."

"You're *forty-seven*?" Summer balked.

"Shut the fuck up," I blurted. Nancy raised an eyebrow. "Sorry. I just mean you look amazing."

"The haircut helps." Nancy said, helping herself to a mini-quiche from my plate.

"Can I get you all anything else?" a waitress asked, approaching the table. I noticed how tiny and plain she looked in the crowd with the rest of us, like Natty Gann at a Dolly Parton convention.

"Yes, another martini for Natalie, and two more champagnes please. In fact, just bring one of the bottles over here, if you don't mind, thank you," Nancy commanded before Summer or I could protest. "Natalie, I understand you come from a stylist background too," she prompted.

"Well, it's funny," I said, downing the last bit of gin. "I work as a stylist and producer now, but I actually come from a design background."

"You're kidding," Nancy said. "That's perfect."

"What? I mean, how so?" I asked.

"I've been working with this pattern-maker, and she's been a bit of a disaster area," Nancy began. "I worked with her on this line, basic pieces that I could describe and have her render as simply and flatteringly as possible."

"And it's all great stuff," said Summer. "We were just saying how gorgeous it is, and how it fills such a niche."

"It must fill a niche, because we're already cash-positive," Nancy told us.

"After how long?" asked Summer.

"Ten months," Nancy declared, finishing her bubbles.

I had no idea what that meant, but Summer seemed impressed. "Wow. In this economy? Wow."

"Investors are finally interested," Nancy reported. "I've managed to raise a fair amount of capital in recent weeks. It won't be enough for a store, but I want to expand into casual clothing and start to establish the foundations of Phoebe Hipp style. Natalie," Nancy said to me. "Do you design plus clothes?"

"I mean, I design clothes for *myself*," I replied, speaking more in the present tense than I probably should have. I haven't been in front of a sewing machine in years, not since I gave up the ghost in New York and moved to Boston.

"I would love to take a look at some of your work," Nancy said, just as the waitress plopped my second drink down on the table. "And as for you," she continued, turning to Summer, "I need some help in my office here in New York. It'll include menial filing, and possibly data entry, but I'm more than willing to let you come in on the big stuff too. Investor reports, balance sheets, fundraising, all of that. How does ten hours a week sound?"

"That would be amazing," Summer replied. She seemed as surprised as I was.

Nancy stood up, reached into the pocket of her sleek white jacket and produced two business cards. "Be in touch, ladies. And thanks again for your excellent work today."

"Thank *you*," I said, stunned. Nancy glided away, and Summer and I looked at each other. I put up my hand. "High five, dude," I said, and she gave it a gleeful slap.

I haven't given clothing design a single serious thought in years. Most of my pieces and my machine are currently collecting dust in my old bedroom at my parents' house. But hell, I've already got a trip down there scheduled for next weekend. And the reasons I gave up on being a designer had to do with the exact prejudices that prompted Nancy to start this company. Coming back to design scares the hell out of me, but if I have the guts to saunter down a runway and call myself a model, I can absolutely put together one measly portfolio. That's something I was willing to do at the tender age of twenty-two, and I managed to keep on doing it for several years, even as door after door slammed in my face. Sometimes it really is as simple as being willing to take an opportunity when it comes along.

Which brings me to how I then proceeded to break my temporary vow of celibacy in order to participate in a threesome.

Halfway through my second martini—and the glasses at this hotel bar were more like V-shaped tumblers than demure little cocktail cups—I made my way over to Gwendolyn to share my news. Most of the models who wore evening gowns in the show had shed them in favor of less formal afternoon attire, but not Gwendolyn. She was bouncing around in all her floor-length, pink glory.

"Hey, you," I said, draping my arm around her shoulder.

"Wow, how many deep are you?" she asked.

"This is my second," I replied, shaking my glass. "I'm fine. I'm probably playing it up."

"You're probably still high from the flawless performance you delivered on that runway," she said.

I nodded. "I feel like I just rode twelve roller coasters."

"Why twelve?" she asked, grinning.

I shrugged. "Seemed like a lot. Hey, you'll never guess what Nancy just said to me."

"Come tell all of us," Gwendolyn replied, leading me toward a large round booth in the corner. "I was just about to join these lovely people over here."

"Yes, come join us," called Deena from her perch in the center. "We'll get cozy. Gwendolyn, pull over one of those chairs."

I crowded around the tiny round table with Deena, Gwendolyn, a couple of other models, and a few guys in button-down shirts. A round of introductions took place, but I didn't retain much of it.

"So Natalie, what did Nancy say to you?" Gwendolyn asked.

"Did she sing your praises for your perfect-ten performance at the show?" asked Deena, stroking the rim of her glass.

"No," I started. "Well. Yes. She did, sort of, but that's not... hang on."

"Take it easy, Natalie," teased Gwendolyn.

"How many of those martinis have you had?" asked a dark-skinned man seated to my left.

"One an nah half," I stammered, giggling. "But I didn't eat all day. Until just now."

"Stage fright," explained Gwendolyn with a wink.

"Yes, Natalie here is a virgin," Deena insisted.

"Hardly," I shot back. "But yes, today I modeled for the first time."

"*Mira*, no, it was your second time," Gwendolyn corrected.

"Do you only say 'mira' after you've had a drink?" I asked with a nudge.

"*Mira*, more like *dos* drinks," she replied. "At least."

"Natalie was fabulous, Mark," Deena vouched to a primly dressed man in a bow tie.

"And do you have representation?" asked Mark, his rimless glasses glinting at me.

"What? Wait. What?" I attempted, totally thrown and easily distracted.

"*Natalie, what did Nancy say to you already*?" Gwendolyn demanded.

"She said," I started. "She said she wanted to look at my portfolio. My designs. Maybe for the line. For Phoebe Hipp."

"You're a designer, too?" wondered the black-eyed stranger by my side.

"Yes, I am, um, I'm sorry, what was your name again?" I asked.

"Ahmed," he replied.

"Ahmed happens to be my boyfriend," Deena informed me.

"Oh," I said. "Nice work, dude."

"I know, right?" he agreed.

"Hang on, Natalie, this is major," said Gwendolyn, leaning forward. "Like, *major* major."

I smiled. "I know, Gwendolyn. I get to dust off my sewing machine, and, like, my *dreams*."

Ahmed chuckled. "Dusting off your dreams? Cheers to that!"

"Here, here!" We all enthusiastically mumbled our own toasts and raised our mostly-empty glasses over the center of our table. I looked outside. A mid-November New York City rain streaked the windows, and the yellow taxis drove past in the dusk light with their roof lights off, overstuffed with brokers, splashing through the narrow winding Wall Street one-ways and their copious pothole puddles. I recalled my blubbering tears over Ben on a similarly gray New York City day and shuddered. My attention returned to the hotel bar.

"What kinds of clothes do you design?" asked Ahmed, turning his attention to me.

"Mostly classics in interesting fabrics," I said. "I add a lot of playful details that make the clothes feel youthful even though they're structured."

"Describe to me one of your pieces," he requested.

"Well, I designed this short-sleeved button-down top," I explained. "The breast pockets are scalloped with complimentary buttons, and the sleeves are cuffed so…I am boring the shit out of you, aren't I?" I blurted, embarrassed.

"No, not at all," Ahmed said with a slow smile. "I'm an architect, so I can geek out on a shape detail like that, too."

"Wow, an architect?" I chirped. "There's this newish building in Cambridge, where I live, and personally I love it. But I guess there were all kinds of problems and controversies about it…"

"In Cambridge, Massachusetts?" he asked. "You mean the Gehry building over at MIT?"

"Yes. Yes!" I replied excitedly.

"Have you visited his building in Spain? The Guggenheim?"

"I have!" I told him, raising my voice with excitement. "It's like the coolest thing I've ever seen in my entire life."

"I love it too," he replied. "Especially the internal spaces he creates. He totally justifies his wild exteriors."

"What are you two gabbing about?" asked Deena, leaning over Ahmed's shoulder.

"Natalie was just telling me how much she loves Frank Gehry," Ahmed explained, giving Deena a squeeze with his arm.

"Did you tell her about the picture?" Deena prompted.

"What picture?" I asked.

"Ahmed has a loft in downtown Brooklyn," she told me. "He's got a huge photograph of Gehry's Guggenheim right across from his front door."

"It's like six feet long," Ahmed said. "You can really see the whole building in context."

"Wow, with the water and everything?"

"The canal, yeah," he replied, his dark eyes sparkling.

A hand stroked my knee under the table. Ahmed was to my left, and Deena sat on the other side of him, draped over his shoulder. It could've been either one of them, or possibly both.

"Did you guys hear that?" asked Gwendolyn, jolting me out of my private party. "Nancy's tab is open for one more round. I'm heading to the bar. Anybody need anything?"

"I'll come with you," I offered, hurrying out of the booth. I could feel the redness on my cheeks.

Deena and Ahmed demurred on more drinks, and Gwendolyn and I turned to the big brown bar.

"They're coming on pretty strong," I said to Gwendolyn.

"Really? Like, as a couple?" she asked, glancing over at them.

"I think so," I said.

"Wow. Another martini?" she asked, leaning her cleavage over the bar and flagging down a service professional.

"How about a soda water," I replied, turning to face the bartender. "With lime."

"So what are you thinking?" Gwendolyn asked me.

I sighed, gripping the bar with both hands. "I don't know. I'm supposed to be taking a break."

"Well, we're not talking about *dating* here, exactly," she argued.

"I'm supposed to be taking a break from sex, Gwendolyn," I said. "I don't really date anyway."

"And why, pray tell, are you taking this break?" she wondered. "I've never quite gotten the low-down. You said you had a bad breakup, or non-breakup?"

"It's because of the thing that just ended, sure, and it's because of that guy I was telling you about on the train too." I hesitated. "It's just my whole sad fucking story."

"Yeah," Gwendolyn said. "So is the idea that you're doing a penance, or taking time to sort it all out?"

"Not penance, no. Sorting it out," I replied.

"That sounds healthy."

"Healthy and *so boring*," I whined.

Gwendolyn smiled. "Natalie, I've been through all kinds of therapy, including some very intense stints, and I'm telling you, it's important to take time out." She handed me two beers to carry. "But sometimes, you have to take a time out from your time out in order to live your fucking life."

Gwendolyn grabbed the rest of the drinks and sauntered back to our group, but I lingered at the bar, contemplating her suggestion. I know myself: I'm about as good at being abstemious as every other failed dieter in America. But honestly, the idea of seeing where things might go with Deena and Ahmed didn't feel like cheating on my vow. For one thing, my actual problem has never been a chronic addiction to out-of-town threesomes with hot plus models and Franco-Arab dudes. And through all my recent reflection on my past, I've started to realize that sex qua sex has never been at the heart of my relationship issues anyway. If you're a woman with an intimacy problem, you're supposed to figure out how sex is to blame. That's what magazines and pop psychology and cautionary teen dramas teach us. But the truth, for me at least, is that sex has always been the most balanced part. It's all the other stuff that throws me off kilter and fucks with my equilibrium.

Besides, I am a red-blooded bisexual. Do all bisexuals fantasize about threesomes? I have no idea. But I've yet to meet one who would pass up such a perfect opportunity.

And so, I made a choice. I granted myself a reprieve from my vow, and I became the sexual creature I'm so used to being, if only for one evening. I returned to the table and slipped my hand across Ahmed's lap to touch Deena's leg. "Tell me more about Ahmed's apartment."

I trusted Gwendolyn to make the appropriate excuses when we didn't join the other models for dinner downtown. November's early darkness gave the three of us a lovely excuse to act like it was much later than six in the evening when the taxi dropped us in Brooklyn. I got the brief grand tour of Ahmed's condo from Deena while he fetched us some water and turned on music.

"And we call this one the 'bedroom,'" Deena said, leading me through the only door in the hallway, just past the panorama of Gehry's masterpiece. She turned on a standing lamp in lieu of the overhead, revealing a king-size bed and not much else. Fiona Apple's voice poured out of the surround sound, and Ahmed entered, closing the door behind him.

"Wow," I said. "That's quite a bed."

"Well. I'm pretty tall," he explained, handing me a glass.

I sipped the water and considered the fact that I'd somehow managed never to do this before. "Do you have, like, tons of threesomes?" is generally either the second or third question posed whenever somebody starts up a round of Ask A Bisexual, and I usually give a condescending, abstract answer, something along the lines of, "Bisexuality isn't about having sex with a man and a woman at the same time, you know." In truth, I'd had zero threesomes, despite how desperately curious I have always been about them. I'd been kissing in tandem for over a decade, and in college I'd engaged in some barely-clad horizontal make-out sessions with more than one fellow undergrad. But this was different. This was going to be sex. And I had no idea how we would get from standing around knowing what was about to happen to the happening itself.

Fortunately, Deena had a plan, or at least enough chutzpah to wing it.

"It's shockingly comfortable," she declared, taking a seat on the edge of the giant mattress. She patted the space beside her, and I joined her on Ahmed's tasteful black comforter. She took the water out of my hand and helped herself to a few healthy gulps, placing the glass down on the floor beside her. Then she turned to face me and climbed up on me like a cat, and I slowly descended onto my back as her mouth met mine. We kissed as Ahmed watched from a few feet away until Deena crawled off me and offered me her hand. I allowed her to pull me up to a standing position, and she and her boyfriend started taking off my clothes.

Moments later, we were all naked and tumbling around on Ahmed's tasteful slate-gray sheets.

I hadn't so much as kissed another person in months. The smell of other human beings, their flesh and sweat and saliva, swirled into my nostrils and intoxicated me. It was a perfect storm: I was so overwhelmed by sensation and stimulation that I just let go and came and came and came. I remember a few moments, like Ahmed sucking on my neck from behind while Deena and I kissed on our knees, or the glimpses I caught of him fucking her hard while she got me off with her hand. As usual, I can't recall very many details. The chatter of my thinking mind fell away and I focused on my pleasure, the remainder of my attention consumed by the two incredible bodies present there with mine.

An hour or so later, I excused myself from the glowing couple to grab a shower. I cranked up the heat and rinsed the slickness off the tops of my thighs and felt like myself again.

Deena and Ahmed invited me to stay, but I declined and slipped away while they lingered in bed. I grabbed a taxi on Atlantic Avenue and stopped at the hotel to pick up the bags Gwendolyn had packed and checked with the concierge for me while I'd been flipping out all morning. I hopped back in the cab and caught the 11:00 p.m. train to Boston out of Grand Central.

The minute I boarded my train, I felt that familiar wall of shame start to creep up on me. I had broken my vow. I signed a contract. With Staze, for christsakes. *What is wrong with you, Natalie?* I scolded. I felt the cruel self-inflicted tension take over my neck and shoulders, and suddenly I was catapulted back into those first few weeks of therapy:

"I counted calories yesterday!" I blurted out one day as I stormed into Jeanette's office. I'd been seeing her for about three weeks.

"Natalie, sit down," she instructed. I perched anxiously on the edge of the couch, unable to comfort myself. "Now tell me, what's going on?"

"I'd been doing so well!" Angry, frustrated tears filled my eyes. My throat tightened around the big lump that had been sitting there for hours. "And then yesterday, I counted calories all day! I kept the running tally *all day*, just like before!"

"Natalie," Jeanette said, leaning toward me. "How old were you when your mother first taught you to count calories?"

"Eight!" I yelped.

"And how old are you now?"

"Twenty-six!"

"And that's, what, eighteen years? Most of your life?" she asked. I nodded. "Natalie, you are not going to recover overnight. You will recover, I promise you, but it's not going to happen on any prescribed schedule. And it will not happen instantly. The worst thing you can do is treat yourself harshly."

"But I'm just so frustrated," I told her. "I'm sick of myself."

"So you counted calories one day!" Jeanette said. "So you're not perfect! Neither am I. Neither are my solutions. I *recommend* not counting calories, but that doesn't mean doing so is not allowed, or that it makes you bad, or weak, or a failure. Giving up dieting is about liberating yourself from all the rules. It's about getting used to freedom. And that's the truth of the matter, Natalie, is that you're free."

It's not hard to see how Jeanette's wise words apply to my current situation. I *am* free, and it's not always wise to follow the rules, even—perhaps especially—the rules I've set for myself.

And so, instead of just shoving down the shame and locking it back up in storage, I engaged with it. I told myself there was nothing wrong with me. *I made a choice, and I had a great experience, and I am not going to feel guilty about wanting what I want.* That was it. And it was completely true. I gazed out the window at the night as the pain in my head and neck melted away.

I reached for my bag and pulled out the scrap of paper upon which I'd written Ahmed's address and apartment number. I have a postcard of the MIT Gehry Building—the Stata Center—hanging on my bulletin board at home. I think I'll send it off to them on Monday to thank them for their hospitality.

This weekend left me invigorated and confident, and, crucially, ready to face the worst parts of my past, when my self-esteem plummeted and the crash diets took hold and my intended career path fell apart. I still don't fully understand everything that's happened in my intimate relationships since high school, but now I believe that doors will open, that solutions will present themselves, that I will not stay mired in this muck forever. That I will be free.

That's just how it works.

Failure and the City

I SNUCK IN AND out of the back of Ben's pantry at least twice a week for the rest of the winter, and, minus the snowdrifts, well into the late-arriving spring. I had an American literature class that semester—*LIT 217: Fictions of the Frontier*—and I often snickered to myself about how obvious it would be to any given Larry McMurtry character that I was trekking between my dorm and Shropner's dumpsters on a regular basis. The worst tracker in world history could've recognized the signs.

The secrecy helped appease Ben's increasingly hysterical fears of our discovery. Even then I recognized that his skyrocketing anxiety was more about the year ahead than the actual fact of my comings and goings. He had accepted a low-paying adjunct teaching job at two of the CUNY campuses in New York. He knew he was going to have to live on a ridiculously tight budget in the city, and, worst of all, finally leave Easton.

"Can you not knock so loud?" he said in a low voice, opening the pantry door for me one April evening.

"Why? Is there somebody here?" I stage-whispered back.

"What? Of course not," he barked.

"Sorry, I just wasn't sure if that was you who called." Ben had taken to ringing me one time and then hanging up in order to signal an invitation to his apartment rather than risking an actual voice-to-voice conversation. It didn't make a lick of goddamn sense, but to this day my adrenaline surges if my phone rings once and then stops. That is some Pavlovian shit. "I got some good news today," I said, trying to change the subject.

"Yeah?" he said, heading for the fridge and opening a beer. He took a gulp, and I stared at him. "Help yourself, Natalie. Come on, you know that by now." He gave me a playful kiss on the neck. Already everything felt so muddled. I was constantly annoying him by assuming too much or too little, by acting too formal or too familiar.

"Thanks, but I'm OK," I said, grossed out by his cans of cheap malt liquor. He was already imposing austerity measures on his food and alcohol budget, getting used to how little he would have to spend in New York. He no longer stocked anything that remotely appealed to me.

"So what's your news?" he asked, taking my hand and leading me toward the bedroom.

"I got an internship for the summer," I said. "My friend at FIT recommended me for the job she had last year, and they accepted me."

"At FIT?" he prompted. "In New York?"

"Yeah," I replied. "The job isn't at the school, it's with a big fashion house in the area."

Ben didn't say anything after that. I closed the door to his bedroom behind us, and he spent a few minutes at his computer, scrolling through his music and checking his email and ignoring me. I sat on his bed, filling up with anxiety.

"Should I leave?" I finally asked, and he turned to me.

"No, I want you here," he said, this time much more warmly and gently. He turned the volume up on his speakers and climbed into bed next to me. My body flooded with the relief of feeling him close to me, and I threw myself on top of him.

Later, as I put my clothes back on, he returned to the earlier topic of conversation. "Congratulations on your internship, Natalie. That's great news. But I don't think we should see each other when we're both in New York this summer."

I felt my throat tighten, but I knew better than to reveal how hurt I was. Besides, I had no right to be. It's not like we were dating or anything. "Oh no?" I said, pulling my sweater over my head, allowing myself a single wince while my face was occluded by my turtleneck. "Why not?"

Ben paused for a moment. He had this way of speaking when pressure got high that sounded more like an overwritten movie script than actual natural dialogue. "I feel I should spend some time getting used to the city all on my own, without any of the comforts of Easton." I felt so flattered to be called a comfort that I nodded my agreement and kissed him on the forehead.

Staze was far less charitable.

"What an ass," she hissed when I reported the conversation later.

"Staze, come on," I argued. "It's not like we're dating."

"And what is it you tell me all the time that you are?" she chided. "'Just friends?' Tell me, Natalie, would any of your other *friends* say they'd rather not see you at all if you were living in the same place for several months?"

She had a point, and I knew it. Minh from TexD had gotten me the internship, and she sent out an email to a bunch of people announcing that I'd be staying with her in the city all summer. Friends I'd barely spoken to since sophomore year of high school were coming out of the woodwork to say they'd love to get together.

"But this is different," I argued, in spite of myself. "He's got his whole adjustment issue thing, his fear of leaving this place. He just wants to be brave and go it on his own."

"Right. We'll see how long that lasts," she retorted.

Sure enough, I'd been in New York for just a few days when I checked my Easton email and found a message from Ben, time-stamped 3:00 a.m. Friday morning.

Natalie. I'd love to see you. Where are you living? —Ben

I replied immediately. I explained that I didn't have Internet where I was staying, with Minh and two friends of hers on East 77th Street. I was subletting the fourth bedroom for the summer while their other roommate took an extended trip to Australia. My internship paid nothing for twenty hours a week, so I got a part-time job at a bookstore and accepted a generous chunk of cash from my father in order to cover the additional costs. I tried to be as friendly and unassuming as possible. Ben was far more brazen in his reply.

Can I come over tonight? I'll bring the wine…

My shift at the bookstore ended early on Fridays, at 8:00 p.m. I raced home to shower and change out of my required khakis. Unfortunately, none of the cool indie bookstores had summer evening openings, so I was stuck in chain-store hell with the blandest of all possible dress codes. So much for my summer of high fashion.

I was sitting with Minh in the living area watching mindless television when the doorbell finally rang. "Oh that must be my friend!" I declared a little too loudly as I flew out of my chair to buzz him in. It took him an eternity to make it up to the fifth floor. At last, I heard a knock.

"Hello there," I said flirtatiously as I opened the door.

"Hey, Natalie," he replied, noticing Minh over my shoulder. "That's some walk-up you guys have." He hugged me with one arm and patted a few times. Apparently just because we weren't on campus anymore didn't mean that Ben was planning to be any less stiff and rigid in front of other people.

"Come on in," I said, obligingly dropping any trace of sexual intimacy. I've always been great at that. I should get a Tony for my many convincing public performances of the role Just Friend.

"Thanks," he replied, handing me a brown paper bag. "Can you grab some wine glasses?"

"Sure. Ben, this is my friend Minh," I said as I walked toward the kitchen.

"Hi!" she said sweetly. She was perched on the couch in powder-blue yoga pants and a purple tank top. Minh has one of those faces that erupts into kindness and light when she smiles. Every one of her features changes: eyes, cheeks, mouth, brow. Even her nose crinkles up with warmth.

I grabbed a couple of wine glasses from the kitchen, and when I came back, Ben was seated on the couch. "Did you want to see my room?" I asked pointedly.

"Maybe in a little while," he said, gazing at the television. "Do these two know each other, or what?"

Minh laughed and started explaining the premise of the program *ElimiDate* while I reached for the wine.

"Do you want some?" Ben asked Minh.

"Um. Sure," she replied, and I scuttled to the kitchen to grab a third glass.

Two hours later, Ben looked at his watch. "You know, I better get going," he declared. "I have to teach tomorrow."

"On Saturday?" I asked, aching inside.

He shrugged. "'Tis the life of a lowly adjunct," he said. "I'll see you soon, Natalie. And it was nice to meet you, uh…"

"Oh, it's Minh!" she said, smiling her sparkles. "Bye, Ben! Thank you for the wine!"

As I showed him out, I stepped into the hall after him and pulled the door shut, hoping a little privacy would prompt him to explain himself.

"Um. So," I began.

"So. Thanks. I'll shoot you an email sometime this week." And with that, he shoved open the heavy stairwell fire door and sped down the stairs. Flummoxed, I turned on my heels and reentered my sublet.

"Your friend seems nice," said Minh, turning off the television.

"He's fine. Whatever," I said, shaking my head. "Good night," I called behind me as I closed my bedroom door too hard, frustrated in every possible way.

Over the next few weeks, I gleefully reconnected with Minh and several other friends from the TexD days and acquainted myself with their expanding New York City circle. David G. was the only David in the group, but everyone still called him David G. Brooke and Xavier turned up from time to time, but both of them had flings going on with boys in other boroughs.

The Pride parade that year remains one of the best times I've ever had in my life. We all dressed up as fabulously as possible—rainbow boas and pink spiked dog collars and false eyelashes—and watched and cheered as float after float rolled past blasting Whitney Houston or Cher. Everybody believed in life after love. After the parade, we headed to David G.'s apartment and drank Long Island iced teas and had our own private dance party. It was so much fun I barely even thought about how I hadn't heard from Ben in two weeks.

Finally, I checked my email at my internship one morning and saw a message from Ben. Like his previous message, he'd sent it smack in the middle of the previous night. He invited me over to his apartment that evening. I had a closing shift at the bookstore, so I told him I probably wouldn't be able to make it to Brooklyn until after midnight. He replied within a couple of hours saying that would be fine. Ten minutes later, he wrote again and said I could stay the night if I wanted to. It hadn't occurred to me that I wouldn't be invited to stay over if I showed up at 12:30 in the morning, but then, such was our story. I should not have assumed anything.

I got off the train in Greenpoint at 12:45, and I had no idea where I was. The station agent gave me some barely audible directions, but I was afraid to ask for clarification lest I indicate to everybody else around me that I didn't know where I was going. I nodded and stepped out onto the street.

Greenpoint is pretty fancy these days, with more than its fair share of fine restaurants and coffee shops and condos. A decade and a half ago, not so much. I wandered around the named streets, past empty lots and desolate parks and seedy bars. I dodged a pair of guys hollering in Polish and taking drunken swings at each other in the middle of the sidewalk.

Finally, I spotted a bodega with a well-coifed goth dude working the register. He had a leather collar and facial piercings and spiked hair. His black lipstick told me that I could trust him. I walked in. "Excuse me, can you please help me find North Henry?"

"That's essentially five blocks away," he said, barely opening his mouth. His sounded a lot younger than he looked. He gave me extremely specific directions and drew me a little map. "Don't worry. You'll be OK," he assured me as I left. I thanked him profusely and followed his perfect directions to Ben's place.

"What took you so long?" Ben said as he opened the door. He seemed more groggy and confused than impatient. I suppose I was visibly alarmed, because once he got a good look at me, he softened. "Natalie, are you all right?"

I walked into his apartment and realized I was shaking. "I got lost." I sucked in my breath and it quivered, and Ben cocked his head with concern.

"Oh, no," he said, gently taking my bag and placing it on the floor. "I should've met you at the train." He perched on the arm of his easy chair and wrapped his arms around me. I was unprepared for how familiar his smell would be. I breathed deeply a few times and started to calm down. Finally he said softly, "Natalie. Come to bed."

Twenty minutes later, as I writhed and arched my back with his head between my legs, I thought, *This is why I do this.* All the frustration, all the disappointments, all the treks through the darkness came down to those moments of bliss and rhythm, of getting to be Ben's lover. And as I fell asleep, safe and sated in the crook of his arm, the way I felt inside seemed worth any price.

I showed up an hour late for my internship the next morning. "Sorry! Trains!" I blurted at my supervisor, who was always on the phone. She smiled and tossed me a list. Two or three times each week, I went out on errands to procure buttons and swatches and yarns. The other days involved mostly data entry and verification, matching shipments with returns and double-checking them against vendor statements. One day I discovered a $2,700 error from Macy's in our favor, and my supervisor was so impressed that she took me out to dinner.

"I know this sounds clichéd, Natalie, but you've got a real head on your shoulders," she said as she picked at her steamed vegetables and brown rice. "Have you given any thought to coming in on the business side?"

"Well," I said, sipping my Thai iced tea and licking condensed milk off my straw. "Design is really my passion. I don't need my own line or anything fancy like that. I'm more than happy to work for somebody else."

"Are you in design school?" she asked.

"No, I go to Easton College," I explained. She shook her head. "It's a liberal arts school? In the Hudson Valley?"

"See, there you go," she said. "You've got broad interests. You should go into production, or maybe even advertising."

I shrugged. "I really like design, though."

"But you're so good with numbers," she said, putting her Amstel Light to her lips. "You've got a great aptitude, Natalie. I'd hate to see you waste it pursuing the same avenue as everyone else."

"What do you mean?" I asked. I naively still believed I could do anything if I was willing to work hard enough. This woman seemed eager to be the first one to burst that bubble.

"Natalie, everyone and their mother wants to be a clothing designer," she explained. What the hell was her name? Vanessa? Veronica? "Trust me. The industry is flooded. And it's very competitive. Smart people like you should exploit the holes. Production, management, back office stuff. It might not be as glamorous, but it's where the money is."

"I guess I've never really thought about—" I started, and she promptly interrupted.

"And I'll tell you right now, it's a very appearance-oriented industry on the design side," she said. "You're way too smart for that. You're not concerned about your image, and that's the way it should be." She took another swig of Amstel Light and I surveyed my own wardrobe for the day: store-bought jeans under a dress I'd sewn for myself. The fabric alternated a blue base patterned with rose and white flowers with swatches of white covered in tight colored stripes: red, purple, pink, blue, green, yellow. I made wide shoulder straps and attached it at the waist in front. It was my personal take on the dress to wear over pants, which was a big trend in SoHo that summer. I'd put it together using the equipment in the warehouse during off-hours one Sunday. Apparently my one-of-a-kind ensemble gave my supervisor the impression that I didn't care at all about style. I also inferred she was trying to politely explain to me that I was way too fat to be a designer.

"Please, Natalie, you are not too fat," Staze lectured into the phone. She was at a writing workshop in a remote castle somewhere in Wales that barely had electricity. They did all their writing in big brown notebooks. On her few free Sundays, Staze would walk a mile into town, buy a phone card, and call me from the red booth at the local pub. I would peal with laughter at her deadpan descriptions of the drunken, leering men who would routinely harass her through the glass. We would gab nonstop until the line went dead without warning, indicating we'd exhausted all sixty minutes. Those conversations were a highlight of my summer.

"I *am*, Staze. I'm telling you, this entire industry is built on the backs of waifs. Even the Lane Bryant designers are willowy," I said, sitting on the kitchenette floor, absently wrapping the curly phone cord around my wrist. "I'm on a new diet, though. One meal a day, and the rest of the time I can have a piece of cheese or a scrambled egg or something, but no carbs."

"Nat, what is a carb?"

"A carb is a carbohydrate," I told her. "Like rice or pasta. They're very bad."

"But I thought you always ate those bowls of rice at school because you said rice didn't have any fat."

"I know, but it turns out that was, like, totally backward," I explained. "All the new diet science indicates that carbs actually make you gain weight, because fat makes you more satisfied or something."

"I do not like the sound of this, Natalie," she said skeptically.

"But Staze, it's really amazing, actually!" I replied, amped up on the promise of this latest trend. "It means I've been doing the wrong thing all these years. Now I just have to do the opposite and I'll be thin finally. And then I can be a designer instead of some behind-the-scenes businessperson."

"Natalie, half the people here tell me that I should go into publishing," she said, raising her voice. "Do you know why? Because I keep my room organized and my notebook is always very tidy. For those reasons alone, they think I would be better off aiding creative people than being one myself."

"What?" I replied. "That's bullshit."

"It's the sort of advice people love to give to smart women with many talents," Staze argued. "They urge us into the supportive roles rather than the substantive ones. And in my field, there's this odd fixation on the authenticity that allegedly goes along with being dysfunctional. If a person is not an alcoholic, or, I don't know, on medication for something, apparently she cannot become a proper writer."

"That's ridiculous."

"Right," she agreed. "And it's ridiculous to suggest that you should not become a designer."

I paused for a few seconds. "Yeah, well. I'm still going to try this low-carb thing. My mom sent me some articles, and—"

"Nat, tell me what else is going on," she interrupted. "We only have a few minutes left."

"OK, so you're probably not going to like this next thing either," I said, preparing her. "But I've been seeing Ben a little."

"Shocking," she deadpanned. "How did that come to pass?"

"He emailed me after the last time I talked to you. It's kind of weird," I began.

"You don't say," she zinged again.

"Come on, Staze," I urged.

"Sorry. How is it weird, love?"

"Sometimes he invites me to his place in Brooklyn, and we immediately have sex. But if he comes over here, we just hang out in my living room with my roommates."

"And then does he stay the night?" she asked.

"No. He always leaves," I explained. "He came to my roommate's Fourth of July party a few days ago, and afterward he just took off. I haven't seen or heard from him since."

"Does he have any friends of his own?" she wondered.

"I don't know, actually," I realized. "I've been hanging out with my high school friends. It didn't even occur to me that he probably still doesn't know many people in the city."

"Ben is a man of habit as well," she said. "I would wager he's still not comfortable being seen with you."

"Do you think he ever will be?" I asked.

"Honestly?" She sighed. "Natalie, I can't—"

And the line went dead.

Thursdays were never my night off from the bookstore, but a coworker traded with me at the last minute that week, so it was actually quite a remarkable coincidence that I was home when Ben materialized to pick up Minh for their date.

"Oh. Hey," I said, opening the door, as surprised to see him standing there as he obviously was to see me. "Did you call?" He just kind of stood there, his lips slightly parted. "Well come in, dude." He brushed past me and stood there, saying nothing.

At that moment, Minh emerged from her bedroom, looking fresh and clean and cute and glowing. "Hi, Ben!" she said to him. "Oh, Natalie, what are you doing home?" she asked.

"I traded shifts," I replied.

"Oh cool," she said absently, shuffling through her purse. "Shit! My wallet's in my other bag. Be right back."

"Are you guys going out?" I finally asked him after she disappeared. He nodded, and I nodded, too. My gaze dropped to the floor, and I heard myself utter, "But."

But she's not even Jewish, is what I thought but did not say.

Minh breezed back in, wallet in hand. "All right, now I'm ready," she said. She smiled sweetly in my direction. "Bye Natalie!"

Ben managed a stiff smile. "After you," he said to Minh, and she walked out of our apartment. He followed behind her, pulling the door shut, never looking back at me.

I stood there in the stuffy eighty-five-degree hallway suddenly covered in goose bumps. For a sweet, fleeting moment, I felt a right to my pain. I knew that I had been wronged, that what Ben had done was cruel, that he'd hurt me. Of course, this unambiguous clarity did not last long. My brutal internal critic had a thing or two to say about the legitimacy of the aching in my heart.

You and Ben are not together. You were never together, and you know that. He didn't even want to see you this summer. You're the one who fucks him whenever he wants it. What's he supposed to do, stop you? And it's your fault you're not skinnier and the kind of girl anybody would want to date. You're lucky to get any attention at all. Maybe if you weren't so lazy and fat, if you finally made yourself worthy…

David G. had a bartending shift downtown that night. I hopped in a cab I couldn't afford and rode to the outer edges of Chelsea. It was early, so the joint was still dead. I found David and, tears filling my eyes, asked if he could talk for a few minutes.

"Natalie, yes! What happened?" He came around the bar and embraced me, pressing me into his newly-perceptible pecs. He settled me onto a stool, checked on the few other customers at the bar, and asked me what I was drinking.

"Soda water?" Alcohol did not sound remotely appealing. "With lime?"

The soda gun blurted and gurgled. My sadness felt warm and watery, the inside of my head pillowy and soft. I took a limey, bubbly sip and started talking.

"And you've been secretly sleeping with this guy for how long?" I'd never captured David G.'s attention so completely before.

"Six months," I told him. It was so strange to actually *tell* somebody all about Ben. Staze didn't count. She'd been following it all from the beginning.

"And he was your professor?"

"Yup." I have to admit that, even in the midst of that nauseating misery, I got a charge out of telling my hot gay friend that I'd spent half my first year at college banging my teacher.

"Wow." He leaned across the bar and propped himself on his folded arms, his black collar grazing his meticulously shaven cheek. "Does anybody else know about this?"

"My best friend Anastaze knows, but in Ben's head, I don't think he can even acknowledge that she does," I explained, surprised by how ridiculous the truth sounded.

"Did Minh ask you if she could date him?"

I shrugged. "I think she might've asked if we were just friends, and of course I would've said yes."

"So she has no idea."

"I'm sure she has no idea. Come on, David. It's Minh! She would never do anything like that to anyone."

He sighed. "She's going to be pretty upset when she finds out."

"No!" I shouted, startling the smattering of other patrons. "She cannot find out. I just need to calm down. It's fine."

"Natalie. Please." David G. was always pretty lucid and wise for such an irrepressible party boy. "You can't still believe you need to protect this guy."

"But we're just friends," I said. "Publicly. The sex is just sex."

"When was the last time you slept with him?" he asked.

I paused. "Four nights ago?"

He shook his head. "Natalie."

I lifted my glass a few times, playing with its adhesion to the cardboard coaster. "This was not the deal. He's single, he can date whoever he wants."

David G. just kept right on shaking his head.

"Can we change the subject for a little while?" I pleaded. "What's been up with you this week?"

Fortunately, David G. relished the opportunity to regale others with his over-the-top stories of batty bar regulars and the crazy antics of his nightlife friends. It felt good to laugh, which I did, hysterically. David G. just kept kicking it up, drinking in the attention.

"Thank you so much, David. I think I'm going to go home," I said after I'd sipped my way through four sodas.

"Are you OK, hon? For sure?" he asked.

I nodded. "I'm good. Thank you. You helped me so much. And please, please don't tell anybody."

I rode the subway home in a souring fog, my mood plummeting ever lower with each station the train passed through. I felt terrified and guilty that I'd told somebody the secret. It was Ben's secret, not mine. He might never forgive me.

Those were my preoccupying thoughts: how I'd betrayed *him*, how I'd violated *his* trust.

Despite how obviously terrible what he did to me was, it's still so hard for me to blame Ben, even now. I try to have honest relationships with people about sex, and I don't believe a person can betray you if he or she hasn't actually made you any promises. Only lame anti-feminist chicks think sex itself is some kind of promise, since sex is for boys to like and girls to carefully guard access to. But I reject that. I have sex for me, for the pleasure, and sex does not equal a relationship. Even months and months of hot, intense sex, and all the talking and all the intimacy... It doesn't amount to any more than simply that, and it would be presumptuous to expect that it constitutes a relationship if neither party ever names it.

It's jarring to realize how much my lame, wounded, teenaged justifications of Ben's behavior that summer have stayed with me for all these years.

The next day, I worked from early morning until very late, in a mechanical, zombified daze. It felt like the tail end of a marijuana high: foggy and not particularly amusing. I rolled into my apartment after midnight and crashed, barely moving a muscle until I heard a knock at my door on Saturday morning.

"Come in," I managed.

"Natalie?" came the sound of Minh's voice as she pushed on my door. Her eyes were as wide as saucers. She looked like she'd drawn the short straw and had to come break the news that somebody had run over my puppy.

I reached over to the window and tugged on the shade. Light poured into the room. "You talked to David G."

She nodded. Her normally bright eyes looked pink and puffy, and big red blotches covered her face and neck, like she was literally allergic to hurting somebody's feelings. "Natalie, I had no idea. I swear."

"Oh sweetie, I know you didn't."

"I never, ever would have—"

"Minh," I interrupted. "I know you wouldn't have. This is my fault. I never told you."

"But why did he ask me out? What is the matter with him?" She sat down on the side of my bed and pounded her cute little fist in frustration. "Asshole!"

"Well," I began, staring up at my ceiling. "Ben is conflicted."

I asked if there was any coffee, and she brightened at the chance to fetch something for me. She returned with two brimming mugs, and we stayed in my bed for hours, talking about my surreptitious affair with Ben and everything she'd been through in the love and sex department since high school. She explained that this episode with Ben and me was not the first time she'd found herself in such a situation.

"This cute guy waited tables at a café near my school. I had a little crush on him, so I was pretty excited when he asked me out. I got all dressed up. When he came to pick me up, this really nice girl who lived on my hall saw us leaving together and just burst into tears. Natalie, she was *sobbing*. And I was like, *what's going on?*" Poor Minh. She was so sweet, so beautiful, and so unassuming. She never meant to hurt anyone. But she attracted attention from guys who slummed around with girls like me but believed they should get to be with a girl like her.

For her part, it turned out she'd been pining away in poetic futility for one of her gay male friends. "Sometimes we sleep in the same bed," she explained. "He cuddles me and we spoon all night and he tells me he loves me. I just want to kiss him so much."

"Oh, Minh." I said. "I think you have to let that one go."

"*Why* does he have to be *gay*?" she whined. "He's so beautiful. Like an angel." She swept the air with her hands in a subtle gesture, imagining the perfection of her beloved's countenance, and I was reminded that my kind of problems weren't the only kind of problems a person could have.

"It's hard for me to imagine you not always just getting whatever you want," I explained. "I'm scared to even try to be somebody's girlfriend. It seems like a pointless pursuit."

"Natalie. I'm in love with a gay guy," she said. "Don't talk to me about pointless."

"I just assume people want to fool around with me, and that's it." I looked at the ceiling. "They'll hook up with me, but they prefer to publicly date somebody better looking. I'm not pretty like you."

Minh didn't argue, exactly. She just paused for a few moments. "There's this girl in my class at FIT. She is *so* pretty. Like, it's hard not to just stare at her all the time."

"Yeah?"

"Yeah. You know I've seen plenty of models and stunning people before, but this girl is exceptional. I guess we're sort of friends. And she always has terrible relationships. Like, even when a guy starts out being normal, sooner or later he turns possessive and paranoid."

"Wow," I said, turning to face her.

"Yeah, " she continued, sitting up and stroking my pillow. "And who wouldn't want to look like that girl? You think being as pretty as possible is the best way to be, and that way all your problems are solved and you have the best life?"

"But of course that's not the case," I said. "We all know it's not that simple."

"It surprised me to find out that dating is so hard for her, like the way she looks turns all these sweet guys into insecure assholes." Minh looked at me. "And you are pretty, Natalie. You're beautiful, and you're so sexual."

"Ha."

"You know you are," she insisted. "You always have been. I'm cute or whatever, but you," she said. "You're really in your body."

I gazed up at my ceiling. I was tempted to start dishing to Minh about the hotness of my down-low sex with Ben, but I thought better of it. She must have been at least a little bit disappointed that she couldn't date him, especially since it sounded like he was her best prospect for distracting herself from that doomed crush on her gay best friend.

So I bit my tongue and waited for the phone call I knew would be coming in a couple of weeks.

"That *bastard*! I cannot *believe* that even *he* would do something so un*speak*ably mean! And crass! The *fucking cheek*!" I pictured tiny Staze raging away in her little red Welsh phone booth.

She never forgave Ben after that.

I, however, still had plenty of slack left on the line I held out for him.

I wish I could say that I at least made it all the way through the summer without winding up back in Ben's bed. But New York City has a cruel habit of throwing you up against the very people you're trying most ardently to avoid. Of course, only the best parts of me endeavored not to see Ben, while the rest of my parts started dragging my ass to artsy movies at the Film Forum at least twice a week. I justified my habit under the highbrow-lowbrow twin guises of intellectual stimulation and air conditioning. One sweltering afternoon during the Kubrick festival, I heard my name called from the line behind me, and I spent that August evening and several thereafter getting sweatily fucked in Greenpoint. I never told Minh, and Ben and I didn't dare discuss any of what had happened earlier that summer.

I wish I could say that I really loved to study film. I do enjoy movies, even a few of the mind-mincingly esoteric ones. But I wound up graduating from Easton with a film studies minor, and I know my primary motivation wasn't a purely academic interest. Film became my proxy for a connection with Ben, an excuse for emailing him to help clarify my argument or find a citation. It was how I kept him in my life, how I legitimized my continued presence in his without asking for too much.

I wish I could say that I went back to college in the fall and had amazing relationships and many meaningful sexual experiences. But instead, I spent the next three years taking occasional weekends in New York or entertaining Ben secretly on campus. I hooked up with a few people here and there, but my mind was always on him.

I wish I could say that I moved to New York after graduation in order to focus on my career, fully exorcised of my Ben demons. But in reality, I took a crappy *unpaid* internship, returned to the chain bookstore, and made sure to let Ben know that I was totally available to him any day, any night, any moment.

And that was college: all Ben, all the time. I never tired of him. He certainly had his flaws, like trying to date my roommate, or never buying me dinner, even after he got a real teaching job and I was still a poor undergrad. But I told myself that the only thing that mattered was the undeniable force of our mental and physical attraction.

And any pain or suffering on my part was, therefore, irrelevant.

Omissions

S TAZE SEEMED REMARKABLY CALM when I met her at the diner this morning. It was borderline spooky.

"I feel like Sister Helen Prejean here, Staze," I joked, gulping my coffee.

"Indeed. Dead blogger dining." She patted some scrambled eggs onto her white toast and took a bite.

"Wow, you're eating and everything," I complimented. "Why so serene?"

"Well," she mumbled with her mouth full. "I suppose right now I'm less focused on my impending loss of anonymity and more focused on my imminent loss of virginity."

"Pardon me?"

She swallowed. "I believe you heard what I said, Natalie."

"Uh. OK," I replied, spreading butter on my pancakes. "Go on."

Anastaze picked up her steaming black coffee and took a sip. "Jeremiah." She placed her mug back down and wrapped both hands around it. "I'm going to have sex with him."

"And you're planning to do this before you reveal yourself?" I asked, raising my eyebrows.

"Yes."

"And this guy is the president of your fan club?"

"He is the *convener* of the *discussion group*, Natalie," she corrected. "It's not a fan club. It's a discussion group."

"Right. Sorry," I said, taking a savory bite of my personal New Town Diner creation: blue corn pancakes smothered in poached eggs. "And is there any chance in hell of me getting to meet this Jeremiah?"

Staze shook her head. "I can't, Natalie. I can't bring him into my life. Not until after I've told him the whole truth, at which point..." She trailed off, hanging her head. "At which point, who knows if he'll even speak to me again?"

"Staze," I said, putting my hand on hers. Her way of handling this situation is so different from what I would do, but based on all my recent introspection, I can't say for certain that my approach would be any better. I'm trying really hard to respect her decisions and offer support instead of judgment. "So which fun facts does he actually know about you?"

"He knows I've never had sex before," she replied. "I played it off as a reason I relate to Broken Hope Chest. It's actually quite logical."

"Indeed," I said. "As you'd say."

"Indeed," she agreed with a smile. I couldn't believe her upbeat mood. Staze seemed downright cheery.

"Anything else?" I asked. "Questions about your *surname*?"

"No. He has never asked if I'm any relation or anything."

"And you haven't supplied the missing link," I presumed.

"No, indeed I have not," she replied. "Perhaps that's a lie by omission, but it's hardly the worst such transgression I'm committing."

"I'm glad you told him it's your first time," I said. "I would certainly want that information if I were in his shoes. But you are still hiding something pretty substantial."

"That's true, Natalie," she said. "I've formed a bond with this person, and I have a plan to reveal the entire truth to him and to everyone. In the meantime, I would like to enjoy my privacy for this."

Privacy. Staze cultivated her anonymity for a variety of reasons, mostly pertaining to her literary lineage and a justifiable fear of overexposure stemming from that. But I realized at breakfast this morning that she's also been withholding her identity in order to be able to live her personal life as it plays out in real time.

"Not to condescend, but do you need any advice or anything?" I volunteered.

"Thanks, but I think I'm prepared," she replied. "Jeremiah's been to the rodeo before."

"What's the plan?"

"He'll be back Friday after spending Thanksgiving in Maine," she explained. "The plan is Friday night."

"Shit! I'll be at my parents'!" I lamented.

"Honestly, Nat, I hadn't planned on inviting you," she joked.

"Oh no?" I joked. "Too bad. You could kill a few birds with one stone." That finally made her break into a bashful laugh. She dipped her fingertips in her water and flicked it at me.

"Stop it!" she giggled. "Yuck!"

"Sorry. I've been thinking about sex nonstop." I paused. "And doing. Also doing."

"So you broke your vow?"

"Indeed," I admitted. "In New York."

"And who was the young man? Or young lady?" she inquired.

"Um. Both. At the same time," I said, feigning bashfulness with a sideways glance.

"Oh, Natalie." She smiled and shook her head. "You're…wow."

"Thank you," I replied, constructing another orange-and-purple bite. "I choose to take that as a compliment."

"Does this mean you're officially back out there?" she asked.

"No," I said, swallowing my mouthful. "It was a lot of fun, but I'm not quite done with my little experiment. I still don't know what's wrong with me, exactly. I've just made so many fucking mistakes, Staze."

"Literally," she replied, and I chuckled.

"Like, with Ben," I began.

"Oh Nat," she sighed. "Are you still fixated on freshman year at Easton?"

"The Ben thing was all of college."

"Really?" Staze asked, puzzled. "Did it go on for that long?"

"Totally," I assured her, raising my voice a little. "And it continued after that," I reminded her. "When I lived in New York."

"But you were involved with other people during that time, Nat," she said. "At Easton, and in the City as well."

"Nobody significant, really," I said with a shrug.

Anastaze banged down her coffee. "Natalie, please! What about Julian?"

"I don't count Julian," I protested. "I hooked up with him a few times in the fall, and then I met Ben right at the beginning of Jan-mester."

"No, Natalie. No, no, no, no, no," she insisted. "You saw Julian throughout the entire year, and sophomore year too. I remember because whenever you would go off with Ben, he would sulk around our dorm like an abandoned puppy dog."

I looked at her. "Really?"

"Well, a stoned one, but yes," she said. "And then junior and senior year, there was Emily. You mean to tell me you don't count Emily?"

My heart sank. "Oh shit."

"How can that be?" Staze asked, perplexed and a little indignant.

I sat there trying to remember Emily's face. I couldn't quite manage to hold her image in my mind. "Maybe she just wasn't that significant to me? You know, like, in the grand scheme of things?"

Staze looked at me with the clarity and calm that she'd been radiating all morning. "Nat, I know the omissions I'm committing mean I'm not being entirely honest with Jeremiah," she said. "Perhaps the bits you leave out of your own story are preventing you from being entirely honest with yourself."

Perhaps.

$\S$

EMILY.

But first: Julian. It's true that my fling with Julian extended beyond the first couple months of freshman year, but in my memory it all blends together with September and October. Anything after Columbus Day was more like a hookup hangover. What can I say? I'm motivated by sex. Julian made sex available, often when Ben did not. Perhaps his laid-back vibe absolved me too much of the sin of…was it using him? Maybe. So perhaps I used him, and perhaps he even cared, as Staze posits with her own recollection of the situation. I don't feel terribly guilty about it, because by the time the first semester of his senior year ended, he was fused at the hip with a gorgeous freshman girl with dreadlocks whose name escapes me. The two of them remained inseparable until the end of the year, and even beyond that. I remember seeing him hanging around the dining halls after he had graduated, and she was never more than three feet away.

Emily, however… Emily weighs on my conscience.

When I remember to think of her, that is.

For sure, she was infatuated with me. I can't say if it was love, because what do I know about that? How love is defined and whether it can truly exist unrequited is a question I struggle with constantly. I felt and still feel so much warmth for Emily. Affection. Tenderness. She was, like, eighty percent perfect, the only problem being that was one hundred percent of what she was. Or, maybe that was all I was able to see.

Emily was my lab partner in Biology 111. She saved my academic life on numerous occasions. She was the energetic freshman, and I was the jaded junior, abandoned by my study-abroad friends and sorely behind on my core math and science requirements. I signed up for a course called *BIO 100: Human Biology for Non-Majors* but dropped out immediately when I discovered it was pretty much a glorified high school health class. So I enrolled instead in *BIO 111: Organismal and Evolutionary Biology*. Counter-current exchanges. Bottleneck effects. It's all a blur of fascinating concepts I only halfway understood and Emily next to me on the lab bench, blushing and explaining. The material came effortlessly to her. After about a month of flirting and brushing hands over the expensive scientific equipment, I invited her over to my bedroom for a study session and ate her out by the light of my clip-on bedside lamp. It was just some random Tuesday.

Sex with Emily was quiet and sweet and always delightful. She hid her inexperience that first time by essentially copying my every move. I went first, and then Emily proved the experiment was repeatable. And we found ourselves repeating the whole scenario on a fairly regular basis for a little while.

Or long while, according to Staze. And she's right, now that I think about it.

At that time, I hung out most days with the gently distressed art kids who operated and patronized the campus underground café, Easton Eden. Staze was the most clean-cut and preppy among them, in her thick black glasses and lavender cashmere sweaters, only partway through her transition from boarding school student to hipster.

All nineteenth-century liberal arts schools have an establishment like Easton Eden: a repurposed below-ground area (or, in some cases, an attic), filled with funky mismatched furniture and student art, lit for womblike study/journal writing/the sort of quasi-dates stoned college students take each other on. Eden had a beat-up old espresso machine and served up a mean English muffin pizza, as well as alcohol, sold with very little regulation. At three dollars for a beer or a glass of cheap red wine, the administration wasn't too concerned that Eden might turn into a go-to destination for getting shitfaced. I would invite Emily down there to help me with my biology homework and slip her a glass of red wine on the sly, even though I myself was only twenty at the time. I enjoyed being the older one for once. Despite my comparatively greater experience, even Heather Boyle was technically my senior.

Emily was sincere and shy and super smart, and I loved all of those things about her. She had ways of surprising me, like when she straight-up recited Ophelia's batshit crazy monologue from Hamlet, complete with creepy singing, as we slaved over our midterm lab report at two in the morning, or the time she nailed a seriously difficult flute solo when one of our campus indie rock bands got it in their heads to ironically cover Jethro Tull.

"Do you think, while I'm in Panama, we could write letters to each other?" she asked near the end of her first year. She was headed out on a summer-long research jaunt to Central America. I was en route to my parents' place, where I would do some admin work at my dad's engineering firm and take the summer *Textile Techniques* course at an art school nearby.

"Emily, it would be my honor to exchange letters with you," I replied, scribbling down my parents' address.

The sheer volume of correspondence I received from Panama that summer cannot be overstated. I started intercepting the mail each day in order to avoid nosy questions from my mother about the myriad red-and-blue-and-white-seamed international envelopes addressed to my attention.

Emily never got sappy or romantic or told me that she loved me, not in her writing or in person. She just kind of bounced from topic to topic, cracking adorable jokes, putting every iota of her vast intelligence to work in the service of making me smile. I enjoyed the rise I got out of reading her letters. I wrote to her, too, every week or so, with one feverish spate of three letters in one week that I knew would leave her positively giddy.

When I arrived on campus senior year, I was fresh off a particularly frustrating Labor Day weekend in New York City crashing with David G. and trying to see Ben. He seemed even more aloof and withholding than usual, and I retreated up to Easton to lick my wounds.

Emily sought me out at an early–school year event, and I was so fucked up on marijuana and vodka lemon drops that I barely acknowledged her. I showed up that year fully committed to my role as the cynical senior, *way* above such inanities as the understated school spirit or the culture of genuine respect for difference that pervaded the Easton community. Of course, immediately after graduation, I would realize how amazing I'd had it in college, but this was a time to be hip and powerful, to throw my seniority around at underclassmen and act artificially chummy with ultra-hip fellow seniors. For the first time in my life, I was cool. And being cool usually sucks.

Despite living in a gentle and kind place, despite having incredible relationships with so many interesting people, despite the fact that I didn't have to cook for myself or clean up after myself or pay a bill or commute or face any single fucking thing in life alone, I fixated on Ben and New York and being so far beyond everything going on around me. I was just there to finish my degree, because I needed it for my big-shot fashion career in New York City, which would begin promptly upon receipt of my diploma, *thankyouverymuch*, and would skyrocket me to the realm of elite cultural relevance for which I knew I was obviously destined.

Awry does not even begin to describe how those plans went.

Once the semester settled into a rhythm, Emily and I started hanging out from time to time. She showed me her photos from Panama, and we started meeting up a couple of times a week to study together. I recall one evening that fall with Emily down in Eden. I sipped a beer and read Proust for class while she flipped through her chemistry book and gulped cheap Shiraz. Then, much to my surprise, Emily stood up, marched over to the counter, and ordered a glass of wine. I watched her carefully, noting the intimate exchange she had with the pixie-like young woman perched behind the counter, who smiled as Emily delivered one witty flirtation after another. I remember thinking, *Look at all the confidence I've given her. She's got that cute girl wrapped around her finger.*

When Emily returned to the table, proudly brandishing the wine she'd procured all by herself, I grinned big. "Nice work!" I praised, leaning back in my chair. I raised my mostly full beer to her, and she clinked her glass against my bottle. I leaned in. "You know, I think she likes you," I said, nodding my head toward the pixie.

"Yeah?" Emily said, her smile widening. "You think she digs me?"

"You should hang out late and wait for her to get off," I suggested, leaning back even further.

"Wait," Emily said, her face falling into a grimace. "Wait, wait. You're serious."

I raised my eyebrows and nodded with encouragement. "Yeah, of course I'm serious. You should go for it."

She slammed her chem text hard, and it startled me enough to bang the front legs of my chair down against the concrete floor. Everybody whipped around to see if we planned to perform the entire opening number from *Stomp*. Emily looked at me angrily until our fellow Eden patrons went back to minding their own business. Finally she spoke: "I like *someone else*," she snarled, and she grabbed her book and fled out the door and up the staircase.

I tried to go back to my Proust, but reading difficult fiction of any kind is hard enough when you're an undergrad, surrounded by the immediate and inane drama of interpersonal co-formulation. And it's even harder when you find yourself embroiled in your own mini-saga, all overwrought and preoccupied and incapable of any modicum of concentration. So much of college is like that. They shouldn't even let you major in English if you're in your early twenties. Bachelor's degrees in literature should only be awarded to bookworm widows and retired high school history teachers. Instead, after a little while, I closed my book, donated my half-full beer to the guy plucking an acoustic guitar in the corner, and silently strode over to Emily's dorm. I swiped myself in with my card key and found her room, which she'd showed me briefly during the first week of classes. I knocked quietly, and after a moment, she opened the door. She looked genuinely surprised to see me.

"Come with me," I said, and she gestured toward her studying roommate over her shoulder. "*Come with me*," I whispered, and she grabbed her shoes and jacket and closed the door behind her.

Emily stayed over in my room that night, and the night after, and the night after that. I took her out to dinner. I cared about her so much. I wanted to show her some tenderness, a good time. And yet it never really even occurred to me to open up to her romantically. What I felt was fondness, a click above friendship but also a click below it. Emily never felt like my peer. I never unburdened my soul to her, and as far as I could tell she didn't really share too much with me either. Maybe she was simply less conscious of her narrative than Staze or Ben or I was. Emily wasn't leaping from crisis to crisis, from obsession to neurosis, from high point to low point. Her life just flowed, and she liked spending time with me.

And I liked spending time with her too.

After our successive nights together, we didn't see each other for a while. A few weeks later, I was making out with some dude at a campus party and I saw her see us. It was the huge annual blowout the night of Fall World Carnival, when everybody got drunk and hooked up and generally made bad decisions.

Wait. That Proust novel wasn't even due for class until *after* World Carnival that year. I distinctly remember the professor making a lame joke about how we should try to find some madeleines at the outdoor food kiosks, how they would flood us with memories to finish our Proust reading or some silly thing like that.

That means that I made out with some dude at a party *the weekend after* spending three days with Emily in my bed. She was with me Tuesday, Wednesday, and Thursday. The party was Saturday.

Was I really that awful to her?

God. I was really that awful to her.

After that, the timeline gets even hazier. I remember Emily turning up tipsy a fair amount, in my dorm on a random weekday evening or late on Sunday nights. I imagine she'd probably sworn me off, and was therefore getting herself fucked up in order to have some half-assed permission to seek me out. A couple of times she was extremely drunk, and I wound up taking care of her instead of just going down on her and falling asleep in her arms.

"Why are you being so nice to me?" she asked, hovering and spitting over the sink after throwing up in my hall bathroom one crisp autumn night.

I stroked her hair. "Well, you're pretty nice to me, too, kiddo," I said with a slight smile. "I remember you were especially nice two nights ago."

"Really? Was it really two nights ago?" she asked, distressed.

"Yup," I replied. "You got up for your Friday lab the next morning."

"Damn," she muttered, still focused on the sink, her white knuckles gripping the cheap plasterboard counter.

"What's the matter?" I asked gently, obliviously, trying in vain to get the front pieces of her straight brown bob to stay back behind her ears.

She shook her head and didn't speak for a long time. "I thought it'd been longer than that," she said.

Clearly I had no idea how to fill my role as this kind of bad for somebody, so I fell back on the tried and true feigned ignorance I'd perfected being other peoples' dirty little secret. It turned out to be remarkably similar: focus on the friendship, treat everything as naturally ephemeral. Pretending to expect nothing is exactly the same as allowing nothing to be expected.

Emily found a girlfriend that winter. I didn't hear about it from her directly, but she and the wide-eyed young lady in question would wind up groping each other squarely in my field of vision on a fairly regular basis. I'd notice them giggling casually next to the door to my French Literature seminar or making out among the stacks during my work-study shift at the library, and Emily's eyes would meet mine, and I'd half-smile, and she'd look away. Eventually I felt so spurned that I stopped giving her so much as a glance. Soon after my campaign of ignoring them commenced, I realized I never saw them anymore at all.

Then, much to my surprise, as I stood there in the middle of a field pumping a keg on a warm night in late May, I felt a familiar arm around my shoulder.

"So is that thing kicked, or is there anything left in it for me?"

"Hey, you!" I exclaimed, throwing my drunken jovial sentimental Senior Week spaghetti arms around Emily's neck. "What are you doing here?"

She grinned, and her eyes sparkled wickedly in the moonlight. "I'm staying the summer. Research. And Easton's throwing me a couple hundred bucks to work graduation and reunion."

"Well, you'd better get to work then," I said, handing her a foamy cup. I grabbed her hand and pulled her toward the bonfire. She hung close by my side for the rest of the night, and around dawn we found ourselves tangled up together in her spacious half-empty double in her nearly-vacant underclassmen dorm.

Over the four days that followed, we were giddy and affectionate—downright *coupley*. The finality of our time together rendered us both unburdened and carefree, and we kissed and cuddled and laughed and flirted and hung around all my college friends pretending that our sudden and intense attachment was the most natural thing in the world.

Anastaze said nothing, mostly because she was all wrapped up in her ploy to lose her virginity to a tragic poet named Lewis. God, that guy. How can I describe him? Inscrutable would be in the right vein, but it's insufficient. This guy was so thoroughly iconoclastic, so deeply strange, that if you told me he was raised by wolves or grew up locked in a room with only Lithuanian television to socialize him, not only would I have believed you, I would've been relieved to finally have a reasonable explanation for his personality. Staze was beyond smitten. She'd spent all of senior year vying for Lewis' attention, and now with only days left she was practically throwing herself at him, or at least doing whatever the Staze equivalent of throwing herself at him might be. Consumed by her own (retrospectively fruitless, of course) pursuits, Staze didn't ask me any pressing questions about what the hell I thought I was doing with Emily.

The night before graduation, I dragged Emily away from the big senior dance party on the early side. I didn't want to hang around long enough for things to get sappy, and I still had a ton of packing to do. We headed back to my room, and I nodded off while Emily carefully placed my clip-on desk lamp into an oversized duffle bag.

"Come to bed," I pleaded, half-asleep, as she opened my closet door and started pulling sweaters down off the top shelf.

"But I'm almost done," she declared.

"You're *deluded*," I retorted. "There's at least five more hours of work. Come on, my mother can yell at me while my dad and I finish up after the ceremony tomorrow."

Emily stuffed my winter hats and scarves into the suitcase and sat down on the edge of my bed. She turned to look at me. "So this is it, huh?"

"Yep, the end of my undergraduate career," I replied, yawning. "I'm a bachelor now, or something."

"A swingin' bachelor?" she asked with a smirk.

"Oh yeah. And in just two weeks, I'll be a swingin' New York City bachelor. So you'd better watch out." I looked out the window of my senior dorm room onto the back of our complex. Despite my terrible luck with the housing lottery, I still had a pretty decent view. Gracefully curved lanterns subtly illuminated the deserted path down the hill. I could hear nearby laughter and the thumping music of our farewell party in the distance. And in that moment, to my great surprise, I burst into tears.

This caught Emily off guard. She scanned the room frantically, then scuttled out the door, returning a moment later with some toilet paper wrested from the holder in a bathroom stall. She handed me the slightly dented partial roll.

"Thank you," I said through sniffles. "I'm sorry, I don't know what's going on with me right now."

"Uh, you're graduating?" Emily pointed out. "You're leaving your home of the last four years and all your friends?"

"Fuck," I said, turning my attention once again to the window. "You know, you might be onto something there." I'd come to terms with the fact that I'd be moving onto a new phase of life. I'd paid a farewell visit to all my favorite professors and contemplated life and friendship beyond the coddling bubble of my liberal arts campus existence. But I hadn't realized how much Easton had become my home. I turned to Emily. "Can I come back and visit you?"

She hesitated, then relaxed into a smile. "Of course, Natalie. You can visit me anytime you want." We curled up together in my standard-issue slightly elongated twin bed. After a few more rapid intakes of breath and an errant sob or two, I fell asleep.

Emily's blaring cell phone alarm startled me awake. She reached over me, grabbed it off the bookshelf and scooted out of bed.

"Where are you going?" I asked.

"I have to shower and get ready," she said, searching for her socks. "I'm supposed to report to the tent at nine to get my marching orders for today."

"So shower here," I argued, yanking on her arm.

"Natalie, I can't," she said, plopping back down on the bed. "The stupid dress I bought is in my room."

"Just stay," I pleaded, sitting up and kissing the side of her neck, "for fifteen more minutes."

Nearly an hour of morning sex later, Emily sprinted out of my room to retrieve her dress, and I followed her into the hall, planning to jump into the shower myself. That's when I realized that my dorm was already teeming with families, parents and siblings of my fellow graduates packing cars full of boxes and getting a head start on the move out. I stood there, disoriented, naked except for my towel, as the commotion swirled around me. A middle-aged woman brushed past, averting her eyes, and a dad carrying a Papasan chair gave me an awkward smile and nod. Finally, I snapped out of my trance and bounded into the bathroom, smacking my unsuspecting hall-mate Alissa with the swinging door.

"Ow!" she exclaimed, reeling back.

"Oh shit, I'm so sorry!" I blurted, my voice echoing off the tiled walls.

"I'm fine," she said, shaking her hand and sucking air through her teeth. "I just banged my knuckles."

"Are your parents here yet?" I asked, pulling my shower caddy out of my metal cubby for the very last time.

"No, they'll show up in a few hours," she replied. "I've just been packing and watching Victoria and her parents try to pretend you weren't having extremely loud sex two doors down the hall from them."

"*What?*" I shouted, causing an even bigger echo. Victoria Overlock had been the odd man out on our hall all year. At our otherwise–very hippie school, Victoria was the one with the Kate Spade purse flat-ironing her hair in the bathroom before her 8:00 a.m. econ classes. She clearly came from New York City money, the summers-at-the-Hamptons kind.

"Dude, it was too funny," Alissa said, shaking her head and grinning. "The whole type A family materialized at 7:30 a.m. on the dot to load up their car, and meanwhile the unmistakable sound of females orgasming lesbionically starts reverberating around the hall." Alissa and her way with words currently work in online media. "I propped my door open just to watch their reaction, which incidentally turned out to be a hilarious non-reaction. I wish you could've seen their squirrelly toil juxtaposed against that soundtrack. Fucking hysterical."

I laughed and turned the water on. "You know, I choose not to be embarrassed by that at all," I declared.

"Good for you, Natalie," said Alissa. "See you on the stage." I pulled the shower curtain closed as I heard the door swing shut behind her.

I can't wait to tell Emily about this, I thought.

But then I ran late getting dressed, and my parents showed up early, and my mother started stomping around my dorm room criticizing my feeble efforts to pack and accusing me of ruining their experience at my graduation, and my father unpacked and reengineered most of what was already done to maximize efficiency, and then it was time to graduate, and then there were reservations two towns over for dinner at eight, and the next thing I knew Easton was receding behind our speeding family Toyota into the late evening twilight. I'd caught a few glimpses of Emily during the ceremony, handing out programs and giving directions to the bathrooms at the back entrance of the tent. When the dean announced my name, I heard her cheer for me, too. But I never got to tell her about the comical situation we'd scandalously caused that morning.

And I never went back to visit her, either.

§

I HEAD OUT TO my parents' place tomorrow morning to celebrate the holiday I've come to call Plastic Surgery–Giving. I finished up all my open projects over at M&S. The end of the year is always a little slow anyway. The next big priority is the company party, where we invite all the models and show contractors and neighbors from the building. That's one of my favorite responsibilities. But first, it's home to cook a fucking turkey all by myself while my mother convalesces in the aftermath of her absurd upper arm reduction.

And earlier today, I had to stop by and see Staze one last time before what I've come to call the Blessed Event. I met her at her place after work with a small-handled shopping bag filled with prophylactics, lubricant, and naproxen sodium.

"Painkillers?" she asked, making a face as she rifled through the bag.

I shrugged. "They might come in handy."

Staze shot me a look and threw the bag onto a chair. "Thank you, I suppose."

"So, the day after the day after the day after tomorrow, huh?" I prompted.

"Yes, Natalie, that *is* when Saturday will arrive," she condescended. "How clever you are, knowing all the days of the week."

"And the order, too!" I retorted with a sly grin. "Listen, I'm sorry if I'm being weird about this. I just feel so protective of you, and of, like, sex, I guess. I want you to have a good experience so we can talk about it and so you'll still listen to me go on and on about it."

"Natalie, you really shouldn't worry," Staze assured me. "I honestly don't anticipate having any problems with the whole endeavor. Look at my parents. I'm a product of all that, you know. A direct result, in fact."

The idea caught me by surprise. "Wow. That hadn't even occurred to me."

"If the apple doesn't fall far from the tree, then I expect to be a natural in that department," she declared wryly. "And this DNA is quite powerful. Just look at what a genius writer I am."

"That you are," I said, grinning again. I thought for a moment about this assertion that our sexual appetites are, on some level, a heritable trait. "I wonder what my parents are like about that stuff."

"Lord. You're lucky not to know," Staze replied, flopping tragically backward on the couch with her arm across her forehead. "Trust me."

I thought back to meeting Alissa in the bathroom. "Hey, remember how Emily and I traumatized Victoria's WASPy parents on graduation day?"

Staze sat up. "I had completely forgotten about that!"

"I mean, you saw them, right?"

"Oh yes," she recalled. "I went out to meet my father, and I saw them and heard you and saw them hearing you."

"Jeez. That day must've been extra-special crazy for you, Staze," I said, remembering her father's strange, disconnected speech that afternoon.

Staze sighed. "When the president of your college calls and asks if you would invite your father to speak at commencement, it's difficult to say no."

"But your mom…"

"My mother was too sick to come anyway," she interrupted. "I knew it was a moot point." She stared up at her apartment ceiling. "She's never said anything about it. But I'm certain it hurt her feelings. Very much, in fact."

"Do you have any idea how she's doing now?" I asked.

Staze shrugged. "Still in India, I imagine. I got a brief letter from her a couple of months back. I keep pleading with her to get on email, but she says she's just not ready to be connected with the world again."

"That sucks so much," I said, shaking my head. "Are you sure you don't want to come down with me? Just for Thanksgiving Day? You can take the train back."

"No, Nat. It's alright," she said. "Your family is lovely, but I want to spend this time alone with my blog, as strange as that sounds. I know we don't have much time left together, and I suppose I want to dwell a bit."

"Anastaze, you can still have your blog after it's not anonymous anymore," I argued.

She looked up at me. "But it won't be the same."

"Awww," I said, plopping down next to her and rubbing her legs. "I'm sorry this is so hard for you." I paused a respectable five or six seconds. "Can I talk about me now?"

"Yes! Please!" she answered. "Let us discuss topics other than anonymity, weblogs, virginity, or my parents."

"I realize now how different Emily was from any of the other people I've been involved with."

"You mean how she was pleasant and accessible and expressed genuine interest in you?" Staze asked pointedly.

"Hey, most people I hook up with are perfectly pleasant!" I demanded. "You were the one chasing guys like Lewis. Remember Lewis, Anastaze?"

"I will never forget Lewis," she said. "Rest assured, Jeremiah is nothing like that, by the way."

"I thought we weren't discussing topics related to your virginity. Or your *blog*," I teased.

"Sorry. Please. Continue."

"There's not much more to say," I replied. "Thinking about Emily, I can picture all these crucial details and pivotal moments, but I don't really lack resolution or closure. I feel plenty of affection for her, but that's it. No loss, no longing, no open wounds. Maybe that relationship was the one that was really everything it could've been."

"I'm not sure she would have agreed with that perspective," Staze posited.

"Probably not," I said, noticing a few snowflakes dancing outside the window. "I just wish I knew how she was doing now."

"Well, you're in luck," Staze said, moving toward the table.

"What, do you see her online?" I asked. I don't have Staze's patience for social media, and I especially try to avoid the people who pepper my sexual past.

"Nope." Staze shuffled around for a while on her coffee table and handed me the latest copy of *Easton Alumni*.

I scoffed. "I've sent those people *how* many change of address notices now?"

"You never received this one?" Staze asked.

"No. That brings my total to *four*. Four quarterly magazines I've missed." I shook my head. "Fucking hippies."

Staze chuckled. "Emily's listed in her class updates." I flipped around for a moment until I found it:

It's been an exciting year for Emily Morgan. She landed a new job at the Coastal Wildlife Preservation Alliance in California, and she and her wife Kate are expecting their first baby in December!

I stood straight up and dropped the magazine on the floor. "A *baby*? What the shit is that?"

"It's like a person," Staze replied. "Only smaller."

"Jesus, Anastaze, you could've warned me," I chided.

"I wonder which one of them is pregnant," Staze mused.

"The other one, the wife. Not Emily," I declared.

"Really, do you think? Because I believe her wife is in medical school, and to me that—"

"Staze! I really need it not to be Emily right now, OK?" I pleaded, and she backed off. I sat back down on the couch slowly, shaking my head. "Jesus. Babies. When did that happen?"

"It really is happening, isn't it?" Staze remarked, shaking her head. "My year's section of the boarding school alumni magazine is just one big birth announcement."

"Incidentally, I still can't believe your high school has an alumni magazine," I said.

"Don't forget the biannual literary journal and the plethora of glossy fundraising materials."

"A *baby*," I said again, returning to the paragraph on Emily. I've spent the past few days imagining her sweet youthful freshman and sophomore self. Fast-forwarding to the present was extremely jarring.

"That's not all," Staze informed me. "If you're ready for it, there's bit about Ben in there as well."

"God. I'm not even done wrapping my mind around everything I went through with him yet."

"Yikes," she said, sucking her teeth.

"You're telling me. So what's up with contemporary Ben?" I asked. I lit up. "Is he getting divorced?"

"Here, give it to me." Staze yanked the magazine out of my hand. "I'll read it aloud, and perhaps that way you can remain seated."

"Agreed," I said, hugging a cushion to my chest.

Staze flipped a couple of pages and took a deep breath. "'Ben Preston-McNally was promoted to Assistant Professor of Cinema Studies at Lincoln College in Ohio. He and his wife Amber Preston-McNally enjoy volunteering with Temple Ner Tamid and spending time with their twin sons, Asher and Ari.'"

"Well," I said. "I guess he's still married."

"Did you ever meet her?" Staze asked as she placed the magazine down on the floor.

"No, I just banged him in her apartment a few million times," I replied. "I'm glad I never met her, actually. If I had, I might feel bad about—"

"Hang on a sec," Staze blurted, interrupting me.

"What?"

"Did I say those kids were called Asher and Ari?" she asked, grabbing *Easton Alumni* and trying to recover the page.

"I think so," I said as I watched her reread the paragraph.

She looked over at me. "Asher and Ari *Preston-McNally*?"

"*Oy, vey*," we said in perfect unison. And then we laughed until we cried.

§

AFTER MY GRADUATION AND a frustrating family vacation on Cape Cod, ("Natalie, all I'm saying is that you're so *close* now. If you could just lose another twenty or thirty pounds, then you'd *really* be ready for New York!"), we headed back to my parents' house together. My mother returned to work for the tail end of her school year while my father helped me load up a U-Haul with some gently used furniture from their basement and my childhood bed. He drove along with me up to my new place in New York City.

I'd found the apartment listed online and asked David G. to scout it out for me, since he worked just a few avenues across town. He gave me a sort of half-hearted, noncommittal thumbs-up, and when my father and I pulled up in front I started to wonder if he'd ever actually looked at the place at all. The Mexican restaurant on the ground level didn't seem that bad at first, but by the time we got up to the fifth floor, the unmistakable odor of marinated beef hadn't dissipated. In fact, it seemed to have gotten stronger.

"Maybe they have a satellite kitchen on the roof," my dad suggested. I laughed at what I thought was his joke, and he stared at me blankly. As usual, my dad was sincerely suggesting what seemed to him a perfectly plausible explanation.

"Yeah, Dad," I replied. "Maybe you're right."

I pounded a few times on the apartment door, and finally a young woman with black hair dressed all in black answered the door. "What?" she demanded.

"Oh, hi!" I said, trying to be friendly. "I'm Natalie. Your new roommate?"

She stared at me blankly.

"I talked to you on the phone?" I attempted. "I'm supposed to be moving in today?"

"You didn't talk to me," she said. "You probably talked to Anne, the chick who was moving out."

"Oh. Well she said her name was Veronica."

"I'm Veronica," she declared. "But you *didn't* talk to me." She stepped aside and let us in. "Key's on the counter," she muttered over her shoulder as she marched back into her bedroom and slammed the door.

My father, who's never quite certain whether a social interaction falls within the normal range, looked at me sideways. "That was weird, right?" he whispered.

"Oh yeah," I reassured him. "Super weird."

We unloaded the truck and brought everything up the many stairs, then tried to fit it all into my speck of a bedroom. I couldn't even keep any of the small tables we'd packed. The room had no closet and barely enough space for my sewing table and bed. In order to sit at the machine and use the pedal, I had to place a folding chair in front of the door.

When it came time for my father to leave, he hesitated. "Sweetheart," he began, blotting his brow with his handkerchief in the early summer New York heat. "Are you sure you're going to be alright?"

"Yes, Dad," I assured him. "Yeah, I'm fine." I walked him down to the sidewalk and shoved him into the U-Haul, smiling and waving and trying to look relaxed. Inside, I was panicking. I had a meeting with the manager of my old bookstore in the morning, but the evening stretched out before me like an abyss of anxiety.

I went upstairs and tried to take a shower, devastated to discover that the water temperature and pressure refused to exceed a tepid trickle. Minh was living with her boyfriend somewhere in the recesses of Queens by that time, and David G. was on my shit list. So I did the one thing I for some reason didn't expect myself to do: I called Ben.

"Natalie," he said right away. His voice through my cell phone flooded me with relief. "Are you in town?"

"Yeah, I am," I replied. "Just got here. What are you up to?"

He invited me over, and I hopped on the L train and hurried along the familiar route from the station to Ben's house through his rapidly changing neighborhood. We ordered pizza and caught up about my final months at Easton and his work in the city. It felt oddly relaxed and unencumbered. It felt chill. *I could get used to chill,* I remember thinking.

"So Natalie," Ben eventually said, in his scripted-sounding way, as he refilled my wine glass. "I've been thinking about us quite a bit, and I've decided that we should no longer have sex."

"Really," I said, raising one eyebrow, cloaking my disappointment like a pro. "And what brought you to such a conclusion?"

"Well, when you told me you were moving to New York, as had always been your plan, of course..." (Did he say that to let me know he'd determined I probably hadn't moved to the fashion capital of the world in pursuit of him?) "When you told me you were moving here, I thought, 'well, maybe Natalie and I shouldn't see each other at all.'" I watched him as he paced around, gesticulating with the wine bottle before returning it to its place on the counter. "But you're my friend, Natalie, and I would like very much for us to remain friends. However, I think we both know that we have a real weakness for each other."

"Do we?" I asked. "A weakness?"

"Naturally," he replied. "A weakness for sex. It's obvious neither one of us wants to keep hooking up, but it's also impossible to deny that we always inevitably still do."

His logic perplexed me. "Hang on a minute," I interjected.

"No, let me finish. Please." He was standing above me in the kitchen, and I was seated at his table. I closed my mouth and nodded at him to continue. And continue he did. "I'm trying to get my life in order, and I've started making some pretty serious changes. Did I tell you I'm running the marathon?"

"Wow," I said. "Is that in the fall?"

He nodded. "October. I'm super psyched. My girlfriend got me—"

"Ding ding ding!" I cried, interrupting, and he pretended to be startled.

"'Ding ding'? What? What's that supposed to mean, Natalie?" he scoffed, offended.

"You don't want to have sex anymore because you've got a girlfriend," I declared.

"No, not at all. Well, sure, to some extent," he equivocated. "But first and foremost it's because you and I need to take some responsibility for our friendship."

"How do you mean?" I asked.

"Natalie, we've been having sex since the week we met," he argued, quite accurately. "And let's not delude ourselves. The power dynamic back then was just plain inappropriate."

"Well, I suppose there's something to that," I began. "But I never felt tha—"

"I've struggled with this for too many years now," he interrupted. "I don't want to feel guilty about taking advantage of your admiration any longer."

"Taking advantage of my admiration?" I shook my head at his interpretation. "I mean, you were my teacher. But I didn't *admire* you. I thought you were hot."

"You were an eighteen-year-old girl from a working-class background, Natalie," he declared, and I tried to wrap my head around the story he'd been telling himself about my upbringing. "You didn't even know what Brie was."

"So my family wasn't a bunch of gourmands, that doesn't mean we were hillbillies!" I said, standing up. "My father has a PhD, Ben."

"I'm just saying, I took advantage of you, and that dynamic has continued as long as I've known you. I want it to stop."

"I don't agree with your narrative here, *Professor McNally*," I sneered. "You didn't 'take advantage' of me. I did exactly what I wanted to do."

"Then tell me you never bragged to your friends that you were banging your teacher," he said, staring me down.

"I never told anyone at Easton what was going on at all," I asserted. "Anastaze knew, of course, but she figured it out herse—"

"But since then?" he said, never flinching. "Come on, Natalie, you expect me to believe I don't factor into the wild stories you tell people at parties?"

"At parties? What are you even talking about?"

"Do NOT bullshit me," he barked, and I looked down.

"Alright, fine. Perhaps it's come up, but I—"

"Natalie, it's simple: you want me to want you. You want to feel desired by me, and I…" he trailed off and sat down. "I want to play a different role than that in your life."

I'd never experienced anything like this from him at all. Hell, he'd just acknowledged out loud that we had a pattern, and a long-standing sexual relationship. It was almost too overwhelming to parse.

After a pause, I sat down next to him. "OK," I said. "I get that, I do. And I just moved to New York, so I really need all the friends I can get."

"New York can be tough at first," he said. "But you get used to it."

I smiled and offered him my outstretched hand. "So, friends?" I asked with a smile.

"Come 'ere, you," he said, pulling me in for a hug. "Say, friend, would you like to spend the night? I can get the couch all set up for ya."

Come 'ere, you. Say, friend. He actually uttered such phrases. To him, they were perfectly natural things to say.

I curled up on Ben's couch that night and slept more soundly than I probably would have in my own apartment, though I still wanted to run into his room and jump his bones with every fiber of my being. As I drifted off, I imagined with dread the impending introduction to his marathon-running stick-thin athletic girlfriend. Then I thought about my carne asada–scented closet of a room over in the East Village and felt deeply grateful for Ben's platonic hospitality.

The summer passed, and despite Ben's assurances, I was still decidedly unused to New York. I didn't see much of Minh or David G. during my first several months in town. They'd stopped hanging out with each other as much, and their own lives and careers kept them both booked fairly solid. In fact, everybody's constant busyness proved a common impediment to making any genuine new friends as well. Veronica the roommate turned out to be nice enough but worked three jobs and didn't offer much in terms of emotional support. I visited Anastaze in Boston as much as possible, but between my internship and my retail job I rarely had two days off in a row.

And then came the anniversary of 9/11. This was one of the relatively early ones, when the general somber mood of mourning was still mixed up with edginess and anxiety and vague warnings peppered with phrases like "mass-casualty event" and "spectacular attack:" the era of orange alerts. I'd never been a particularly anxious person, but the emotional twitchiness of a densely populated city coupled with the overall shittiness of my situation in life at the time conspired to render me downright hysterical by the end of my bookstore shift at 3:00 p.m.

I called Ben in tears. "Natalie? Aw, Natalie, it's OK!" he assured me through the phone. "Meet me at my place in a couple of hours."

Grateful, I hung up and took the train to Brooklyn. I spent an hour in McCarran Park, reading an Allen Ginsberg collection I'd bought double-discounted off the bargain table at work. When Ben came home, I was waiting on his front stoop.

"Well, you seem to be doing better," he said, embracing me.

"Yeah, I was just having a meltdown. That's a thing people say here, right?" I joked.

"Are you alright now, friend?" Ben asked with a nod.

"Yes. Let's get some dinner."

"Do you want to just go upstairs?" he offered. "I've got a ton of food. I'll cook."

"Sure," I replied, and I followed him up.

We sat and drank orange-flavored seltzer water and talked about our mutual frustrations with American foreign policy and our various neurotic fears. I revealed that I hated riding in a subway car with anyone hauling a rolling suitcase. "Even an eighty-year-old grandma," I admitted. "I still try to slip out at the station and into the next car."

"I avoid the bridges," he said, pushing onions around a cast iron pan. "That's part of why I'm excited about the marathon. It'll give me a couple of opportunities to conquer that fear." He looked over at me and smiled, and suddenly all my blood rushed into my loins.

I didn't quite know what to make of myself in that moment. I'd been doing a pretty good job of being Ben's benefits-free friend, though he'd still never managed to bring me around his lady, even though the two of them were allegedly inseparable. But something in his countenance that evening had shifted me so dramatically off that course that I decided it must be mutual.

I sidled up behind him at the stove and wrapped my hands around his waist. I placed my lips gently against the back of his neck and moved my hands down the front of his body.

I definitely heard his breath catch. He exhaled, *he made an audible sex noise*, and his neck stiffened. Then he grabbed my hands firmly.

"Natalie, what are you doing?" he demanded. He turned to face me, looking more besieged than angry. "What is this? What is the matter with you?"

"I'm sorry. I'm sorry," I said, showing him my palms. "I thought there was a moment is all." I stumbled back a few paces, grabbed my seltzer and gulped down the rest of the glass.

He shook his head. I backed away even further, and he returned to his onions without a word. He seemed to be getting angrier and angrier, and I thought he was about to throw me out of his apartment.

"Fuck!" he shouted, kicking his foot against the broiler. Then he flipped off the stove, slammed the pan onto a cold burner, whipped around, and grabbed me by the waist. He stepped all the way through my personal space and into my center, knocking me off balance. I stumbled backward, but his grip was too tight to let me fall. He jammed his tongue into my mouth so far that it would've been a bad kiss if it weren't instead hands-down the hottest kiss of my whole entire life.

We made out like that for a long time, like teenagers, like people who'd never had sex with each other before, or even at all before.

We leaned against the kitchen wall, drinking in the deliciously familiar tastes we'd managed to render even more intoxicating by explicitly forbidding.

Eventually Ben maneuvered me out of his galley kitchen and through the only internal door, to his bedroom. He pushed me down on the same bed from that first relatively uncomplicated encounter, back before he tried to date my roommate.

Ben thrust his body into mine more forcefully than he ever had, and my diaphragm and core muscles and abdomen and pelvis began to push loud vocalizations, deep moans, out through my lungs. Then Ben did the craziest thing I'd ever seen him do: he reached up with his right hand *covered my mouth* with it. My eyes grew wide and I came almost immediately, watching him fuck me while he brazenly demonstrated that he didn't want another living soul to know a damn thing about it. He didn't avert his eyes or hesitate as he stifled my cries of pleasure; he just fucked me even harder and let me wail into his open palm, and he came too, ending with a few convulsive full-body shudders.

The silence that followed was lengthy and near-total. Every fifteen seconds or so, a car would pass or a breeze would blow or the neighbor's dog would bark. Aside from that, I couldn't even hear him breathing. After an interminable stillness, he finally rolled over and spoke.

"Natalie." There it was. There was my name, alone, as its own sentence. "You. Are a woman. Of substance."

So much for Plato.

I always preferred Aristotle anyway.

S

I STILL CAN'T DECIDE if this weekend will go down in my family's lore as the worst Thanksgiving ever or the best.

I rolled into town around 11:00 p.m. on Tuesday, having stayed up until the wee hours on Monday night contemplating my Great Leap Backward with Ben, and by the time I arrived my parents had already gone to bed. I let myself in at the silent house and found a note from my father:

Natalie, Your mom and I will go to the hospital before you wake up. She's scheduled for prep at eight, and the procedure begins at ten. I will keep you posted on your cell phone. We should be home before dinnertime. Your mom has done all the shopping for the holiday. See you tomorrow night. Love, Dad.

He always punctuates his messages the same way: *Love, Dad.* Just like that, with a period on the end. It's one of those technically incorrect things that look so much better wrong than right.

I felt kind of bad. In flagrant defiance of my father's advice, I had managed to time my departure perfectly, and by that I mean I left at the absolute worst possible time on one of the worst travel days of the year. Fortunately, or unfortunately, Sean from down the hall left me a bag of those chocolate cranberry cookies, ostensibly to share with my family, but they were so delicious, and I-95 was so maddening, that I polished them off before I even hit Rhode Island. Wired from all the coffee I'd downed to keep awake in the stultifying traffic, I crept upstairs to my former bedroom with my laptop and started the process of digging through my old design trunk.

I logged into my parents' wireless network using the password my father had typed (with a typewriter) onto an index card and affixed to the refrigerator with four identical round magnets. I set my computer's volume to the lowest setting and put on some CDs from my high school collection, still reliably collecting dust in the same black waist-high stand. Liz Phair rocked out barely audibly as I shuffled through my old swatches and patterns and measuring tapes in search of items to show Nancy at Phoebe Hipp.

I'd uncovered my favorite button-down cuffed short-sleeve and my seriously fierce asymmetrical A-line dress when I picked up a vaguely familiar item that turned out to be a Morbidica T-shirt.

My curiosity sparked, I turned to my laptop and googled Tyler, which I'm pretty sure I hadn't done in at least a year. I tabbed through page after page of liner notes and publicity photos. (Yow. Still.) Finally, I clicked on the most recent tour schedule.

"Holy shit," I said out loud to nobody but Liz as she fucked and ran her way through my laptop speakers. Tyler's band, Follow the Reader, will be playing downtown this Saturday night. An article in the local alt weekly makes several references to the fact that this'll be a homecoming for Tyler, although the other members of his band all hail from Texas and Louisiana.

And the show, interestingly enough, will take place at the historic Elmwood Lounge.

I contemplated hanging around town long enough to go, but then I thought better of it. I've got it on my schedule to swing through a few not-mandatory-but-strongly-encouraged department store holiday parties in Boston this weekend, and, of course, there's Staze's drama to attend to. And I really don't think it's a great idea for me to hang out here beyond Thanksgiving, watching my mother scrutinize her new arms in the mirror for hours on end.

After a few more minutes of googling, I closed up my laptop and headed downstairs to the guest suite. My old room is more or less intact, except, of course, for the bed, which succumbed to New York City. I fell asleep on the comfy queen-sized guest bed wrapped up in my parents' gently used spare comforter, and the next thing I knew the sun was up and my parents' landline was ringing off the hook.

"Hello?" I said groggily into the startlingly cumbersome receiver. I haven't had a landline in years.

"Oh, thank goodness. Natalie, it's your father." I could hear the sound of doctors being paged in the background, which meant that my father was making a phone call from inside the hospital. My father, the biggest rule-follower I've ever met, was talking on his cellular telephone within the confines of a designated hospital zone.

Something was very wrong.

"Dad?" I replied, now wide awake with adrenaline. "What's the matter? What's happening?"

"I don't know, Natalie, something about anesthesia, and a seizure. They're telling me they've moved your mother into intensive care."

"I'll be right there!" I blurted, hanging up. I threw on some clothes and leapt into my car, experiencing total recall of every shortcut and back alley route I learned as a teenager to navigate around the many traffic lights of my over-safe suburban hometown. I parked my car and was running up to the concrete slab of a hospital when suddenly I realized had absolutely no idea where to go. That's when I noticed my father milling around outside.

"Dad!" I screamed, jogging over to him. He walked briskly toward me, his breath puffing out in clouds against the early morning November chill.

His face revealed deep concern. "Natalie, where are you coming from?"

"What? The house, Dad. From the house," I replied, my heart racing.

My father looked at his watch. "Natalie, speeding is extremely dangerous. Now, I hung up with you less than ten minutes ago, which means there's no way you could've safely driven—"

"Dad!" I interrupted. "What's wrong with Mom?"

His face softened, and he remembered himself. "She's fine, Natalie. It turns out she's fine. She just had a reaction to the anesthesia. A fairly common one, they tell me."

And in that moment, I reentered my own body and realized how frantic I'd become. Tears welled up and streamed down my face.

"Oh, sweetheart," my father said. "It's alright. She's alright." He hugged me amidst the pillars framing the ambulance zone on the parking lot blacktop, patting my back with an engineer's rhythmic affection.

"Can we see her?" I asked, wiping away my tears.

"The nurses told me it would be about an hour," he said. "That's why I came out to look for you. I wasn't sure you'd know quite where to go."

"I'm glad you did, Dad," I told him. "Once I parked my car, I realized I had no idea where to find you."

"Well, I found you, instead," he said, and he put his arm around me and walked me up to the waiting area.

We sat there for an interminable hour, after which point they told us it was going to be "a little bit longer." Antsy and irritable, I actually stooped so low as to purchase coffee from one of those old-school drip vending machines. I carried my Styrofoam cup of lukewarm brown water back to the main waiting area and sank into the chair next to my father.

"You know, I feel really guilty," I confessed. "Like I willed this misfortune on her by hating the idea of this surgery so much, you know?"

My father sighed. He removed his glasses and rubbed the bridge of his nose. "Natalie, I know you and your mother haven't always seen eye to eye on these things," he began.

"And I should be supportive, I guess," I replied. "But it's not easy, Dad. I just don't understand what her problem is."

"Neither do I," he said wearily.

"Really?" I asked, and it occurred to me that I'd never heard a single word out of my father on the whole body-and-weight issue.

"I think your mother's beautiful the way she is," he told me. "She's perfect to me. Always has been. And that goes for you, too, baby."

I gave him a half-smile. "Thanks, Daddy, but of course you have to say that."

"Natalie, I'm serious," he said, pulling out his wallet. Inside he had a picture of Mom and me taken at a Sears portrait studio when I was a little baby. I smiled as he showed it to me. Then he reached into the billfold and produced a meticulously trimmed piece of computer photo paper with a picture of me from backstage at the Phoebe Hipp shoot.

"Dad!" I exclaimed. "How did you get that?" I still hadn't even seen any of the photos from that day myself.

"I printed it up off the Internet at work," he explained. "I saw somebody tagged you, so I looked at the picture. My goodness, Natalie, this is really something. You modeling? I'm so proud of that."

"Mom didn't mention it to you?" I asked, taking the photo and examining it.

"Nope. It turns out neither of my girls saw fit to say anything to me about it. I had to find out instead from young Mr. Zuckerberg."

I chuckled at my father's quasi–pop culture reference. "Well, she's not too happy about the fact that it's plus-size clothes I'm modeling. She's still ashamed to have such a chubby daughter."

Dad sighed again. He took off his glasses, rubbed his eyes, and replaced them. I know I'm sick to death of the battles Mom and I have been waging against each other and ourselves for all these years. I can't even fathom how exhausted my father must be by it all. "Sweetheart, your mother has always thought there was something wrong with her appearance. And so she does all these things to change it and control it and perfect it and all of that. The problem with you is that she feels responsible for the way you look as well. And you've always been so much more confident and at home in your own skin than your mother ever was. Poor thing. I tell her all the time, she ought to leave you alone and let *you* decide what you want to wear and how you want to look."

"I really feel like I jinxed her on this surgery," I said, squeaking my thumb against the rim of my cup.

"No, this is my fault," he replied. "I never should have gone along with it. But she said if she didn't get this procedure, she wouldn't go on our anniversary cruise. And then there was all the pulling and yanking at her arms in the mirror..."

He trailed off, and I passed him the tepid coffee. He took a swig like it was bootleg whiskey, like we were old war buddies reminiscing about the front lines. All these years, I've thought it was me against Mom, me and my feminism and my wide-hipped frame duking it out against her body dysmorphia and her impossible standards. I never realized my father had been squarely in my corner the entire time.

Finally, a nurse led us up to see Mom. She was still pretty weak, but she managed to reach out and grab each of our arms.

"I'm sorry," she mouthed before either of us even got a chance to hug and kiss her. Dad leaned in first and then held up a pink plastic cup filled with water, which she sipped through a straw. I leaned in for a hug, and her mouth was moist enough to speak.

"Natalie, I'm sorry to wake you," she said, groggy and doped up enough to still be confined to nonsequitors.

"Grace, do you understand what happened?" my father asked.

She nodded, her eyes taking long blinks as she struggled to stay awake. "Anesthesia?" she said. "They say I had a reaction." She nodded off and then opened her eyes suddenly. "Is Natalie here? Oh, Natalie," she said, noticing me again, and I couldn't help but giggle.

Mom laughed too. She was just plain loopy.

"You know, this was actually kind of fortunate," Dad said to Mom, but probably more to me. "If you'd needed emergency surgery and had this type of reaction, it would've been much worse. Now at least they know what anesthesia to avoid."

"Mmmmmm, sing to me, Tommy," my mother said to my father, at which point I just plain laughed out loud. Mom laughed again as well.

"I think I'm going to head home and start prepping for tomorrow," I announced. I felt tired and twitchy, and it seemed like doped-up Mom was more my dad's department anyway.

"Alright, sweetheart," Dad said, giving me a kiss on the cheek.

I leaned in and pecked my mom on the forehead. "See you soon, Mama."

"Mmmm, go back to sleep," she said with her eyes closed, and I turned toward the door. "Natalie," she said, and I looked back at her. "I think, no surgery," she declared, forcing her eyes open to meet mine. Then she closed them again, mumbling, "Mommy's arms are fine. Mommy's arms are fine."

"That's right, Mommy," I said, smiling at the absurdity of the entire morning. "Your arms are just fine."

I exchanged amused looks with my father and strolled back down to my car. I spent the rest of the afternoon chopping carrots and peeling potatoes and baking pie crusts for tomorrow's big feast. I assume Dad and I will be the only ones eating, but I want Mom to have plenty of options for leftovers when her appetite returns.

And I decided I want to stick around at least until Sunday. Driving will be hell, but I'd like to talk to Dad about the modeling stuff and tell him the good news from Phoebe Hipp. He's always been so supportive of my goals, both personally and financially. It would be nice to have some time alone with him while Mom sleeps it all off.

Still, Dad is a pretty early-to-bed kind of guy, so I'm sure my Saturday night will be wide open. I guess that means I'll be heading down to the Elmwood for the Follow the Reader show.

I better find something to wear.

§

TWO YEARS AFTER MY first relapse with Ben, much had changed in my life, though none of it for the better. My original housing situation with Veronica fell apart soon after a water pipe burst on the second floor, turning the whole building into a breeding ground for cockroaches. Just as the vermin were becoming too overwhelming to fight, another pipe burst and our bathroom ceiling caved it, filling our tub with plasterboard and covering everything in toxic dust. Our landlord gave us back our security deposit and rent for the month and chased us out. We didn't have a lease, so we didn't have a choice.

After that, I lived for six or eight months in a place in Park Slope, Brooklyn until the building's bedbug infestation struck my poor, unsuspecting childhood mattress. I hauled it out onto the street on garbage day and found a new apartment on 57th Street in Manhattan the next week. I passed my nights in a sleeping bag on the floor until I could pull together the funds for a cheap *new* futon. Buying a used bed in New York City in the mid-00s was far too risky a proposition.

The midtown place proved expensive and inconvenient, so I found somebody to take over my sublease and hauled my ass back across the East River. Prospect Heights was a long trip from my Union Square retail gig, and it was in a different dimension than Bryant Park, but I found an apartment there that I could afford, and I wound up staying for almost eighteen months, my New York City continuous residence record.

To make matters worse, I kept getting promoted at the fucking bookstore. Shift leader, shift supervisor, *assistant manager*. Eventually I had enough responsibility to keep me occupied for more than forty hours a week. This was most definitely not the plan.

"Come talk to my boss's boss," Minh said to me on the phone one afternoon as I complained to her about my derailed life a million light-years away from the garment district. "She's nice. She'll love you."

"I don't know, Minh," I replied, rushing through the Green Market for yet another late-day shift in retail hell. "I don't know if your brand is a good fit for me." *Fit* being the operative word.

"Just come in. You'll wow them," she assured me.

Instead, the slender, tan Asian woman who Minh thought was so nice looked me up and down skeptically and tossed my sketches onto her desk as I sat uncomfortably on the ultralow couch in her office.

"I don't know, Natalie," she said. "You know, we're not one of these houses with a hundred junior associates. In fact, we don't even have twenty." She looked out the window, fascinated by the paper bag blowing past her third story office.

"Well, thank you for your time," I said, mortified, preparing to leave.

"Did you say you went to fashion school?" she asked, turning her back to me as she reloaded her inbox.

"Um, no, I didn't. I went to a liberal arts school. Easton College?"

"Oh. I went there," she said.

"You did?" I asked. "You went to Easton?" I was shocked. Most alums from my school greeted each other with a hug or at least a warm smile. This woman just seemed annoyed that she'd inadvertently given me another reason to remain in her office.

"Well. I transferred," she said, picking up a paper clip and unbending it. "To NYU."

Of course you did.

"I'll just be going," I said, gently pulling my sketches off her desk.

"I'd put your name in for one of our internships, but generally I find it difficult to recommend somebody unless I've really seen them shine, you know?" She looked back out the window and absently rolled the ankle of her top leg a couple of times. "I'm just not a very good liar."

"She said *what* to you?" Minh exclaimed later, as I recounted my experience over the phone.

"Yeah, it was pretty crazy," I admitted. "Though not the worst informational interview I've ever had." I'd become so inured to devastating meetings with waifs that I didn't even cry anymore. "The best part was when she said she wouldn't recommend me for an internship that I've already completed."

"Oh my God," Minh said, stunned. "She must not have even read your résumé."

"Whatever, it's fine."

"Natalie, I wish I could do more for you," Minh said. "After I get ten more promotions, I promise I'll hire you."

I chuckled at that one. "Thanks, Minh. It helps to know you're on my side."

"TexD forever!" she said before hanging up the phone to go slave away some more.

And that was pretty much how it went: bad apartments, discouraging interviews, and soul-killing retail shifts.

That, and fucking Ben.

And gaining, like, twenty or thirty pounds.

At least.

Granted, after my first six months in New York, my size twelve pants were nearly falling off me. Running around the city being broke and busy made the inches disappear, but after that initial metabolic peak, my increases in pay and stress contributed to some very poor comfort-related eating habits. I never cooked in those days. My groceries consisted of microwavable mac and cheese and screw-top red wine that I could stash in my room, away from the reach of grazing roommates. For the most part, I ducked into delis and cafés and bagel shops and pizza parlors in search of my three (or six) meals a day. After the first year, I stopped visiting my parents altogether for fear of what my mother would say about my weight.

And all the while, Ben kept calling me, at least twice a week. He'd continued his athletic pursuits, completing two marathons and then switching to a popular training program involving lots of very heavy weights and several different kinds of push-ups. He would tell me about completing workouts named after women, like "Ruby" and "Eleanor." "I did Jessica today," he'd say, and I'd wince until I remembered that his girlfriend's name was actually Amber.

The elusive Amber had a standard nine-to-five job, in finance or corporate real estate or something. This made it extraordinarily easy for me and Ben to find time together, with my sporadic retail shifts and his adjunct professor's free afternoons. We would rendezvous mid-day. Our sex timetable read like an academic department's office hours schedule. *Mondays and Wednesdays 2:30 to 4:00 p.m., or by appointment.*

It felt awful that he was cheating and I was the other woman. After the first year, I noticed that I'd started yelling at myself *out loud*, actually forming the words of the thoughts I used to only toss around my brain. "You fucking bitch," I would hear myself mutter as I walked down the street contemplating the evil I was doing to poor Amber Preston. Poor, unsuspecting, hot, blonde Amber Preston.

When I found out she was also his former student—that she'd been his student far more recently than I had—I actually had the balls to say something to him about it.

During those first two years, Ben and I met up for our trysts almost exclusively at his place. He came to my apartment in midtown on 57th a couple of times since he taught classes on 68th Street, but I didn't even stay there for an entire season. When I moved to Prospect Heights, we encountered that bizarre Brooklyn "you can't get there from here" problem. In order to travel between my place near Prospect Park and his apartment in Greenpoint, one either had to take the unreliable G train for about a million stops or travel all the way into Manhattan to grab the L. Fortunately, or not, Amber lived alone very close to where I worked in Union Square. Ben, being her very special public meet-the-parents kind of boyfriend, had his own key.

I'm not going to mince words: doing bad things is extremely hot. There is no book, no play, no tale of sex and betrayal in human history that doesn't make reference to the erotic power of transgression. The ten thousand times I'd cringe or wince at my own awfulness during the week after I fucked Ben on Amber's chocolate brown Crate and Barrel couch did not constitute a plausible deterrent. My life had in New York become lonely, stressful, and pointless. I had nothing else to look forward to.

The fact was, after nearly three years of living there, Ben was the only person I really felt close to in the whole city. I still loved Minh and David G., but the other TexD kids had all moved away, and I almost never hung out with the two that remained. There were many weeks when I saw Ben more often than the semi-strangers I shared an apartment with.

The umpteenth time Ben brought me to Amber's, I felt brazen enough to peruse her bookshelf: *Alfred Hitchcock and the Making of Psycho, Deconstructing Disney, For Keeps* by Pauline Kael. "Are these your books?" I asked him when he returned from the kitchen with two glasses of water.

"Uh, nope. Those are hers." I could tell he was uncomfortable talking about her, especially when we'd just finished doing it on her red and brown and beige-striped carpet.

"I guess you guys have a lot in common," I said, gulping water and bending down to tie my shoes.

"Yeah. Well, um, yeah," he hesitated.

"What?" I asked.

"Those are the books for my class, obviously," he said.

"I thought you said they were hers," I replied.

"Yeah, they're hers," he said, pulling his messenger bag over his shoulder. "You ready?"

"Hang on," I said, standing up, my shoes half-unlaced. "Are you telling me that Amber was one of your students?"

"Yeah, like, three years ago," he muttered. "Listen, I'd really like to get out of here."

My mouth fell open. I grabbed my bag and followed him out of the apartment, stunned. We jogged down the stairs (the elevator was off limits, of course), and when we got out onto the street, I just looked at him.

"What?" he demanded.

"I thought the whole teacher-student thing was the fucked-up dynamic that *you and I* had, Ben," I argued.

"Well obviously it is," he shot back.

"But your *girlfriend* was your student much more recently than I was," I said.

"Natalie, I have to go to the train," he said, shaking his head.

"Fine. I'll walk with you," I told him.

"No. Please don't make a thing out of this," he pleaded. "It's different with her. Trust me."

"Is she even *Jewish*?" I demanded.

"What does that matter?" he snorted back.

"I thought that was all that mattered," I replied. "I thought that was, like, your main criteria."

"Criterion," he corrected. "And yeah, maybe when I was nineteen years old." He furrowed his brow and shook his head at me, puzzled and hostile. "What are you even talking about?" Then he swung his messenger bag around his body and turned toward the train.

I stood there and let him walk away. He hadn't said anything I didn't already know in my heart: that all his concrete reasons for never officially dating me were just convenient excuses or, perhaps more maddeningly, retroactive justifications that he came up with in order to rationalize his own bad behavior to himself. It didn't actually matter to him if a girl was a shiksa or a former student or "working class." But with me, all of that mattered, because it added up to what he had long ago decided: that he was never, ever going to be my boyfriend.

It's different with her. I kept turning that phrase over again and again in my mind, thinking about how different our sex was from the way it used to be. When I was at Easton, Ben deployed all these skills and moves and suave lines. But by the time we were meeting up regularly in Amber's apartment, the whole tone had shifted. He wasn't quite violent, but things got pretty damn rough. We went at it. Often he would hold my arms over my head or push me onto the couch or throw me down on the floor. I dug it, but standing outside that apartment, I started to realize the role I was playing in his life: Natalie the workhorse, sturdy and substantive and reliable. His show pony, by contrast, was probably very delicate and fragile. He rode me hard because he wasn't afraid to break me.

I wasn't stupid. I knew he loved to fuck me but he was never going to date me, at least partly because I didn't look like the kind of girl he wanted on his arm. As I gazed at my reflection in the shop window, fatter than I'd ever been before, wearing mandatory khakis and no makeup, how could I blame him? How could I blame any of the looks-conscious fashion industry people who rejected me? I was no display model. And appearances mattered tremendously to everything that mattered to me.

I kept seeing him. Even after that day, even after all his various excuses for how he regarded me had been obliterated, pulverized, turned to ash. I realize now that I did this because I believed his actual reason was still out there and that it was something I could ultimately overcome. I believed—I *knew*—that the real obstacle keeping Ben from taking me out on his arm was my weight. And I believed with a religious fervor that I could change it, that I could figure out how to control it, that if I could just string him along as his side piece for long enough, I would lose the weight and become beautiful and he would finally, finally fall in love with me. I craved this outcome with such a manic passion that I'd long since forgotten to ask myself if Ben was even the kind of guy I'd want to be with in the first place.

Late in my third winter in New York, a huge storm blew through and dumped a ton of snow, and a couple of days later it was sixty-five degrees. The weight of the snow must've snapped the stretch of gutter directly above my fifth floor window, because as the snow melted, water started seeping through the top of my storm window and dripping into my room. I first noticed the drops in the morning, but in my fragile and depressed state I had no idea what to do about it, so I just went to work. When I returned home at 7:00 p.m., water was pouring in on all sides, the melting snow following the path of least resistance directly into my room.

The floor beneath the window was completely destroyed, and the walls around it bulged and cracked. My wooden and plasterboard furniture had all been inundated by the streams of water pouring down my slanted floor toward the door. I had no idea what to do. I started dialing every number in my phone, but nobody was picking up. Desperate, I called Ben. When I went to voicemail, I hung up and hit *resend* on my phone, hoping that two calls in a row would signal that I was in trouble.

"Hey, what's up?" he said in his table-reading voice. I knew he must be with Amber.

"Hey, I'm sorry to bother you, it's just that my room is flooding with all this melted fucking snow! I have no idea what to do, and—"

"Did you call your landlord?" he asked.

"I called the property manager, but they're not picking up, and none of my roommates are home, and my stuff is getting all soaked, and—"

"Well I'm kind of busy right now," he interrupted, sounding chipper. "How about I give you a call back a little later?"

"Ben, I know you're busy, but I really need help right now, so if you could just make an excuse or something, because you're the only person I—"

"Yeah, I'm hanging out with my girlfriend," he said as if he were responding to a low-key inquiry as to his whereabouts.

"*Ben, my bedroom is filling with water. This is an emergency. I need your help. Please?*"

"OK, talk to you soon," he said. And he hung up.

I stood there in a puddle on my warping floor, breathing shallowly. And I called Staze.

"Get on a bus!" she yelled into the phone. "Pack a bag and get on a fucking bus."

I did her one better than that. In that moment, I decided to give up on New York City altogether. I rode the train to the nearest rental car place and slapped down my credit card. I was twenty-five, after all, old enough to rent a car and quit a job overnight and walk out on an apartment. I shoved my clothes and my sewing machine into the tiny American sedan they gave me, leaving all my furniture sitting there in the flooding bedroom and my key on the kitchen table. I made it to Staze's apartment in Allston, Massachusetts, around 4:00 a.m. I unloaded the car in the morning, then dropped it off at a rental location in Cambridge. On the bus back across the river, I called my bookstore and told them I had to leave town for a family emergency and wouldn't be coming back. I tried not to feel too bad about the confusion and genuine concern I was causing: this behavior was very unlike me.

I noticed six missed calls from Ben on my cell phone, four from the night before and two from earlier that morning. When I got back to Staze's place, I sent him an email explaining what had happened and where I was. He wrote back apologizing for not helping me right away and told me he'd tried to call me fifteen minutes after we'd spoken so awkwardly. He offered to go to my apartment and move all my furniture out onto the curb on trash day so that maybe I could get my security deposit back, but I told him not to bother. I was done bothering Ben, done nagging him for those scraps of attention and acknowledgment that he had always been so reluctant to give. His ambivalence, on top of everything else I had to deal with, had at last ceased to motivate me, to catapult me into the throes of manic fixation or lust or desire to impress him with my intellect. Suddenly it just made me feel fucking exhausted.

We emailed back and forth a few times after that, but I haven't actually seen him since I left New York. Sometimes he shoots me an email on my birthday, and I endeavor to reciprocate. But it always depends on my mood. Sometimes I'm too angry. Sometimes I'm too sad.

By letting Ben off the hook that one final time, I doomed myself to eat my last month's rent and security deposit, along with the cost of the car rental and whatever it would take to get started in a new place in Boston. In total, my abrupt departure from the

Big Apple cost me roughly $4,300, all of which, given my paycheck-to-paycheck lifestyle, wound up on my credit cards.

And I wound up at Staze's, crashing on her tiny couch for the better part of three months.

Follow the Reader

I T SEEMS MY MOTHER is a changed person. Her brush with catastrophe, despite how routine a medical emergency hers apparently was, has given her a new perspective on everything. Or perhaps that's just the codeine talking. Either way, it's extremely refreshing.

"Oh my *word*, you look *gorgeous!*" she exclaimed as my father showed her the pictures from the Phoebe Hipp shoot. It turns out the ones he found online were snapped backstage with Summer's little cell phone camera. Even still, we all look pretty incredible.

"Thanks, Mom," I said, realizing it was probably the first time she'd ever given me an unqualified compliment.

"And these carrots are *delicious*," she gushed, her mouth full. "Where did you learn to cook like this?"

"Uh, from online videos mostly," I replied. When I first started seeing Jeanette, she suggested cooking as a therapeutic way to heal one's relationship with food, and since then it's become my favorite hobby.

parmesan

"The meal you made really was wonderful, Natalie," my father reiterated. *That's because I used olive oil instead of low-fat butter substitute*, I thought. Poor Dad has been unwittingly forced onto all of Mom's crazy diets over the years. He must forget what normal food tastes like.

"I hope the food will be this good on the cruise," Mom piped up, taking another bite of mashed potatoes. Dad cannot stop beaming at both of us.

After three days of unprecedented nuclear family bliss, I threw on some black tights and that fierce asymmetrical A-line dress I made and headed down to the Elmwood for a show.

I can't tell if the place has changed or if it just seems smaller and seedier to me now than it did back in high school. The neighborhood around it has clearly been through a lot. Insomnia's long gone. The storefront was taken over by what appears to have been a small art gallery, but it's now vacant and up for rent. The marquis that used to jut out from the top of the Elmwood has been replaced by a chalked sandwich board out on the sidewalk. I walked up to the outside window and found the box office closed, so instead I stepped inside and paid my ten dollars directly to the bouncer who stamped my hand without even checking my ID.

Nearly every one of my fellow concert-goers was a dude in a plaid shirt and tight black jeans. Follow the Reader has clearly been enjoying some time on the heavy-rotation list at every college radio station in America, as evidenced by the scores of barely-legal male music nerds all around me.

I ordered an overpriced bottled beer and watched the tail end of the opening band with my back against the bar. I wandered over to the wall during the lull between bands, and eventually the lights went dim, and I saw Tyler walk out on stage and take a seat at the drums.

He looks really different than he did in high school, though he's still so attractive to me. His hair is darker, and his freckles have faded, but his dark eyelashes still contrast with his light eyes. I watched him the whole time, giggling at the way he stuck his tongue out and sometimes mouthed the lyrics. He seemed much more rough around the edges than the other members of his group, whose "instruments" included a Mac laptop. The lead singer picked up a guitar from time to time, but she usually just played a riff and then looped it with her foot pedals. Still, she had a beautiful voice and she was captivating to watch in her dark red mini-dress and low-healed suede boots.

At one point in the set, the singer cued up a low whirring riff and started to talk.

"As some of you may know, our drummer Tyler here is a local boy," she remarked, and the audience vocalized our support.

"He graduated from…Wilson High School," she said, and a pretty large portion of the crowd cheered at the mention of our alma mater.

"What was your mascot, Tyler?" she asked him.

Tyler stepped out from behind the drums and walked over to the second microphone at the front of the stage. "Panthers," he said, and the anonymous scattered diaspora from my hometown, including me, dutifully hooted again.

"Sounds like we've got some Panthers in the house," she said with a mischievous smile. The same crew of us cheered, chuckling at the irony of our collection of weirdos speciously laying claim to suburban high school spirit.

Just then a guy came out of the wings and handed Tyler a bass guitar, and everybody went nuts. He started plucking and thumping on it absently.

"Yup, Wilson High School," he said into the mic, to another smattering of hoots and applause. "Class of," he paused, "…1999."

And he stopped playing just as my lone "woo-hoo!" filled the sudden silence. Mortified, I slapped my hand across my mouth as forty bearded faces whipped around to look at me. Fortunately, I was too far away from the stage for any of the band members to see my face.

"Whoa. Uh. Whoever that was, come see me after," Tyler said, and his very young fans all laughed. "Wow. I really hope that was who I think it was. Anyway," he concluded, and he launched into a song to a cacophony of cheers.

Tyler and the lead singer conjured up a great deal of sexual tension during that performance. And of course, thanks to the conservatory, he's got unbelievable skills with the bass. It's like he was born with one in his hands. After the one number, though, he climbed back behind the drums and stayed there for the rest of the night.

I was sure Tyler had no notion that I might have been the person in the crowd cheering for our graduating class, but I thought he might get a kick out of seeing me anyway, so I milled around the emptying club, hoping he'd crop up. After the lights had been on for about fifteen minutes, I noticed him step out of the wings to pick up a few sheets of paper he'd thrown around, and I walked over to the stage and called his name.

He spun around and his eyes widened. "Holy shit," he said, and he took two big steps and jumped down next to me. "Natalie," he said, and we smiled and embraced each other for a long time. "How's it going, rock star?" I said into his ear.

He pulled back. "I *thought* that was you," he said. "That was you, right? Who cheered?" I nodded, and he hugged me again.

"I can't believe you recognized my voice," I told him.

"Well, I've been thinking about you lately," he replied.

"Yeah? That's funny. I've been thinking about you too."

"Can you hang out for a while?" he asked. "I'd love to introduce you to my wife."

"Uh, sure," I responded. "I don't have any other plans."

He climbed back up onstage and gave me a hand up. "Just let me take care of a few things and we'll find a diner or something," he said. He gestured for me to follow him backstage. "Come on."

"Was that your wife?" I asked, trailing behind him. "The singer?"

"Amy? No," he replied as he gathered scattered drumsticks and cables and tossed them into a black backpack. "No, she's more your type than mine." He glanced at me with raised eyebrows.

I shadowed him for a little while longer as he bopped around backstage and pulled out his iPhone. "Can you get a table for three? I'm bringing somebody I want you to meet." He firmed up plans and gathered his crap for another minute before turning to me. "OK, she's got us a booth at the twenty-four-hour place down the street," he said. He threw on his backpack, and we walked briskly out the side door and down the street in the cold night air. "Where are you living these days?"

"Boston," I told him. "I've been there for a few years now."

"Cool town," he said, pulling the restaurant door open for me and pausing. "Man, it is good to fucking see you."

"Good to see you too, dude," I said with a smile. We stepped inside.

The place was pretty full, and a number of the hipsters at the booths did obvious double-takes, recognizing Tyler as we walked past. They all clearly came from the same place we'd just been. Fortunately, they were far too cool (or neurotic and aloof) to come over and say anything. It's pretty nice, actually: Tyler can be perfectly relaxed in a crowd of his fans.

Tyler stopped at a booth populated by a lone black woman typing furiously into a phone. She looked up at him, smiled, and leaned in for a kiss. Tyler turned to me.

"This is my wife, Angela. Angela, this is my friend, *Natalie*."

"Oh my God, are you *the* Natalie?" she asked, grinning electrically at me. She stood up, revealing herself to be quite curvy and rather short, though her natural hair gave her an extra three inches at least.

"Um, I don't know!" I replied, shaking her hand.

"Yes, she is," declared Tyler, sitting down on the inside of the booth.

"Natalie as in *bisexual* Natalie? Natalie is in *v-card* Natalie?" Angela asked wickedly, and Tyler blushed.

"Dude, I haven't seen this person in, like, a thousand years," he said. "Can you please be polite?"

I was a tiny bit embarrassed that this stranger knew her husband had taken my virginity, but I really enjoyed the fact that she was such an extroverted firebrand. Given Tyler's high school proclivities for ghastly gothic skeletons, Angela was very different from what I'd expected, in all the best possible ways.

"What do you do up in Boston?" Tyler asked as he passed me a menu.

"I do fashion production stuff," I explained.

"Yeah? I wondered if you were still making clothes," he said.

"Well, not quite. I run events mostly," I began. Then I remembered the look on my father's face when I told him about Nancy's interest in my portfolio, and how my mom reacted to those backstage photos. I decided I might as well own it. "Lately I've been getting into modeling."

"Badass," Tyler replied.

"Yeah, and it looks like I'll be designing for a label in the New Year," I said. "A plus line?"

"Ooo, which one?" Angela asked.

"It's called Phoebe Hipp."

"Shut up!" she shouted, flipping on her ten-thousand-volt smile once again. "Tyler, that's where I got the dress I wore to your brother's wedding!"

"Wow, how is Jason?" I asked. The conversation was moving at a million miles an hour.

"Jason's good," he began. He shut his menu, and Angela looked at him. "Jason's in Afghanistan."

"Oh shit," I said.

"He's good, though. You know Jason." Tyler chugged his glass of water. "He went to Iraq twice, and I think that was a lot harder. This deployment isn't so bad. No patrols. But he's married now, so he misses his wife."

"Jesus," I said.

"She's really nice," said Angela. "I like her a lot. She was one of the nurses who took care of him when he got hit."

"He got hit?" I gasped.

"Yeah," Tyler said, helping himself to Angela's water, as well. "Yeah, that was about the worst phone call I've ever received."

"I cannot even imagine," I said, shaking my head.

"But he's totally fine now. Fully recovered, well enough to deploy again," Angela assured me.

"Yeah. Totally fine," Tyler scoffed. He shook is head and looked at me. "I'm not a huge fan of the United States military these days. Not after what I've watched him go through."

"Of course not." I marveled at the horrendously disproportionate burden of my generation's wars: Jason is the first person I've really known who's gone to fight, and he's had to go back again and again.

The waitress came by and took our orders. She explained that the kitchen was extremely backed up, so it might be a while.

"No problem," Tyler told her. "We've got a lot of catching up to do anyway."

We sat there and talked for hours, about Jason and his injuries, about life in Austin and New Orleans, about Angela's work as a digital content and social media consultant.

"I'm not into any of that stuff," Tyler said. "She takes care of all of it for me."

"Yeah, I don't know if we're even friends online," I told him. "I feel kind of bad about that."

"I joined Facebook one day and a couple months later I had the maximum number of friends," he explained. "I didn't even do anything but accept. People in Austin are crazy about that stuff."

"It seems like your band is pretty damn popular," I said, nodding at all the kids in the diner around us.

"I like this project a lot," he told me. "Our next album comes out in a couple of months, and I think it's going to be a pretty big deal."

Angela nodded enthusiastically. "It sounds fan*tas*tic. And you should see the list of guest performers."

"Yeah, we all called in a bunch of favors," Tyler said.

"So Natalie, are you single?" asked Angela. Tyler elbowed her. "Not to pry, I'm just wondering about your life," she explained. She was so unassuming that it hadn't even occurred to me to be annoyed by the question.

"Yes, I'm decidedly single," I replied. "I've always been single, in fact."

"Well, except in high school, right?" Angela asked, looking back and forth between Tyler and me. "Weren't you two a couple?"

"No, I was never Tyler's girlfriend," I said, pouring myself some more hot tea from the tiny personal pot.

"Yes you were," Tyler declared.

"No I wasn't, dude," I insisted, raising my voice, surprised at the force of my own assertion.

"You know what, I'm going to give you guys a minute," Angela volunteered, and she zipped away and sat down with the Mac player, who was eating a couple of booths over.

"She's amazing," I told him.

"Isn't she something?" he said with a shy smile.

"It's a little weird that she knows you took my virginity, but whatever," I said, taking a sip of my tea.

"What?" He furrowed his brow. "Oh, the 'v-card' thing?"

I nodded.

He shook his head. "She was just giving me shit because she knows *you* took *my* virginity."

"Excuse me?" I said, a little too loudly.

Tyler chuckled. "Don't look so surprised."

"But you had condoms in your car!" I argued.

"I was a cocky musician!" he blurted, and we both laughed. "So it was your first time too?"

"How could you not know that?" I asked, shaking my head.

"I don't know," he said. "You were always so...sexual."

"Yeah, I hear that a lot," I replied.

"You were my girlfriend, though, Natalie," he told me. "Freshman year, I mean, and that summer. That whole time."

"But what about what's-her-face?" I asked, pretending I had to reach for her name. "Gretchen?"

"Oof," Tyler said, shaking his head. "I'm sorry about that. I was shitty and stupid. Jason gave me hell for it, and he was right, too."

"And what about when we did have sex? Didn't you have a girlfriend then as well?"

Tyler shook his head and rubbed his temples. "Natalie, I have to be honest. It's pretty fuzzy," he said, looking up at me. "I've smoked. A lot. Of weed." And we cracked up.

Tyler and Angela paid for my tea and scrambled eggs, and when I left we exchanged business cards and hugs.

"So amazing to meet you!" sang Angela, my new favorite person on Earth.

"You too!" I exclaimed, turning to Tyler. "And please send my love to Jason."

"I definitely will," he said, standing and wrapping his arms around me. "He'll be so glad to hear you're doing well."

I scurried back to my car in the freezing cold, giddy and aching with nostalgia at the same time. I can't wait to bring Staze backstage the next time Follow the Reader comes to Boston. I'm sure they'll be right up her alley.

§

AFTER I FLED NEW York, I landed in Boston in early March and quickly discovered that winter stuck around well into April. Spring wouldn't spring until May. The gray dreariness matched my attitude as I lamented to Staze about what a failure I was.

"Nat, you cannot be a failure at twenty-five," she argued.

"Maybe not as a writer, but in fashion, I'm finished," I declared, having basically no idea what I was talking about.

The good thing about living in New York is that, once you leave, all the experience you gained there that couldn't get you the time of day in the City actually becomes valuable to your job search. The internship with M&S was the very first gig I applied for, and Melanie and Stephanie gushed about how overqualified I was. It helped breathe some life into the bloated corpse formerly known as my self-confidence.

However, another unpaid internship meant I had to find another low-commitment day job. Reluctant to call upon my bookstore colleagues for references, I instead found work in a coffeehouse, based on my one summer occasionally steaming milk and tamping espresso in the cafe attached to the store in Union Square.

After a few months in Boston, I decided I was feeling so spectacular that it was probably a good time to try a crash diet. How clever I was in my mid-twenties! I spent a few days drinking a latte for breakfast and another for lunch, then eating a little actual food for dinner. I'd single-handedly invented replacing shakes with caffeine in the Slim-Fast plan, for that extra 1950s housewife amphetamine punch.

After a week of that, I started googling and found out about the lemon and cayenne pepper thing, so I went out and purchased a shitload of organic lemons and de-ionized water or whatever they recommend. Then, as I rushed around the fabric store trying to find several yards of the pink and white paisley that Stephanie wanted for tablecloths, I suddenly realized I could no longer see the floor. Or the ceiling. I stopped dead in my tracks as the rest of my field of vision was eaten up by whiteness, and when I came to I was on my back with a crowd of people hovering over me.

"Oh my God!" I heard over and over, as a chorus of crafters cried out in concern.

"Are you all right?" asked a middle-aged woman in a yellow employee vest. "Do you need an ambulance?"

"No," I replied, slowly sitting up and leaning myself up against some sturdy-looking rolls of blue felt. "No, I'm OK. Maybe just some water."

But then, I hesitated, because the water they brought me was teeming with ions, and therefore constituted cheating on my diet.

That's when I realized I probably needed some help.

Staze found Jeanette through a combination of Internet searches and the various connections she'd made in Boston over the years.

"My supervisor's sister found this woman quite helpful," Staze told me as she handed me the phone number.

"Is your supervisor's sister extremely fat?" I asked. Non-dieting is definitely the best way to go, but when you're starting from where I was, it can be terrifying. I don't know anybody on this path who wasn't initially worried that, as soon as they stopped counting calories, they'd wind up weighing a minimum of four hundred pounds.

"Natalie, she's normal," Staze assured me. "Just give it a shot."

Of course, Jeanette turned out to be amazing and wonderful: whip-smart, earnest, helpful, *lesbian*. And I dutifully read all the books she recommended, and wrote all the journal entries, and cried all the tears. After a little while, I got a decent raise at my café job, and M&S started paying me a little bit for weekend and evening events. Soon, I managed to get all my credit cards paid off, and I treated myself to a full set of pots and pans and started teaching myself to cook.

Slinging coffee and helping Melanie and Stephanie and getting head-shrunk kept me pretty busy, but I still managed to find the time for a little nookie here and there. After a couple of years at the coffeehouse, I'd (at a minimum) kissed all the eligible-to-Natalie employees, meaning none of the gay guys and only a couple of the straight girls. Having exhausted my prospects among my coworkers, I started flirting more flagrantly with customers. One regular came in each day in a crisp button-down shirt and ordered a nonfat latte. Her blonde hair fell past her chin and tickled at the tops of her starched collars. She was Jodie Foster in Brooks Brothers, and I had fun embarrassing her with my winks and innuendo.

"Large nonfat latte?" she said, every time, as if we didn't recognize her.

"A nonfat latte for the beautiful lady!" I would yell at the barista, and the regular would scoff and avert her eyes and grin at the ground.

Time flew by those first years in Boston. When M&S finally hired me, I felt a little sad about leaving my café job. I'd wanted to burn the Union Square bookstore to the ground, but the coffeehouse in Cambridge had a lot going for it: cool coworkers, respectful and generous customers, perfect cappuccinos.

On my last day, the blonde in the button-down came in for her latte, and I gave it to her for free.

"It's on me," I said.

"Oh. Thank you," she replied, a bit taken aback.

"No problem," I said with a smile. "I'm not going to be working here anymore, so I just wanted to say thanks for being awesome."

"Oh, you're leaving?" she asked. "That's a shame."

"Well, actually, I just got a really cool job, so I'm pretty happy about it."

She didn't say anything for a moment, then forced a strained smile. "Well. Congratulations," she declared with a nod, and she scuttled out the door.

Forty minutes later, much to my surprise, the blonde in the button-down came back. She marched up to the counter, handed me her empty paper cup, and bolted back out onto the street. I examined her odd gift and found some fascinating information scribbled on the side: her number. And a little note:

I.O.U. 1 drink. —Alex

Alex turned out to be Dr. Alexandra Hamilton, and yes, she was named for the would-be King of America. I called her the day after her bold move.

"Hi, I'm calling for Alex?" I pronounced into the phone.

"Speaking," she said. She cleared her throat. "This is Alex."

I know, you just told me, is what I didn't say.

"Oh, hi!" I said with as much warmth as I could muster. My heart was racing. "This is the girl who gave you a free latte the other day. My name is Natalie, and—"

"I know, Natalie," she said, lowering her voice. "I mean, I know your name."

"Oh, OK. Wonderful!" I've never really dated. These conversations are supposed to be awkward, right?

"So," said Alex. "Um. Let's meet for a cocktail."

I agreed, and we scheduled a time at a place near Copley Plaza. I spend a surprisingly small percentage of my social time on that side of the river, but I thought, *What the hell? This is dating, right?*

"This is not a date," Alex blurted as she mounted the stool next to me at the appointed place and time.

I sat there at the big brown bar with the chrome fixtures in my skirt and blouse feeling a little foolish. The bartender came over, and we each ordered different glasses of red wine. I struggled for something to say.

"Well. This place is certainly lovely," I said, not knowing what else to talk about.

"It's not a date," she said again. She picked up her pinot noir and took a sip, then a swig. "At least, I don't think it's a date."

"Well, if you don't want it to be a date, then let's call it not a date," I replied, deciding to relax and go with the flow. I raised my glass. "To friendship!"

"Friends," she said, clinking her glass against mine and taking another generous gulp.

"So. I left the café because I just got a new job at a fashion production company," I said.

"Oh. That's nice," she said. "I'm a doctor."

"Wow, really?" I asked. "What kind of doctor?"

"Well. I trained as a surgeon. That's what I did for my residency. But I've worked almost entirely at clinics in the developing world."

"Which countries do you work in?"

"Haiti, most recently," she began.

"No way! Do you work for Partners in Medicine?" I asked.

Alex looked surprised. "Yeah I do, actually. How did you know that?"

"It's the first organization I ever donated to," I explained. "Paul Keller came to speak at my college. He's, like, the most inspiring person I've ever seen."

She raised her eyebrows and laughed. "Yeah, Paul's incredible. He's a good friend of mine."

"Oh my God, really?" I gushed. "It's so amazing what your organization does, especially in Rwanda," I said, raising my dark Malbec to my lips.

"Gosh," Alex replied. "And you said you work in fashion?"

We laughed, and I hoped I was simultaneously challenging her misconceptions about both fashion professionals and girl-kissers. I asked about mosquito nets and their effectiveness and listened carefully as she explained the difference between mortality and morbidity. She ordered a second round and followed that up with another for herself.

"So," Alex said, tucking into her third glass of wine. "You're a lesbian."

"Not exactly," I explained, swirling the bourbon I'd asked for after my first drink. "I'm what is known as a 'bisexual.'"

"Oh. Really?" She seemed skeptical and edgy, but then she seemed skeptical and edgy about lesbianism as well, so I reasoned that she was generally nervous and judgmental about the entire situation.

"Yeah," I said. "But I've had plenty of experiences with women."

"You've dated women before?" she asked.

"Actually, I haven't really dated anyone before," I replied.

Alex sighed and picked up her glass. "Me neither," she said. "I'm thirty-six years old, and I've never had a relationship." She sat there, stressed out and rigid, and I hoped with all my heart that Heather Boyle had managed to come out in college.

"No?" I prompted, expecting to hear a tale of woe.

"I mean, I've slept with guys," Alex informed me. "Plenty of guys. In college. And med school." Her eyes danced.

"Oh really," I said, taking a sip of my bourbon.

"And residency. Forget it. Surgical residency? It was horny alpha-male central," she deadpanned, and I laughed at her naughtiness.

"Well. Congratulations to you, I suppose." I raised my glass.

"Can I get you another one of those?" she asked. She had loosened up considerably.

"No, I'm alright," I said, waving off the bartender. "I should probably get going anyway. I've got big plans for the evening."

"Oh?" she asked, surprised. "Where are you headed?"

"Well, I was thinking I'd take you back to your place," I replied in a low voice. "I figured we could get some important work done."

The next thing I knew, the bill was paid, and we were back in Alex's apartment building near South Station, anxiously riding the elevator. We arrived at her floor, and I followed her into her apartment and through to the bedroom. She sat me down on her bed, and I waited there obediently as she walked away. I didn't quite know what to do with myself. She dashed into the bathroom, brushed her teeth, came back, adjusted the lighting, and put on some music.

The next thing I knew, she was standing in the middle of the room looking at me. Then the music started, and she dropped her hips down to the ground, stood back up and undid the top button on her shirt.

Is this a fucking striptease? I wondered to myself.

When she put her hands behind her neck and lifted her highlighted hair with both hands, I had my answer.

The truth is, the trappings of scripted female sexuality don't really do anything for me. The truth is, they do nothing for me. Less than nothing. They turn me off. Alex undid her crisp pink button-down to reveal a black lacy (and certainly very expensive) bra covering her evenly tanned breasts. I was more excited by her visible pectoral muscles and the contours of her neck, by the physical strength that complimented her softness.

I fought the urge to avert my eyes as she painstakingly unbuttoned her shirt and tossed it across the room. If there'd been a hint of playful irony in any of this, I might've been able to stomach it. Alas, Alex was dead serious about the whole thing. Finally, I stood up and reached my hand around her waist and started dancing with her.

"What are you doing?" she demanded. The music should've record-scratched and stopped right then, but the MP3 of Sade played on.

"I'm sorry, am I not supposed to touch the talent?" I asked. She looked at me like I'd flipped on the lights to reveal an audience of her friends and family. "Kidding! I'm kidding. Stripteases just aren't really my thing."

"Oh! Well, uh," she stammered. "That's OK. Let's just start here," and she gestured to the bed.

We transitioned, somewhat awkwardly, to a horizontal position, and the situation started to improve. Her iPod sex mix definitely revealed some cracks in her heterosexual façade. I imagined all the smart male doctors she'd brought home before me cocking their heads *en flagrante* and puzzling over the soundtrack. Or perhaps she'd made a new playlist especially for tonight.

Our making out got hot and heavy, and she was already shirtless, so I moved my mouth down and started kissing her stomach. Her tan skin covered muscles so toned and taut that it felt like she'd just swallowed a bucket of rocks. Teasingly, I unbuttoned her pants and felt her heart rate speed up. But when I ran my tongue along the top of her (black lacy expensive) panty line, that's when it started.

"Oh! Oh! Oh! Oh! Oh!" she cried, panting.

I stopped cold. "What's wrong?" I asked.

"What?" she replied, raising her head off the pillow to look down at me. "Nothing. Nothing's wrong."

I resumed my previous activity, and after a few seconds, she started again. "Oh! Oh! Oh! Oh! Oh!"

"Alex, what are you doing?" I demanded.

"What? It feels good," she said.

"It does not feel that good," I argued.

She sat up. "I'm sorry. I feel like everything I do is wrong. Maybe this girls thing just isn't right for me, Natalie."

"First of all, Doctor," I began. "'Everything' you do is not wrong. You've done, like, two things."

She smiled. "Fair enough."

"And I guess, I don't know," I began. I wasn't quite sure how to phrase it. "Some of the stuff you're doing feels like it's for show rather than what feels good or comes naturally."

"Like I'm performing sexuality," she filled in.

"Well, yeah, if you want to get all post-structuralist feminist theory about it," I teased.

"I did go to Smith, you know," she said.

"You went to *Smith*?" I asked, incredulous. "And you never did it with a girl?"

She shook her head. "I was too busy trying to get into Harvard Medical School, which, mission accomplished," she said with a self-effacing smirk.

"I admire your sacrifice," I joked, but I think she took me seriously. I realized I was really going to have to watch it with this one.

"So," she said with a sigh. "Is this ruined?"

"Well, tomorrow's Saturday, but I know doctors don't follow the normal days of the week."

She smiled. "I'm off tomorrow. I work a standard week when I'm in the US. It's mostly putting together a plan for my next international rotation, plus some development stuff."

"I'd love to hear more about what you do," I said.

And so we curled up on her bed and talked until we were both yawning and closing our eyes. I slipped off my skirt and blouse and she pulled off her pants, and we slept beside each other without touching.

In the morning, I woke to find her sleeping soundly next to me. I slid up next to her and started kissing her neck. Her eyes fluttered open.

"Good morning," I said, and I leaned in to kiss her.

"Mm!" she cried, jerking her head away. "No! I haven't brushed my teeth!"

"Alright, alright," I relented, and instead I worked my mouth down the length of her body, kissing and licking and nibbling. She let me slip off her bra, then her panties. She remained completely silent until I finally moved my mouth down between her legs, at which point her breathing got a little heavier. When she came, she grabbed the bed frame and pulled hard, and I felt her body contract around my hand.

I crawled back up next to her and put my head down on her spare pillow. She was staring at the ceiling, her eyes wide and alive. She turned to look at me.

"Can we do this again sometime?"

Out

THIS HAS DEFINITELY BEEN the craziest week of my entire life. I got back from my parents' place late Sunday night and headed directly to Staze's.

"Well?" I inquired as she opened her apartment door.

She took a couple of steps back, spread her arms, and did a little twirl. "Do I look different?"

I laughed and hugged her. "So everything worked out OK?"

She nodded. "It was perfect."

I know the proud smile that erupted on my face was probably borderline creepy. But I couldn't help it. It seemed like we'd been waiting for this for so long and now it had finally come to pass. And everything went well! I could hardly believe it.

"I think I'm in shock," I said, floating through her dining area and collapsing onto her couch.

"I know. It's surreal," she agreed. "And by the way, thanks for the painkillers. They came in quite handy the morning after."

"*OH MY GOD YOU HAD SEX!*" I screamed.

Staze giggled. "Natalie! I have neighbors!"

"Sorry," I laughed. "But it really happened! You really, actually had sex!"

"Indeed," she replied. "For the first and what's certain to be the last time."

"Oh, come on," I argued.

She shook her head. "He's going to break up with me, Natalie. I'm sure of it. As soon as he finds out all the things I haven't told him, he's going to be crushed. Who wouldn't be?"

"Staze, I think he might surprise you. Once he realizes everything you've been through, there's a good chance he might understand what motivated your secrecy."

"Natalie," she said. "He is the president of my fan club."

"He is the *convener* of the *discussion group*," I corrected.

We debriefed some more on the weekend, and then we talked about December the First, which was coming up in just a couple of days.

"And you're sure you want to go through with this?" I asked.

She nodded. "I've got to, Nat," she said. "I can't keep lying to Jeremiah."

"Maybe you could just tell *him*, and ask him not to tell anybody..." I suggested.

She shook her head. "President. Fan club."

"Point taken," I agreed.

"Besides, Natalie, I thought you wanted me to do this," she said.

"Well, I do and I don't," I answered. "I want you to be unburdened and free and, yes, as celebrated as you deserve to be. But I don't want you to be stressed out and miserable, and I don't want you to have to give up your blog."

Staze shrugged. "I think *Broken Hope Chest* has run its course. I get to write two final posts, and they'll be the ones my readers have been waiting for ever since I started the thing twelve years ago," she said.

"God. We were in college," I said. "You were the only one who knew what a blog was."

"It was called an online journal back then. I transitioned to blogware when the free platforms became ubiquitous." She batted the air with her hand. "Anyway, none of that's important right now. I have no idea what I'm going to say to Jeremiah."

A couple of days later, I packed a bag and showed up to spend the night of December the First with Anastaze. We stayed up late talking and laughing and crying and remembering all the insanity her parents have put her through over the years. She asked me to review the post, and I gave my approval, but it would be several more hours before she could finally muster the courage.

"Can I really do this, Natalie? Can I?" she asked. We were half-delirious with exhaustion as the sun peeked over the horizon.

"Staze," I said to her. "It is now most definitely December the Second."

At that, she turned to her computer, hit *publish*, and collapsed into hysterical sobs. I held her as I watched as the words appeared on her homepage: *posted December 2 at 4:37am.*

And the phone started ringing at five.

Here's what the whole world now knows: Staze's full name is Anastasia Mill Kaplan. Her father is Leo Kaplan, who won the Nobel Prize in Literature. Her mother is Margot Coombe Mill, the famous English sculptor who is perhaps much more famous for the brutal public spurning she received from her husband, Nobel Laureate Leo Kaplan, in the decade after he received the Prize.

Staze's father got the call from the Nobel committee a few years after the Berlin Wall fell. She was around ten years old. At the time, she and her parents lived a television-free and occasionally cosmopolitan life in England. Her father wrote dense novels and lectured on literature at Cambridge, and Staze's mother was actually far more famous than he was. The Coombes are an old family. When Staze's grandmother married the heir to the Mills retail fortune, the result was that great dyad of English society: money plus a name.

After the fall of communism, the world took a renewed interest in the Eastern European diaspora, and Staze's father and his body of work fit the bill. He brought his wife and daughter along to tour Warsaw, Krakow, and Prague. Leo was welcomed as a native son and a hero, and for a while the whole family traveled back and forth between Eastern Europe and what I prefer to call "that *other* Cambridge." Their new lives in the wake of his sudden notoriety initially seemed so exciting and full of promise. But before long, cracks started to appear.

Following the tense situation at Staze's bat mitzvah, she was shipped off to boarding school, allegedly in the interest of keeping her out of the public eye. After that, her father started jet-setting around Europe all on his own, turning up in gossip magazines and tabloids in a dozen different languages, always surrounded by young women. He refused to confirm or deny rumors of his public and flagrant philandering, and Staze's mom began her long, slow fall off the deep end.

Margot started to drink heavily and self-injure. She was admitted to psychiatric hospitals on several occasions. Still, Staze's parents remained married, and the tabloids lurked around every corner.

Not long after Margot's four-part series on her sex life with Leo and the impact of his many transgressions appeared in the *Manhattan Review of Books*, a tabloid reporter and a very young-looking photographer posed as a prospective student and her guardian in order to gain access to Staze's boarding school and snap pictures of her. The reporter apparently marched right up to Staze in the dining hall and jammed a tape recorder in her face, asking awful questions. "Have you seen your father with young women? Does he ever make passes at your schoolmates?" After that, Staze's whole campus was put on lockdown, but the damage to her sense of safety had already been done.

During Staze's last year at boarding school, her father accepted a guest appointment at Harvard, and her mother was supposed to come along. Hoping the family might make a fresh start in America, Staze decided to matriculate at Easton. However, not long after Staze mailed in her acceptance, her father served her mother with divorce papers.

Then things got really bad.

Staze tried to maintain contact with both her parents, but her father was unreliable and sporadic with letters and calls. Sometimes she wouldn't hear from him for months at a time. Meanwhile, her mother had retreated to a remote part of England to recover from the very public dissolution of her marriage. Staze would see her occasionally when she went back during school vacations, but for the most part, both her parents had dropped out of her life before she turned twenty-one.

Staze invited me to come to England with her during Christmas break of our senior year, and I agreed. I had never been to Europe, and I was excited to travel around a little and see the sites. When we arrived, however, Staze's mother looked half-dead. Apparently, she'd been diagnosed with breast cancer and had started chemotherapy a couple of months before. She didn't tell Staze, but she had written several letters to her ex-husband, begging him to take her back and care for her in what she was sure would be the final phase of her life.

Instead, he hadn't called either of them in months. Staze's mom really did almost die. Apparently one particularly vile tabloid even did a spread of the once-famous, now fallen artist and beauty sitting in a Barcalounger getting chemo pumped into her veins. It's the most atrocious shit imaginable. And all the while, Staze's father didn't breathe a word to either of them.

Staze dutifully called her father and asked him to speak at our commencement when the president of Easton asked her to do so, and that was the only time she saw him that year. Or the year after that.

I worried she'd move back to England after graduation, but she was going through a big Tom Robbins phase at the time (he's one of few writers Staze and I actually agree on), and she assured me she was destined for the Pacific Northwest. However, she didn't want to indenture herself to either her father or her mother, so she had to find a way to earn money at a place that would be willing to hire a foreign worker. Given the tight job market at the time, she had to take work wherever she could find it, and most of her connections were on the East Coast. She heard about a graphic and web design firm in Boston through some of her computer geek friends on campus, and the company was willing to sponsor her visa, so that's where she went.

Margot recovered from breast cancer and found religion and became a vegan and a yoga fanatic and fled to India to hide from the media. Leo continues to be famous and brilliant and churn out thick tomes full of complicated imagery and epic run-on sentences. He's in his eighties now, and he's still running around with much younger women. And he never calls his daughter, even though she lives ten minutes away from his office.

Now you know my name, Staze wrote in her final post. (She had written an ethereal, dreamlike meditation on her night with Jeremiah and posted it a couple of hours before.) *You are free to research my parents if such things interest you. I won't bore my faithful readership with my own jejune version of the details. I believe that what you now know or may come to know about my history will provide some explanation for my reluctance to reveal*

*my identity over these years. I'm confident that this secrecy will
be understood and forgiven, just as I've come to forgive those who
engaged in hurtful speculation with regard to my identity.*

*However, there is one person reading this who I know will be
wounded by this revelation, and I hope with all my heart that he
can appreciate what a tremendous catalyst for change and liberation
he's been in my life, and how very grateful I will always be to him for
everything he's given me, and how terribly sorry I am for any pain I
may have caused him.*

I've learned a lot in the past week. For example, when the *New
York Times* calls you, the number displays as all 1s on your phone.
111-111-1111. That means it's the *New York Times*.

And I've learned that Sam Elliot Jacobs is actually a fabulously
nice person! After Anastaze's landline and her cell phone and her
work phone and her blog email and her personal email were all
inundated with calls and messages, we put out a little press release
directing inquiries to me, and she shut off her phone and went on
leave from work and moved into my place, all within the first few
days of December. After the press release went out, I received a
very warm phone call from *the* Sam Elliot Jacobs. He introduced
himself and explained who he was to me with charming and
genuine humility, and we wound up having a terrific conversation.
We both gushed about Anastaze and what an awe-inspiring and
brave and fiercely talented person she is. I told him I'd do my best to
convince her to give him a call back, and he thanked me profusely.

"'*Profusely?*'" she said, perking up from her state of
overwhelmed anxiety. Staze does not take kindly to the media
hounding her, for obvious reasons.

"Anastaze, he *pleaded* with me to tell you that he called," I said.

"'*Pleaded?*'" she repeated, her eyes widening.

And so she returned that particular phone call, and she did the
only other job she really had to do, which was to go see Jeremiah.

I handled everybody else, and I started compiling a dossier of the articles written about her, online and in print. I think my favorite quote actually comes from the *New York Times* article. The writer reached out to her father for comment. Apparently, this is what he said:

"Anastasia? A website? *Why*?"

§

ALEX AND I SOON found ourselves spending the night together two or three times a week, and the sex had become quite excellent. She was increasingly uninhibited and adventurous, and she just seemed much more relaxed in general. Of course, we were both stupid busy, so I would usually show up at her place pretty late at night. Weekend days gave us a bit more time to hang out.

"I'm starting to get soft," she commented one Sunday morning, standing in front of the mirror and banging on her still rock-hard stomach. "I need to get back with my trainer."

"You're nuts," I said. "You look amazing."

"Do you work out at all?" she asked.

"Uh, I like yoga," I replied, flipping through one of her magazines.

"Yoga's not really exercise," she said. "I mean, some styles are pretty intense, but in an hour-long yoga class, you waste a lot of time."

"Well, I enjoy the slow pace," I said. I'd been working with Jeanette for a while, but I still wasn't quite prepared for where this conversation was going.

"Have you ever considered intense cardio, like running, or maybe some resistance training?" she asked, shoving sneakers into a small black duffle bag. "If you found the right program, the inches would fall right off."

"Alex, I don't really feel comfortable talking about this," I said. "I've had some serious food issues in the past, and I'm only just starting to get better."

"Oh yeah?" she asked, almost in a clinical way. "Was it anorexia? Bulimia? What's your diagnosis?"

"Uh, well, most recently, I fainted in a fabric store while attempting the lemon juice cleanse."

"Hm. Yeah, some of those fasts can be a bit tricky," she informed me. "You need at least five hundred calories a day, even when you're restricting."

I really didn't want to hear any more of her pro-extreme-diet medical opinions, so I tried to change the subject. "Hey, do you want to meet up and see a movie after your workout?" I suggested.

"Oh, no. I have all these movies here that I need to watch and mail back," she said, referring to the red envelopes filled with DVDs all over her coffee table.

The situation had its less-than-perfect elements. But there were many good things about Alex too. She always called me back, always showed up when she said she'd be some place, and I knew for certain that she wasn't seeing me on the side. I left clothes in her apartment and a toothbrush in her bathroom.

"I want to meet your new girlfriend," Staze would nag. "If you must be so frequently indisposed, I at least want to know who this person is that you're spending all your time with."

"She's not my girlfriend," I'd reply. "And we don't really go out too much. We just hang out at her place and have sex and watch Netflix."

"Ergo she's *not* your girlfriend?" Staze teased.

I remember one time when I actually did convince Alex to go out with me. The World Cup was happening, and I'd discovered a bar in Cambridge where people from all over the world convened to watch the matches on television.

"It's incredible, Alex," I explained. "I caught the tail-end of the Italy versus Argentina game, and suddenly all these people with rising sun headbands starting pouring into the place. And then a big group of guys comes in brandishing a giant inflatable kangaroo, and it turned out the next game was Japan versus Australia."

"Ghana is playing this afternoon," she said. "I'd love to catch that game. I spent a year there once. Best people in the world."

Later that day, we shoved into the crowded bar, with its wooden floorboards and tables that smelled like they'd been deliberately cured with beer. Alex managed to wrangle us up a couple of drafts, and we stood against a tall table with a bunch of other fans.

"No!" Alex cried as England scored a goal.

"You're for Ghana, then," the blue-eyed man standing next to us asked in his English accent. His buddies were still busy cheering.

"Well, she used to live there," I replied. "I'm trying to remain neutral. My best friend is English, and she might kill me if she found out I rooted against them."

"Tough call for you," he said with a wink, returning his attention to the game.

Alex looked uncomfortable. She leaned in close to me and whispered something inaudible.

"What?" I asked, unable to make her out in the din.

"That guy, Natalie," she said, gesturing toward the bloke on my left. "Do you think he knows?"

"That you're not actually Ghanaian? Yes," I teased.

"Ha. No, I mean, do you think he can tell, you know…" and she gestured at the two of us with her hand.

"You mean that we're *doing it*?" I stage-whispered.

"Shh! Keep your voice down, Natalie!" she demanded, looking side to side like a silly cartoon villain.

"Alex, I don't think anyone has any idea," I told her. "And I don't think they care."

Still, whenever the celebrating crowd would press me in her direction, she would always move away. By the end of the match we'd circled halfway around the table.

"Well that was fun. Shall we?" she said as she started toward the door.

I sighed. "Sure, let's go."

Not long after that, I started condo hunting. My realtor, Dagney, was a total riot and also just about the most helpful person I'd ever met.

"She's done amazing legwork," I told Alex in her bed one night. "She really listened to everything I wanted."

"I wish I could hire somebody like that to help me pick out a dress," she said absently.

I stared at her. "Are you kidding?"

"No," she sighed. "We've got our big black tie gala fundraiser event coming up, and I never have any idea what to wear to these things."

I sat up. "First of all, there *is* a person you can hire to help you find a dress. We call such a person a *stylist*. And secondly, that is *my* job. I am a *stylist*."

Alex's mouth fell open. "Oh my God, Natalie. I'm an idiot. Jesus, I'm so stupid sometimes."

"It's fine," I say. "You're not the first person I think to ask when I find a weird mole."

"Well, if you ever wind up with guinea worm, feel free to give me a call," she said, and I laughed. She'd really loosened up a lot. It helped mitigate the impact of such non-events as our World Cup viewing.

"So, shall we make a shopping plan?"

I called Claudia, and she was kind enough to reserve us a private room at Bloomingdale's. I showed up a little while before Alex was scheduled to arrive and grabbed half a dozen potential gowns for her. I'd done some research on the event ahead of time, and it looked like she would receive an award on stage and perhaps give short speech. She needed something distinctive but understated.

I met her among the makeup counters and led her back to the private dressing room. "I pulled a few looks. It's important that you feel totally comfortable, so just let me know if you need a different size."

Alex nodded and started trying on dresses. "Wow," she said, looking at herself in a midnight blue gown with silver threading on the left shoulder and on the right side of the skirt. "This definitely beats my tired old black frock."

I smiled. "You look beautiful."

"Thanks," she said, and I helped her get the first gown off so she could try on a few more.

After she cycled through four or five, I crossed my arms. "Let's take a look at the first one again." She slipped back into the midnight blue. "Yeah. I think we have a winner," I said.

"I think so too," she said, glowing.

"Before you get undressed, do you need shoes?" I pulled the top hook closed above her zipper.

"Oh, probably," she said. "Right? Whatever you think." She could hardly take her eyes off herself in the mirror, except to glance over at me with warm gratitude. I decided to take a risk.

"Do you need a date?" I asked, adjusting the seams on her shoulders.

"No, my friend Peter always comes along with me to these things," she replied. It took her a moment to realize what I'd meant. "Oh, you mean… No, Natalie, no, I can't, I'm sorry," she stammered. "I'm not… This is a work thing. You know?"

I nodded. "Sure."

"But actually, if you wanted to come," she began. "I was talking to our event coordinator, and she said she could use some help getting the materials and decorations in order. I was thinking we could hire you."

"Oh, no," I said, waving my hand. "I'd be happy to volunteer."

"No, we have a budget," she urged. "I know you're really great at your job, and I want to make sure you get compensated." I could tell she felt bad about never really acknowledging my work before, and the fact that I'd just pointed out how she wasn't really acknowledging me in other ways probably made her feel even worse.

"Please, Alex," I insisted. "I want to support the organization and all the good work that you guys do. Let me donate my time."

In the weeks that followed, I contacted the events team over at Partners in Medicine and spent a number of hours coordinating with them on the gala. I toured the event space and made some lighting decisions, ordered flower arrangements for the stage, and decided on a look for the round tables, banquet tables, and printed materials. It was a lot of work, and it meant that decorating my brand new apartment had to be put on the back burner. I'd barely even unpacked. Still, owning my place made me so happy. Alex worked nearby in Cambridge, so we'd taken to spending nights in my bed rather than hers.

The night of the gala, I had to rush over from another event, so I made sure Alex knew how her dress was supposed to fall and told her I'd see her there. I arrived in the event hall thirty minutes before it was time to open the doors, and I scrambled around rechecking all the decorations and the lighting. I perched myself behind the registration table and watched as the well-appointed guests descended on the space.

Everything worked out splendidly. Long-time Partners in Medicine supporters seemed enchanted by the extra attention to detail at the event. "Oh, how lovely!" guests would exclaim as I handed them their place cards. Using a few tricks and connections, I'd even kept the price tag down to a few hundred dollars under budget. *More money for mosquito nets*, I thought.

Alex, being one of the guests of honor, didn't come over to registration. She worked the crowd, visiting each table during the hour before the various speeches began. It was impossible not to notice her. She looked spectacular, and I found my eyes coming to rest on her for most of the night. *Shit*, I thought. *I think I'm in love with her.*

Toward the end of the evening, I saw Alex and a gentleman heading straight for me. At first, I thought he must be her beard, but then I realized I recognized his face.

"Are you the person responsible for all this?" he asked with a kind smile. I stood up to meet him.

"Natalie, this is Paul Keller, our founder," Alex said. "Paul, this is Natalie, my…" Her face fell as she realized he had no idea how she planned to introduce me.

"Friend!" I said.

"Dog-walker!" she blurted simultaneously, utterly inexplicably, and Dr. Keller and I both turned to look at her.

He let out a warm laugh. "Well, whoever you are, I cannot thank you enough. What a beautiful job you've done with this event! And I understand you volunteered your time to do it, too." He offered me his hand, and I shook it.

"It was my pleasure, Dr. Keller," I said. "I so admire the work you do."

"Please, call me Paul," he replied. "You've really helped us out. Our big donors have been very vocal about how much they've enjoyed all the extra little touches this year."

"I'm so happy to hear it," I said, looking at Alex, who did not look back at me. And with that, they walked away.

I didn't see her again for the rest of the night, and I realized I really didn't want to. After all the guests had gone, I grabbed a flower arrangement, headed down to the street, and hailed a cab back to my very own apartment.

An hour later, my buzzer rang. I was plodding around in my yoga pants drinking tea. I really hadn't expected to hear from Alex for at least a couple of days. Reluctantly, I buzzed her up.

"I'm sorry, Dr. Hamilton, I'm not available to walk your dog right now," I snarled the moment she walked through my door.

"Natalie, I'm so sorry," she said, stepping out of her shoes. She still looked stunning in her gown, but with her three-inch heels off she stood a lot more like her usual self.

"It's one thing to pretend we're not fucking," I said. "It's another thing to act like we barely know each other." I didn't realize how hurt and angry I was until I started laying into her.

"Natalie, he's my boss! And my friend!" she cried. "What can I say? I panicked."

"I think Paul Keller can imagine that you have a friend or two he doesn't know about, Alex," I argued.

"Actually, we're quite close," she said. "And he knows my parents, Natalie. In that instant, I just pictured him calling them, and—"

"And saying what?" I conjured a phony voice and held a fake phone to my ear. "'Gee, Dr. Hamilton, I noticed your daughter Alex seemed awfully chummy with that woman who styled our event. Perhaps they're lesbians together.'"

"I don't know, maybe!" she said.

"Please," I replied.

"I freaked out. I'm sorry. And you don't know my parents," she argued. "They can never know about anything like this. They'd be devastated."

"Aren't your parents Massachusetts liberals?" I asked. "I think they probably know a gay person or two."

"My parents are a retired couple in Orleans," Alex declared.

"Orleans is five minutes from fucking Provincetown!" I cried. "What is wrong with you?"

"You don't know the people I know," she said. "You don't know how they'd react. Do you know that being gay is a crime in some of the countries where I've worked? That you can go to jail? Or get lynched?"

"This is Cambridge, not Kingston, Alex," I argued. "Nobody here cares if you're a dyke."

"What did you just call me?" she growled.

"'*Dyke*,' Alex. *Dyke*. It's a word that people use for people like you and me, only lately we've co-opted it, and now we use it for ourselves, and each other, and at our bars, and at our Pride Parades!"

"Oh, but you're not a dyke, Natalie," she said bitterly. "No, you're a *bisexual*, lucky you. You can just go be with a man anytime you want, isn't that right?"

"Except that I don't think there's anything *wrong* with being with a woman," I said. "Do you know what year it is? We could get fucking *married*, Alex!"

"Oh my God! You want to get married now?"

"I'm saying, *I'm* the out one here. My parents know who I am. All my friends and coworkers know who I am," I said. "*You're* the closet case."

"So, what, I'm supposed to make a big-to-do about coming out of the closet? Another lesbian Smith alum? Another lesbian working in international development? You want me to give everybody the satisfaction that they've been right about me all along?"

"Why the fuck do you care?" I hollered. "So some surgeon you hooked up with says 'I knew it' to his wife, so what?"

Alex looked like she might explode with rage. She clenched her fists and flared her nostrils. "Well, maybe it's not about me, Natalie. Maybe I just don't want my very first girlfriend to be somebody so *overweight*!"

And in that moment, my heart gave up. I'd heard it and felt it and seen the writing on the wall too many times. I thought of my mom scrutinizing my portions at every family dinner, of Tyler going off with Gretchen, of Ben and Amber running marathons and posing for wedding pictures, and I just gave up. I couldn't do that anymore.

"Go," I told her. "Just go."

And I wish I'd left it there, with my resignation and surrender and refusal to defend what has always been and will always be my appearance, my shape, my figure.

Instead, I marched over to my closet and pulled out the handful of dry-cleaning bags she'd taken to leaving in my apartment. I looked into her eyes, and just as she was about to speak, undoubtedly to apologize for her cruelty, I thrust the wire hangers into her hand.

"And if you really don't want people thinking you're a lesbian, then maybe you should stop dressing like one."

We glared at each other for a few more seconds. Then, she picked up her shoes and walked out of my life.

I haven't heard from her since.

§

THANK GOD FOR HOLIDAY parties.

Almost every suite in our building participated this year. One of the artists cleared a huge space in his studio and set up his DJ equipment. I bribed Sean, the chocolatier, with his own stash of bourbon, and he baked all damn day: hand-tossed pizzas topped with thyme and linguiça, beet and goat cheese tarts, roasted butternut squash empanadas, and more cookies and cupcakes and pies than we could fit on our tables.

Melanie and Stephanie gave me a huge budget, so I invited pretty much every person I've ever met.

Gwendolyn arrived with her entourage just as the party started to pick up.

"Gwendolyn!" I said, giving her a big hug. "I haven't seen you in a billion years."

"Try three weeks," she replied. "And I believe you were wearing the exact same outfit you've got on right now."

"Guilty," I said, giving a twirl in my teal and silver Phoebe Hipp dress. "I love it. I'm so glad I wound up wearing it in the end that day."

"I'm pretty sure you weren't wearing anything in the end that day," she replied with a wink. The woman loves to wink. "What happened with Deena and her boyfriend?"

"I never told you?" I said. "We had a fun time."

"Spare no detail," she begged.

"Gwendolyn, I'm hosting this thing!" I argued, walking away from her and over to the "bar," which was just a table covered with handles of alcohol and a hefty tower of Solo cups. "Everyone help yourselves!" I announced.

What a difference three weeks makes.

I milled around the warehouse, checking on the various sub-parties. Then I ducked into the darkened chocolate suite and grabbed a cookie off a tray of treats reserved for later.

"Hold it right there!" came a voice from the darkness. Sean stepped out into the dim hall light and took a swig directly from his bottle of bourbon. "I caught you red-handed."

"Ha," I laughed, my mouth full of cookie. "I can't fight the crowds at the food table in our office anymore."

"Fair enough," Sean shrugged. "Hooch?" he offered, and I took a hefty swig. "There's our girl," he praised, his blue eyes twinkling in the light from the hallway.

"Your food is amazing," I gushed. "Not just the desserts, all of it. Where did you learn to cook like this?"

"Do you want the real answer or the official answer?" he asked.

"Both?" I replied, raising my eyebrows.

"Officially, Johnson and Wales," he told me. Then he broke into a bashful smile. "Truthfully, my grandma. My mom's mom, on the Portuguese side."

"Aww, that's adorable," I teased. "I can picture it now: little Seany in the kitchen with his apron and his rolling pin."

"It's true!" he insisted with a chuckle. "My brothers would all be out playing baseball, meanwhile I'm inside with a bubbling pot of fish stock." He shook his head. "My dad was never too happy about it."

"Pretty brave to stick to your guns," I said.

"Well." His eyes met mine, and he winked. "I know what I like."

It nearly knocked the wind out of me.

"Wow. Uh. I need to keep moving," I said, pulling myself together. "Playing the hostess. You know how it is."

He nodded. "I expect to see you out on the dance floor later."

"No promises!" I called as my heels clicked against the concrete floor of the hall. I scurried back to the M&S suite, no longer quite sure of what to make of that candy man.

When I turned the corner into our office, I saw Melanie and Stephanie stepping up to stand on their desks. Their husbands were giving them a boost. The four of them were in rare form. They'd sent their kids to sleepovers with grandparents and rented hotel rooms down in Boston for the night. Mel and Steph each took a shot of vodka as soon as I finished setting up the bar table. That's when I knew it was going to be a very fun night.

"Excuse us, everyone!" Stephanie said, attempting to raise her tiny voice.

"HEY!" hollered Melanie, and everyone startled and quieted down.

"We just want to take a moment to thank the woman who made this event happen," Stephanie began.

"As she makes *many* events happen!" Melanie interjected.

"And we want to thank her for everything she's done this year and wish her luck on her little side gigs as a model and fashion designer," Stephanie continued. I felt myself starting to blush.

"We're sure she won't be slumming around with us for too much longer," Melanie said.

"Oh, stop!" I shouted.

"*Any*way," Melanie continued. "We just wanted to say that we love her."

"And she'll always be welcome at our parties!" added Stephanie. "To Natalie!"

Everyone raised their red cups and cheered me, and I smiled and sipped my vanilla vodka.

"Thanks, you guys," I said, hugging Melanie and Stephanie as they dismounted the desk and all the other guests turned their attention back to Sean's ridiculous food.

"Oh, we forgot PR person in your list of new jobs!" Stephanie said, tipsy.

"Yeah, how's your friend doing?" Melanie asked.

"Anastaze? She's OK. I tried to get her to come out tonight, but she's still feeling a little afraid of the world," I explained.

"Poor thing," Stephanie said.

"Yeah, her dad sounds like a real dick," said Melanie.

"Well," I said. "He's got his issues."

I chatted with my bosses for a bit longer, and their spouses came along and chimed in. It was so fun to see them all loosened up and excited for their big night on the town.

"Hey," I said, finding Gwendolyn again about an hour after I'd left her. "Where's Jeff?"

"I don't know," she said. "We haven't been seeing as much of each other lately."

"Really?" I asked. "What happened?"

Gwendolyn shrugged. "Oh, it's just one of those things. I don't always call him back right away anymore, and it's the same on his end. I guess we've both been busy."

"If somebody stops calling me back, that automatically becomes the only thing I can think about," I confessed. "It's like the bullet train to obsess-town."

"Yeah, I used to be like that," she admitted. "Now, I just really like my life as it is. It's fun to have a guy like Jeff around, and maybe someday I'll have what they have." She pointed at Melanie and Stephanie and their husbands, who are all so clearly the very best of friends. "But I'm not interested in forcing it."

"I think you really are my hero," I said.

Gwendolyn laughed. "Thanks, Natalie. You're a pretty fantastic person yourself. He definitely seems to think so," she said, and she nodded over my shoulder. I turned around and caught Sean looking at me. He winked again, and this time, before I knew what I was doing, I winked right back.

"So," Gwendolyn teased. "How's that vow of celibacy going?"

A few hours later, I found myself pressed against the freezing brick of the back wall of our building with Sean's tongue in my mouth. His beard tickled my chin as he ran his hand around to the back of my neck and pulled my lips deeper into his. He slid his other hand under my emerald green winter coat and started pulling up my Phoebe Hipp dress. I laughed right into his mouth.

"What?" he asked

"I'm ticklish," I replied, willing my teeth not to chatter.

"Come home with me," he implored. "I called a cab."

"Can they send two cabs?" I replied. Even as I said the words, I could barely believe what I was refusing.

"But one would be so much warmer," he said, tucking his face under my hair to nibble on my neck.

"Sean," I said. "Sean, Sean, Sean."

"Yes, yes, yes?"

"I can't go home with you," I stated firmly, surprised once again by my own resolve.

"Yes you can," he replied. "You can, *and* you may!"

I giggled. "I want to, I just... I made this vow."

"Vow? Are you married?" he asked, pulling away.

"No! Married? No. No. Not married, never married," I sputtered. He relaxed a little but continued to study my face. "It's as simple as I can't go home with you. Not tonight." A green and white taxi pulled into the parking lot. "Another time, if, you know, if this comes up again, but tonight I—"

"Natalie," Sean said, interrupting me. "That's my cab. Let me drop you at your place."

"No, Sean, no, I'm sorry," I sputtered. "I can call my own taxi, for real, I—"

"Natalie," he interrupted. "It's cool. Get in the cab. It'll still be warmer this way." He pulled open the door, and I ducked in and slid across the backseat. We kissed and nibbled our way to my apartment door. It took every ounce of my vodka-weakened will to hug him goodnight and leave him in that cab. The taxi lingered until I was safely inside, when I heard it pull away.

And I spent the night alone, in my very own bed, contemplating the stillness of my alabaster ceiling fan.

February

"HAPPY VALENTINE'S DAY!" I cried as I pried open a Tupperware filled with strawberry balsamic mascarpone cupcakes.

She reached in and took a bite, and I realized I'd never actually seen Jeanette eat before. "Oh, Natalie!" she exclaimed. "These are delicious! Did you make them?"

"No, the guy I'm seeing did," I explained.

"You're seeing a guy?" she asked, delighted. "How's that going?"

"Good," I said. "Really good, actually. He says I'm a dream come true: a model who eats."

Jeanette laughed. "Does that mean you plan to continue with the modeling?"

"I'm not sure," I replied. "I think I'll take the gigs that fall in my lap, but right now I really want to spend the bulk of my spare time on design."

"Now, where can I find your designs for sale?" she asked.

I reached into my bag and produced a postcard-sized flyer for Phoebe Hipp's website. "Click on the Hope Chest Collection.

It's just a few items for now, but we should be expanding in the coming months."

"Hope Chest. That reminds me." Jeanette stood up and walked over to her desk, picked up a clipped newspaper article, and handed it to me. "Isn't this your friend?"

"Yes, indeed," I replied, reading the words *Anastasia Mill Kaplan* from the headline. "I'm impressed that you remembered."

"I saw it in the *Times*, and I exclaimed to my wife, 'I *knew* about this!'" she said. "Natalie, I had no idea that this weblog was such a huge thing."

"I don't think Staze did, either," I said. "But I had a hunch it was going to be big news."

"So how is she?" Jeanette asked. "I can't imagine how overwhelming this all must be for her."

"She's doing pretty well," I replied. "She agreed to one book deal already, an edited volume of entries from her blog. Her agent is pushing her to get to work on a memoir, but she's not too sure about that."

"And her father?" Jeanette asked.

I shook my head. "Nothing."

"Unbelievable," she said.

"Yeah, it's pretty terrible," I agreed. "And she and her boyfriend are having a rough time with it all, too. Right now they're taking a break, and he's on a fellowship in India for the spring anyway, at a monastery. The good news is they'll only be able to communicate through letters. I suspect that after a few months of handwritten exchanges, they'll wind up back together."

"Well, it sounds like *you're* doing remarkably well," Jeanette said. "Honestly, for me the biggest surprise is your mother."

"She's started to slip back," I said. "The other day she forwarded an email about how to avoid gaining something called 'relationship weight' when you're dating someone new."

"Yeah," Jeanette said. "Your mother's been a dieter for her entire life, and that means she might not ever really change, even after a scare like the one she went through."

I shrugged. "I just wish she could be happy with herself the way she is."

"Natalie," she replied. "What can I say? Some people just never quite get there."

I left Jeanette's office in the wintry cold and strolled down to the Charles River. My breath formed white clouds as the wind bit my cheeks. I thought about writing an email to Emily, and maybe one to Ben. That's the next goal for me, I think, is to tie up those loose ends, to apologize to both of them for the way things went and especially for how they ended.

I walked up onto the Weeks Footbridge and watched as a single insane sculler emerged from under the bridge and cut a sharp line through the barely unfrozen water, gripping her oars with gloved hands. I looked back at the path along the riverbank where I'd been sitting a couple of months before, on that unseasonably warm December day, when Alex had jogged by, just a few feet in front of me. It shocked me to see her again, and I was stunned by how surreal it felt to be so close to her. She didn't even turn her head. I'll probably never know if she chose to ignore me that afternoon, or if she simply couldn't recognize me in the light of day.

I started home toward my apartment and pulled out my phone to check in on Staze. I noticed a new text from Sean: *Grendel's?* I told him I'd be there, and I invited Staze to join us in the hopes that she might finally be ready to leave the house. I walked back along the river toward JFK Street, crossed Memorial Drive, and found my way to the familiar yellow awning over Grendel's Den. I spotted Sean in one of the big booths on the corner, surrounded by a lively group of tattooed beer drinkers.

"Natalie!" Sean called as I approached the table.

"Holy *shit*!" exclaimed the dude with the jet-black pompadour seated to Sean's right. "You mean we finally get to meet this Natalie you will not shut the hell up about?" His eyes danced as he offered me his hand.

"That's Matty," Sean said to me. "You can ignore him."

"Oh, I bet I can't," I replied. Matty pumped my hand vigorously and grinned.

Sean pointed around the table and rattled off more names. "And this is Kate, Riley, Andrea, Billy, and Franco. Everyone, this is Natalie."

"Hi!" I chirped, trying to soak it all in. Sean pulled out a chair for me. "What are those?" I asked, eyeing a plate of small round appetizers.

"Devils on horseback," he said, sliding them over to me. "Perfect for February." I popped one in my mouth and chewed slowly as the sweet and savory flavors of bacon and dates swirled over my tongue.

"That *is* perfect!" I blurted. Sean beamed.

"Um. Hey," came a quiet but familiar voice from behind me. I whipped around and saw Anastaze hovering next to my chair, gripping a cardigan in one hand and signaling a tiny wave with the other. I stood up and hugged her as hard as I could.

"Welcome out!" I whispered into her neck, and she wrapped her arms around me and squeezed me tight.

Acknowledgments

M Y PROFOUND GRATITUDE GOES first to Reiko Davis and Julia Callahan, the driving forces behind the publication of this book. Thank you so much to Josh Gondelman, Emily Pullen, and Noah Ballard for helping me find Reiko and Julia. Thanks also to Tyson Cornell, Alice Marsh-Elmer, and Winona Leon at Rare Bird, and to the team at DeFiore & Company, particularly Miriam Altschuler. Huge thanks to Leah and Bea Koch who run The Ripped Bodice in Culver City, California, one of the most exciting independent bookstores anywhere.

In 2005, Samantha House put me on the cover of the *Improper Bostonian* magazine and exposed me to the captivating world of Boston luxe and in-store fashion shows. Those experiences inspired this story and changed my life. Over the years, Bethany Van Delft, comedian and storyteller, shared insider tidbits about life as a model; her own tales of the runway are hilarious, heart-rending, and, best of all, true. Jessica Mozes never let me give up on this book. Karen Pittelman's counsel was realistic, heartening, and indispensible; writers in need of clear-headed support should

visit her at writersremedy.com. Heather Havrilesky was generous
with her help early on as well.

Thanks to my family, especially the wonderful McCauleys and
the amazing Rosses, and to everyone from Wellesley, especially
Dead Serious, Shafer, and Whiptail alums, the American Studies
program, the Women's and Gender Studies department, and the
incredible Lisa Scanlon. Susan Reverby offers me endless support—
indeed, I edited this manuscript at her kitchen table. Paul Fisher
told me I could be scrappy and write a book. Genevieve Brennan,
Charlotte Cooper, Lian Dolan, Monica Byrne, and Baratunde
Thurston offered strategic input. To Rick Jenkins, Myq Kaplan,
Baron Vaughn, Josh Gondelman (once again), Carrie Gravenson,
Abbi Crutchfield, Kaytlin Bailey, Mehran Khaghani, Andrea Henry,
Tim McIntire, Zach Sherwin, Caitlin Durante, the Comedy Studio
community, the Pillowfighters, a Tribe Called Sketch, the Great
and Secret Show, Wendy Liebman, Jonathan Katz, Nick Zaino,
Lizz Winstead and everyone from Wake Up, World!, Chenoa
Estrada, George Gordon, Emily Heller, Rojo Perez, Rebecca Trent,
Marianne Ways, Mindy Tucker, Molly Hawkey, and all the terrific
comedians, journalists, and bookers I've had the pleasure of
working with over the years: you have contributed to the creative
process that lead me to this book in profound ways. Maryanne
Watson, Joanne Greenfield, and Caitlin Tonda have helped me
so much. Ailin Conant, Caitlin Conboy, Mike Crissey, Takara
Ketton, Neha Ummatt, Nancy Smith, Lizzie Nichols, and Shaun
Joseph know how long writing a novel has been a dream of mine,
and their support and friendship mean the world to me. Much
love to my Nexleaf family, to my Plano (Carpenter, Clark, and
PESH—especially IB) family, and to my Ithaca family (now spread
throughout the world). Thanks to every early reader who offered
feedback and perspective: Alana Devich, Lisa Larson, Nancy, Ailin,
Chloë, Mandy, Jessica, Myq. Thanks and love to Jenny Chalikian,

who stands by my side on stage and beyond. Your presence makes everything so much better, so infused with comedy and love and chaotic good.

Jesse Ross saw Natalie and me all the way through, from the inception to the publication of this book, and everything in between. His unwavering support for this project, and for me, keeps me going. Thank you forever, Jesse, for believing in me, and for loving me. I love you and believe in you too.